ERIC SCOTT FISCHL

THE TRIALS OF
SOLOMON PARKER

ANGRY
ROBOT

ANGRY ROBOT
An imprint of Watkins Media Ltd

20 Fletcher Gate,
Nottingham,
NG1 2FZ
UK

angryrobotbooks.com
twitter.com/angryrobotbooks
Toss the bones

An Angry Robot paperback original 2017

Cover by Steven Meyer-Rassow
Set in Meridien and Insane Rodeo by Argh! Nottingham

Distributed in the United States by Penguin Random House, Inc., New York.

ISBN 978 0 85766 641 3
Ebook ISBN 978 0 85766 642 0

Printed in the United States of America

9 8 7 6 5 4 3 2 1

This book is for my mom.

"*The passing moment is all we can be sure of; it is only common sense to extract its utmost value from it.*"

W Somerset Maugham, The Summing Up

"*But ye should say, Why persecute we him, seeing the root of the matter is found in me?*"

Job, 19:28

The old sorcerer breathes in, his medicine hot in his chest. He sits atop a mountain shaped like an ear, listening to the dreams that cross from the west when Sun goes to his sleep.

A child burns and is saved and burns again.

A man dices with gods.

A hollow mountain is aflame.

The old sorcerer is tired, but he knows an end finally comes. He has been called many names during his long life. Black names, evil deeds clinging to them with sharp fingers. Names bright with fire. Names wet with tears. But the name of a thing is not important, and he must do what he must do. He is ready for this end, whatever it will be. He is ready.

He breathes in, smells the smoke. Hears these things:

The wailing of an infant.

The rattle of bones.

The prayers of burning men.

The laughter of spirits.

The cry of lovers.

The drums, the stomp of feet.

The sorcerer holds the cut bones in his hands, feeling their warmth. They are a powerful part of his medicine, given to him in the long-ago, kept next to his skin. He casts them upon the ground, three times.

He knows that, just past the end of things, there is a beginning. That is the way of the Above Ones.

It is I who sings you this tale.
Breathe in, then.
Listen.

Release

1900

Stevensville, Montana

Flame and smoke. It's all she can think about, most days.

It's always so hot and the room is so close. A fiery summer the likes of which she's never felt. Smoke from the wildfires to the west floats lazily in air that feels like treacle in her lungs. She can't breathe. Always the smell of it in her nose. With the back of a sleeve she rubs the sweat from her forehead, blinking in the dim light that seeps under and between the curtains. He hates that she keeps the room dark, the drapes shut, but it's just so hot and the light so bright. The air so thick. When he comes home from the tavern, the first thing he'll do is throw the windows open, pull the curtains aside, yell about fresh air. He'll push past her, reach down into the crib, pick the baby up, swinging it around and making sounds like everything is normal. Nibble a belly, tickle toes. Like everything is fine.

She feels hollow, wrung out. Filling up with smoke, burning up from the inside out. So hot all the time. So tired. This isn't right, she isn't the way she should be, but some days she just can't stop crying. It's hard to think. Sometimes, some days, she just doesn't think she can do this, can't continue.

She stands over the baby, listens to it wail. A sharp keening of need. She breathes in its milky, musty smell. Night after night, she pushes the pillow down over her ears, tries to hide from the baby's constant screaming, until her husband forces her to get up, to tend to it. *I'll get you some more help, soon,* he says, *but you need to feed him now. He's just hungry.*

The baby leeched to her, like a coal at her breast. Night after sleepless night.

At first, her husband found a woman to help, but she'd chased the old bitch out for the knowing looks, the snide remarks. That woman, all sweetness and light when *he* was here, sure, sure, but, as soon as the door closed, the bitch stared dagger eyes at her, sharp and judging. *You poor thing,* she'd said. *You sad, weak fool,* what she meant. *Crazy girl, crying all the time. Curled up in the dark.* The woman would hold the baby, coo at it. *There, there,* she'd say. *There, there.* The two of them looking at her with big, blue eyes.

Her husband came running when the neighbors found them. Pinned her arms, took the knife away from her. The old bitch crying as hysterically as the baby in her arms. *Sad, weak fool.* Is that right?

She rubs her wrists, feels where the old hurt was, long gone now. The tears are wet on her face as she looks down into the crib where her son sleeps, the child that she and her husband made. The red, squalling thing. Whimpering, feverish. It wasn't supposed to be like this.

They'd tried for so long, she and her husband, years and years that started sweet and then soured like bad water. She learned that whatever was inside her wasn't right, and each new child would dissolve and fall out of her in a hot rush of blood. Her body was poison, toxic ground in which nothing wholesome could grow. But they tried and tried and tried. They'd both wanted a child so badly, and now they had it.

The women at the birth, pushing the baby out towards her, pressing it hot and slick to her. Insistent. *Take your son*, they said. She barely felt the doctor's fingers between her legs, checking her for damage. *Take your son*. Her husband, half drunk, holding the child, refusing to believe. Even now, he refuses to stop pretending. *Take your son*.

She stares into the crib. In one hand she holds the unlit lantern, feels its weight, the sloshing of the fuel inside. It's so hot in the room and she can barely breathe and it's hard to see through her tears. He won't be home for hours yet.

A clatter at the window, scratching. That raven is outside on the ledge again. A big, ratty black thing with flat, shiny eyes. It's been coming around for days. Gone crazy from the fires, blown in on the smoke, maybe. Trying to get inside, cawing, a rough, almost human sound. *No, no, no.* But it's just a bird, that's all. Its noise quieter, now. So quiet she can barely even hear it over the pounding of blood in her ears.

The baby squirms, red-faced, looks up at her with wide eyes.

As she swings it by the wire handle, the lantern's weight stretches at the ends of her fingers, as if seeking release, so she lets it go. There's the crack of glass, the bite of kerosene. A thin puddle slops across the dry wooden floor towards her feet, pooling around a leg of the crib. Hazy waves shimmer in the air, climb up her legs, or maybe she just imagines it. Watching the child, she pulls the matches from the pocket of her apron.

Flame and smoke, she thinks.

The matches scratch against the wood of the crib and

there's another sound, the bird again, something else. She ignores it, one last thought blistering through her brain.

Burning.

Flame and Smoke

1916

Pennsylvania Mine: Butte, Montana

1.

Sol stamps down on the abandoned candle stub that's burning dangerously near one of the timber shorings, squashes it under a heavy boot until he's sure it's out, rubbing his sole against the smoldering patch of timber to smear mud and wet, just in case. Flame and fucking smoke, seven hundred goddamn feet under the goddamn ground. If it isn't one thing, it's something the fuck else.

"Goddamn it, who left this here?" Sol Parker shouts back towards his boys, trying to be heard over the crash of the rocks into the ore car and the ratcheting of the drillers down the other end of the drift. "*Who left this fucking candle?*" He kicks it towards Michael, who's nearest, liberally spattering him with mud and muck.

"Aw, Sol, it weren't me," the boy yells back.

"*Who was it?*" He looks around balefully, pointing a gloved finger from man to man, coughing through the dust.

"Aw, Sol." Michael, always the loudmouth.

More mouth than fucking sense, that one. He kicks more muck at him. "I don't care if it's wet in here," he says. "I don't care if there's the goddamn fucking Columbia river running under our goddamn feet. *You put out your fucking candles.*" He gives them another glare. They're a young crew, stupid at times. Sol is old enough to be their grandfather, most of them. He turns back to work, disgusted, knowing they'll follow.

More mouth than sense, some of these boys.

The dust is ever-present, even wet as it is, down in the dark. Water seeps down from the drift ceilings, up from the depths as the aquifers battle the pumps; it puffs out from their mouths, damp and steaming in the hot air, with every labored breath. The wet – laden with chemicals, caustic, skin-burning – slops down the dust some, but it's never enough. Every inhale feels thick and sharp in lungs which never seem quite full. The drillers at the widowmakers raise the dust a hole at a time, clouds of pulverized rock billowing out over the racket of the bit against the drift face. When the powder monkey blows the face at shift end, the whole level will fill with yet more fine, particulate silica and whatever else is in the rock. Short break between shifts so the monkeys can double-check any bad blow and the crowfoot boys poke and prod the ceilings to see if they're going to collapse; thirty minutes to give the dust time to settle, but when the muckers start shift, the air will still be thick with the stuff.

Sol hacks, spits between his feet. His teeth feel gritty and there's a pain under his ribs. He's an old fucking man. Some things you just have to admit. Ancient, really, for a miner who's been down the hole more than a few years. It's a job that uses you up quick. Wrings you out, breaks you. He spits again, coughing into the crook of his elbow even as he tosses a rock the size of his head into the cart, slapping Michael on the shoulder with his free hand in passing. Some days Sol's back hurts so bad he can barely stand up in the mornings, the arthritis in his knees and shoulders crying out, badly healed broken fingers gnarled like roots. More than once Quinn has offered him a spot as station tender, but Sol always refuses, out of stiff-necked pride, old fucking man or not. He could damn well use the extra bit of money and, at times like these, which come more and more often, his busted-up body certainly calls out for the break. Feels like giving up, though. Let the other old men and the injured stand there all shift, sending the ore up. Packing the boys when needed into three cages at a time, seven per cage. Pull the bell-cord, send them up and down the shaft, level by level, telling the hoistman up the top of the headframe where to put the cage, ring by ring.

– 2 rings and 2: five hundred level.

– 4 and 2: a thousand feet.

The two long buzzes back from up top: didn't catch that, repeat.

– 4 and 2, slow and sarcastic. Fucking pay attention, you lazy bastard, sat up on your ass up the top of the world. 4 and 2, it ain't hard.

Confirmed from up top and the cage goes down, too fast, stopping too sharp, dropping the boys hard so they're pissed off when next you see them.

– 13 rings, sharp and bitter: you motherfucker. Maybe see you later, after shift.

Let some other brokedown old bastard do that work. Stand there all shift, by yourself during the middle hours more often than not, when most of the boys were where they needed to be, bored and lonesome and to hell with the extra fifty cents an hour. Sol's proud to be a mucker, crew boss of a good goddamn group of boys and he'll be damned if he'll let a bit of soreness and a hack of a cough and lungs that are damn near fucked keep him from it.

They're the lowest of the low, the muckers – barring the crowfoot boys, who are usually just getting started down the hole, auditioning as it were for one crew or another – lowest in the eyes of the miners if not by official ACM policy. The timber boys look down on the muckers and the drillers look down on the timber boys and the powder monkeys look down on them all, because they, the dynamite layers, they're the specialists. And then there are the engineers and geologists and cartographers and every other bastard that helps get metal out of this hill. Over all of them are the bosses and managers and, above all of *them*, the big-shot fuckers in their gilded offices and the rest of the rich political cunts on the board, lording it up from their mansions, lining their pockets with gold grown from the copper pulled out of the mines.

After the dynamite blows, twice a day, the lowly muckers are the ones who bring that copper-thick rock out, though, fill cart after cart, roll it down drift rails and into the cages to be pulled up out the hole to the headframe – *2 and 1: rock coming up* – and loaded on railcars. The drillers and dynamite boys think themselves swells, the timber boys fancy themselves as keeping the whole place together, but that ore isn't going fucking nowhere without crews like Sol and his men pulling that rock out. To Sol's mind, that's something to be proud of, no matter how hard the work is, no matter the dirt and mud seamed deeper into your face every day and the constant, hacking cough that's going to kill you before too long.

Silicosis. Everyone – everyone but the Company, that is – everyone knows that miner's consumption, the miner's con, is caused by that ever-present dust settling in your lungs, hollowing you out as it fills you. The big drills are called widowmakers not because they're dangerous in and of themselves but because they raise so much fucking dust. If a man saw fifty years, after a few down the hole, he was elderly. At sixty-two, Sol is as old as Methuselah.

For a miner, if a cage doesn't cut loose and drop you into a wet squidge from a thousand feet, a fire burn you out, or a blast accident bring a drift down on you, the dust will kill you. It's that simple. That your job will kill you, sure enough, slow or quick: that's the real miner's con.

Later, crammed into the cage at shift end with six other men, Sol rolls his head on his neck, trying not to cough at the same time. He's so tired he can barely stand upright; the fact that they're packed in so tight is a help. He's able to subtly lean on Big Nancy to one side, using the boy's bulk as a bulwark of sorts. Sol runs his hand down the greasy wet metal of the cage wall, scrapes his boots on the grating to cut loose some of the mud and muck, ignoring the cursing from the car below. The car drops down to allow the one above to load, the three cages hung like beads on a chain, each dripping grime and wet down on the men in the car beneath, swaying on the cable.

– *3 and 1: run slowly, men to be hoisted.*

The buzzer loud in the tunnel: *ack-ack-ack, ACK.* Up top, at the headframe, it's a sharply ringing bell, the better to cut through the racket of ore clattering into railcars and the whine of spinning machinery. Down here, though, in the dim, the buzzer's always startling to Sol, even after long familiarity. The red light affixed to the tender's station winks in and out in time with the signal.

– 1 and 2: up and out.

Per usual, there's that first quick jerk when the cage gets started and Sol's heart falls into his belly, wondering if this will be the time when the cable will break, drop them to the bottom of the shaft, splash them down hard into the seeping water, the car above crushing them into the one below, down into the sump.

– 7 and repeat.

– 7 and repeat.

Accident. Accident.

But no, not this time, and they slowly make their way up from the 700 level, out into the cold, clear, February air. The wind is whipping across the hill, as it usually does, scraping across Sol's wet, muddy face as he and his boys make their way to the lockers to wipe down and change into clothes more resembling clean. Michael is running his mouth about something or other, as he generally does, speech more akin to the function of breathing for the boy; the two Dans, Young and Old, are pretending to listen to him although, really, it doesn't matter if he has an audience or not, as far as Michael Conroy is concerned. Big Nancy and Flynn plod along silently, no doubt thinking of the first drink of the night. Owen, Sol's boy, new to the crew and otherwise wet about the ears, sticks close to Sol. He's young at sixteen and the newest member of the crew so, his parentage notwithstanding, Owen is already something of a mascot. This enables Young Dan, at eighteen, to assume an air of fatherly wisdom, seasoned old salt that he is. Old Dan, nineteen, watches the youngsters with the tolerant amusement of the aged.

Billy Morgan brings up the rear and Sol gives him a wink. He and Billy have been friends for fifteen years but Billy looks like he hasn't aged a day, to Sol's eye.

Maybe, like a lot of his kind, he'll look young and a little weathered until one day he just looks weathered, going to ancient overnight, face seamed and shrunken like a winter apple. Sol knows that he himself looks about eighty, or at least feels that way now, at the end of twelve hours mucking ore down the hole.

Without the press of rock overhead, it's easier to stand upright, easier to breathe without the clouds of dust and the drip of burning water. As they walk from Finntown towards the East Side, though, the press of worry pushes upward from the depths of Sol's thoughts like the steam rising off of his body and his wet clothes, which threaten to freeze him in the winter air. One thing about working down the hole is that it's easy not to think, or fret and mull and pick at the problems a stupid, reckless man – like Sol – has brought down onto himself. The kind of problems that can get a man killed just as fast as a dropped hoist cage, but not likely as cleanly. The kinds of problems that live, as he does, not far from the East Side.

2.

Marked Face squats with the rabbit under the little overhang of rock, trying to get himself farther out of the wind. His fire, a small and feeble thing, snaps and dances, whipping over from side to side in the gusts and threatening to blow itself out. He pauses in his skinning to feed it more sticks, trying to coax more life out of it, build up enough heat so he can cook the scrawny jack that found his snare earlier. He cuts around the back feet, works his fingers under the hide and, with smooth tugs, the rabbit's fur comes off like a wet glove, hanging loose from the neck and dangling head. He cuts the head and feet off, wraps them in the hide and throws it all as far away from his camp as he can manage. Stepping farther away from the fire, Marked Face opens the belly and guts the animal, hurling the offal after the head. He rubs his bloody hands clean in the snow and returns to hunker under the rock, spitting the carcass on a stick and waiting on the fire. Even though he's hungry and cold, there's a pleasure in these simple tasks, done so many thousands of times during his long life, and pleasures are few and far between in this world.

He leans back against the rock, pulling his old blanket

tighter around him. The wind is bitter, his breath steaming and puffing in the fire's dim light. Marked Face wishes he had some tobacco, something better than cold air to smoke. But he does not, and he long ago learned to live with disappointment. He is a patient man.

Even though the hour is late, the moon high, the hill on the horizon to the east of him glows with electric lights. It never stops, that place, rattling loud, steaming the air with foul smoke and sickening the earth. All day and all night the whites burrow and scrape and dig under that hill, searching for whatever it is they search for. They say it is metal they dig but Marked Face knows that really it is only greed, that those people are simply trying to fill the aching hunger in their bellies. More, more, always more. He has seen those people for a long time, watched them. He understands them, in a way, though he wishes he did not. He knows that what they find there under that hill will not stop the gnawing in their guts.

The boy is there, somewhere.

Marked Face does not like to get too close to that place but, soon enough, he will have to. For now, where he camps tonight is plenty near. He has camped here many times over the years; it is a good place to stop and sit while traveling. Not the best, of course but, so near to the city, good places for a man to stay have become few. Even as far away as he is now, he can smell the stink of that town.

The fire heats up and Marked Face cooks his rabbit, listening to the flesh sizzle until his hunger becomes too great and he takes it from the spit, still half-raw. The meat is stringy and has an odd, unpleasant flavor, perhaps because of this sick land so near the city, all the spoiled things the animal had to eat during its short life.

Marked Face himself has eaten much worse over the years, though, in times of famine, of which there were plenty. It's hard for him, sometimes, to even recall the better times, the taste of other flesh. Red and glistening, rich with fat, giving his body its power with every morsel. Perhaps that is the way of old men, though; the before times were always better, eh. While he knows not to call himself wise, he has learned a thing or two about himself over all these years.

He picks the rabbit to its bones, sucking every bit of meat, and then hurls the leavings away toward the head and guts. Warm food in his belly, Marked Face feels a little better now, still cold but better. All day he has felt low, off. It is because he is so close to what he must do; that is no mystery. The ache in his gut is no longer only hunger, but fear.

Pah, he tells himself, *this is not me*. He knows who he is. This is only a small feeling, no more than the icy, nervous, twinge in the balls before jumping off a high rock into cold water. It is normal, after all. Starting a thing is sometimes more difficult than finishing it.

He closes his eyes and sings, trying to calm himself. The Above Ones watch him as they watch all of the world. Let them see him sing, let them know that Marked Face listens and has no fear. He is their instrument. The boy will learn, soon enough, he will learn to open his eyes and see the world as it truly is. He will see and he will choose his path and the world will go the way it goes, ever pitiless. As in the old tales, the Above Ones have spoken.

The boy, and the old man who moves him, are on that burning hill, somewhere. Soon, he, Marked Face, will come to them, pouring dreams into their ears. He will come bringing stories and lies. He will come bringing chaos. He will come bringing fear.

He is the twining root that cracks the rock.

He is the one who pushes the stone that starts the slide.

He is the instrument of the Above Ones.

3.

Billy Morgan comes back from wherever his mind has wandered off to and takes a sip of his beer. Even in the raucous din of the Stope, it's easy to drift one's thoughts away when Michael Conroy is chattering – which, to be fair, is most of the time.

"I don't know why we gotta come all the way down here, every night," Michael is saying, now, pausing to wipe beer foam off his lips. "If there's one thing this damn town don't lack, it's places to get a fuckin drink. There's a hundred thousand people in this town, and places to drink for every last one of them, but me and Nancy and Flynn still gotta walk back up to the Gulch after this to get home. Plenty of places to drink in Dublin Gulch, is all I'm saying."

"Drank in the Gulch last week," Young Dan mutters.

"Surrounded by all you fuckin Micks," Old Dan adds.

Billy watches the boys over the lip of his glass, the beer inside he's nursing just enough to slide some of the grit from his throat, the whiskey side of his Sean O'Farrell untouched in front of him. Billy is a rarity, not much of a drinker, usually. He rarely wants more than just the beer.

"Oh *all you fuckin Micks*, that's right, Dan, all us fuckin Micks. Leastwise *we* know who we are, hey? The fuck are *you*, boy-o? Some kind of Russian, maybe? Fuckin Croat? I don't even know how to *say* your fuckin name so don't you be talking talk at us sons of Saint Fuckin Pat. Right, gents?" Michael looks over at Nancy and Flynn, who are focusing on their drinks, trying to ignore their countryman. Without missing a beat, he resumes. "The fuck *is* your name, anyway? Hey? How d'you say that, again? Wanker-vich, is it?"

"Watch yourself, Mike," Old Dan, Darko Jankovic to his mother, says, raising a finger.

"Oh and what is it I'm watching now? *I'm* not the ill-mannered sod who don't want to drink in a better class of establishment, closer to where the civilized fuckin folk live, instead of this Christ-forsaken shack. Full of questionable characters from the *darker* corners of Europe, like whatever little benighted scrap of a country your people are from." He waves an arm, vaguely, in what he figures to be a somewhat easterly direction.

"Would you just shut it, Michael," Flynn says, looking up after draining his glass. "Sweet merciful Jesus, every fuckin night with you. You've must have got the fuckin tongue of Hercules on you, the way it never stops moving. My own hurts just listening to you, not to mention my poor fuckin ears."

Michael assumes an expression of affront. "Well, *excuse me*, Johnathan, *excuse me* for standing up for our blessed homeland," he says, airily waving an arm again. "The art of intelligent conversation is a *gift*, which flows deep in the blood of the sons of Erin and I, lad, *I* – unlike you – am a natural racketeer. You and Nancy both should be ashamed to call yourself Irishmen, you disgraceful fuckin mutes."

"You're a natural fuckin eejit, Mike," Flynn says. He gets up, looks around inquisitively at the table. "My round, boys, if you can get this fool to shut his hole for five minutes." All hands but Billy's go up, including Michael's own.

"Raconteur, son," Sol says, as Flynn walks off. His head leant back against the wall, eyes mostly closed. "Word's *raconteur*."

"Jesus, Sol, don't get him started again," Eamonn Mallon, Big Nancy to the boys, mutters.

Billy smiles to himself. Every night after shift it's more or less the same: weary, good-natured carping and bitching at one another, pouring a good chunk of their day's wages down their dry throats – save Billy himself – until they get so tired that it's a struggle to drag themselves back to their respective rooms for a little sleep before another twelve hours down the mine. Sometimes, once or twice a week, the boys will get to feeling their oats and will drain that paycheck a little more, one round at a time, maybe find a working girl, maybe blow off a little steam with a fight behind one of their usual haunts. Muckers against the timber boys, maybe, or some drillers who look to get shirty. Maybe Penn crews against those of the Orphan Girl, the Speculator, the Neversweat, for no reason other than pride of one mine against another.

Billy takes another sip of his beer, looking around the crowded little tavern. The Stope is like most of the other places they go after shift: dim, loud, smoky, with a sawdust floor, mediocre beer and indifferent whiskey, but full of men like themselves, the rank and file from one mine or another, brothers in Labor and proud of it. Some crew foremen, like Sol, maybe a few of the better sort of level bosses. Not for them the like of the Atlantic, with its fancy, gleaming bar a block long, fifteen bartenders

behind it for each shift, nor the saloons where the
engineers drink, or the smeltermen, or even the ethnic-
only miners' enclaves in one part of town or another.
Here at the Stope, Croats rub shoulders with Cousin
Jacks, Swedes with Serbians, Slovenes with Syrians, and
everything in between. Antti, the proprietor, is himself
some kind of Finn who'd leaked out of Finntown to
parts slightly eastward; he maintains a strict policy of all
are welcome, as long as you keep drinking and take the
fights outside, thank you very much, gentlemen.

Billy looks over at Sol, who seems to be asleep, like
Owen, who has yet to master the knack of a drink or two
after a full shift's hard work without immediately passing
out. As Billy watches, Sol opens his eyes, blinking for a
moment back at him.

"What?"

"You all right?"

"Oh, he speaks."

Billy isn't much of a conversationalist, as a general
rule. A closed mouth gathers no flies, his father had told
him. "You all right?" he repeats.

"Tired, is all, mother. Just goddamn tired."

Tonight, most nights lately, Sol looks his years, and
then some. Billy wonders how long the old bastard is
going to be able to keep up with the work, if he'll have
to take Quinn up on a station-tender job, sooner or later,
or find something else entirely. Plus there are the other
difficulties Billy knows that Sol's brought on himself,
which weigh on the old man, even though he tries to
hide it. Sol's a bad liar, though, and the kind of trouble
he's in right now isn't the kind of trouble you can lie
your way out of anyway.

"Maybe let's go, then," he says now, draining the
warm dregs of his beer.

"Nah, one more drink, Bill," Sol replies, closing his eyes again. "Just one more drink."

Sol isn't tired *now*, that's plain enough to Billy, later. He, himself, wants to do nothing but sleep. He aches and his eyes feel heavy and gritty. There's a headache nestling at the back of his skull and his jaw is sore from yawning. But Sol is on a tear, again.

A game of dice, of course, that's all it takes to perk Sol up. Dice or cards or dominoes or anything else, and Sol Parker is a new man. Alert. Awake. A gleam in the eyes. Most everyone has something that makes them stupid. For some it's booze or women or dope. Religion, social movements for others. You name it. It's not always clear just where the stupidity lies, for some people, what it is that has hold of them, but it's obvious for Sol. He likes his drinking and girls and the rest of it but, seeing him sat there wagering money he doesn't have, shiny eyed and wet-lipped, hollering out numbers and slapping the table, it's no mystery where his deeply stupid-making enthusiasms are.

That goddamn Michael. There are going to be some fucking words about this tomorrow, that's for certain. Maybe more than words. The boys know by now, have been told in no uncertain terms by Billy, with Nancy's bulk backing him, to keep the fucking dice away from Sol. No dice, no cards, no dominoes. Hell, no bingo. Not even rock, paper, fucking scissors. None of it. Sol looked out for all of them, down the mine, least they could do was try to look out for him up top. Keep him away from that blind spot he has, that little bit of stupid hunkered down in his belly. It wasn't shameful to have a weakness; what's shameful is when your friends won't help you fight it.

They'd been damn near finished with their drinks and ready to head out when that idiot Michael brought out the dice, looking for a game. There wasn't any malice in it, not really; Michael's just a fucking moron. The words weren't half out of Michael's mouth when he realized his mistake, but still that was enough time to wake Sol up, lean him forward, one hand reaching out automatically for the dice, the other digging into his pocket for a small, grubby wad of bills. Eyes open, smile creeping across his face. Michael afraid to catch Billy's look, and for good reason. It's too late now, though; once Sol is going it's hard to stop him. Best they can do is try to cut the game as short as they can, before things get out of control. Keep others away from the table, prevent the game from growing, as it tended to do when Sol was around. Everyone loves to gamble with Sol Parker. He's the lame elk the wolves cull.

Flynn is frowning, the Dans look worried. Billy can feel his own teeth grinding. He reaches over and takes Michael's whiskey. Knocks it back, hissing around the burn.

There are definitely going to be fucking words about this tomorrow, Michael. Maybe a foot up the ass. Maybe something more stern. Goddamn fucking idiot.

It's not just stupid and reckless, Sol tossing dice and hollering, spending money he doesn't have. It's dangerous, is what it is. Plain and simple. Word of this gets back to Sean Harrity, and Sol is in more trouble than he already is, if that's even possible. The money Sol doesn't have, the simple idea of it, belongs to Sean. *Sol* belongs to Sean, until his debts are paid. Spending Sean's money at a dice game – and Sol *will* lose, rest assured; he's that sorry type of compulsive gambler who can't stop playing and who is lousy at games of chance, hence his popularity – is disrespectful. Sean Harrity is big on respect.

Goddamn you, Michael.

It's getting on for midnight, fortunately no later, by the time they manage to get out of the Stope, parting ways with the boys: Michael, Nancy, and Flynn off north to the Gulch, the Dans and Owen to their boardinghouse farther east, Billy and Sol heading southwest, towards the shitty shack they share in the rats' nest that is the Cabbage Patch.

The town of Butte smells like the fires of Hell itself, most times, a dank, sharp, sulfurous reek from the smelters, which settles over the hill in a low fog. The Company will tell you that the eggy, stinking cloud is beneficial, that sulfur itself is an element vital for health, which will make your bones strong and your teeth hard. *The people of Butte don't suffer flu or colds or lassitude,* they say, *the very air of our town is fortifying.* Never mind the hollow-eyed, consumptive miners hacking their lungs out shift after shift, the families missing fathers and brothers and uncles; never mind the stunted and dead vegetation for miles around Butte. *That smell: that's the smell of prosperity.* To Billy, Butte brings to mind nothing more than a rotting carcass, the hill burrowed out underneath, hollowed like a dead thing swarmed with carrion beetles, the stink of decay rising up.

But, if Butte smells like Hell, the Cabbage Patch is a level yet lower, the close streets reeking of festering garbage, overfull privies, dead animals. Even in the freezing temperature tonight, their boots squelch unpleasantly through muck best left unexamined. Ramshackle boarding houses press up haphazardly against cabins and gambling houses and the type of saloon that makes the Stope look like a gentleman's paradise; on the streets, drunks and thieves and the more used-up sort of whore rub elbows with poor – frugal, Billy likes to think – workingmen like him and Sol, packed in more often than not with their raggedy families, too many to a room.

Why do you live in that shithole? the boys ask them. Sol blusters about saving money and *Hell boys, it's just a place to sleep and I'm hardly ever there. Why spend the money when sleeping is just sleeping.* But the boys know that the truth is more complicated.

Cabin is a flattering word for the shack in which they live. It has a decided lean in at least two separate directions and is largely propped up by the building it slumps against on the downhill side. The place isn't much bigger than the outhouse out back and, to Billy's nose, smells about as bad, though he tries to keep the cabin as clean as he can. Years of neglect and filth and a residue of hopelessness seem to cling to every surface, though, which he figures will only come out when the shack finally burns to the ground. The entirety of the inside is taken up with their two cots, between which sit a low table; a couple of rickety and spavined wooden chairs are pushed up against the walls. A fly-specked bulb hangs naked from the center of the room, although Billy ignores it and lights a kerosene lantern, preferring the warm quality of its glow to the harsh electric light.

Sol sinks onto his cot with a groan, slumps over to wrestle his boots off. "Another goddamn day, huh?"

"Another day." Every night this is their closing ritual, as if each day is a thing they've conquered, a victory to be remarked on before tackling the next in a few short hours. After getting out of his own boots and skinning down to his longjohns, Billy reaches over from his cot and turns off the lantern. He can hear Sol already wheezing in what sounds like sleep, breath whistling in and out of his nostrils.

Tired as he is, Billy can't drop off. He envies Sol his ability to be asleep as soon as his eyes close, damn near anywhere. Billy's never had the knack of slipping away like that; even as a kid he'd be up long after everyone else was snoring, his mind on edge, churning away on thoughts he couldn't cut loose for one reason or another. Maybe it came from being woken up so often by his dad or his uncle on another one of their tears, trying to get out of their way or calm them down enough to back off from one another. Later, at the government school, it made sense to not sleep too soundly lest you wake up with a pillow pressed over your head as the bigger boys, or sometimes the night wardens, tried to get their cock up your ass.

It's been a long time since Billy's thought of the government school, where they tried to scrape the Indian out of him, turn him into a brown-skinned white man. To a large degree, it worked: Billy has only a rough, choppy remnant of his first tongue, what they didn't slap out of his head to make room for English. He dresses like a white man, works like a white man, thinks like a white man in most ways. When he reflects on it, rare as that is, it saddens him some, but he knows that's just the way things are. Billy doesn't see the sense in chewing on it: the old ways are gone. That's why his uncle is so bitter, maybe that's why his father is the way he is, too.

He himself is just trying to make the best of a bad game. That's really all you can do. He's mostly content with his lot. He's a miner, no worse off than the impoverished immigrants that wash up in Butte looking for steady work and a better life. The job is hard, dangerous, will kill him sooner rather than later but, for now, he has food in his belly, friends, a place to live – mansion that it is – and a little money for a drink or a woman when the urge for either takes him. That's about all there is to ask for in life. All the rest is just extra. And you don't really need it, the extras, not when it comes right down to it.

Still, he remembers the old stories that his father sang, his uncle, night after night, before he, Billy, was taken off to the government school to learn to be white. He's been dreaming about them, lately, almost every night; strange, vivid dreams that seem to stretch the night too long. The dreams exist somewhere in a place just shy of nightmare, at times. When he wakes in the morning they stick to him for hours, they taint the flavor of what he does. Now, as he fights his way towards sleep, his mind finally starting to drift loose from the day, Billy can hear the drum and a low, breathy voice, singing.

4.

I remember the East Wind was howling, pushing Maatakssi and his brother Siinatssi across the great water on a skin boat. They were coming to the place of the People, they were coming to our lands. This I remember: on a skin boat they came, fleeing the wrath of Old Man, for what I do not know. The People were not here, then, but these were their lands.

I remember the wind and the raging water. I remember the fear of Maatakssi and Siinatssi, who were sure their skin boat would sink beneath the dark sea. They cried and prayed to the Above Ones for succor; they cried and prayed to Old Man for forgiveness. "Let us come home," *they cried,* "take us from these waters."

Old Man turned his ears from his sons and instead the brothers came to this place, battered and wet, tired and sore. They pulled their boat to shore and kissed the land; they gave thanks to the Above Ones for saving them even as they cursed Old Man for abandoning them. I remember this too.

But some say Old Man did not turn his ears from his sons Maatakssi and Siinatssi at all, that he himself came to the lands of the People, in another form, searching for his lost children. Some say that he made the People his new children when he could not find his lost sons. The old women say this is not so, but some say it is true.

Maatakssi and Siinatssi came to the lands of the People then, and, for a time, it was good. Game was plentiful and the weather still. They talked to Raven in the trees and Beaver in his lodge. Particularly, at that time, they reverenced Siyakohah, Black Bear, who reminded them of the place from which they had come.

For a time, yes, it was good, but Maatakssi and Siinatssi became lonely, for they were the only two in the lands of the People, and the brothers longed for wives. They asked Siyakohah where they could find wives to give them sons and daughters, but Black Bear did not know, nor did Beaver in his lodge. Raven, though, had seen many places in his travels.

"I have seen a people," *he said,* "east along the great river. They are traders from the north lands. Maybe they will have wives for you."

"Are their women strong?" *asked Siinatssi.*

"Are they beautiful?" *asked Maatakssi.*

Raven shrugged. "Truly, it is difficult for me to tell you two-leg walkers apart, but look east. Now, I myself must get back to my own wives, who will be missing me." *And with that he flew off.*

Maatakssi and Siinatssi headed east along the gorge of the great river. They decided to race, that the first to reach the northern traders would have first choosing of their women. They ran, racing towards their new wives. Maatakssi was the faster and took a great lead, but he lacked the stamina of his brother Siinatssi, who gradually made up the distance between them. Neck and neck they were for a long time, but Maatakssi's strength started to fade, and his brother pulled ahead. Sure that he would lose the race, Maatakssi became full of anger, from which he suffered at times, and struck his brother before Siinatssi could outdistance him, driving the point of his spear into Siinatssi's hipbone.

Siinatssi fell, and hit his head on a stone. The life fled from him, seeking the Other Lands, and his brother Maatakssi wept.

"Father," *he cried,* "I have murdered your son."

The Above Ones heard Maatakssi's cries and saw his tears. They came down to the gorge of the great river and said to Maatakssi, "Lay your brother to rest in the proper way, so that his spirit can go free to the Other Lands. When this is done, you will be given one boon, for easing your brother's spirit, but you must also be given one punishment, for releasing it before its time. Do not worry, Maatakssi," *they said,* "you will always be beloved of the Above Ones, if you reverence us in the proper way. We will watch over you, in this life and the next and the next. You will find wives and have many sons and daughters to carry your name. You will live many years. This we promise."

Sharp-eyed Raven saw this pass from his perch atop a tall pine, where he could look across all of the land and see its workings. He saw the smile of the Above Ones and felt a grief, knowing that mischief was afoot. He was a wise bird, and knew the nature of those people.

Maatakssi wept, but did as he was told, placing Siinatssi's head to the east and saying words over him. Precious things he gave his brother to ease the journey, and Maatakssi cut his own hair and sliced his arms in his grief. "Goodbye, my brother," *he said.* "Would that I could take your place. Would that my own place had been taken by a better man, so that things had not passed this way."

The Above Ones saw that Maatakssi had done well, and eased his grief. They led him to his new wives, who gave him many sons and daughters. Maatakssi lived many, many years, as the Above Ones had promised, surrounded by his sons and sons' sons, his daughters and daughters' daughters.

But first, the Above Ones gave Maatakssi, the murderer of his brother, one boon and one punishment, as they had promised they would do.

The old women say that these things were one and the same.

5.

Sol is dreaming again of Lizzie and fire and smoke, monsters and cut wrists and shouting, empty bottles and gunfire. The scene shifts and there's an Indian crying over a body in a hole. Another shift, another Indian, then, an old one with bones tied into his hair, standing on a mountain; the man is singing something wordless and in one bloody hand are two shining white things, like plucked eyes. The other palm is held out as if in offering and burning, in the middle of it is a flame that's black and twisting. The old man's gaze bores into Sol, his face looms close and Sol thinks maybe he himself is shouting when Billy shakes him awake, although that could have been in the dream. Sol isn't much of a dreamer, but lately they're coming hard and fast; they cleave to him for a while after he wakes up. He can still smell smoke, hear the echo of that song.

Giving his head a shake, he opens his gluey eyes for a moment before wearily closing them again; he swings around on his cot, the blanket draped over his shoulders. He rests his bare feet on the cold, dirty wooden floor of the shack, taking a deep breath before straightening his back. The morning inventory of his myriad aches and pains takes longer and longer these days, his various poorly healed injuries and bodily insults draped over his innards in an accretion that thickens with every passing year. Pulling his spine straight and his shoulders back is a jagged, crackling, muscle-stretching process that requires some time; rolling his head around his neck produces ominous chattering pops from the base of his skull down to his clavicles, which at least provides some relief from stiffness.

All of this is accomplished with his eyes closed and he can smell the kerosene lantern Billy's fired up. Without needing to look over, Sol reaches out for the tin cup of cold water that he knows Billy has left on the table between their cots, as he does every morning. As he swallows, Sol can feel the icy water spreading out inside him, refilling needy cells desiccated by whiskey and overwork and exhaustion. Billy, who seems to need little sleep, is already gone; Sol himself struggles with the desire to just lie back down for a minute or two, to put off the stabbing, cracking pangs that will come to his knees when he stands upright. Bright, sharp pain to welcome in another day.

He still sits there when Billy comes back a little later with two steaming mugs of coffee and a bag of sandwiches. He wordlessly passes a cup to Sol and sits on his own cot to pack up their lunch pails. The smell of the coffee brings Sol's eyes open but he doesn't need to look over and catch Billy's pointed glance at the rusty little clock that sits on the table between them to know what the man is thinking.

"Yeah, yeah, I'm getting up, goddamn it." They're like an old married couple sometimes, Sol thinks, with their tired routines and – mostly one-sided, to be fair to Billy – squabbles.

Billy says nothing, merely sips his coffee. They have plenty of time; Billy well knows by now exactly how early to get Sol up, to give him time enough to grumble his way to vertical, get dressed, thunderously shit at the privy out back, do all the other little chores it takes to get awake and to the mine before the start of their shift. Billy is the sort of man to whom sleep clings lightly, who merely opens his eyes and gets on with the business of the day, rather than having to peel and shrug out of bleariness. A lucky gift that Sol tries not to resent as he mutters and struggles into something resembling human every morning.

A short while later they leave the cabin, Sol pausing in the doorway as he always does to look around for Mickey or Faraday or one of Sean Harrity's other men. Sean's taken to sending them out to find Sol at odd hours, to remind him of his obligations. The reminders are coming thicker and sharper, and Sol knows it will one day end with him dead in some messy way, if he can't figure out a way around it before Sean's patience finally runs out. It's a thought that occupies much of Sol's mind when it's not pushed out by work or drink or exhausted sleep. His carcass slumped in a shit-strewn Patch alley somewhere, neck open, hole in the skull, what have you, left there to rot like a dead cat, swollen belly nuzzled by the rats and the flies.

It's still dark as they make their way through the frozen muck and stink, lunch pails in hand. Heading north to the Penn, flowing along with the crowds of men going to one mine or another for the start of shift. By the time they come back out, twelve hours later, it will be night again, this time of year. From dark to dark they work, deep down in the earth. As they walk along with the others, Sol looks up; there are no stars and the moon is only the faintest gleam through the press of stinking clouds hanging low over the hill.

From the shadows of an alley, a man watches them.

The buzzer rings in the day.

The hoistman rattles the cages down, seven men per cage, three cages stacked like beads on a wire.

– *3 and 2: men on, to be lowered.*

– *4 and 5: 13th level.*

Picking up their tools, eyes squinting through the rock dust that has yet to settle from the blast at the end of the last shift. Down the drift, ore cart rattling along beside them.

– *2 and 1: hoist rock.*

– *2 and 1.*

– *2 and 1.*

As sore and beat-up as he is, once Sol is going, the work wakes his body up. Muscles loosen. Some of his old strength comes back. Low and squat, with strong shoulders, he fits well to the work, like the Cousin Jacks who, over generations of mining in Cornwall, have been bred to the job. Sol fares better than Big Nancy, who's always cracking his head into things, as is lanky John Flynn. The Dans and Owen are still growing; Young Dan in particular looks to be the kind of boy who still has a ways to go, who might grow to an awkward size for mine work. Billy isn't a large man but even after their years down the mine has never entirely shucked himself of a wide-eyed fear of close spaces. Though he never complains, just gets on with the work. Sol himself doesn't *enjoy* the work, as such, no one does – no one entirely sane, anyway – but he's good at it and it fits his strengths, physical and otherwise.

Just get on with the work, that's what they do.

Coughing and cursing, griping and hollering at one another over the racket of the drillers and rattling cars, they push through the dust and muck and stink to get the ore out, down the drift to the vertical shaft, to be sent up the cages so the copper can be bashed and sucked out of the rock. They burrow through the ground of the Richest Hill on Earth, so it's called, hollowing out under the city like ants, digging for the metal that makes the Amalgamated Copper Mining Company rich, the swells and shareholders anyway. The Company owns Butte and, if men want to work, the Company owns them too.

Michaels, Johns, Antons, Olafs. Amads and Peters and Svens and Jacks. Pauls and Alvars and Davids and Hirams. Men from a dozen countries, more, drawn up to the Montana mountains and down into the mine shafts. Brothers in Labor, the lot of them: Butte is the Gibraltor of Unionism, it's said, a place where a man can do honest work for an honest wage. In reality, they suck rock dust and chemical residue twelve hours a day, the mine getting inside of them over the years as they do to the mine, day after day, giving their health and, eventually, their lives, to line the pockets of the likes of that fucker William Clark and his rich cronies. Now, with the war in Europe, the men are being pushed even harder to expand productivity, safety be damned, and the fight of Labor against the ACM is heating up once more. Rumor has it that Frank Little, a bigshot with the IWW, is coming out to Butte to help organize the men against the depredations of the Company.

Sol shakes off the rest of his morning aches, focuses on the job to hand. Thirteen hundred feet underground, today, in a drift tunnel barely wide enough for two men to walk abreast, in spots, wet, dark, and reeking of rock dust and dynamite residue, is no place to lose concentration. Just do the work. Get the rock in the cars, rattle down the drift to the cages at the shaft, have old Torsten – whose age, younger than his own, Sol tries to ignore – send the cages up.

– 2 and 1: hoist rock.

Rock in the cars, down the drift, up the shaft.

Again, again, again.

– 2 and 1: hoist rock.

Coughing and hollering, bashing knuckles on stone, scraping skin. A back that, after a while, doesn't want to straighten, knees that feel frozen, iron spikes jammed up under their caps. Wet muck everywhere, sweat streaming stinging down into eyes. Air so damp and thick it's like breathing underwater, if it weren't for the constant dust scratching its way down your throat to roost in your lungs. Head pounding, ears humming from the noise of the drills and the cars and your own hoarse shouting.

But laughter, too, from time to time. Jokes, a mucky finger jammed into an unsuspecting ear, the time they'd convinced Owen that each car had to have exactly fifty pieces of rock, no more, no less. *Goddamn it, Owen! Get that fuckin rock counted so we can send the car up!* After, they'd laughed so hard that Flynn claimed he'd pissed himself, just a little bit. *Although it's too wet to tell for sure, boys,* he'd said, which had started them off again. Michael's nonstop chatter about this or that, often irritating but sometimes hilarious, intentional or not. *Did'ya know, boys, that your Chinese fella eats birds' nests? Some kinda fuckin soup, if you can believe it. Sparrow fuckin soup, hey?* From time to time Young Dan can be prevailed upon to sing a bit for them, when the racket will allow, the boy having the kind of voice that one came upon but rarely. *Are you* sure *you're not fuckin Irish?* Michael would ask, every time.

– 2 and 1: hoist rock.

Rock in the cars, down the drift, up the shaft.

– 2 and 1: hoist rock.

Hour after hour, day after day. Just get on with the work.

"I saw a thing once, boys," Michael is saying, now. "Was in Denver, I think it was, if I'm remembering rightly. There was this workin gal who would put her whole fuckin fist up herself, like. No, no, I'm not kidding. I saw it myself. Whole fuckin fist!"

Clatter of rock into the car. Rattle of the metal wheels on the rail as Owen pushes it back down the drift towards the shaft.

"Right up her cunny, I swear, to the wrist, and I'm thinking *now why the fuck would you want to do something like that, girl?*"

"So she can get ready for me, son," Flynn says, pausing from where he's loosening up a spill of rock with a bar to grip his crotch suggestively.

"Nah, I seen that little thing, John," Nancy chimes in, "looks like a wee carrot from what I remember."

Sol coughs around a laugh, helps Young Dan shift a heavier stone, while Flynn makes a trenchant, however accurate, remark about Nancy's predilection for lithe boys.

Down the drift, Sol can faintly hear the buzz of the cage signal. The dim bulbs on their string overhead flicker, once, twice.

– 2 and 1: hoist rock.

"I'm serious, boys," Michael continues, "what kind of woman can get her whole fuckin hand up there–"

– Repeat, 2 and 1: hoist rock.

"–and could you even *feel* anything, if you got yourself in her, like? I mean, I'm no carrot-cock like your man

Flynn here, but I'm not a giant neither–"

– *Repeat, 2 and 1: hoist rock.* A bit slower, more insistently. The lights flicker again, longer this time, making Sol pause and look up.

"–so I thought, this is something I need to settle for myself, for science, right? Anyways, so I ask this girl, when she's got her hand back out, mind–"

– *Repeat, 2 and 1: hoist rock. Repeat.* There's a longer pause this time, and then the overhead lights go out entirely.

"Shut up, Michael," Sol says. "Just shut up for a second." He lifts his head, sniffing, but Billy is already ahead of him.

"Fire, Sol." His voice wary, tense.

Just then Owen comes running back down the drift, the light of his helmet candle bobbing crazily. "Fire! Sol, shaft's on fire!" From the end of the drift they can now hear the buzzer going insistently.

– *7 and repeat. 7 and repeat.*

Accident. Accident.

The crew goes still, eyes widen. They each have the same thought: *the shaft, the way out, is on fire and they are thirteen hundred feet underground.* The thought of burning or suffocating deep underground comes a close second in the long list of terrifying miners' deaths, after being buried alive in a cave-in; neither are prospects to relish. After a long, drawn-out second they all start in at once.

– "Oh, Jesus."

– "Fuck, fuck."

– "Sweet Jesus."

– "Sol, what do we do?"

– "*Fuck*, fuck, *fuck.*"

– "Sol, what do we *do*?"

"*Goddammit shut the fuck up*!" Sol yells. "Calm down,

just calm down!" He reaches over and shakes a wide-eyed
Dan by the front of the shirt, slaps Michael on the chest.
For a crazy second he thinks he hears laughter, a voice
he doesn't recognize. He looks around for a moment but
no one else is there, just his boys. "All right," he says,
turning back, "just calm down and we'll be fine."

Flame and smoke.

They can all smell it now, the acrid reek of burning
timbers, smoke beginning to thicken the air. "Owen, did
Torsten know where the burn is? Owen!"

"I don't know, it's in the shaft, though. It's in the
fuckin shaft!"

"What level, boy?"

"I don't know, Sol, I don't know!" Owen's eyes are
wild, too much white showing. *Thirteen hundred feet
underground and the way out is on fire*. He looks to be
having a hard time breathing.

"It's OK, we'll be OK. All right?" Sol looks around.
"All right, boys. All right. We're going to get to the cage
and Torsten will pull us up to a safe level, get us out
another way. I'm sure Quinn's already got things going
on that front, right? He knows his stuff. Now let's just
be calm and make sure to keep your fucking lights lit,
hey? OK?" Sol meets each man's eyes, trying to display
a confidence he isn't sure he feels. His heart is pounding
in his chest. *Flame and fucking smoke, again.*

They only make it about halfway down the drift when
Rob Quinn and a number of other men, including the
old Swede, Torsten, come stumbling out of the billowing
haze, hunched over, coughing, eyes round in their dirty
faces. "Fire's just a level up, men," Quinn says, when he
can draw a breath. "Cage ain't going nowhere for now.
We got to work our way up the manways, climb 'em
up a level or two, away from the shaft, get above the

burn and then we can get out. Crew bosses, get your fuckin men organized and follow me. Gonna be crowded getting up there so we got to be careful."

The men push forward, Sol's crew going back the way they've already come, working their way along the drift until they get to the first manway, the ladders that run perpendicular to the drifts, where the drillers can follow the seam of ore. From the manways, the stepped stope tunnels move out laterally where the rock is drilled and mucked out, to be brought down to the drift and eventually up and out via the shaft cages. Now, dozens of men, and who knew how many more in the other levels, were going to have to climb out these narrow passages, only slightly wider than a man's shoulders, some of them. Crawl a couple of hundred or more feet up, get above the fire and hope there's a working cage. In the dark, and smoke, and wet, caustic heat that only will get worse as the fire grows.

Quinn stands at the base of the manway, sending the miners up one at a time. "Don't fuckin crowd up, goddammit!" he yells. "Don't fuckin rush, just get up slow and steady." The men are already hunching, pushing and shoving one another, yelling and cursing.

Sol watches for a minute, before pulling Quinn aside. "It's too fucking slow, Rob. If it's taking this long to get up this first bit, there's no way we're all going to get up there in time. No fucking way. We need to split up, it'll go faster. Because we need to get out, quick." *Before the air burns out*, they both know. That's the real danger.

Sol thinks for a moment. "I'ma take my boys out the Tramway."

"Tramway's half a fuckin mile away, Sol… you sure?"

"Course I'm not sure, Rob. Best idea I got, is all. My boys are young and spry, though, hey?" *Unlike me.* "We'll be all right." He nods at the manway. "You think you can get them all up there, quick enough? Why don't you come with us?"

"Nah, I'll get them up there, if I have to kick all their fuckin asses up the goddamn fuckin ladders my own fuckin self."

They shake hands, quickly, and then Sol grabs the arms of his boys and they stumble away.

The Tramway mine is connected to the Pennsylvania, its shaft rising out of the ground a half-mile or so to the east. Sol's thought is that, instead of trying to fight their way upwards along with all the other men trying to get out, they'll go *down* a couple of levels, via the manways, work their way across the drift to the Tramway and ride its cage up. All this while in the dark, before the fire catches up with them and roasts them or, more likely, burns out all the air and they suffocate a quarter-mile or so underground.

Easy.

They run. Down the drift a ways they reach another of the manways but there are crates and tools and timber and debris stacked all over in the little notch in front of it; miners being miners, various crews have just moved this detritus out of the main flow of the drift tunnel so that they can continue working – war production, right – rather than clear it out properly and stack it in one of the storage areas. The boys frantically start to pull the boxes and heavy timbers free until Sol stops them. "No fucking time for that, go! We'll use the next one. Go, go!"

Back down the drift to the next manway, only a little distance away and mercifully clear, the ladder open but, when they get down a few feet the stope is full damn near all the way through with more rubbish, a big pile of timber that bisects the path of the ladder. *Fucking lazy fucking goddamn fuckers,* Sol silently shouts as they pile their way back upwards again. He vows that, if he makes it out, he is going to find and kick some fucking asses, and that's for goddamn sure. The smoke has gotten noticeably thicker already and he's coughing more than even he is used to. They all are.

There's only one last manway, down at the very end of the drift. It's the perfect kind of place for lazy crews to pile more shit up and block the way, he knows. *Killed by sloppy fucking laziness,* Sol tells himself, *and whose fucking fault is that. Put that on my headstone. Killed by lazy fucking shitbird miners.*

When they get to the end of the drift, though, the ladder is clear, and down they go, Sol pushing the boys down in front of him, counting to keep track. Seven men, plus himself. Before Billy starts to descend, somewhere near the middle of the pack, Sol grabs his arm. "Eight of us, all together, right?" he yells. "Help me get them out. *Eight of us.* You keep an eye on these boys, Bill."

Billy looks back at him, eyes white in his dark, dirty face. "Jesus, Sol." He starts down the ladder, looking back up. "Fucking shit."

Owen is the last to go down the ladder, aside from Sol himself. The boy's nearly frantic by now, coughing and gasping and quite possibly crying around it, though he tries to hide it from the others. Sol knows the boy has always had a terror of fire, Ag had told him that much. That Owen knows the story of his mother, has the puckered scars down one arm and leg in lieu of a memory of it. The boy hasn't even been on the job two months yet; he'd spent most of that time as a crowfoot, prodding the rock overhead with a long pole, waiting for a rotten ceiling to fall in on him, before Sol had taken pity and added him to this crew when he was short a man. Now, Owen can't breathe and he can barely stand up for coughing. They're going down, not up, and Sol knows the boy won't understand. Down, down, down into the dark where they might never come out. He'd just wanted a job, Owen.

Sol grabs him for a second, squeezing him hard around the biceps, giving him a quick shake. "Hey! *Hey!* We'll be all right, son, huh? Look at me!" Gives him another shake, tries to fashion something close to a smile, something that resembles confidence. Sol realizes yet again that he doesn't know this boy, his own son, that he'd mostly let his brother Ag raise up. Given how the boy had jumped at the first opportunity to head out on his own, though, Sol thinks that maybe Owen has something of himself in him after all, that maybe all that time with solid, reliable Ag and his quiet, godly family hadn't quite stuck. He's done not a goddamn thing for the boy until now, unless it's just giving him a job, but Sol vows that he's going to make up for lost time. The lot of it. Once they're out of this fucking mine.

"We'll be fine," he says. "Just down this ladder a smidge and then a quick jaunt over to the Tramway and up and out, good story at the end of it, hey? Drinks are on me tonight, so you need to try to stay awake for once, OK?"

"I'm scared, Sol."

"Hell, Owen, that's how you know you're alive. I'm damn near shitting my pants, but we're going to get out, don't you worry. Hey, right? *Don't worry.* You just keep Billy in front of you and I'll be right behind, OK? If you don't see Billy you'll damn sure see Nancy banging his head on the ceiling every other step. Worst case, you just listen for fucking Michael because you know his gums will be flapping, right?" He slaps his son's shoulders again. "You're doing fine. I'm proud of you, boy." When he says it, it feels wrong in his mouth, like he doesn't have the right to say it, not yet anyway, but chooses to ignore it. He gives Owen a little push. "I'm right behind you. Now, go!"

Down the manway ladder and the drift, having to backtrack once because of another pile of timber – *fucking lazy bastard timber fucks* – onto another manway and then, finally, the drift of the 1400-level, full of smoke but ominously quiet, aside from the hacking coughs of the boys gathered around the base of the ladder. Sol makes another quick count: *seven plus me. Eight. OK.* The Tramway connects to the Penn, far as he remembers anyway, on 1500, which means one more descent, which this time passes mercifully quickly, unblocked and a straight shot down. On 1500, he counts again – *eight* – and takes a moment to orient himself, checking the wall signs before heading them off in a direction that had to be east.

Half a mile, give or take. 2,500 feet or so. Easy.

They run, gasping through the smoke. Sure enough, Nancy and Flynn spend a goodly amount of time banging into things, given their height and the fact that they can see fuck-all in the dust and haze. After the first few minutes, Sol can barely stand, he's coughing so hard. More than once he slips in the muck and has to be dragged upright by one of the boys. His headlamp has gone out, as have those of several of the others. Billy, always careful, has kept his alight, at least. It's hard enough to see now, but running from a fire in the absolute dark of the deep is something too fearsome to contemplate.

The minutes drag, stretched long and tight with

fear. The mine is empty, quiet over the gasping of Sol's breath, the coughing of the boys. Someone is muttering nonsense, someone is cursing *fuck fuck fuck* over and over again. Tunnels that always feel tight seem to be closing in, the smoke and dust wrapping around them in an embrace no one wants. Sol concentrates on the bobbing of Billy's light in the middle of the pack. Finally, they reach the end of the drift where the bulkhead that connects to the Tramway intersects.

"*Oh you motherfuckers! Sweet Christ's cunt you cunting lazy motherfuckers!*" Michael is screaming at the blocked door as Sol staggers up. Already Nancy and Flynn are attacking the stack of crates and timbers, hurling them to the side as fast as they can, hacking and coughing all the while. "*Jesus fuckin shite fuck you sheepfuckin timber cunts!*" Not pausing in his nonsensical cursing, Michael joins them. In a moment, the rest are at the pile, digging out the door so they can get it open. Sol pauses to make another count. *Eight.* For a moment, Billy's eye catches his and they share something akin to a smile, a kind of panicked, mindless thing that flashes bright and crazy for a second.

The smoke is as thick as a wall by the time they get the door open, so dense and airless that Sol weaves for a moment, having to bend over and hack into his shoulder, his vision going hazy, ready to just pass out and stay there. *At least Sean fucking Harrity won't get paid now*, he thinks for one wild instant. *Let him come down here and threaten his money out of my goddamn corpse.* Forcing air into his lungs, he hollers at the boys to get down the tunnel to the Tramway, shaking off someone's arm – Billy's, no doubt, but it's too dark to see – as he coughs into his shirt again. "*Just goddamn go! All of you, move! I'm right behind you.*"

He looks back at the mass of smoke behind him, which parts for a second. An old Indian man steps out of the gloom, singing something hoarse and breathy and wordless. There are small bones tied into his hair and in one palm burns a black fire. The old man is smiling around his song, his teeth white as new china, gleaming through the smoke.

Sol heels over, gasping for air, knowing that the old man isn't there, that he's just an artifact of his own oxygen-deprived brain, the smoke and dust in his chest, a product of the terror that's knuckled his asshole shut. A hallucination, that's all, just a memory of a bad dream that he'll forget soon enough. The old Indian isn't there, so Sol steps into the tunnel and drags the door shut behind him. He won't look back; he doesn't need to. The Pennsylvania is burning but he's gotten his boys out, and that's the thing.

Later, Sol doesn't know just where Owen was lost. How, even. When the Tramway hoistman finally responds to their frantic signaling and pulls them up, they come piling out of the cage at the top of the Tramway and the count is seven.

The old sorcerer smiles in the dark and smoke, warming the carved bones in his hand, tracing the outlines of their marks with the tip of a bony finger. They are pregnant with possibility, these bones. He sits and casts them to the ground, listening.

A boy, burning.

The echoes of that act are building, moving. It will be soon, now that he has set things in motion. He has pushed the stone and the mountain of time begins to slide, rumbling and slipping, inexorable, pushing all before it, towards another boy and a new angle of repose at the end.

After the long years, it comes fast now. As these things are measured, it will be soon. He must prepare.

The Above Ones have spoken and the power to end this thing has been given to him. Because of the strength of his medicine and depths of his sins, it belongs to him, until it must be given to the other. The pouch where his medicine lives is hot against the skin of his chest, hidden under his shirt.

Memory

1902

Warm Springs, Montana

It lingers on her skin, her hair, even after all this time.

Her over-washed clothes, fabric scrubbed thin as gossamer over the tight spots at elbow and knee, still contain the hint of it. Smoke, the whisper of burned wood, charred cloth, the meaty slick of melted fat. It covers her, clings to her, memory made substance.

Those memories, the smell of them, they twist and change, blow away on the dead wind. First one thing, then another. Things that happened and didn't happen and will happen or won't. Strange things that make no sense until they do.

She's not sure what she knows any more.

Sometimes it's hard for her to breathe. There are times when she wakes up at night, sweating and gasping for breath, feeling the press of burning air on her eyelids, flame sucked down her throat, into her lungs, scalding them into collapse. She remembers the small hairs on her arms crisping, her eyelashes singed to powder. During the day, when she feels the fire thoughts coming, she can usually fend them off: slow her breathing, shut her eyes and think *cold cold cold* until it passes.

But not always, and the smell and touch of smoke

never leaves her, day or night. It has marked her like some sister of Cain: murderess.

Owen, my son.

For a time, in the beginning, her husband visits. Alone at first, and then, for some unknown reason, in the company of a skinny Indian boy she doesn't know. The boy hesitates outside the room, shuffles his feet, frets his hands around the edges of a ratty hat. She can tell the boy doesn't want to be there but perhaps he feels obligated. Her husband has the habit of taking people under his wing, making them feel beholden to him. As he did with her, she knows, rescuing her from some imagined peril, years ago, and then never letting her loose.

She thinks she loved him, once. Now, nothing is clear because the smoke covers everything.

He talks to her about the child, as if Owen was still a living thing. He says the boy is a handful – *full of vinegar, now that he's walking* – he's running poor Mrs Malloy ragged. *You remember Mrs Malloy*, he says. Of course she remembers the old lady. She remembers everything.

The fire bursting upwards. The shrieking of the child in her hand. The pork smell of burning flesh. The screams of the bird at the window.

She still sees the bird. It's there so often, as if it knows her. As if it's waiting for her to let it in. Or, if not that one, another. Watching her, tapping at the window. Trying to get inside.

They catch her with a knife again, cutting her arms. They take it from her – *where do you keep getting them, girl* – and submerge her in an icy bath. When the attendants are alone with her, they hit her, do other things. It doesn't matter. She always heals. Once, as a younger woman, she was very sick, dying, but now she is an unnatural thing, tight and swollen with life. Overfull with something noxious.

In the freezing bath, submerged in water that smells like smoke, she screams for her boy, for Owen, for forgiveness.

Get Your Hands Up

— 1917 —

Warm Springs, Montana/ Butte, Montana

1.

"Owen!"

The sound comes from outside the barn, a thin and plaintive wail drifting on the wind from the main hospital. Billy shakes his head, knowing the source.

"Owen, no, no, I'm sorry, no –"

The sound cuts off abruptly.

The barn is warm, humid, the dairy cows packed in their stalls, munching hay with bovine contentment. The grassy smell of cowshit fills Billy's nostrils, dank but somehow comforting. He shrugs out of his coat while he watches the old man at work.

The whites call him John Bird but, in the old tongue, his father's given name is Bad Bird, which means *bat*. Not for the first time Billy thinks about the fact that the name he himself was given at the school, William Morgan, doesn't mean anything. It's just a name, drawn from a hat for all he knows. Billy never thinks about his old name. Lately his father has taken to calling himself *Crazy Cow*, a joke at his own expense, given where he is. *Chief Crazy Cow*. Bad Bird hums to himself as he mucks out the last stall, moving with slow, precise efficiency.

"You've been all right then?" Billy says now, taking

out a cigarette paper and clumsily rolling tobacco into it. He rarely smokes but knows that his father will enjoy one. The old man still has a reverence for tobacco and is not allowed it here.

Bad Bird shrugs. "Don't let them catch you with that," he says, without looking up, speaking the old tongue. He understands English just fine but refuses to use it, the opposite of his son. "They say that tobacco winds us crazies up. Or maybe it winds up the cows. I don't remember. A lot of stupid things are said here and it's best to not listen too closely."

"You're not crazy." Although of course he is, which is why he's here at Warm Springs, the Montana State Hospital for the Insane, why he'll never leave. A humane place for the ill in mind, those needing rest and recuperation. Or so they say.

It's also a place for those who need to be kept away for the safety of others, and for their own. Those like his father, Bad Bird. Those like Elizabeth Parker, Sol's wife, calling again for the son she thought she'd killed all those years ago. He doubts that they've told her that, now, Owen truly is gone. What's the point in that.

Eventually, deeming the shit-mucking complete, Bad Bird straightens up, resting his weight on the pitchfork's handle and taking the proffered cigarette from Billy. He leans forward to accept a light. The old man's seamed face crinkles into a satisfied smile as he pulls the smoke into his lungs. For a long while they don't speak, his father simply enjoying the cigarette, humming under his breath again.

Watching Bad Bird smoke, looking at the sharp implement in his father's hand, Billy wonders again about the wisdom of allowing a lunatic the use of a pitchfork. Once, he'd asked Dr Rideout about it. *The work, the animals, it helps keeps him calm, Billy,* he'd been told. Billy isn't inclined by nature to doubt Dr Rideout, Sol's brother, but he, Billy Morgan, still has the scar on his shoulder, the one his father put there years ago with the business end of a hatchet.

His father does seem calm, though. Lucid, right now anyway, so Billy supposes the doctor is right. This hospital, with its various failings, the accusations of mismanagement and corruption, is still a better place for his father than the reservation is, after all; here, people can look after him, make sure he eats and, most importantly, keep him from mischief. If Bad Bird is kept content shoveling cowshit in a dairy barn, so much the better.

His father is saying something now, which takes Billy a moment to translate. "The job is fine, Father," he replies in English. "I'm safe." Safe enough. For now.

Bad Bird glares at him, his eyes buried deep in the hollows of his leathery face. Billy's father doesn't ever seem to age; he'd looked ancient when Billy was a boy, and that was a long time ago now. Bad Bird is like old wood, merely getting denser and harder, more himself, as the years pass. He looks it, his rough, dry skin the brown-orange of ponderosa bark, his long grey hair the color of a cottonwood.

"That place is poison, boy. Remember the story of Rabbit Woman."

Billy doesn't reply. The last time he'd seen his father, Bad Bird had been far less sanguine than he is now, screaming from the little room in which he was being held, given another of the series of icy baths that are supposed to calm him. Apparently the cowshit therapy doesn't always work.

The People had a story: Rabbit Woman, who dug up

Moon's carrot, even though Sun had told her that doing so would unleash great ills on the world. For whatever reason, Bad Bird believes that Moon's carrot had lived in the hill under Butte, that it had turned to gold and silver and copper and, now that it had been dug up, there would be nothing but sorrow and pain and death unleashed on the world.

When Bad Bird is finished with the first, Billy rolls and lights up another cigarette for him, making one for himself as well. For a long time, they smoke in silence, he and his crazy old man, breathing in the smell of hay and warm cow farts and the taste of stale, cheap tobacco.

Later, Billy walks the grounds with Dr Rideout.

"He seems better."

Ag Rideout just shrugs. John Bird is a dangerous and unpredictable man who, although given to long bouts of lucidity, will remain here until he dies. Given the old man's years, that won't be long. Really, John Bird shouldn't even *be* here, should be on the reservation, an awful idea, but state bureaucracy is what it is. Fortunately, Dr Rideout had been able to pull strings as a favor to his brother.

"How's Sol?" Ag says now.

It's Billy's turn to shrug. The brothers rarely see one another, so how to describe the last year? *Sol's angry* doesn't begin to explain things. *Sol's ashamed and full of guilt about Owen and broke and drunk all the fucking time* are the facts of the matter, but that doesn't scratch the surface of what it means, even for a brother. *Sol is in trouble* is about as close as he can get, but saying it feels like a betrayal. If Sol wants his brother to know, he'll tell him himself.

"He's been better," is what he finally settles on.

Dr Rideout seems to understand; he reaches his hand over with a long arm, giving Billy's shoulder a squeeze, sighing.

They walk the grounds for a while longer, Dr Rideout giving him the latest on Elizabeth Parker – *she's having a bad spell again, lately* – a report that Billy knows Sol will never ask for, and which Billy will never offer.

Billy's not entirely surprised to see his uncle, Marked Face, squatting outside the squalid little tavern in Anaconda, just down the road from Warm Springs. Billy just wants a beer, maybe a few, today; he's tired of talking and merely wants some quiet, some time to himself before he has to get back to Butte for Nancy's fight. He wants to be alone but, more often than not, lately, whenever he comes through Anaconda after visiting his father, his uncle is somehow there, waiting for him. For an old man who decries the ways of the whites, and who lives God knows where up on the reservation, Marked Face is in Anaconda often enough. If his uncle had been a normal man, Billy would just assume he was here at the tavern to cadge a drink, but Marked Face is different, and did things for reasons of his own.

"Uncle," he says, checking a sigh, trying to push down the unease he always feels around the old man. His uncle is as crazy as Bad Bird, crazier maybe, given to rants and curses, violence; the fact that he isn't locked up somewhere, or dead, maybe just means the scary old fucker is too wily.

By way of response, Marked Face spits in the dirt between Billy's feet, then reaches out a hand to rub the mark away, drawing a circle in the dust when he's finished.

Billy tries to ignore whatever witchcraft the bastard

thinks he's just laid on him. "Buy you a drink?"

Marked Face rises to his feet, moving smoothly and gracefully, given his age, drawing the ratty old blanket he wears closer around himself. Billy notes that, again, for a man who claims to hew to the old ways and who hates whites, his uncle has on a store-bought Pendleton shirt, jeans, and a decent, if battered, pair of leather work boots. The old man tosses his chin towards the southeast, towards Butte, the long white braids he wears flipping across his neck like dead snakes. His eyes are black river-rocks, flat and empty.

"Did my brother ever tell you what the People called that place, that place you and your white friends are digging up?" He speaks the old tongue, his voice low and graveled, full of contempt.

Billy thinks back through the stories that he'd heard before being sent off to the government school, most of them only dimly remembered by now. He has no idea what the old name for Butte's hill is, doesn't care, really, so he shakes his head, shrugging.

There are a long few seconds as Marked Face just stares at him with what seems like – to Billy – unreasonable anger, even for an old lunatic like his uncle. *So I fucking forgot the name, if anyone ever even told it to me*, Billy thinks. *And you know what? The place is called Butte now and that's what it will always be; it doesn't matter what name the tribes gave it, because they're gone, so to hell with you.*

Marked Face stares, looking like he wants to slap him out of pure disgust. Billy takes a short, involuntary step backward and then his uncle laughs, sharp barks that the old man wraps up with another spit between Billy's feet, an oystery gob that he leaves there in the dirt this time.

"We called it a hill, boy. Just a hill, somewhere to hunt. A place to cut poles for lodges. There was good rock for arrowheads there, too, in the old days, they say." He cackles again. "How's your father?"

Billy just shrugs again, wanting to slap his uncle now. "He's OK. Working with the cows."

"He try to kill anyone lately?" Marked Face says, scoffing, rubbing the thick scar that runs from the corner of his eye down his cheekbone. Billy has to keep himself from rubbing at his own shoulder.

"He's working with the cows."

Marked Face spits again. "Haven't seen you for a while, boy. I heard about that fire. Bad business. Lot of people dead, they said. Not a place for men to dig, that hill, to crawl around like ants in holes, for no good reason. What was under the earth didn't matter, before the whites came. You remember that. What lived underground was put there at the beginning of things, and there it should stay."

Billy's tired of it all, his family and the stories and crazy old men. Every time he comes to see his father he winds up feeling this way, worn out and disgusted and vowing to never come back, and yet here he is, again, skipping back to the same old shit like the needle on a scratched phonograph.

"You should maybe go talk to your brother, then, Uncle," he says, "because I've heard it all. Two of you old fuckers can talk until you're blue in the face, tell your old stories, sing your fucking songs. Worked for you pretty well up to now, all that bullshit, hey?" He spits on the ground himself. "I got to go find a ride. I got to work tomorrow."

He's surprised to see Marked Face smiling at him. He forces himself to stay still as the old man takes a step closer, leaning in to whisper into his ear, his breath oddly sweet.

"You should have some respect, Nephew. You're not as white as you think you are, so you listen to your old uncle, hey?" Marked Face steps back, holding Billy with his river-rock eyes. "You remember this word, white man: *omanaahstoo*?"

"Raven." Billy mutters it, unwilling to hold his uncle's gaze. He feels small and wonders if he'll ever lose the fear he still has of Marked Face, of his father, or if he'll always be that same scared, bleeding little kid he was before the school, trying to fight them off when they went on a tear, getting beat to shit for his troubles. They're old men now and Billy is as big and strong as he'll ever be, but just the sight of them peels the years back, leaves him a puny, weak thing again. He forces himself to look up into his uncle's smiling face. It isn't a smile he likes, has never liked; it's a smile that hides black things behind bright white teeth.

"You'll see Raven, soon enough, you'll see him at night. That's what I came here to tell you, Nephew. I had a dream. I had a dream of you and Raven." Without another word, Marked Face turns and walks away, pausing after a few steps to spit again. "Be seeing you," he calls over his shoulder.

Billy has no idea what that was all about but, as he watches his uncle walk away, he wants that beer, maybe a few, even more now. For fuck's sake, why does it have to be like this all the time? And why does he even bother with these sad, lunatic bastards any more. Just die already, you old fuckers. Give me some peace.

He pushes the tavern door open, steps inside into the cool, smoky dark. Curses old men and crazy Indians. Fuck them, fuck them all, fuck the lot of them.

2.

"Goddamn it, get your fucking hands up, Nancy!"

Fist meets flesh with a hollow, meaty thump. Big Nancy folds over into the follow-up punch that tears across the stub of his ear, is lifted back up upright with the left to his chin. Sol can see Nancy's legs start to buckle, and he rubs his hands across his own face, gritting his teeth and squinching his eyes shut. *Come on, not yet.* When he opens them, Nancy is still standing, somehow, but his eyes are glassy; he stumbles into Faraday's next combination to the body, absorbing the blows with stolid distraction. Left, right, left, left, like a butcher pounding steak, and then Nancy lets loose with a wild, looping right of his own, which Faraday calmly ducks before chiming the side of Nancy's head again. Nick Faraday is a fair bit older than Nancy, if a shade smaller, but has experience, skill, guile. An actual boxer. *Jesus Christ, Nick, the fuck are you doing?* Sol isn't sure how much longer Nancy's going to last at this rate. He glances surreptitiously at his pocket watch and, when he looks up, sees that Sean Harrity is looking over at him, tapping his own, as if to say *third round*.

Goddamn it.

"Get your fucking hands up, Nancy!" Sol yells through his cupped fingers. "Don't just fucking stand there and let him hit you!" If Nancy hears, he makes no sign, just ducks his head and mulishly wades into another series of blows. If Faraday was a better puncher, this fight would have been over long ago, had it been on the level. Once, a fighter had told Sol that each punch had to have the weight of a baby dropped off a building, a disturbing – and yet surprisingly apt – description of how a fist should land. Nick Faraday, the fucking moron, is quick and has some technique but, for a relatively big man, his punches still lack some mustard. Which is fortunate, as Nancy has to last at least another minute.

"Goddamn it, Nancy, hands up!" Sol glances at his watch again. He and Sean have set the fight to three two-minute breaks and then, if the fighters are still going after that, last man standing. Which would be Nick Faraday, by prior agreement, in the third fucking round. *Not now.* The final break is still over a minute out and Nancy is never going to make it at this rate. Sol glances around the crowd, looking for a path to the exit, just in case. He looks back up just in time to see Faraday plant his forehead into Nancy's already broken nose.

"The hell!" Sol shouts, waving a hand. "Pat, the fuck are you doing? That's a goddamn foul!"

The referee, a loose title at best, gives Sol a disgusted look. "You shut your hole, Parker, and let the boys fight."

Jesus Christ, Pat. It's not like you don't know what's going on here. Keep Nancy up or I'm well and truly fucked. We all are.

Sol needs a drink.

3.

The year since the fire hasn't gone well for Sol Parker.

Twenty-one men died in the Pennsylvania fire, twenty-one of their brother miners. Of the two-hundred plus men working the Penn that February day, nineteen never came out; later, most of their bodies were found up on the 300 level, lying where they'd finally suffocated. Two other men, who'd gone back into the mine with the rescue parties, died because their Draegers hadn't been serviced and primed with enough oxygen. The fire wasn't fully contained until the first week of April, concrete bunkers built to keep the burn and smoke from spreading to the other mines, the Penn itself requiring tunnel collapses and hollowed-out levels to finally smother the blaze.

The body of Owen Parker hasn't yet been found.

Sol had been responsible for the boy, way he was for all of his crew; Sol had told his son that he'd get him out, had *promised*, and failed, completely and thoroughly. The name of his son now one more to add to the long and storied list of the people Sol's let down in his life. He doesn't know, still, just how he'd lost him, so close to safety, but it doesn't fucking matter because he had.

Owen is still just as dead, his bones somewhere down there in the dark, alone. His boy, for whom he'd done fuck-all over the course of Owen's short life, aside from dumping him with Ag and his family to raise, when Sol's own grief over Lizzie had gotten too sharp. Maybe that was the best thing he could have done at the time, but now it feels cheap and miserly, selfish and weak. Just when the boy had come back into Sol's life he'd failed him again, one last time.

It couldn't be helped, Sol, the boys said, through their own tears. *It was an accident* and *you got all us out* and *we'd be dead without you. The kid knew this job was dangerous, Sol.*

No he hadn't, though, not really. He was just a fucking kid looking for some work, maybe saw that his dad was doing all right down the mine and thought to try it on for size, a way to get out from under his uncle's thumb, see something of the world, make his own way. Just a kid wanting to put food in his belly, but fucked by the mine. By the Company, by his failure of a father. Fucked for a few more dollars of copper.

The miners were angry, getting angrier. All of them. Twenty-one of their brothers, gone. This wasn't a freak accident, a cage cutting loose or a bad explosion. These men died because the ACM cared so little for basic safety precautions, because that costs money. That's it. A fire suppression system, sprinkler lines at the collars, might have stopped the burn cold. It's not like the technology didn't exist. Their brother miners, dead for the fucking bottom line; they will be one day too, most likely. Rumor has it that Frank Little is pushing forward his trip to Butte, to use his weight and savvy to try to keep the workers from letting anger burn into something reckless and destructive, something that wouldn't help Labor, another repeat of the Union Hall debacle or something even worse. He's coming to Butte to channel their anger into something sharper, something stronger.

After the fire, Sol begins to find in the movement – the Movement – an outlet for his own anger and grief and shame. He begins to pay attention. To go to meetings, listen to speakers, even stand up and talk himself, once in a while. When he isn't too drunk, that is, a state he found himself in more often than not in the weeks and months after the fire.

His crew worries about him; Billy, ever the mother, tries to keep Sol sober when he can, ignoring the snapping outbursts of anger and the sullen silences. He worries that Sol is slipping away from them.

It's not your fault, Sol.

But it is, Sol knows. Just like it had been with Lizzie, all those years ago.

"It's your own fuckin fault, Sol."

Sol just looks down at his hands, waits for whatever is coming. Fat Mickey Doyle and Nick Faraday had pushed their way into the cabin just before dawn, rousted him out of bed, ignoring Billy after a flat, warning glare. *At least it's my day off,* Sol had thought, struggling into his clothes, dry-mouthed and gut-sick, a new hangover pounding behind his eyes once more. As Mickey had dragged him out of the shack, Sol tried to give Billy a look that had something like assurance in it. *Don't worry, I'll be fine.* Regardless of the fact that he knew it to be a lie.

Sean Harrity shrugs now, raising his eyebrows in a helpless sort of way. "Sorry, but there it is: *it's your own fuckin fault,*" he repeats, slowly and with grave emphasis. He nods his head in time with the words. Brightening falsely then, raising a bottle. "Too early for a drink?"

"I'm awake, ain't I?" Sol looks around Sean's office, a squalid little space at the back of the Piper restaurant, barely wide enough to accommodate the battered desk Sean sits behind. Sol himself sits on a rickety dining chair that's too low to the ground, as if someone has taken the time to shorten the legs by a couple of inches, forcing the chair's occupant to look up at the man behind the desk. A penitent's chair, a supplicant's. Fat Mickey is squeezed in between that chair and the door; Sol can feel the hot press of the man's belly uncomfortably close to the back of his neck. It's hard to resist the urge to crane his head around so that he can keep one eye on Mickey, but instead he reaches up to take the glass of whiskey Sean pushes across the desk.

"*Sláinte.*"

"Cheers, Sean." Sol drinks, nods appreciatively. "Good stuff."

"Only the finest for my friends, Sol." Sean smiles across the desk, laces his fingers together.

An uncomfortable silence. Sol looks back at the smile, wondering where this is going. All in all, he'd prefer an angry Sean Harrity to this smiling fuck sat up across from him. The man of quiet threats and noisy menaces he knows too well, from long association both public and private. Sean Harrity, the pimp, shark, thief; a criminal generalist, one of the enterprising class of lowlifes who exist to suck the paycheck out of the working man like the Company sucks the metal out of the hill. More worrying, to Sol, is the fact that Sean's a murderer when he needs – or wants – to be. When he feels affronted or his interests are compromised or for any number of other reasons. Sean Harrity has never balked from using his power to the fullest extent and fuck the consequences, what little there are.

Mining the pockets of his fellows has made Sean Harrity a wealthy man: he has gambling, drink, and prostitution interests throughout the red-light district around Chinatown, as well as owning a number of the shittier variety of cribs, hop-houses, and the like in the Cabbage Patch. Sean's parlayed this wealth into a number of legitimate holdings, too: a portfolio of shops, boarding houses, and cafes, mostly up around Dublin Gulch, catering to his fellow Irishmen. Rumor has it that Sean is in tight with Company managers as well, providing unaffiliated and deniable muscle when heads needed cracking. Certainly Sean's boys aren't afraid to use their fists, or more, when collecting from recalcitrant debtors who have run the string out on their obligations a bit too long.

Men like Sol.

They look at each other for a solid minute. The dank, stuffy little room is so quiet that Sol can hear the faint whistle of Mickey's breathing, the tick of the ornate, ostentatious pocket watch Sean wears on a thick gold chain.

"I'll get your money, Sean," Sol says, finally. "I don't got it now but I'll get it, OK?"

Sean winces, looking up, as if seeing something unpleasant off in the distance. "Well, Sol, I don't like to be that man, but, you know."

"I said I'll get your money."

"You'll forgive me if I admit I've heard that before." He shrugs. "I've got a business to run, Sol, a business. Now, I think I've been more than patient, particularly given your recent losses and griefs, but ..." He trails off, shrugging again. "It's been fuckin months now, over a year, and your debt is doing nothing but rise."

"What do you want me to say, Sean? I'll get your

goddamn money. I don't have it right now, and all the threats and bullshit in the world ain't going to *get it* right now, so maybe spare us both the jawing, yeah? I said I'll get the money and I will."

Sean leans back, looking aggrieved. "Threats? What threats?" He looks over at Mickey. "You hear any threats?" He leans forward. "Sol, I don't make threats, but I'll have that money. D'ya understand me?" He lowers his voice. "I've been a patient man, Mr Parker, out of respect for your age and station and the losses you have endured but, like I said, I have people who rely on me and, dare I say it, a certain image, a reputation, to maintain, you understand, and *I'll have that money*." He looks over Sol's shoulder, gives a small nod.

The bolt of pain shoots from Sol's kidney up to his neck, making him lurch forward with a gasp. The second punch hurts even more than the first, and a low groan slips out from between his gritted teeth.

"Let's talk about repayment, Solomon."

4.

"Hands up!"

This fight isn't going well and Sol needs a drink.

The air inside Heaney's, one of Harrity's joints, a hole on the south edge where the shittier parts of the East Side rot into the arms of the Patch, is hot and close, containing more tobacco smoke than oxygen. The tables and chairs are pushed to the walls, patrons crowded tight against one another around the periphery, the room sweaty and smoky and reeking of unwashed bodies. Without looking, Sol reaches backwards into the crowd, yelling, "*Drink!*" until someone's pint is put in his hand. He takes a long pull of the warm, sour muck that Heaney passes off as beer, knocking some of the dry from his throat.

"Get your *FUCKING* hands *UP*, Nancy!" he shouts, watching his man lean into another series of fists: left, left, right, left, left, one coming after the next with quick, calm precision. Nancy's never been much of a fighter, even back when they'd fought straight; he's merely big and tough, with a tolerance for abuse that would kill any two other men. When he lands a punch, though, rare as it is, it's truly that baby dropped from the building, the dead weight of his huge fist propelled by a tree trunk of an arm. Nancy's slow, though, and has nothing in the way of cunning. The fighters around town figured him out soon enough and simply dance around him now, pick him apart piece by piece until he eventually crumbles. Which had accelerated Sol's bad series of bets, of course, as he'd been too stupid to see it for what it was, naively trusting to Nancy's heroic capacity for mistreatment.

Even Nancy had his limits, though.

He's going down now, swaying, lurching to one knee as that excitable southpaw idiot continues to ring his skull with lefts. Sol looks at his watch, screams *"Time! Time! Time!"* He steps forward and tries to push himself between his fighter and Faraday's fast left hand. Nick Faraday will get him killed if this keeps up.

"Time!" Sean shouts, flat-eyed and angry, though he's trying not to show it. Sol wonders just who has actually been dumb enough to put money on this fight, the fix being so obvious. Although, from personal and repeated experience, he knows that the human capacity for stupidity is limitless.

"You want to call it now?" Sean calls over to Sol, fuming, trying to maintain at least a modicum of subterfuge about the events at hand. "Your man seems done, Mr Parker."

Sol looks down at Big Nancy. One of the boy's eyes is swollen shut and he's huffing out of his broken nose like an animal, raking in air through a bloody mouth. Sol takes a handful of Nancy's thick red hair and leans down, pulling his fighter's face close to his own. "You OK, Nance?" he says, as quietly as he can over the din of spectators yelling at one another. "You don't look so good, son, but just a little bit longer, hey?"

Nancy's good eye rolls around for a bit in its socket

before coming to rest on him. "Fuck you, Sol," he mutters through puffy, split lips. He spits a glutinous red dribble of blood and mucous between Sol's feet. "Got him right where I want him."

Sol feels that isn't really the point, but does his best to heave Nancy to his feet, leading him over to the chair someone has placed in their corner, passing him a beer when the big man sits. Nancy knows the score; going down doesn't sit right with the boy but he'll do it. Sol himself isn't particularly troubled by the sporting implications of what they're doing, because he knows that he has no choice. As he'd explained it to Nancy: *you do this or you boys are going to find me in an alley somewhere.* Nancy taking the dive won't square Sol with Sean – far from it – but it's at least showing some due diligence towards his obligations and, when it comes right down to it, Sean owns him, at least for now. Fucking owns him, body and soul. Sol has to do what he's told and to hell with his pride.

Nancy, weaving on his chair, leans over to one side and pukes up a thin stream of beer, blood, and bile.

Sol squats on his haunches in front of Big Nancy, feeling the sharp crack in his tired knees. Nancy's bloody face has gone vacant; Sol reaches up and gives him a few gentle slaps to focus the boy, wiping sweat and snot and blood off of him with his sleeve at the same time. "Goddamn it, someone get me a rag," he shouts back over his shoulder. When one is passed into his hand he spends a moment trying to smear Nancy's face back towards clean, stanch the flow of blood as best he can.

"Fighters, one minute!" O'Toole calls.

"Fuck off, Pat," Sol mutters, slapping Nancy's face with his free hand again until he sees the gleam of focus coming back into his open eye. Nancy raises his own hand, tries to push Sol's slaps away.

"You got to get your hands up, son," Sol says, cupping the back of Nancy's head, steering that one wavering blue eye towards his own. "Up, up. I don't want you to get hurt."

"I am hurt," Nancy mumbles.

"Ah, come on, now, Nance, don't be such a fairy. You're fine. Just hold on a little longer, and you know what to do."

There's a long, wavering pause as Nancy's battered brain processes this. "But I *am* a fuckin fairy, Sol," he said.

Sol slaps him a little harder. "Not tonight, you're not! Come on, boy, I need you to focus."

"Quit hitting me, Sol," Nancy says, waving his hand loosely in front of his face, blowing blood out of his broken nose. "I know what to fuckin do, OK?"

"Time, gentlemen!" Pat calls out. "Fighters!"

Nancy stands up, rolling his head on his shoulders, pushing Sol out of the way as he watches Faraday step back into the open space between them. It's shameful, what they're doing, but it needs to be done and he won't let Sol down. Nancy turns away to spit again, catching Sol's eye for a brief moment and then moving forward, gritting his teeth as he gets ready to absorb some more punches. He hopes that he can go down in a realistic enough manner, and that it won't hurt too bad when he does.

Later, he isn't sure exactly just what happened. He remembers one fist after another smacking into the side of his head – *left right left left left* – and then the lazy loop of his own punch and then somehow Faraday is on the ground, twitching, eyes rolled back in his head as a bemused Pat O'Toole counts ten. Across the room, Nancy can see Sean Harrity staring at him, no expression on his face at all.

Heaney's is too loud, the air is too close and his head feels huge and swollen, throbbing from the punches he's absorbed. Behind the crowd, an old man with long white braids is grinning at him. It's hard to catch a breath and, for a moment, Big Nancy worries he's going to pass out. *A little late for that*, he thinks, as Flynn and Michael hustle over to him, drag him to the edge of the crowd, push him towards the door.

As they pull him away, Nancy swings his head around, mouth open, still trying to catch a breath. He looks for Sol, but he's nowhere to be seen.

5.

Fuck you, Sean, Sol says to himself, those days after the fight, as he scans the crowd that's gathered at the picket around the Neversweat. He knows Sean Harrity will be here, and is trying to plan accordingly. *Accidents goddamn happen, so fuck you.* For a moment he thinks he sees Mickey Doyle, but on closer inspection it proves to be just some other fat Irishman. Regardless, he ducks a little farther behind Nancy and Flynn. From where they are, to the left of the flatbed truck that the speakers will stand on, Sol can see a good portion of the men gathered on the road, without most of them able to see him.

He hopes.

"You boys spot anyone?" Michael is keyed up, shuffling from foot to foot as a cheap substitute for actual pacing. From time to time he pops a fist into the palm of his other hand, nervously cracking his knuckles.

"Yeah, Michael, there's a whole host of them right in front of us, with bats and fuckin axes," Flynn says, "but we just thought to keep it quiet, like. You know, as a surprise for you. You fuckin eejit."

"Well *excuse me*, Johnathan, you and your keen fuckin eyes—"

"Goddamn it, you two, shut up," Sol says. "Just shut the goddamn hell up for a minute and keep an eye out."

It's been like this for days, since the fight and Nancy's looping, misplaced fist. He can't hold that errant punch against the boy, not really. Accidents happen, after all, and the likely concussion Nancy's wearing, on top of an enormous helping of guilt, is more than the boy deserves.

It was supposed to have been easy, but now everything is fucked and Sol's hiding out, doing his best to avoid Sean Harrity. Shuffled to and from the mine every day, surrounded by his crew as de facto guards. Moving from room to room at night, never sleeping in the same place twice. It's embarrassing and emasculating, is what it is. Old Sol Parker, the welcher, idiot, and coward. The boys try to press a pistol on him, but he and pistols don't agree with one another.

Besides, it doesn't matter. There are two ways this thing will go: he'll find some way to square things with Sean or, more likely, Sean will merely wait him out and exact whatever punishment he sees fit when the chance finally presents itself. The boys – and Sol himself – can't keep this up forever. It's only been a few days and already they're damn near ready to kill one another from too much nervous proximity.

There's one other thing he can do, though, and that's leave. He'd left his problems behind more than once in his life, after all. So maybe best to not take the high road now, either.

The miners mill around the picket blocking the Anaconda road to the Neversweat which, along with several other mines, is shut down by the Union on the urging of Frank Little. The Company isn't happy. No one is happy. The mood is ugly and it won't take much for things to spill over. Already some fights have broken out, for no good reason. When the scabs and the police and the Pinkertons show up – and they will, for sure – Sol doesn't know just what will happen. The mine guards on the other side of the picket line are armed with rifles, the Pinkertons aren't shy to use their own guns, and the police are in the Company's fucking pocket. It doesn't look great, as situations are measured.

It's a year, to the day, from the Pennsylvania fire. All Sol wants to do is go find a bottle and not think for a while, but here he is. He's tired; he can't remember the last time he's had a good night's sleep, what with all the moving around and the terrible dreams he keeps having. If anything, the dreams are getting worse. They're full of fire, big black birds, a field of cut-up bones.

He'd been surprised to discover how much he liked Frank Little when the man showed up in Butte. Somehow Sol had been drawn into Frank's orbit, grudgingly at first through Rob Quinn but, later, he was unable to resist the appeal of the man and his message. At some point, an honest wage for an honest job seemed not just desirable, but a right. Something that could actually be accomplished, maybe. Or maybe all this is just something Sol is using to take his mind off of other things. He doesn't really know, when he looks closer at it.

A murmur in the crowd heralds Frank's arrival, surrounded by an honor guard of the miners who are looking out for his safety. Quinn's at the head of the procession, gaze swiveling through the crowd. There are hundreds of men at the picket, and no doubt some undercover Pinkertons salted throughout. Quinn and Frank and some of the other organizers have taken care to station levelheaded, trusted men at strategic points throughout the mob, in an effort to maintain a modicum of control if things go south. The Company guards on the other side of the picket look restless, passing their rifles from hand to hand as Frank and the others make their way to the flatbed. Before he steps onto the back of the truck, Frank gives Sol a wink and then, with a light hop, he jumps up. He raises his hand for a moment to acknowledge the cheers and whistles of the crowd, before making pressing motions downward, to silence the commotion.

Lining the truck's bed, facing the miners, are twenty-one helmets. One for each man that died a year ago in the Penn. For a long moment, Frank is silent, looking out at the now-quiet crowd.

"Brothers!" He pauses, looking up, and collects his thoughts.

"Brothers. Today we remember those men lost, one year ago, in the Pennsylvania." Silence, head down now. He lifts his hat, runs his hand through his hair. Sol turns his eyes from Frank to the crowd of miners, who stand there motionless.

"We hope," Frank continues, raising his chin again, "that our brothers are at peace, wherever they are. But you know they're watching us now, that they're full of hope for us. They hope that we will stay strong, stay organized. They hope that we never give up our struggle for the things that are our due."

"Hope ain't gonna cut it, Frank!" someone calls out from the crowd. Sol sees heads swivel, trying to find the source of the outcry. That will be the Pinkertons.

"No, brother, you're right," Frank replies, spreading his hands out. "You're right: hope *won't* cut it, not by itself. Listen, men, I won't lie to you: I'm frustrated. I'm angry, just like you. But we're here now, together. It's that simple. The Neversweat, these other mines, they aren't pulling ore out of the ground, so the Company *is* sweating, if you'll excuse a bad joke. The Company without production is like a hophead without his drug, and when you threaten to take that production away, they get sweaty. They get nervous.

"Listen: the Company wants an excuse to break this strike, to shut us down. Those scabs are coming. They're coming, sure as anything. I want you men to hold your ground, when they show up. Keep your anger in. Hold it inside, where you can use it. These scabs are men, workers like all of us. Maybe they're scared, yeah, maybe they've got babies and wives – like we all do – but maybe they're just scared because they can't feed them. Fear makes men do stupid things, weak things. Not every man can be brave. Not every man can be strong. But we can. Those men are going to make you mad, I know." He pauses, nodding.

"You see those men, though," he says, louder and with more grit to his voice, "you see them, with the goons the Company will have with them, and you're going to block their path, calmly and without violence. Don't give the Company any excuse. Don't even call those men names, if you can. You just say *not today, brother*. Repeat that now."

"*Not today, brother!*" several hundred miners yell, together. It's stirring, but Sol wonders just how easy it's going to be when the Company men show up, with their truncheons and rifle butts swinging, to escort the scabs in. A polite *no* is only going to go so far. Sol tries to put his trust in Frank, a veteran of plenty of strikes, but it's hard.

"I want you to think about the men we lost," Frank continues, gesturing at the helmets. "Our brothers, our friends. Twenty-one of them. Twenty-one lost to a fire that never should have happened. Think about that, and think about what we're trying to do here. I wasn't here a year ago; I didn't know those men, not personally, so I've asked some of our brother workers, men I'm proud to call my friends, to come up and say some words about the departed. So I'll stand aside for now." Frank looks down at Sol, waving him over. "Come on, Sol, why don't you come on up here first." He leans over, extending a hand down and helping Sol up to the back of the truck.

Sol takes his place at the center of the makeshift stage. He's nervous; he pauses for a moment, looking out over the silent crowd, looking past them to the headframes of the nearby mines. It makes him think again about how the ground they all stand on is hollow inside, decaying, and yet this hill is the reason why they're all here, in one way or another, damn near every last person in this town. It's a hell of a thing when you think about it.

A raven is perched atop a stack of timbers. It cocks a bright eye at him, head atilt as if it's listening.

"I ain't really much for speeches," he says now, looking away from the bird. Something about it makes him uneasy. "That's Frank's line and we're lucky to have him, lucky that a sharp fellow like him is on our side." A shrug. "Some of y'all know me but, for those that don't, I'm just a mucker crew boss. I do my job and help the man at my side and he helps me. We all help each other. That's how we get the job done and stay as safe as we can. It's that unity that Frank is always talking about; it ain't nothing more or less than that. You men are my friends and there ain't a damn thing I wouldn't do for you. That's unity right there."

He points at the helmets in front of him, pausing at the one he'd set out for Owen, feeling his eyes tighten. "We do dangerous work. Things happen and sometimes that's just the way it is. Sometimes we can't stay safe."

There's a shout, and Sol looks down, distracted by the sight of Nancy and Flynn, waving, trying to push their way through the crowd that has pressed close to the flatbed.

Raising his head again, Sol sees Sean Harrity who, along with Mickey Doyle, has stepped out from behind the stack of timbers the bird sits on. Sean nods at Sol and then shrugs, apologetically, almost. He raises a pistol Sol's way and whatever Sol is going to say next is lost in the sound of it firing.

6.

Later, Company men will say that Bloody Tuesday had started when unruly miners, incited to an illegal work stoppage by IWW anarchists, rushed the headframe of the Neversweat mine, bent on destruction of ACM property and intending to cause bodily harm to Company employees. The police and Pinkertons will say that the riot started when they'd been suddenly attacked by those same men, no doubt urged on by the hidden Bolsheviks in their ranks, and that they'd opened fire and raised their truncheons purely out of self-defense. The miners themselves know that it had all kicked off when Company men – or their Pinkerton thugs – attempted the cowardly assassination of Labor leader Frank Little, while they, the workers and union brothers, were gathered in peaceable, legal assembly.

Sol Parker knows the real reason: that, by the end, fifteen good men are seriously wounded, two are dead, along with who knows how many lesser injuries, simply because he can't control his gambling, because he made a series of bad bets and is in debt to the wrong sort of man. Sean had simply chosen a public setting to make an example of Sol. To restate the case that he, Sean Harrity, collects his debts, always, that he'll have his money or the proverbial pound of flesh.

It's also possible, likely even, that the Company hired Sean to start up trouble at the picket so that they can once again crack down on uppity workers, that Sean used the opportunity of that happy confluence of circumstances to deal with the chronically delinquent Sol Parker.

See, the Company will say, *these men are anarchists, animals. We, the Amalgamated Copper Mining Company, must keep a firm hand to ensure production remains steady and the Company profitable*.

Whatever the reason, a year to the day after killing Owen, down in the Penn, Sol knows yet more deaths are laid at his feet.

7.

Sean Harrity raises the pistol and fires. Once, twice, again.

A well-honed instinct of self-preservation flares up inside of Sol and he hunches and leaps to the side, barreling into Frank and knocking both of them from the flatbed stage. Either it's too long of a shot for a pistol or Sean has simply missed due to poor marksmanship because, when he moves, Sol hears the distinct metallic ping of a bullet hitting one of the helmets lining the front of the bed. The echo of the shots rings out and, for one long, stretched second, nothing happens. Then the moment caves inward upon itself, the mass of miners bursting in several directions at once like a startled flock of starlings, that same self-preservative instinct scattering them across the road in one frantic motion. At the same time, the line of mine guards on the other side of the picket, most of whom are no doubt as frightened of what is unfolding as the miners are, raise their rifles uncertainly. A supervisor hollers at them to *hold their fire*. At least one jittery guard hears only the word *fire* and then, once one or two have started shooting, the rest follow suit, rifles cracking off like fireworks at a

Chinatown parade. Pinkertons in the crowd, along with the police already on site to await their brother officers escorting the scabs, draw their own pistols in the mayhem, ready to shoot, certain that the strikers are firing on them. It's a terrible, comical mess.

Those miners that run laterally, away from the road, downhill, come off the best. Some of the men, disoriented in the scrambling crowds, wind up running *towards* the firing rifles but it's those that attempt to flee directly away down the Anaconda road who wind up taking the brunt of the bullets. Shot in the back for the temerity of trying to run away from gunfire. The Pinkertons are everywhere, dozens of them, maybe, firing in all directions, including inadvertently towards the police, who respond with shots of their own, then wade into the mass of men with batons raised. Men are tripping over the fallen, or locked in fistfights or wrestling, some with their own side. There's no reason to it, no order. This is a mob in the truest sense of the word: men reduced to an animal state, fighting with whatever comes to hand.

Some of the miners who've escaped in the first rush come bravely back, throwing rocks and bricks, flying into the mess wielding pieces of lumber or scrap metal. Sol sees one large man hurl a barrel into the crowd, screaming like a madman. A policeman takes a crowbar to the head, turns, slowly, gracefully even, eyes rolling up, staring vacantly at Sol as he crumples to the ground, and then is buried under kicking boots.

The raven on the stack of timber is squawking, stretching up with wings extended.

"Sol! We got to get Frank out of here! Sol!" Quinn is shaking him, screaming in his ear. "We got to get Frank out! They're going to be coming for him!"

Sol feels dazed, distant. The cracks of gunfire and the

shrilling of whistles, men screaming in pain and fury and fear. The air smells like cordite and dust and something sharp and bitter, over the stink of the mines. Sol shakes his head, tries to cut loose the ringing in his ears.

"Sol!"

He shakes his head again, brings back the focus that's deserting him. He looks into the wide-eyed faces of Quinn and Frank.

"We got to get Frank out, Sol!" Quinn yells again. "They'll be coming!"

"Yeah. Yeah." It's hard for Sol to concentrate, and then it isn't, some inner resolve, lost for a moment, taking back over. He turns to Frank. "*Yeah*. Quinn's right, we got to get you out, someplace safe. They're going to pin this shit on you, don't say they won't."

The whistles are getting sharper, closer maybe. Sol sees Nancy and Flynn and the rest of his crew hunkered nearby, behind some pallets. He puts two fingers to his lips and whistles as loudly as he can, over and over, until Flynn turns and sees him. Sol waves a hand, trying to steer the boys his way.

He looks back at Quinn and Frank. "Quinn, my boys are yonder, coming over. They can get Frank somewhere safe. Maybe you best hole up for a bit with him, too. There ain't nothing more we can do here. We was on that truck, and they'll come looking for us." It feels good to be making decisions, doing something rather than just squatting scared in the dirt.

Michael Conroy, looking twitchy, is the first to arrive. For once his mouth is shut. The others follow after, Young Dan ashen-faced and bleeding, carried by Nancy. Sol feels a wash of sick in his belly. "The hell happened to Young?" he says, leans closer.

"I'm OK, Sol," Dan says, trying manfully to smile.

"Got shot's all." He angles over and pukes a little, then wipes his mouth, still working on that smile.

"Got his leg, Sol," Billy says, distractedly, looking at the big, ratty bird cawing over the fight. "Think he'll be fine. He ain't bleeding so much."

"They shot Young Dan, Sol!" Old Dan says, voice quivering. If anything, he looks worse than Young, pale and shaking, eyes shining too white in his face.

Sol reaches over, giving his shoulder a squeeze and trying to will some calm into the boy. "It's all right, Dan, we'll see him sorted. Young Dan will be fine, hey? Right, Young?" Young Dan has passed out, though, cradled in Nancy's arms like a lanky baby.

"Listen, boys," Sol says. "Flynn, Michael, Billy, I need you to help get Frank and Quinn here somewhere safe. No, I don't want to know where, just get them the fuck out of here before the Pinkertons come sniffing. Swap coats with them, find them different hats, whatever. Quinn and Frank will figure all that out, so you just do what they tell you, OK? Keep them safe." He turns to look at Nancy and the Dans. "Nance, you and Old Dan get Young over to the Stope and talk to Antti; he'll know someone who can get the boy's leg taken care of, right? It don't look too bad and it's probably best to not just stroll up to a doctor with a gunshot hole about now. Antti will steer you right. Got it?"

"What are you going to do, Sol?" Nancy asks.

"You should come with us. So we can keep an eye on you," Old Dan adds. He nods a bit too fast. Sol knows the boy would feel safer with him around, but he needs to grow the fuck up, and now is as good a time as any. He gives Dan's shoulder another reassuring squeeze.

"Nah, I'll be fine, boys. We shouldn't all be together, just in case. Best if we let Frank and Quinn figure out what to do without everyone clustering around them, at least until this shitstorm dies down some. Besides, old bastards like me have still got a few tricks left. That's how we live to be old. I'll come find y'all soon enough."

"I'm going with you, Sol," Billy says. "Flynn and Mike will be fine without me."

The look in Billy's eyes tells Sol not to bother arguing. If Billy decided to do something, he would do it, no matter how much you tried to push him different.

"Fair enough," is all Sol says.

A round of nods and some slapped shoulders, and then his crew takes off, hunkered over, crossways down the road, skirting the edge of the melee as best they can. Sol follows their progress until they're out of sight, turning back around from time to time to peek over the truck he still hides behind, watching the riot finish tiring itself out. It feels like it's been going on for hours, hours of noise and stink and pain but, really, Sol knows that it's only been a few overlong minutes. More police have arrived and are swept around into a kind of U-shape now, corralling an unlucky group of miners who sit on the ground, bloody and dirty, hands in the air. Some of the other cops, along with the Pinkertons, are still fighting small knots of workers but, thankfully, the gunfire seems to have ceased, the fights continuing with truncheons and saps and fists.

"You OK, Sol?"

Sol turns to look over at Billy, crouched down there beside him. "No, I'm nowhere close to OK, Billy." He pauses. "You saw it, didn't you? Sean."

Billy looks down, not wanting to catch Sol's eyes. "It wasn't your fault."

Sol laughs one humorless bark, waving a hand out at the carnage. "You know, I'm getting tired of hearing that, and I damn sure don't want to fucking see what happens when something *is* my fault."

The road is littered with wounded men, some ominously motionless, some being dragged into the Mariahs that are pulling up and disgorging more police. If the men get medical attention at all, Sol knows, they'll have to wait until the lawmen are satisfied that the riot is well and truly over. Cops queuing up for their pat on the head by their Company masters, like the fucking dogs they are. He wants to scream, maybe more than that.

Billy must see it, because he says, "It's trouble, Sol, but we'll get past it. We'll make it right."

Sol wants to say that it's more than that, that it's not that simple, that it's more than just fucking *trouble*, but a whispered curse is what he settles on, before he slinks away with Billy. When he looks back, the raven is gone.

8.

The old women say that, after his troubles, Maatakssi became the father of a great tribe of the People, that he had many sons and daughters. The Above Ones had favored him in this thing. They made Maatakssi's family strong and their medicine powerful. This was back before the time of the stories, even, but the old women say they know this.

But first, before that came to pass, the Above Ones gave Maatakssi one boon and one punishment, as they had promised.

"Maatakssi," *they said,* "you have done a terrible thing, killing your brother, as you did in your anger. Old Man is our friend, and killing his son was an evil act. For this you will be punished. But you have reverenced your brother, Siinatssi, in the proper way, and released his spirit to find the Other Lands. So, after you have been punished, we will grant you one blessing."

"I am sorry, Above Ones," *Maatakssi said, sinking to his knees, rubbing dust in his hair.* "My anger was upon me and, now, I am filled with shame."

Two birds, the small ones the People called niimatsoo, *upside-down walkers, cried from a tree just then.*

The Above Ones – even those people – were great gamblers, and they could not resist the chance for a game, whenever the opportunity arose. The place where the Above Ones lived could be dull at times. The old women say that the outcome of one game or another between those people decided the shapes of many things on this Earth. They say that, many times, the world itself had taken a new face on the turning of a bet, those worlds that had passed before this one.

"Maatakssi," they said, "do you fancy your luck? Can you see those two birds there on that branch? Let us bet on which bird flies first, you and us. Where is the harm in that? If you call it rightly, you will not be punished for your sin. If you do not want to bet, though, we understand, and will make the punishment you have earned easier for you to bear. For, as we have said, Old Man is a friend of ours and we do not want to trouble him overmuch with the suffering of his remaining son."

Maatakssi smiled to himself, as he could see that one of the birds had a turned wing and could not fly. Why endure a punishment? For such mighty beings, the Above Ones were fools. And Maatakssi himself was one who would not turn down the chance to gamble although, at times, that habit had caused him grief and the loss of precious things.

"Very well, I choose the bird to the left," *he said, picking the one with the healthy wings.* "That bird will fly first."

Just then the crippled bird on the right straightened its wing and flew off, spiraling up into the sky.

It is a very stupid thing to bet with gods.

At the faraway place where he lived with his wives, Raven watched this pass from his perch atop the high pine and was troubled. For that old bird, of all creatures on this Earth, saw the world as it truly was.

He lifted his shining black wings and flew.

9.

Billy comes awake to the sound of tapping at the window, a dry rap like a fingernail against the glass. Moving slowly, eyes closed, he reaches under the pillow for the large knife he'd placed there. The tapping hasn't woken Sol, given the sound of his snoring. The amount of whiskey Sol had consumed – over Billy's objections – since they'd arrived at this little room in the Gulch is no doubt helping with the old man's slumber. Billy is surprised to find himself woken up, given that he'd never meant to sleep in the first place. Exhaustion and the emotional crash after the danger of the riot and running, combined with – he'll admit – a bit more whiskey than he himself was accustomed to, must have put him out.

He'd been dreaming about Maatakssi's bet with the Above Ones, one of the stories his father used to sing to him in the days before the government school. It was a good story and, as near as he could tell, the moral was that the house always wins.

Words to live by, if ever there were such.

The tapping continues at the window. He isn't quite ready to look yet, although, if they've been found by the wrong person, the door would already have been kicked open, most likely. Billy hopes it's just a lost drunk; he doesn't want to show his face, in the hopes that the man will give up and wander off without catching sight of just who is holed up in this little room. At first Billy had questioned the wisdom of hiding out in the Irish stronghold of Dublin Gulch, where Sean Harrity maintains such a presence but, upon reflection, he has to admire Sol's cunning. No one will likely think to look for them here, of all places. Probably Sean will figure Sol has finally wised up and cut out of town. Billy isn't quite sure just what the next play is, but tomorrow is another day.

Tap tap tap. Tap-tap. Tap.

Go the fuck away, he thinks. *Keep on moving, rummy. No one here, no one that you're looking for anyway.* He levers one eyelid open the slightest bit. From the darkness of the room he can see it's full night still, dawn far away. Sol's ratcheting, wheezing snores judder up out of the sagging easy chair he's wedged himself into, in the far corner of the room.

Tap-tap. Tap tap tap.

Goddamn it. Billy tightens his grip around the knife, taking comfort in its heft and, in one smooth motion, rolls himself out of bed and onto his feet. He crosses to the window in two long strides, yanking back the tattered lace curtain.

"*Jesus fuck!*"

He staggers back, shouting before he can help himself, tripping over the leg of Sol's chair and nearly stabbing himself in the kidney as he falls clattering into the bed table, which is kicked aside with the shriek of wood against floorboards.

"*What now what!*" Sol, coming awake and upright from a dead sleep, hollering, swinging an arm out. "What!"

He bashes into the table himself, shoves it back the other way with another squeal of legs on floor, yelling something incoherent again.

A long, confused second, then Billy gets his legs under him and his wits somewhere back to close. "No! Sol! It's fine! It's fine." He heaves himself upright, tossing the knife onto the bed before someone gets hurt. "Sol, it's fine. It's a bird, it's just a fucking bird."

Sol looks at him, eyes wide and crazy, shining in the dim light coming through the window. "What?" He takes a step back, bumping the back of his knees into his chair, letting his weight collapse into it. "The hell are you yelling about, Billy? You scared the goddamn shit out of me."

"Startled me, is all."

"Sweet Jesus, boy."

"I said it fucking startled me." The bird is looking at them, head cocked to one side like an inquisitive dog, black eye gleaming. It taps its beak against the window again. *Tap-tap-tap. Tap tap.*

"The hell's a goddamn crow doing at the window, middle of the night?"

"It's ain't a crow: it's a raven, Sol. It's omanaahstoo." Billy's voice is hoarse, whether from being woken from a sound sleep or something else, he doesn't know.

There's a knock at the door.

10.

Sol looks from Billy to the old man, the man Billy says is his uncle. Marked Face is his Indian name, apparently, and it's easy to see why. Twist of a scar, oily skin like old saddle leather. He's an evil-looking fucker, built low and broad like Sol and, even though he looks to be somewhere north of two hundred years, it's plain that there's plenty of muscle left on him. He squats there on the floor, back against the wall, a tatty blanket pulled over a flannel shirt. From time to time he looks over at Sol with a shine in dark eyes that are flat and otherwise empty, like badly silvered mirrors. He wears his white hair long, in two thick braids, wrapped at the end with leather and what look like rabbit or bird bones, small bleached things that softly chatter against one another when the old man moves his head.

The old man looks somehow familiar, but maybe only because all old Indians look a bit alike to Sol.

He and Billy are talking Indian at each other; Sol can't follow any of it but he doesn't like the tone. Billy is stabbing a finger towards his uncle now, saying something in a harsh voice. Marked Face laughs, coughing out a few words of his own, pausing to spit afterwards. The

Indian language always sounds to Sol as if they're short on breath.

"That he said, Billy?"

Billy ignores him, which Sol feels is reason enough to get up and find his whiskey bottle, which still somehow has a few inches left at the bottom. Now that the excitement of being scared awake has mostly worn off, Sol realizes he has a thirst and is also still about as drunk as he'd been when he passed out earlier. No reason to go dry then, now, particularly when they have a guest, uninvited and as sour-looking as the man is. Pulling the bottle out from where it's wedged between the arm and seat of his chair, he uncorks it. He politely wipes the rim with the tail of his shirt, offering the first drink to the old man, whose hand extends outward in a peremptory manner.

Marked Face takes a long drink without looking at Sol, busying himself with sneering at his nephew. Billy is still arguing in Indian, his voice somehow getting both louder and more breathy, the sound sinking down lower and deeper in his chest, rumbling through his breastbone. Instead of responding, the old man merely leans forward and spits a stream of whiskey – to Sol's dismay – on the ground between his feet. He repeats the act two more times, makes a complicated gesture with the hand that doesn't hold the bottle, muttering something under his breath.

Sol badly wants the bottle back. He notices that the raven is still at the window, which is open now, although Sol has no memory of any of them raising it. The bird watches the proceedings with eyes that are the same empty, shining black as Marked Face's own. The old man reaches into his shirt, pulling out a handful of the same small bones that are tied into his hair; he scatters them into the whiskey he'd spat on the floor. The room feels colder.

Sol takes a step back. It isn't that he's a superstitious man, per se, but in his youth he'd learned a respect for ineffable things.

"Oh, bullshit." Billy says in English. He stands up, breaking the spell of the moment, stepping past his uncle to push the bird out the window. It dodges him with an indignant squawk and hops down onto the bedside table, eyeing them warily. Billy shuts the window with a bang anyway, taking the bottle of whiskey from Marked Face's hand as he comes back over, pulling a long drink before passing what little is left back to Sol. "Bullshit, old man."

Marked Face gives an ugly cackle, spitting again on the ground and rattling off a long, hoarse sentence, cocking his chin Sol's way.

"Hell's going on, Billy? What's that he said?"

Billy shakes his head, muttering something in Indian that sounds like a curse, which makes the old man cackle again. "Don't worry about it, Sol. My uncle is fucking crazy and full of shit, not to mention a bastard. It runs in the family."

Marked Face slaps his hand down on the whiskey-wet floor, making the bones bounce. His cheeks twist a frown deep into the canyons of his wrinkled face, and he starts in on another gravelly, panting sentence.

"*No*, old man, just get the fuck out of here," Billy says. He leans forward, pointing down at his uncle. "You're not a fucking sorcerer and whatever medicine you think you had is long gone. You're a broke, crazy old man with a trained fucking bird and a line of shit as long as I am tall and who has nothing better to do, in the middle of the goddamn night, than to fuck with me, apparently.

You're a pain in my ass, you and Bad Bird both. Two of you should have done me a courtesy and died a long time ago. You don't belong here, you belong out at Warm Springs with him. Maybe you can see which one of you can finally kill the other, hey? You know what, why don't you go there right now, get started." He reaches into his pocket, pulling out some limp, crumpled bills, throwing them at his uncle. "Here. Just get the fuck out. I don't care where you go, come to think of it, just as long as it's not here. Go."

"Billy," Sol starts to say.

"No, Sol, no. You have no idea. *No goddamn idea.*"

Sol hasn't seen Billy, normally so quiet, like this before. He reaches out to put a hand on Billy's arm, but is shrugged off.

"Don't fucking touch me, Sol. I don't need *no one* touching me." He absently rubs at his shoulder.

Sol's known Billy for years, knows that his childhood had been less than ideal. Which is why he'd wound up in Sol's orbit, after all. He'd never asked details, and Billy had never offered. Fair enough; every man had been a boy once and every man has a right to the privacy about things past. Lord knows Sol had gotten up to some stupid shit as a youth, things no one needed to hear about.

What he realizes now is just what Billy puts aside, a couple of times a year, sometimes more, to go see his father up at the asylum.

Sol hasn't been out to Warm Springs to see Elizabeth in years.

Marked Face squats there, listening to his nephew rant. The boy is as soft as sun-warmed shit. *Poor, poor little Sagiistoo. Such a hard life you have had!* Once, when the boy was small, he'd maybe seen something hard and fierce in the one his brother had named Sagiistoo: Owl, the Night Announcer, who now calls himself by an English name, one that sounds like the patter of piss on dry grass. *Billy Morgan*. Piss on grass followed by the plop of dung. A boy afraid of his own true name. But the name of a thing didn't matter when it came down to it, did it? Regardless, whatever strength had been there in the boy was squeezed out of him at the white school, that's clear; the young man who came back with his short hair and his Jesus-god Bible wasn't the one who had left. Strange that the Above Ones have singled him out in this way, although, perhaps, that is the point.

Sometimes Marked Face feels that it is too bad, in a way, that his brother's hatchet hadn't cut a bit deeper when the boy had gotten between him and Bad Bird that time, one of many times, to be sure. But that's how the world is: you are strong or you are weak. Sometimes you get caught between the strong and discover a fact about yourself, discover what you are. That is how you are tested, that is how you choose your path in this world.

Poor little white Sagiistoo with his scars and his crying now.

His nephew has never understood – never believed, as a wise man does – that the whites are nothing but an evil trick played on the world by cunning Nihaat and foolish Maatakssi, to spite his brother Siinatssi. Those stupid old ones, back in the time before other things. The stories are clear. Seeing things as they are now, what kind of man would not believe their truth? And, knowing the stories, what kind of man would want to *be* one of those whites: empty, evil creatures, even given the power of their medicine. What kind of shortsighted fool would choose that, as his nephew does? Better to be nothing at all.

It was a good trick, though, with the bird, Marked Face thinks, chuckling to himself. He's always had an affinity with the ravens. The father of those birds, Raven himself, has long been beloved of the People.

But, ah, Sagiistoo, Sagiistoo. His nephew isn't only empty, he's stupid, although maybe that is merely another aspect of the same thing. He is also disrespectful, Sagiistoo, carrying on in such a way, and that is a thing that should not be tolerated, for the boy's own good. He is weak, he is stupid, but he is family, nonetheless, with all that that entails.

It is time that he learned that hiding from medicine doesn't make it any less strong.

There is a way things must go. Marked Face knows the task in front of him. His time is coming to an end, after all. This is the thing he must do. The Above Ones have spoken and he fears their judgment. Marked Face fears his own failure, as all men should. To fear a thing is to respect it.

"Nephew, let us have a game," he says, in the language of the People. He understands the white tongue well enough, but does not dirty his mouth with it, whenever possible. Marked Face knows that his nephew thinks him just a foolish old man, weak with age, but he will learn. He is old, true, but far from weak. *Marked Face* is not his name because of the scar; no, these are the old words for Badger, a powerful, dangerous animal, possessed of a fury, who makes his own way in the world, on his own terms. Badger is built low and heavy, strong in the legs and shoulders, as he is.

But more powerful than Marked Face's body is his medicine, the power songs that he'd learned, at great price, long ago. It is the thing that makes him who he is.

"Let us have a game," he repeats.

"A game?" Sagiistoo answers in the lying white tongue. "Old man, you need to get the fuck out of here. *Go!*"

It's tempting to put this disrespectful, stupid pup in his place right now, with something harder than the long medicine. Maybe just stand up, push a knife in the boy's belly, like in the old days, taste in his nose the hot reeking rush of shit-sharp blood, feel the heat as it washes over his hands, hear a last, womanly whimper in his ears. He feels his power building up inside him, seeking escape. The anger that sends him to black places. He remembers other times, before the whites had finally finished breaking the People; he remembers other men who crossed him, to their sorrow. He is Marked Face, and this cur of a nephew, this hollow man with his white, piss-streaked name, is giving him orders? The boy will learn. Perhaps he had been too lenient in the past, thinking that his weak brother, Bad Bird, would somehow impart strength into his even weaker offspring. That is a foolish thought: since the old times, each generation of the People has been born softer than the one before. It is no surprise that, after the whites were created from Nihaat's trick, even those empty people had overpowered the People.

He relaxes his clenched fists, calms himself. Things must be as they must be. The Above Ones have shown him the path and he will obey.

"We will have a game, Sagiistoo," he says. "We will have a game or, when I leave this place, I will tell those whites where to find you." He doesn't particularly care whether his nephew or the old white man are found, but he knows, as he knows many things, that other evil men seek them out. If this is the goad that is required, to teach his shit-soft nephew the way of things, then so be it. In his many years, Marked Face has learned that to come at a thing sideways to achieve an outcome is often the better way. He glances at the white man. It is only the fool who rushes headlong into things.

Marked Face sees the fear and disgust alight in his nephew's eyes, like corpse-flies on a body. "You wouldn't do this thing, Uncle. Not even you." Sagiistoo lapses back into his first tongue, now, which makes Marked Face smile. The tongue of the People is the tongue of power, of anger, when such is needed. The tongue of true things. The white language is hollow, like those people themselves. It isn't suited to real things, only to shadows and lies. This is why the word of those people is as worthless as a mouse fart in a strong wind.

He shrugs. "Why would I care what happens to your pet, Nephew? He means nothing to me. Nor do you."

"You talk from your ass, Uncle. We are family, like it or not."

"Why would I give thought to you, boy? Because you give me tobacco, sometimes? Pretend to listen when I speak? Your mouth and your ears are full of shit. Besides, I think maybe your mother fucked some other weakling, maybe one of the camp dogs, and not my brother Bad Bird, to get you. I fucked her enough times myself – everyone did – but you're certainly not one of mine." He spits. "Now we'll have our game."

"Get the fuck out of here, Uncle. Go tell the whites, then, coward, if that's what you want to do. If I see you again, though, I'll kill you myself."

Marked Face is unable to hold back a peal of laughter. The puppy is finally showing some teeth. It's far too late, though; one kick will send him whimpering off quickly enough. The boy is not yet strong enough, whatever he might think. Swallowing his distaste at making the liar's tongue, although of course that language is just the thing needed now, he addresses the old man.

"Old man. We will make a game, me and you. My nephew Sagiistoo is afraid to play, because he is a coward." He glances towards his nephew, then back. "So you will play with me. We are old men, too old to be afraid of games. Where is the harm in a game?" He opens his hand to show the white man the flat bones, notched and marked by long-ago people. They are very old, and Marked Face has had them a long time.

Sagiistoo strides over to the door, opens it. "Get out, Uncle!"

Marked Face ignores his nephew, quickly showing the white man the rudiments of the game. It is a simple thing.

"Now hang on, Bill," the white man says. "We'll just play the one and then your uncle here will leave, right? That right, partner?"

Marked Face keeps his face impassive. "We will play one game tonight, yes."

"See, Billy, let's be polite. We're gentlemen, right? Of a sort, anyway. What's the bet, then, sir? I ain't got much in the way of money, so what are we betting?"

Instead of answering the white man, Marked Face looks over at his nephew, still standing stupidly by the open door. Like a dog needing a piss. "Here is the wager, Sagiistoo," he says, slowly, in the real language. "We will cast these bones, your pet white father and I. If I win, I will leave this room and find those men that are looking for you. I will say to them: *Here is where my nephew, Sagiistoo, stays with one of the ones for whom you search. Why you want him, I neither know, nor do I care, but there that man is, with my disrespectful dog-spawn of a nephew.*" He nods. "Maybe I will also tell them: *White men, when you go to them, make sure to beat the shit out of my disgraceful kin, although probably he will like this. Even as he cries like a woman, he will like it, thinking that if you beat him enough he'll become one of you, finally, that you will beat the color from his skin and the sweetness from his blood."*

Sagiistoo stands in the doorway, breathing in and out through flared nostrils. Marked Face can see the tendons creaking in the boy's knuckles.

"Maybe you wonder, still, why I would do this, hey, Nephew?"

"And if Sol wins?" Sagiistoo asks.

Very good, Marked Face thinks. *Enough talk*. Even the language of the People can only go so far to make another understand. Certain things, the strong things, need to be felt with the liver. Maybe little Sagiistoo is finally starting to feel the bite of the lesson there. Feel the gnawing of things to come.

"If your white man wins, Nephew, I will give him whatever he wants. Whatever is in my power to give, and then I will leave."

Sagiistoo shuts the door, letting loose a hard laugh. "Whatever's in your power to give, hey? Shit." He shakes his head.

"Here's the wager, Sol," Sagiistoo says in English, then. He walks past his uncle, sits down on the bed. "Here's the wager: if he wins, he's going to tell everyone where we are. He's going to tattle on us, tattle like a little girl whose dolly got stole. That about right, Uncle? But here's the good part, Sol, here's the good part: if *you* win, right, he's just going to leave. Poof, gone. That's good enough for me. Go on, then. Let's just get the old fucker out of here, as quickly as that can be done, so we can get some fucking sleep."

Marked Face shakes his head. Perhaps the lesson isn't

biting yet, after all. For a moment, he feels sorry for little Sagiistoo, and then hardens himself to his purpose.

Holding the bones in his hand, feeling their heat, Marked Face stares into the eyes of the old white man until he understands what the man wants, right now. Not what he thinks he wants. What burns in his heart.

"You sure you don't want to sweeten the bet?" the white man says, reaching out for the bones and shaking them in his hand. "I feel my luck coming on, I'm not afraid to tell you that, partner."

Marked Face keeps his face blank. The greed of these people, always. He nods. "If you win, yes, I will give you what you want. Within reason."

"*Reason* is a broad word," the white man says, smiling.

"I will give you what you want," Marked Face says, his own smile coming now. "Now, let us play."

With great ceremony, and unnecessary flourishes, the white man tosses the bones. He picks them up and tosses them again. Picks them up once more and, on this last throw, one nearly perfect, he shouts, as if he'd done a great thing and not that which was simply ordained, long ago. The arrogance of these people, always. Twigs floating on a stream, who think they direct the course of the waters.

"Let's see you beat that," the white man says. "Let's see you, son."

"Truly you have thrown the bones before," Marked Face says, his true feelings hidden. "What skill you show." He takes the bones back, relishing the feel of their warmth on the skin of his palm. He feels more complete with them in his hand. Quickly, he makes his throws, knowing the outcome even if some small part of him wishes the result could be different.

The white man, his hand raised in victory.

"You have won," Marked Face says. "Yes, yes, you have won. Tell me now, what is it that you desire from me? Within reason, recall."

"Well, how much money do you have in your pocket, son? Let's start there."

Marked Face is already reaching for the coins he carries. The stack of worthless gold he'd picked up long ago. Money, always money with these people. The greed, again. He sets the coins on the floor in front of him, watching the white man's naked want. *I am not your son, you stupid old man,* he thinks.

"Where the fuck did you get those, Uncle?" Sagiistoo says, leaning down to examine the metal.

Marked Face shrugs. "I have many things, Nephew. More worthless things like this, yes. Other, more important possessions." He doesn't have to look at the white man to hear the snare close.

"You say you have more of these, partner?"

Marked Face shrugs again. "Of course."

The eyes of the white man gleam with avarice. They are such simple people.

"How about you want to bet some more, then?"

"Sol–"

"Now, Billy, now, let's just think here. Your old uncle won't turn us in, will you sir? That was just talk. We're all friends now, hey? Just having a game. So how about we change the bet, maybe? What do you want that I have, up against more of that gold of yours? Within *reason*, of course," he says, bending forward, grinning, eyes bright.

There is only one thing that Marked Face desires.

"I will bet with you again, yes, but you are too skillful with the bones," he says, putting them back into their pouch. "Perhaps, though, there is another thing we can gamble on."

"Son, I'll bet on any game you like. My luck is sitting up with me, I'll tell you."

"Sol–"

"Damn it, Billy, just pipe down. You're a goddamn wet blanket sometimes. It's just a fucking game."

Marked Face stretches his arms out in front of him. "Take my hands," he says. After a pause, the white man does, an odd expression on his face.

"Look into my eyes," Marked Face says, gathering his medicine inside him. "Look, Solomon Parker."

Deep in his chest, he starts to sing. The song swells and builds, growing stronger with every breath.

The world drops away, the room falls into his medicine. And then:

The sound of men yelling. Of fists, hitting flesh, a hollow thumping.

The smell of smoke and spilled beer.

Heat and sweat and greed.

Marked Face sees the eyes of the white man widen, feels him try to pull away, and tightens his grip. No, it is too late for that. Sagiistoo reaches toward him, his movements slow and stretched.

The medicine burns around the song in Marked Face's chest. The bones in their pouch are fiery against his skin.

The room falling away and a sound, then, as of a great bird, pecking at a branch.

A shout, faint, from a long distance away: *"Goddamn it, get your fucking hands up–"*

A Kind of Dance

1917

Butte, Montana

1.

"Goddamn it, get your fucking hands up, Nancy!"

Fist meets flesh with a hollow, meaty thump. Big Nancy folds over into the follow-up punch that tears across the stub of his ear, is lifted back up upright with the left to his chin. Sol sees Nancy's legs start to buckle and rubs his hands across his own face, gritting his teeth and squinching his eyes shut. *Come on, not yet! Third fucking round.*

There's an affronted shout from the crowd as one of Nancy's huge fists slams into Nick Faraday's groin. Faraday backs up, wavers for a second, heeled over and looking like he might puke.

Jesus Christ, Nancy, what the fuck are you doing?

"Goddamn it, Nancy, hands up!" Sol shouts. He glances at his watch again, studiously avoiding Sean Harrity's gaze from across the room. *Stay on your feet and keep fighting, Nick.* Sol gives a quick look around the crowd, looking for a path to the exit, just in case. He glances back at the fighters just in time to see Faraday plant his forehead into Nancy's already broken nose, bellowing incoherently.

For a second Sol's thoughts seem to hitch and stutter

with something, a memory, out of place. There's a word for it, something French that Elizabeth had once told him meant that feeling of reliving a moment that had never happened. It's been happening to him lately, a feeling of *I've been here before;* sometimes it's like the aftershock of a dream, just out on the edge of his mind where he can't quite catch it. *I remember that, I dreamed it once.* Other times, like now, it's as if his perception of a few seconds of time is out of sync with itself, like the ghostly afterimage on a photo, one of those things that Spiritualists show to claim proof of the soul. Maybe it means his own soul is loose inside him, can slip free of his body and look around. Lord knows that there isn't much holding it there any more. After Elizabeth, after Owen, there's no one but Sol himself to lay claim to it, and he isn't even sure how much he wants the thing.

An image, for a moment.

An old man, holding his hands. A noise, a tapping becoming a banging becoming a booming. A sensation of falling.

The image, gone then. Another remnant of a dream maybe. He's out of sorts, is all it is, with everything that's happened, with the reminder that the anniversary of the Penn fire is coming up. All Sol wants to do on that day is to go find a bottle and make deep acquaintance with it, but he's promised Quinn and Frank he'll speak at the fucking memorial.

Another shout from the crowd brings him out of his reverie. Nancy is taking punch after punch, weaving woozily backwards; the stutter in Sol's thought cuts free and he begins to shout again.

"Hands up! Up, goddamn it!"

• • •

Billy winces as Faraday's knobby head cracks into Nancy's face. He's broken his own nose enough times to know that Nancy's eyes will be streaming tears, that he won't be able to see the rain of fists that are now following, landing one after another, rocking his head from side to side on the pivot of his neck. Nancy's backing up, frantically, finally appearing to hear Sol's shouts to get his arms up, although the boy looks too dazed to be very effective at following the instruction. Nancy stumbles backward into the crowd; a heaving shove pushes him forward again, propelling him mouth first into another oncoming fist, snapping his head back once more.

If this continues, there's no way that Nancy will make it to the six in the third. The sick feeling Nick Faraday must have in his guts from the fisted insult to his balls has sent the man into a frenzy, making the idiot forget his own part in this charade. *Left, left, left, right, left, left.* It's no longer a boxing match but has devolved into an alley brawl. Only Nancy's capacity for absorbing punishment is keeping him upright.

Billy's head feels thick and rummy and his own guts are sick; there's an echo in his ears, whistles and men shouting. He's felt off all day, since waking up before dawn to half-remembered nightmares that had left him in a sweat, bedding twisted around him like a shroud, throat hoarse as if from yelling. Something about violence, a bird at a window. He must have a cold, some kind of flu maybe. He doesn't want to be here now: he wants to be in bed, maybe with a hot whiskey, trying to sweat out whatever has gotten into him, which has done nothing but get worse since he woke up. It's to the point, now, where he isn't sure how long he himself is going to last on his feet, never mind Nancy. But Billy had told Sol that he'd be here, so here he is.

"*Nancy*! Don't just fucking stand there and let him hit you!" Sol is apoplectic, looks like he might step into the circle himself. Flynn must be thinking the same thing, as he reaches forward and grabs the old man's shoulder, which Sol shrugs off. "Jesus, Nancy! Hands!" he shouts.

Everything feels distant to Billy, almost serene, filtered through his rummy head as it is. Dreamlike, as if he's watching from underwater. Each movement slow, disassociated from the rest. He sees Sean Harrity, eyes tight, leaning over and muttering to fat Mickey Doyle; Sean's lips open and smack shut, chewing each word as it comes out, taking an age to say whatever it is he's saying. No doubt he's as concerned as Sol that the fight last another few minutes. Two men on the far side of the crowd have their arms around each other's shoulders, and look to be singing, swaying as lazily as dry windblown stalks of summer mullein. Peaceful and quiet, mouths moving silently, like trout sipping at flies on the surface of a lake. A man over by the bar drops his glass: it floats slowly towards the sawdusted floor in flashes of gold as the beer spills out in a rain of perfect globes, before splashing upward in an explosion of dust.

Billy thinks of Imiinatssi, from the stories, who once had run so fast he'd outpaced his shadow; he'd spent the rest of his days trying to put it back on, but it no longer fit and would drop off at inopportune times, causing mischief. Now, for Billy, sick as he is, the world isn't fitting quite right. Like Imiinatssi's shadow.

All the while he's looking blearily around, trying to take in this ill-fitting room, Billy feels more than hears the pounding of Faraday's fists into Nancy's head and body. Each blow thrums Billy's chest until his heart is pounding to the rhythm of the punches. *Left, left, left, right, left, left.* Slow, hard, methodical, like the steps of his father's dancing that he, Billy, had watched as a boy, before he was sent away to the government school. He'd tried to mimic it, but never got the knack. *Left, left, left, right, left, left,* each foot raised deliberately, placed down with equal precision to a rhythm like a heartbeat. His own dancing nothing more than a stumble.

Nancy takes a hard shot to the temple. His legs cross and he staggers a long, uneven step sideways, another, looking like he'll finally fall. Billy, in his fevered haze, remembering his father and the other men, thinks to chant the boy upright with the old songs that keep the dance together, *left, left, left, right, left, left,* the dancers carried and buoyed by the rhythm, slick with sweat and panting for air, like Nancy is now. A fight is a kind of dance, after all, an abbreviated story: action standing as shorthand for a more complicated thing, told with movement and breath and the sound of men in motion.

Sagiistoo, Billy hears. *Sagiistoo!*

He comes back to himself for a moment, head clearing briefly. He looks around, sees only the room full of shouting, drunken men. He's dizzy and wants to puke out the nausea in his guts, get some relief. Billy can see that Nancy has somehow kept himself up, with the help of the crowd, and is now being shoved back towards Faraday's fist again. This isn't going well.

Sol is shouting something back over his shoulder, words that Billy can't understand. Shit, he's sicker than he thought. Maybe he should find a drink.

Sagiistoo! he hears again.

"Drink!"

Without looking, Sol reaches backwards into the crowd, yelling, until someone's pint is put in his hand. He takes a long pull of the warm, sour muck that Heaney passes off as beer, knocks some of the dry from his throat.

"Get your *FUCKING* hands *UP*, Nancy!" he shouts, although he can tell the boy is past hearing, his heroic talent for taking abuse notwithstanding. Even Nancy has his limits, though, and he's going down now, swaying, lurching to one knee as that excitable idiot Faraday continues to ring his skull with lefts. Sol looks at his watch, screaming *"Time! Time! Time!"* He steps into the circle, trying to push himself between his fighter and Faraday's fast left hand.

"Time!" Harrity agrees, elbowing Mickey Doyle forward, who grabs Faraday's arm, taking a wild right cross for his trouble. For a moment it looks like the fight will continue with Doyle standing in for Nancy, but the blood fury drains out of Faraday's eyes in the face of Doyle's shouting, to be quickly replaced by indignation.

"He hit me in the fuckin bollocks! Right in the fuckin bollocks!"

Sol shakes his head, looking down at Nancy, who Flynn and Michael have helped drag onto a stool in the corner. Michael's barracking Nancy about his stance and Sol tells him to just shut up, shut the fuck up. That boy, the mouth on him.

One of Nancy's eyes is swollen shut and he's huffing out of his broken nose like an animal, raking in air through a bloody mouth. Sol passes his beer to the boy, which Nancy sucks down in one long gasp. Nancy belches mightily and then, weaving on his chair, leans over the side and spits out blood.

"Few more seconds, Nance," Sol says quietly, hunkering down with a crack of tired knees. "Just a few more seconds is all and you go down and this is all fucking over. You done good." For some reason, even as he says the words, Sol feels uneasy. They've done what they came here to do. What they had to do; what *he* had to do, really. He feels lower than a grasshopper's asshole, putting the boy through this. A fight to fight was one thing, but this is just brutality and, the shit of it is that it's by proxy, that Sol can't take it on himself.

It's his own mess, after all, the long series of fuckups and his disrespect to Sean Harrity that's brought him to this pass but, instead poor, good-hearted Nancy Mallon is taking the medicine for him. A man should wear the punishment for his own sins, no matter how much the garment pinches.

Sol's belly is tight and there's a pounding behind his eyes that maybe rivals Nancy's. He's felt strange all day, really, ever since Billy had woken him up in the dark, screaming in Indian, fit to wake the dead. Sol had calmed him down but never got back to sleep himself and has spent the day stuck in that space one gets caught in sometimes, when awoken at the wrong time, not fully awake and with the leftover flavor of an interrupted, unremembered dream clinging like smoke.

It's just nerves, he tells himself. Few more seconds and it will be over. All Nancy has to do is walk out there, get hit a couple more times, and let himself give up. Drop to the floor and get counted out. Wasn't nothing that could happen to fuck this up.

"Time, gentlemen!" Pat O'Toole hollers. "Fighters!"

Sol helps heave Nancy back to his feet.

Wasn't nothing that could happen. It's just nerves.

Sol and Billy watch Nancy's fist swing in a big, looping, lazy arc. From where Billy stands, he sees it pass almost in slow motion, the hard, meaty mass hanging there at apogee for one long, dying moment before crashing back down, into the side of Nick Faraday's skull.

A baby dropped from a building, that one.

Billy feels the impact in his chest again, his sternum vibrating with the aftershock like a deep drumbeat. Faraday's eyes roll back in his head and he sways, out on his feet. Sol's own eyes are wide and his lips, moving silently, Billy can easily read.

No. No, no, no, no.

Sean Harrity, across the room, mouth hanging open in disbelief.

Nick Faraday, the victor, in the third round. As decided. Cash on the nail, obligations met. Due diligence.

Not this.

Nick Faraday, stumbling towards a fall. Nancy, wild-eyed and wheezing, standing there staring at his fist. The bet that was never a bet, falling away.

Obligations.

Oh, fuck.

2.

The bet lost, Maatakssi pressed his face into the dust and awaited his punishment. He could hear the singing of the once-crippled bird as it flew away. His belly was tight with fear, and with anger that the Above Ones had tricked him in this way.

"Ila, Maatakssi," *the Above Ones said,* "we have won the wager. Don't you know not to gamble with those more powerful than you? Sometimes we wonder why we bothered to make you people. Although, the place where we live is sometimes dull, yes, so perhaps it had something to do with that. But you are fools, nonetheless." *In their pride, the Above Ones would not admit that they were a people who made mistakes like any others. Some of the old women say that humans were one of these mistakes, that the Above Ones had tried to create something better and failed, and that this is why our natures are as they are. Perhaps this too is why we are such sources of amusement to those gods.*

"Forgive me, Above Ones," *Maatakssi said.*

"You and your people are very foolish, Maatakssi," *the Above Ones continued, warming to their subject.* "We, who have seen the making of all things, do not lose our gambles."

"Perhaps this is why the place in which you live is dull," *Maatakssi said, forgetting himself, for he was angry and his own pride was stung.*

"What is that you say, Maatakssi?" *the Above Ones answered. They were troubled, for they themselves had thought this very thing. The worlds upon worlds that were given their shape by the games of those people were, at heart, merely the same flawed creation, over and over. Above all else, the Above Ones craved novelty.*

"A game is not a game if the result is certain, Great Ones," *Maatakssi said, sensing an advantage. The Above Ones were great, truly, but it was obvious that even with their strong medicine they were simple creatures.* "Let me put this thing to you, mighty Above Ones. Let us wager again, what we have bet before: if you win, you will punish me as you see fit but, if I win, I will escape any penalty for killing my brother, Siinatssi."

"And how do you look to change the game, Maatakssi?" *the Above Ones asked, trying to hide their excitement, because new things were truly rare for those people.*

"Mighty Above Ones, I ask you to release your power over this wager. We will look to my friend Raven, Omanaahstoo, to serve as judge, for we both know Raven to be a clever and honest being." *Maatakssi hid his smile, for he had a plan.*

The Above Ones talked among themselves for a few moments. They did know Raven, who was indeed an honest creature, if somewhat crotchety. The prospect of this new game made them excited, though, and also perhaps a bit foolish. But who are we to judge the gods?

"Very well, Maatakssi," *they said.* "We will call on Raven."

Just then, Raven arrived, out of breath, having seen, before, what was passing and making the long journey from his perch far away. "I am already here, Above Ones. What do you require of me?" *he asked, hiding his unease behind a mask of irritability.* "My wives are for once feeling lustful, and I would like to get back to them."

"We will have a game, Raven," *they said,* "and Maatakssi here has recommended that you be the judge of it, as you are known to be honest and impartial in these things."

Raven doubted that this was his entire reputation, but he was worried and, in truth, did want to return to his lusty wives. But one does not balk the will of powerful beings. Still, he said, "Maatakssi, surely you have learned your lesson. One does not make bets with gods."

"The Above Ones have agreed to new rules, Raven," *Maatakssi said, trying to hide the smug feeling he held.* "This game will be different."

Sometimes, there is no arguing with the foolishness of others. Raven knew that things would pass as they must, regardless of his own worry and concern. He was a very wise bird, Raven, seeing the world truly as he did. "Very well," *he said, sighing, pushing his fear away to another place.* "What is the game?"

"I have here in my hands the bones that Old Man gave me when I was a child," *Maatakssi said, showing them all the carved pieces in his palm.* "We will play the dice game, where no man may cheat."

Raven inspected the bones, prodding them with his beak. They were warm and flat, but weighted properly. He was a great gambler himself and knew all the tricks. The dice were fair, and he pronounced them so.

"Now you players will wager on these bones," *he said.*

The Above Ones went first, as was their right. Three times they threw the pieces, and made nearly perfect tosses, being gods. It was only an imperfection on the ground that fouled their final throw but, this time, they abided by the result, playing the game as fairly as they had promised.

They passed the bones to Maatakssi, who stumbled over a root when taking them in his hand. As his did so, he substituted those bones for another set he had in his off hand, a shaved set that would always throw perfect.

Raven, whose eyes missed nothing, saw this deception. Do not do this thing, two-leg walker, *he thought to himself.*

Once, Maatakssi threw the bones, twice, perfect each time. On the third throw, he held his smile as he looked at the foolish Above Ones, and then made a final toss, as perfect as the others.

"Above Ones," *Raven said, then, sighing in his heart,* "you have been cheated. Look to the hand of Maatakssi, where you will find the original bones. These ones he has thrown have been shaved."

The Above Ones seethed in their wrath at Maatakssi's treachery, and took him by the arms, readying a terrible punishment.

"Raven, Raven, help me!" *Maatakssi cried, weeping, as the Above Ones dragged him away.* "I will make you the totem of my tribe, and reverence you above all animals! I will leave you the prime parts of my kills and never will you or your family go hungry. These words are my promise, if you will help me now!"

"Foolish Maatakssi," *Raven said. He was a wise bird, as I have said, and far-seeing.* "Do you think I would cross the Above Ones, who were witness to the creation of us all? The reverence of you two-leg walkers would be a pleasant thing, true, but your kind are thick upon the ground. There will be others with whom I will be friends and they will keep me and my family fed. One day soon, too soon, you will learn that words are nothing more than air." *He shook his head.* "Now I must get back to my wives." *With a bow to the Above Ones, Omanaahstoo flew off, hoping that his wives were still feeling their lusts, with which he could distract himself from his worry.*

The Above Ones held prideful Maatakssi, the fool, and prepared to bestow their terrible punishment.

"You have betrayed us, Maatakssi," *they said.* "We, who have shown you forbearance. This is how we are repaid. It was a simple thing we agreed to, and you have betrayed our trust. You, who are as nothing before us. For that, we will punish you but, first, as we have promised, we will give you a blessing."

Maatakssi shook and shivered, fearing the punishment to come. He shook so hard that the pouch that held the marked bones, the true ones, slipped from his neck and fell to the ground. The bones spilled out and he said, "Look there, Above Ones, look! That is my final throw. That one there. Not that other! It is a weak and wretched throw, suitable for one such as I. You, Great Ones, must certainly see that. I did not cheat you, Great Ones! You have won the bet! You said that the place you lived was dull. This, all of this, was only a thing to amuse you, O powerful Above Ones!"

In his fear, Maatakssi tried to weave dung into something more and, sometimes, that is all a man can do when in the presence of his betters. We flawed men are nothing if not liars. That is the way of us, that is how we were made by the Above Ones.

Those people looked at the throw on the ground, then, and talked among themselves. Maatakssi, sensing that his lies would bring his salvation, hid his smile, his fear forgotten, just like that. Fuck you, Above Ones, *he thought to himself, full of pride at fooling the gods once again.*

Because we are liars, we men rarely learn from our mistakes. There can be no lesson without consequence.

3.

Fuck you, Sean, Sol thinks, scanning the crowd.

He can see Sean Harrity off to one side of the mass of men, the ever-present lump of fat Mickey Doyle at his side. Nick Faraday is there, too, the side of his head an unwholesome-looking shade of mottled blues and yellows, the white of one eye still a hemorrhaged red. Faraday is an idiot and a piece of shit, but Sol has to give him credit for being far tougher than anyone had suspected, staying on his feet as he had. Nancy's punch should have killed him. After the fight, Nick had slept for two whole days and it was anyone's guess whether he'd ever wake up. Or, if he did, if he'd come out of it even stupider than he'd been before the fight. But now, here he is, at least together enough to stand there.

"Fuckin tetched, Sol!" Sean had screamed, after the fight, spittle spraying Sol's face. "Doc says that if that fuckin boy even wakes up, he's probably going to wind up… what'd he say, Mickey?"

"Simple, Sean."

"Fuckin simple!"

"Well, Nick wasn't so sharp to begin with, Sean," Sol murmurs, before he can stop himself.

"Are you getting fuckin smart, old man?" Sean leans forward, prodding one finger into Sol's sternum. "Are you getting *fuckin smart now?*"

Sol shakes his head, tries on an expression that he hopes combines respect and contrition into a tidy shape. Really, he doesn't give a good goddamn if Faraday ever wakes up. The fool had done his part and, maybe, if he hadn't punched Nancy's own head all to rummy shit, confused him, Nancy wouldn't have let loose the haymaker that had damn near stove in Faraday's skull. It was only luck and – again, he has to give some credit – Faraday's native toughness that allowed him to stay up long enough for the shaky, weak follow-up cross to Nancy's jaw. Which the boy had fortunately taken as an invitation to drop, as ordered, in the goddamn third. Although, in retrospect, perhaps it's merely the fact that Faraday hadn't much in the way of brains in his head that kept him going for a few more seconds after being hit, that the muddling of same was less of a trauma than it would have been for a man with the full complement of wits to begin with.

Regardless, Nancy took the cross and flopped theatrically to the canvas; Faraday stood there swaying on his feet for another couple of seconds, eyes rolled back in his head, before collapsing himself, a state of affairs that sent Pat O'Toole into a tizzy, suddenly having two men to count out. Sean and Sol made it clear in no uncertain terms that Nancy had hit the canvas first and so, by the rules, unconscious Nick Faraday, blood leaking from his ears, was hoisted upright and one bruised hand raised in victory.

As a spectacle, it was sporting gold.

One that Sol himself hadn't taken the time to enjoy, realizing wisely that he was better served to get the hell out of there with his boys before Sean took exception to what could have been read as betrayal instead of simply drama, inadvertent though it had been. Sometimes the wise course is to make the best of a bad situation by fucking off and hoping one's own inherent talent for bullshit will smooth things over later, which of course it had, yet again. A telling-off to endure, later, and some false regret that hid a hearty *fuck you* to Sean Harrity and that was that. That particular can kicked down the road one more time.

Now, looking at Faraday, Sol wonders just how much addling poor Nick's brains have taken, as he stands there by his boss with what seems to be more than the usual amount of blankness in his gaze. Although, with him, it's hard to tell. Nancy himself had only needed a day or so to recover from the fight, battered though he was, and is now bruised and sore but hale. The boy wouldn't be buying his own drinks any time soon, that was for goddamn certain.

From the edge of the crowd, Sean catches Sol's eye, gives him a sober nod. Sol isn't entirely sure why the man is even here at the picket, but it makes him uneasy. Perhaps, like many men, Sean is simply drawn to the prospect of imminent violence, the feel of which hangs heavy in the air today like the crouching clouds of sulfur from the smelter stink-pots. So many men gathered into a close space: miners, ACM guards, the Pinkertons and, soon enough, scabs coming under escort to push their way through the picket in an effort to break this nascent strike.

Nothing good is going to come of this, whatever Frank and Rob Quinn and the others think. Sol can feel it. Nothing. A series of minor fuckups and inconveniences that morning meant that Frank and the others arrived late. The speechmaking is behind schedule, which means this mass of men has been stood there too long with only their angry, nervous thoughts for company. The scabs would be arriving soon.

Looking around, Sol has that sense again of his memory stuttering, that what he sees in front of him has somehow gotten out of phase with what he remembers, although there was no way he *could* even remember anything yet, because it hasn't happened, has it? The thought is just to the outside of his mind, somewhere just out of reach; he tries to sidle up to it from an angle but, when he gets closer, it slips away. The memory, or whatever it is, is a confused series of things. Noise and dust and fear and violence. Hands, again, holding his own. Black empty eyes like pits, drawing him in.

A raven sits atop a stack of timbers, watching him.

"Think they're coming, Sol." Billy points with his chin towards the Anaconda road. Heads in the crowd turn, the men watch the dust kicked up by the trucks they know are full of the strike-breaking scabs, trucks escorted by Mariahs, no doubt packed to the gills with police. The miners watch the trucks and the guards on the other side of the picket watch the miners; the Pinkertons strewn throughout the crowd do their best to watch everything.

This isn't going to end well. Billy knows it, can feel it like he feels the pull of north. Like Sol, he has a pit of dread festering in his belly, which he doesn't entirely understand but chalks up to good sense, or maybe just being out of sorts still. He feels sick, half-feverish, with pukey guts and watery bowels; since the night of the fight he's gotten no better, merely holding the same. Billy has always been one of those lucky sorts blessed with a robust constitution, rarely ill but, finally, days of feeling like pounded shit finally sent him in search of a doctor, who merely told him to rest. *Rest*, and this from a doctor who catered to miners and should have known the impossibility of the order.

Frank Little looks to be wrapping up his speech now, which is good, as Sol can see that he's losing the audience to the distraction of the scab trucks coming up the hill with their police escort.

"You see those men, boys," Frank is saying, "with the goons the Company has with them. Now, we're going to block their path, calmly and without violence. *Calmly and without violence*. Don't even call them names, if you can. You just say *not today, brother.* Repeat that now."

The silence is ominous until, finally, someone cries out: "*They're here to take our fuckin jobs, Frank!*" The shout is picked up by other men, again and again, until Frank is barely able to quiet the men down enough to hear his reply.

"Those boys are scared, men! They are scared and weak but they are our brother workers, even if they don't –" Whatever he's going to say next is lost in an outburst of jeering and curses.

– "*Fuck them!*"

– "*My family needs to eat too!*"

Sol nudges Billy. "This is going to get bad," he says, watching a man in the crowd brandish a length of rebar he's pulled from somewhere.

"Yeah, we should get out of here, Sol," Billy replies, looking uneasily at the mine guards on the other side of the picket, nervously passing their rifles from hand to hand. "We should go."

Sol looks around, tries to get an eyeball on all his boys, make sure they're still together. Billy is right, they need to get out of here. Not just them, though: everyone. Things are going to kick off. The mood is ugly and whatever Frank thinks he's going to accomplish here isn't going to work. The ACM doesn't have enough scabs to keep production going to the levels they need for the war in Europe; not skilled men, anyway. Maybe the workers don't need to shut down production entirely, he thinks. Maybe instead just slow it down enough for the Company to feel the pinch. He's no organizer, though. Frank knows what they should be doing; maybe he's right but, right now, Sol can feel that something very bad is about to happen.

"Sol! Sol, get on up here!" Frank is shouting at him now, waving an arm, inviting Sol up on the back of the pickup. He remembers that he's supposed to speak, to talk about the men lost at the Penn. Talk about Owen. He hadn't wanted to do it, not at all, but somehow Frank and Quinn convinced him. He's no speechmaker. Looking out over the angry crowd, he wonders just what the fuck he'll even say. These men don't care about the dead, not right now anyway. They have one thing on their minds, and that's breaking the heads of the men coming to take away their jobs, coming to take food out of the mouths of their families.

Sol climbs up onto the back of the truck, knees aching from the effort. For a long moment, he merely looks stupidly out over the crowd. He sees the anger, the rage simmering in their bellies, and then sends his gaze down to the twenty-one miners' helmets which line the truck bed, pausing at the one he knows belonged to his son. It's the old, bashed-up spare, a hand-me-down from Sol himself. Owen's own helmet is buried with him, somewhere down the Penn, melted maybe, buried under the tons of rock that came down when the timbers burned. One day some unlucky mucker would find his boy, perhaps, or maybe his body will just stay down there, if the seams of ore lead elsewhere. Eventually, when it finally plays out, the mine will be allowed to flood and whatever is left of Owen by then will remain forever underwater. It's rare that they aren't able to get a body out, but that's most likely to be his boy's fate, left interred inside the mine that took him. This whole town his headstone.

Sol looks up again, feeling heavy and tired inside. Whatever is going to happen here is going to happen. It doesn't matter what he has to say, so there's no point trying to use words to stop anything. Frank asked him to talk about the fire, about the men who had died because the Company found safety to be an embarrassment to the sanctity of the profit line. Sol will tell these men, then, about the miners that died. He'll tell them about his boy and, if they want to bust heads with scabs and the police, let them. Owen and the others deserve at least to be heard, even if it all turns to shit by the end.

Sol straightens up, takes a deep breath. As he does, he catches the eye of Sean Harrity, who nods back, and then, shrugging, reaches inside his jacket.

The raven atop the timbers stretches, extending his wings.

4.

Billy comes half-awake to the sound of tapping at the window, a dry rap like a fingernail against the glass of their cabin's one, grimy little pane. He'd been dreaming of some kind of fight, masses of men pushing and striking at one another, gunfire and screams and the dry, metal smells of snow and bloody dirt. A raven, flapping atop a stack of timbers. The dream had been a confusing, inchoate collection of ideas, only loosely wrapped together in the kind of tortured logic that dissolved upon waking, the way such things often are. Now, his heart is racing, the bedding wrapped and twisted around him so that he feels trapped. He has the sense that he's shouted himself awake, but then he hears the tapping again and realizes that there's something outside the window.

A bird, something about a bird, in the dream. Something about his uncle and a bird, before all the rest but, when he tries to come closer to the thought, it scuttles away.

Sagiistoo! he hears, although he knows he hadn't, not really, and tries to shake himself the rest of the way to consciousness. For once, sleep isn't easily dropping him free of its grasp, until it finally does and the voice and the dream fall away.

Sol is snoring in his own bed across the room, a ratcheting buzz that's amplified by what must be amazingly capacious sinus cavities, punctuated by irregular gasps for air like a drowning man. Billy had long ago learned to ignore it, even given his own tendencies towards light and fitful sleep. With a quiet groan, he swings his legs over the side of the bed and blearily sits up, feeling half-drunk still from the boozy celebrations that broke out after turning the scabs away at the strike; he has a stabbing pain in his head and feels as if all the water has been leached out of his body, leaving him shaky and as dry as gristle. He's never been much of a drinker, for reasons both temperamental and constitutional and, now, he remembers why.

The tapping at the window continues, soft and sharp. Moving slowly, Billy reaches under his pillow for the large knife he'd started keeping there a few days ago, for reasons he doesn't entirely understand. The damn thing is big enough that he can feel it pressing painfully on his skull through his flat, tired pillow when he tries to sleep. But, somehow, he doesn't feel quite right lately if it's not there. It's an uncomfortable comfort, he thinks, holding the knife in his hand now, feeling the cold, hard weight of it. Listening to the quiet rapping at the glass, which is still loud enough in Billy's dried-out, ill-used skull to hurt. *Go away, whoever you are. Let me fucking sleep.*

For a while that afternoon, it had looked like what had begun as a memorial would end in bloodshed, riot. More death, more miners to mourn. The work stoppage had done nothing but send already keyed-up, angry men that much more out of sorts. Working men will say that they want their leisure and, to a point, that's true. But what men want even more is the safety of routine. It felt wrong, somehow, to be outside in the cold February sunshine on a working day, no matter what the justification. No work means no pay which means no food for your family. No end-of-shift Sean O'Farrell and the companionship of friends equally worn out from twelve hours down the hole. No work means restlessness, unease; combine that with the memory of brothers killed by Company negligence and combine *that* with a passel of strikebreakers come to take your pay and you have a bad, bad combination.

Trust Frank, Sol had said. *Man knows what he's doing. Trust Rob.* From the beginning, though, the idea of the strike, combined with the memorial, had seemed like a bad idea to Billy. But what did he know? He wasn't even particularly attentive to the Labor movement. Just a man who did his job, paid his union dues, maybe listened to the occasional speech down at the Hall. He's no dummy though, he knows, and shit and damn, today had been a close one.

No wonder he let himself get so fucking drunk afterward.

Frank said his piece about unity and focus and a fair wage for a fair job and all that, ideas that smell sweet but lack real taste when chewed, Billy's always thought, and he'd damn near lost the crowd before he was done. But then Sol stands up and, although Billy shouldn't have been surprised, knowing him as he does, knowing Sol has a touch of the poetic in him, at times, he is: the old man speaks calmly, elegantly even, with feeling. Brings the crowd back in, quiets the restless and angry with just a few simple, heartfelt words about the son he'd lost, the friends he'd feared for, down the burning Penn a year ago.

Sol hadn't been much of a father to Owen; it was Dr Rideout and his wife who had raised the boy. Maybe, had things with Elizabeth not happened as they had, Sol would have done better. He'd damn near raised Billy, after all, rest of the way up, anyway, after Billy had left that school and Bad Bird had gotten too dangerous to be around. Maybe it was a flavor of guilt at his failure with Owen that'd made Sol take Billy in, those years ago, and maybe he could have started over with Owen, picked up some of those pieces, had the fire not happened. Maybes were worth jack shit, though, Billy knows, no more than that. Sol can be a pain in the ass, that's a truth; but, under the bullshit, is the man that Billy still, these years later, shares a shitty little room with, by his own damn choice. He wouldn't have called it in so many words, but he loves Sol Parker, plain and simple. He knows that Owen loved him, too. Or would have, if he'd had the chance to know him.

So, when Sol starts speaking about the fire, about getting his boys out, except for the one person that, in a perfect world, would have been first to the mine collar, Billy can't help but feel his eyes burning. Something in Sol's words, or maybe just his tone, communicates itself to the unraveling mass of angry men who are looking to take out their frustrations on the easy target of the scabs coming up. Cowards, thieves, escorted by the police in the pay of the ACM, to take their work, steal food from their babies' mouths.

Billy sees Sean Harrity, smoking a cigar he's drawn from a pocket inside his jacket, eyeing Sol from within the cloud of smoke he's making, puffing away like a freight train. Just a cigar, nothing more than that, and never mind the look in his eyes. Above his head, squatting on a stack of timbers, a big raven frets and mutters.

The crowd is ominously silent when the scabs start to hop out of the back of the trucks, looking at the ground for the most part, not willing to meet the eyes of the men they are betraying. Their police escorts grip their batons so tightly that, even from here, Billy can see whitening knuckles. On the other side of the picket, mine guards are shifting nervously, rifles pressed to chests. Between them all, the working men are packing closer together, trying to fill the space with as much human mass as possible, to build a wall of muscle between the collar of the Neversweat and the scabs that have come to go down her.

One burly, red-faced police sergeant steps forward, close to the protesters. The man raises his baton, points to the headframe of the mine, widens his legs. He sucks in a deep breath of air in preparation for whatever he's going to say.

"Not today, brother!" From the bed of the pickup, Sol bellows the words, shaking his head, arms crossed over his chest.

The shout is immediately picked up by the strikers, individually at first and then with greater cohesion, a staccato beat from hundreds of hoarse throats.

– "Not today, brother."
– "Not today, brother!"
– "NOT TODAY, BROTHER!"

The sergeant can't help but take a step back. He raises his own voice, but the words are drowned out by the chanting miners. The scabs still stare at the ground, shrinking into themselves even more.

– "NOT TODAY, BROTHER!"
– "NOT TODAY, BROTHER!"

After a while, Frank pushes his way through the miners, flanked by a wary Rob Quinn. He takes the sergeant aside. They huddle together, Frank pressing his case, from time to time gesturing back to the mass of yelling men packed between the putative workers and the mine collar. The sergeant's face gets yet redder and he stabs a finger into Frank Little's breastbone, making his displeasure known, waving vaguely towards town where the ACM offices are. Even from a distance, without sound, it's clear what the conversation entails.

And then, just like that, it's all over.

The sergeant shouts towards his men and then washes a last baleful glare over the strikers, no doubt memorizing faces as best he can. With a sneer towards Frank and Quinn, he turns his back, directing the scabs into the trucks with a minimal amount of curt, disgusted gestures. The trucks cough back to life and, a few minutes later, the miners are left to themselves, wedged between the Company and that day's profits, still shouting.

– *"NOT TODAY, BROTHER!"*

– *"NOT TODAY, BROTHER!"*

Later, of course, the festive, comradely spirit devolves into pure, drunken celebration, the miners of Butte reveling in one brief, surprising victory over the forces of Capital, washing the dust out of their tired, sore throats with round after round of drinks. There are songs and bar bets and, likely, another generation of miners planted into the bellies of willing women that night. There are fistfights, of course, mostly good-natured except when they aren't. The whores are walking bowlegged by night's end, picking up the slack for those miners lacking a wife or a steady.

Tomorrow will be another day but, tonight, Labor is king.

Tap. Tap-tap-tap. Tap. Billy sits on his bed now, listens to whatever drunken fool is tapping at his window, and vows to never drink again. Never, ever again. Eventually, with a determined, unsteady movement, he flings himself upright, weaving for a moment. Knife held behind his back, he yanks aside the tatty lace curtain, heaving up the sash.

No one's there.

Whichever asshole had stumbled up to rob Billy of his sleep and introduce him to this hangover must have finally moved on. Cursing liquor and all who consume it, himself most certainly included, Billy staggers back to his bed. He drops into it, searching again for slumber.

5.

Uninvited, Marked Face sits down across the table from his nephew Sagiistoo, next to his pet white man, Solomon Parker. It's early, the sun just up, and each man is staring bleary eyed into a steaming mug of coffee. Searching those depths for relief from the white sickness. Marked Face himself is an old man, who needs little sleep, for whom drink has largely lost its savor; he relishes the feeling of health that a man has when sober and in the presence of suffering drunkards. It's a small pleasure.

Here, again, he is come to do the work of the Above Ones. That which must pass is moving ever onwards, creeping inexorably to the end. Marked Face thinks, as he has many times before, how strange it is that such massive things like the shape of a world can be determined by such tiny actions. Again, the thin searching root that splits the boulder, the pebble that starts the slide that destroys the mountain. Bones, clattering on a table. Such tiny actions, all of them, to do so much. But, then again, to the Above Ones, men are all tiny. They are as ants to those people.

He feels the bones warming in his chest. Best to get on

with things, then.

"You look unwell, Nephew," he says, in the true tongue, over-loudly, not bothering to hide his smile as the drunkards wince. "Perhaps you indulged in too much of the white man's medicine, hey? Did my crazy brother Bad Bird ever tell you the story of the Old Ones and the sacred ear mountain? I will tell it to you now. Listen. You see, one day, the daughter of Siinatssi's brother, Maatakssi, came to the old man and said…"

This old man needs to pipe the fuck down, Sol thinks. Billy must have the same thought, as he says, "Shut up, Uncle," holding his head on one palm as he has been since they got to the diner. It's all Sol can do to keep from reaching across the table and throttling the old Indian. If he felt better, himself, he might have done so. There's nothing worse for a hungover man than the presence of the loudly sober. Whatever the old fucker is saying in Indian is most likely not complimentary, anyway; his very presence seems to stir up unpleasant half-memories, although Sol himself has never met the man, so far as he knows. Some relation of Billy's, apparently. He seems familiar, maybe, but Sol feels too wretched to study on it.

Sol had dreamt of Owen last night, no doubt due to the feelings cracked loose at the memorial, from the cage in his chest where he keeps them. He almost never speaks about Owen to anyone; Billy maybe, once or twice, but not even to the other boys in his crew. His surrogate little family, Owen's briefly adopted brothers. Certainly Sol's never before stood up in front of a mass of men, mostly strangers, and talked about the boy. Doing so has broken a poorly mortared dam inside him, and the thought of Owen has crawled its way into his head, infected his dreams.

"Coffee," he croaks out, remembering his manners. He waves a waitress over, points at his cup, nods at the old Indian.

When it's brought to him, the old man stares at his cup of coffee. He picks it up, briefly blowing on it before taking a long, loud, slurping sip. In English, he says, "I heard that you white miners won a great victory yesterday, against your masters. Congratulations." He tries another taste of the coffee but then makes an unpleasant face and blows a long breath across the mug. He sets it down and pushes it away.

If Sol hadn't been so hungover and out of sorts to question his own senses, he would wonder just how that cup of coffee the old Indian pushed away, after blowing on it, has frozen solid into a black mass.

"Yes, a great victory, Uncle," Billy says. "No one got their heads cracked, for once, just for standing in a road. The fuck are you here, anyway, old man? Shouldn't you be on the reservation?" He just wants to be left alone, left alone to nurse his aching head and grumbling guts with a cup of coffee and the greasiest eggs and potatoes a Butte diner can provide, some salty, meaty corned-beef hash, something to help him wait out the hours until he can return to being merely sick instead of both sick and hungover.

"Why am I here? That's my own counsel, boy. Maybe I just wanted to see my beloved nephew, Sagiistoo. Are you sure you are well, Nephew? You look pale, even for a white man."

Billy manages as much of a glare as he can, trying to keep the contents of his stomach where they belong. He will never drink again, he vows. Never. His uncle sits there, across from him, smiling wide enough that

Billy wants to do nothing more than slap it off him. From time to time the old man looks around the room, nodding amiably whenever anyone catches his eye. This cheerfulness is more disconcerting than Marked Face's general surly anger, and Billy is uneasy that it's the mad smile that prefaces the fist, as it often had been when he, Billy, was small. Both his father and uncle have dangerous, unpredictable natures, as shared scars attest.

Their food arrives and they tuck in, Marked Face refusing to order with a smiling shake of the head. The hash and eggs are oily and hot, thick with salt; the taste is a small shine of heaven. Billy knows that he'll shit himself inside out later but, now, he can feel the food sucking some of the whiskey from his innards, steering him on a course towards human again.

Marked Face has taken something out from a pouch inside his shirt and is shaking it in his cupped hands, as if praying. When he lets them go, Billy sees that they're his old bone dice, and he feels a twist of unease in his belly, and not simply because he can see the look on Sol's face, the familiar gleam coming to his eye, the gleam that he gets when he's about to lose something. That same gleam that put him in this current mess with Sean Harrity. There's something more to this, but he doesn't know what. He doesn't know why Marked Face is here and the unease is deepening now. Billy glances outside the window without knowing what he's looking for.

"Do you gamble, white man?"

When Billy turns back, his uncle is smiling wider.

"Let's go, Sol," Billy says, pushing his empty plate forward. He tosses some money on the table. "Let's get out of here."

"Now hang on, Billy, hang on," Sol says.

• • •

Sol looks at the old Indian, cocks his head a bit. "Let's not be rude to your uncle here." He reaches out a hand. "Solomon Parker, sir. Don't believe I've had the pleasure." The Indian merely stares at Sol's hand, still smiling, and then mutters a couple of syllables in his language, whether his own name or what Sol doesn't know. Sol reels his unshaken hand back in, feeling foolish but telling himself that one must allow for differences in customs, after all.

Billy stands up. "Come on, let's go."

The old man explains in broken English the rules of the simple game, pointing out the markings on the yellowed old bones. Sol nods along, pausing once to wave a hand at Billy. "Goddamn it, Bill, either sit down or go. Making me nervous, you looming over me like that. Like the damn shadow of death."

Billy sits again.

"What's the bet then, sir?" Sol asks, picking up the bones, rattling them in a loose hand, getting their shape and heft. He has a lucky feel about himself this morning and his hangover seems to be crawling away.

The old Indian's smile grows wider, the scar on his cheek pulls his lip up and out of true. The base of a shining white tooth gleams wet. Instead of responding, he looks across at Billy again, pulling a handful of gold coins out of a pocket of his shirt, setting them carefully into a stack on the table. Then, as if changing his mind, he picks them back up and returns them to his pocket.

"Cigarette," he says.

"Pardon?" Sol's disappointed to see the coins go away; there were a fair few there, more than he'd have thought a shabby, broke-down chief like this old boy would have had. Sol needs money, needs it bad. The fight has chipped away at his obligation to Sean Harrity but he's a long, long way from straight with the bastard and Sol won't sleep entirely easily until he is.

"Tobacco. I win, you give me a cigarette."

"That's it?" The old man doesn't reply, just takes the bones from Sol's hand, giving them a rattle. He's looking across at Billy, still smiling, but with an unpleasant gleam in his eye, that one long tooth still shining slick. "You wouldn't want to sweeten the pot a bit more, partner?"

"Cigarette," he says again.

"A cigarette, OK, OK." Sol shrugs, breathes out a little sigh of disappointment, but sometimes games start small like this and build of their own momentum. If that's what it takes to loosen up this miserly old bastard's pockets then so be it. "What if I win?"

"I will do you a favor, Solomon Parker," he says, the smile stretched tight. "I will give you what it is you most desire."

"Excuse me?"

"Sol, come on, this is bullshit," Billy says. "Let's go." He stands up again.

After a glance, Sol ignores him, directing his attention to the old man in front of him.

"Let me make sure I understand this," he says. "If I win, you'll do me a favor, that right? Cigarette for a favor, huh?" Sol doesn't really get it, but maybe it's another Indian thing. Difference of culture again. Offhand, he can't really think of anything this old bastard can do for him but, again, maybe it's just a thing to get the game going. He's starting to get that familiar itch; he can tell that the luck he feels creeping up on him has come to stay for a while. He's had a run of bad, lately, but it'll be different now. He's due. Goddamn it, he's due. Hell, the favor will be another game, Sol decides, and soon enough he'll cut loose this tight fucker from that gold in his pocket. The day is off to a good start, and his hangover is entirely gone now. Poof, just like that, like magic.

"It is your throw," the old Indian says, reaching forward with the dice in his palm. "Now we wager on these bones."

He's due, all right, and that luck of Sol's holds true and the bones chatter on the tabletop, winning, winning, winning. He's due and his luck is changing and then the old Indian takes his hands again. Differences in culture, some kind of ritual, maybe, and it doesn't matter because he knows that when he picks up those bones again for the next game he'll win again and again and again. This is a new day and he's goddamn due and, finally, he can feel his luck digging in to stay and he looks into the old man's eyes, so black they're like holes in the world.

They're like holes in the world and then he's falling into them.

A tapping that becomes a slow boom.

He's falling and there's the smell of burning timber.

Boom.

Boom.

Boom.

It's coming.

The Smoke and the Dark

— 1916 —

Pennsylvania Mine: Butte, Montana

1.

Flame and fucking smoke.

It's coming.

Sol knows it, this time. He can see it ahead of himself clear as fucking day, thirteen hundred feet underground. Down here in the wet, dusty stink of the Penn, again, again. Over the rattle of the ore car and the chattering shatter of the widowmakers on the rock face down the end of the drift, he can hear the screams and curses and gasping for air that's coming, soon enough. His nose tests for the acrid bite of burning wood, his lungs pull tight inside him, searching for the tickle of ash in the breath he sucks in.

He knows it: it's coming.

Flame and smoke. Flame and fucking smoke and twenty-one men dead. Twenty-one men will die today, Owen among them.

It's coming.

Sol hears the clatter of a dropped prybar, sees Billy looking back at him from a few feet away, eyes wide with fear. Billy knows too. A moment ago they were drinking coffee and fighting down hangovers with greasy hash and eggs; a moment ago Sol was throwing dice with

Billy's old uncle, the scar-faced, smiling bastard who can freeze a cup of coffee with a breath. A moment ago, a year from now, a year that had happened and would happen again, unless Sol does something.

It's crazy and makes no sense but Sol can see it shining back at him from the look in Billy's eyes. Fear of a memory of a time that doesn't yet exist. It makes no sense but Sol's guts are in a tangle, his asshole tight as a saddle knot, sweat pushing through the grime on his forehead.

It's coming, flame and smoke: the mine is going to burn.

"*Go!*" Billy shouts, pointing down the drift. "*Fucking go*, Sol!"

There's no time to think it through, no time to wonder if he's gone completely batshit and is going to wind up down the road at Warm Springs, under the care of his brother; maybe in a day or two he'll be swapping stories with old John Bird, Billy's dad, about the times their heads cracked open and all the sane leaked out, laughing and hollering about what a great hoot that was, dragged away screaming about fires and futures and all sorts of fucking things. *No time for that now, John Bird*, Sol thinks as he sprints as best he can down the drift, hunkered down, elbowing the boys out of his way, ignoring their odd looks, *no time for crazy talk because this mine is going to burn, ha-ha, I know it, going to kill a passel of men, and Owen, and how about that brother of yours, Whatshisname, with the scars and the dice and the cigarette bets, owes me a favor, that one does, and I guess this is it.* Maybe soon enough he and Lizzie can rest on some porch stairs at the hospital, of an evening, enjoy a smoke and a lemonade and talk about whatever it is that lunatics talk about. *How's Owen?* she'll say, *How's my baby that I burned up?* Sol will laugh,

squeezing her shoulder and drawing her closer, her head
to his chest, scratch of her hair against his beard. *Oh, he
wasn't burnt up, girl, I saved him that first time, didn't I, and
then I saved him again, that time I went crazy down the Penn.
Saved the lot of those boys from a fire that never happened, hey?*
And they'll hug closer and swirl their crazy thoughts
together and things will be as good as it was when they
both were sane, years and years ago when they were
young.

Best not to think about it, not right now anyway, best
to just take this chance and leave the thinking for later,
once Owen and the rest of the crew are up at the Stope,
tonight after shift, alive and not burnt up at all, drinking
their Sean O'Farrells and bitching about the day's work,
making rude jokes about their respective heritages and
the rest of it, griping about the Company and maybe
looking for a girl or a fight or just a good drunk to try on.
Leave it till then and then maybe, *maybe*, take Billy aside
to a quiet place and talk, low and lunatic, about *what the
fuck* and that smiling, scarred-up old bastard of an uncle
of his, with the evil looks and Indian magic and the crazy
that's crawled into Sol's head and all of that.

Right now, though: *run.*

Coughing around the dust in his chest, trying not to
bang into anything, too hard anyway, Sol sprints and
staggers down the line of the drift towards the shaft,
looking for Owen. Soon enough he finds him, hunched
over, body sprawled out at a forty-five-degree angle as
he pushes an especially overfull cart of ore towards the
shaft to be hauled up to the headframe. As the new boy,
Owen gets the shit jobs and it's a bit of a game for the
others to see just how heavy they can make the cars; the
drift is mostly level but the cart itself is heavy enough
even empty, the wheels and rails thick with muck,

and stuffed as full as possible. That car can get damn oppressive, pushed back and forth over the course of twelve hours. Sol knows it from experience, years and years ago when he was the low man, doing all the scut-work and shit details, but it's an expected part of the job and Owen needs to build up some muscle anyway. The boy takes after his mother, lean and narrow-boned. Pushing a heavy cart won't kill him.

Owen's heeled forward, palms on the cart, arms stiff, legs spraddled out behind him, taking one steady step after another. The startled look on his face when Sol grabs the back of his shirt, pulling him upright, would be comical if Sol himself wasn't so terrified about what is coming. "Are you OK, boy? Are you OK?"

"What?"

"Goddamn it, just follow me!"

"What? Sol, what the hell is going on?"

"*Just follow me, boy!* Don't fucking *argue with me*, just follow and don't get out of my sight, you hear, Owen? *Don't get out of my fucking sight!*" Sol's pulled the boy close, screaming the last into his face, knowing he won't understand but trusting in the power of volume and spittle-flecked proximity to trump logic. Without further discussion, he runs off down the drift, dragging his son behind him, ignoring whatever it is the boy is saying.

A moment or two later they're at the shaft, where old Torsten sits on a stool, reading a detective magazine under the dim shine of an overhead bulb. He looks up with placid unconcern, marking his place with a finger. "Sol," he says. "And whatever your name is." Torsten doesn't stand on ceremony; he's been down the mines for almost forty years, seen plenty of boys come and go. It's too much work to remember all the fresh ones, he says, so he doesn't even bother to learn the names of the new kids until he's reasonably sure they're the kind that are going to stay. "What can I do for you, Sol?" he says.

It's then that Sol realizes that he has no idea *what* to do, how he's even going to stop whatever is coming, now that he has the chance. Some screaming part of him just says *take Owen and get the fuck out of the Penn, quick fucking sharp* but, as soon as he thinks it, he knows that he'll never let what's coming find Billy and the rest of the boys. Or any of the other men, for that matter. *But Billy* knows *what's coming*, that nervous, fearful part of him is saying, *he'll get the boys out. Might already be doing so, right now.* Sol knows he can't leave his crew, though, those boys that look to him, not even in the hands of Billy. It wouldn't be right. They're his responsibility. His.

He casts his mind back – *forward?* – trying to remember – *what?* – whatever it is he knows about the fire down the Penn, what happened – *will happen, Sol, you crazy fucking old man* – a year ago. Now. In the aftermath, before, in the half-assed Company investigation, they figured that the fire broke out on the 1200 level – *right? am I remembering that correctly?* – and it started from an electrical short or an abandoned miner's candle or who the fuck knew what else. But 1200. Two hundred plus men down the Penn that day, scattered across levels, the fire starts, they pull most of them out from safe levels and Sol and his boys go out the Tramway, a half-mile away. Most of Sol's boys. He grabs Owen by the collar, pulls him closer.

"Send me up to 1200," he says to Torsten.

Torsten leans back, scratching one gnarled, yellow-nailed hand across the stubble on his cheek. "Why you need to go up to 1200, Sol?"

Sol doesn't pause, just lets Owen loose and steps forward, grabbing the old Swede by the shirtfront. "Send me the fuck up to 1200, Torsten, or get ready to count your fucking teeth, old man. *Get me up to 1200!*"

Torsten assumes a look of affront and peels Sol's fingers from his shirt, brushing down his chest with wounded dignity. There's no call for this kind of behavior, his expression says. None at all. He's a senior man, after all, proved himself down these mines for years added on years. Sol Parker should show him some respect. General courtesy.

"I ain't no old man, Sol," he says. "And you're older than me, yeah. Older than me. No need to be rude, friend, I was just askin. But I send you up there, don't worry." He gestures towards the cage, still wearing his mournful, hurt expression, face like a slapped ass. Once Sol and Owen are inside, Torsten joins them – *I go with you, yeah* – taking what seems to Sol an inordinate amount of time ringing the hoist operator up at the headframe. By the time the confirming buzzes finally sound, Sol is ready to throw the old fucking Swede down the shaft.

– 4 bells and 4: 1200 level.

There's a jolt and the cage starts moving upwards.

"Sol, what's going on?" Owen hollers over the rattle of the lift.

Sol ignores the boy, trying to frame some kind of strategy. He can't very well just start telling the miners to get out of the Penn, on no evidence at all, to just drop tools and fuck off up top because old Sol Parker has a scare up his butthole; when the fire starts he knows that the Company will damn sure try to hold him accountable somehow, if he does that, as a saboteur or on some other horseshit charge, negligence, maybe, no matter what he has to say. They'll frame him up as a Wobbly anarchist or secret Bolshevik, burning up their mine. If, for some reason, the fire *doesn't* start, if he's wrong or just straight-up crazy, as he half suspects, the ACM will haul him over for that, too, and he'll never find work again; they'll tear up his rustling card and put him on the blacklist. Either of those options are fine and good, he'll take them happily if it will keep all these boys safe, but the better bet is to just find this fucking fire and *stop it before it happens*.

And how in the hell is he going to do that? Just stroll around 1200, asking *hey now have any of you boys seen a fire?* Strolling around is about the extent of his ideas, just yet, though; maybe something better will come to him but, so far, that's all he's got. Best not to overthink it and, given the fact that he's here at all, it seems wrong that he won't be able to straighten things out. Best to shy away from *that* thought, too, though, wrapped up as it is in crazy or whatever kind of goddamn Indian witchcraft or acts of God or what the fuck ever. It's too big of a thought to get in the head all at once without pushing something else out, so Sol just figures to ignore it for now and trust that he's here for a reason, and that reason is to stop a fucking fire.

"Come on, boy," he says, as the cage rattles to a halt on 1200. He steps out, dragging Owen behind him, leaving Torsten to his magazine. "Just shut up and follow me."

Owen has no idea what's happening. He walks behind Sol, who shuffles along, head swinging down low, side to side like a bear. For several minutes they work their way down the drift, the old man pausing at timbers, from time to time kicking them with his boot. Sol ignores the miners they encounter, who look at them curiously and then go back to their work. Whatever they're doing, Owen is at least enjoying a break from pushing that heavy goddamn cart up and down the drift all day. It's bullshit that he's the one who always has to do it but

Owen also gets it, that he's the low man and gets hind tit, workwise. It's paying your dues, he guesses, but at the same time he looks forward to the day when he's not spending all shift at the ass end of a heavy ore cart.

If he even lasts that long. Owen isn't sure that the miner's life is the best fit for him. Maybe it just takes some getting used to, but the work is hard and, he hates to admit it, being down inside the earth scares the shit out of him. His dad and the others seem to pay it no mind, but Owen can feel the weight of every single foot of dirt and rock overhead, pressing down on him; sometimes the shaft walls, already narrow enough, push tighter and his breath catches in his chest, his eyes go a bit swimmy, until he can relax some. Just the thought of that that makes his head get a little light now, so Owen tries to focus on his dad, who's still shuffling along, muttering to himself.

It's strange being here with him, though, finally getting to know him some. Owen isn't sure if he really likes Sol, not yet, anyway, given that the old bastard shunted him off as a kid because he was inconvenient or because of his mom or whatever the reason was, but he can see that there are at least a few things to admire about him. Which is a grudging thought but there it is. The other men look up to Sol, and he's good at the work and seems fair and all that. He can be a pain in the ass and he's a fucking taskmaster, but all and all there's less to dislike about his old man than maybe Owen wanted to find when he first came to Butte.

His thoughts are interrupted by the sight of a big, big, man, damn near as tall and wide as Nancy, maybe bigger, even, blocking the drift in front of them. A pissed-off look on his face, fists the size of sledgehammers at his hips.

"What the hell you doing here, Sol?" the man says, his accent twist-mouthed and sharp around the edges.

Jesus fuck, not now, Sol thinks, looking up from his scan of the timbers. He's never gotten on with this big fucker. Vlad, foreman of another mucker crew, who he crosses paths with more than he'd like, given their mutual animosity. Never got on with most of Vlad's whole crew, really, Russians or Serbs or whatever the hell they were, the lot of them insular and distrustful of non-Russians or non-Serbs or non-whatevers. Pride in your heritage is fine and good but if you won't drink with a man because he doesn't speak whatever vowel-bereft language you speak, well, that's just bullshit. Plus Vlad's crew are a bunch of big, hard-knuckled bastards and Sol and his boys have come off second best in a scuffle or two with them over the years, of an evening, and that rankles.

"Vlad. Hello, son. Just looking for something is all."

"Rob knows you are here?"

"Goddamn it, Vlad, don't worry about what Rob knows or don't know, OK? Now come on, brother, I need to get past you." He tries to edge around the big Russian but Vlad moves back in front of him.

"Maybe I think you should be back at your level. 1200 is my crew today."

Goddamn all fucking Russian bastards and their bastard Russian fucking crews, Sol shouts quiet inside his head, but instead says, "Just looking for something, Vlad. Just give me a minute and I'll be out of your hair, hey?"

"You tell me what is you want and I find it for you."

Sol eyes a prybar that's leaning against the drift wall a few feet away. In another minute he's going to pick it up and crack it across this stupid asshole's thick Russian skull, is what he's going to do, ring his chimes and then be about his business.

"Not sure what it is just yet, Vlad, OK?" Sol raises a placating hand, edging a bit closer to the prybar.

"You look for something but what you don't know." Vlad frowns theatrically, shaking his head.

"About the size of it." A step closer.

"Best you look for it then at your level, Sol, *khorosho*?" The big man reaches a hand out to take Sol's shoulder, none too gently but, when Sol takes a step away, he sees it, a thick wodge of candle, still burning, resting up against a timber that's beginning to char at the bottom.

"*You motherfucker!*"

He pushes past Vlad, who's caught by surprise; Sol takes three quick steps forward and brings his muck-caked boot down on the candle, squashing it into the rock and mud, twisting his heel and then scraping down along the timber until he's sure that any spark is out, cursing more or less incoherently all the while.

"The hell are you doing, Sol?" Vlad steps close, his face darkening.

"You stupid Russian motherfucker," Sol says. "Stupid big square-headed dipshit. *Stupid.*" He points to the timber and the smashed candle. "You'll burn this whole fucking mine down around us, you dumb asshole. *Do your fucking job, hey? Pick your fucking shit up.*"

"Is one candle. Half candle." Vlad kicks up a pat of wet, gluey mud, hitting Sol in the shins with it. "Is wet everywhere, old man. Nothing burns."

Before he can stop himself, Sol steps forward, slamming his palms into Vlad's wide chest, knocking the big man into the drift wall. Even though the Russian has most of a foot and seventy-plus pounds on him, not to mention being thirty-odd years younger, all the pent-up fear and teeth-grinding emotion from what's happened

has Sol ready to tear the bastard apart, or at least give
it a good shot. Mercifully, Owen takes the opportunity
to step in front of him, which gives Sol a brief splash
of sanity, making him back down a shade. He contents
himself with pointing over the boy's shoulder, yelling.

"*Do your fucking job, Vlad.* You'll get us all killed."

"You don't tell me how to do my job, old man."

Vlad is pressing forward against Owen's outstretched
hands. Owen looks a bit like he does when he's pushing
the ore cart, although he never has to worry that the ore
cart is steaming furious and going to beat the shit out of
him. "Hey hey hey, fellas, come on now," he says, tries to
calm things down. Even though standing between these
two must be the last place he wants to be and is probably
going to get him killed. Sol knows he isn't being fair to
the boy but his thoughts are still jumping hot and crazy
in his head.

"You stupid Russian fuck," he says. "You stupid fuck."

"Fuck you, old man. You say that again, you say that
to me."

"*What the fuck is going on here?*" Rob Quinn is standing
in the drift, hands on his hips, looking every shade of
annoyed. Vlad and Sol turn to look at him, Vlad fuming,
Sol guilty because he knows he's acting like an asshole,
right then, even if he can't help it. But there are goddamn
circumstances, right, circumstances.

"Sol, what the hell are you doing up here?"

"Old man is looking for something he don't know,
Rob." Vlad spits a mucousy glob on the ground between
Sol's feet.

Quinn points a thick finger. "Goddamn it, Vlad, didn't
ask you, I asked Sol. And what the fuck are you doing
standing here? If you're done playing fuckin grabass
maybe you can go do some work, huh? That's what

you're paid to do, dipshit, not to stand here running your fuckin mouth. Now get the fuck out of here." He points down the tunnel and Vlad slumps off, shouldering Sol out of the way, muttering to himself.

"Thanks, Rob," Sol says. Sheepish.

"Fuck you. And Jesus, Sol, save that fuckin stuff for after shift. You know that. The fuck are you doing here, anyway? Why aren't you down with your crew?"

Sol doesn't really know what to say, so he mumbles something about hearing that someone needed some help with something, vague bullshit that trails off into something approaching incoherence. Quinn is looking at him with an expression somewhere between annoyance and just plain disgust by the time Sol finishes.

"Jesus Christ, Sol, get the fuck down to your crew." He nods at Owen, standing there mostly ignored now. "Hope you don't take after your old man here, kiddo. We're here to fuckin work, right? Jesus, you two." He walks off, shaking his head.

"Hey Rob," Sol calls after him. He thinks he's done what he needs to do, but there's some worry still, a nagging feeling scratching at the inside of his skull. It's not like he has an instruction manual for any of this. Quinn turns, face still sour. "Just keep an eye out today, OK?" Sol says. "Got a funny feeling, is all."

"You got a funny feeling."

Sol shrugs. He knows he sounds stupid, but needs to say it anyway. "Yeah, I got a funny feeling. Woman's intuition or something. Just look out for the boys, OK?"

"Fuck, Sol, don't tell me to do my fuckin job, because, of the two of us, *I'm the only one who's fuckin doing it* right now. Now take your boy and your fuckin woman's intuition down to Thirteen and do *your* fuckin job. Jesus." He turns and strides off down the drift. "Get the fuck out of here, Sol!" he calls over a shoulder.

Sol and Owen walk back down the tunnel. Sol feels hollowed out inside, shaky on his legs now. He's trying not to think. From time to time he glances over to Owen, who's walking next to him and, then, from one step to another, he knows that his words to Quinn are unnecessary. There is no fire, there will be no fire. If he's done one good thing in this life of legion and numberless mistakes, bad choices, here it is. He just feels it, feels it in his belly, warm and hot like a shot of whiskey. How he managed it, how he stopped the fire from a year on, back now from a bet, he doesn't know and isn't nearly ready to study on it, not for a long goddamn while, really, but there it is.

Torsten is still sitting in the cage, reading his magazine. He doesn't look up as Sol and Owen get into the lift. Must still be in something of a snit, because, when he rings them down, the car drops sharp and hard and then heels up fast. It bangs Sol, unprepared, into the side of the car, where he cracks into a shovel that's propped, against all regulations for sure, in the corner. The handle of the shovel knocks painfully into his shin and he curses the brokedown fucking Swede as the lift descends again, more slowly this time.

"Don't blame me, Sol," the old man mutters. "I'm not the one who runs the machine, I just send the ring, yeah."

Yeah, you already sent up the drop-hard signal, you old fucker, Sol thinks. *Notice you didn't get all crashed around, braced as you were.* It's fine, though: Torsten will get over himself and Sol had been an asshole earlier, after all. He'll buy the old Swede a drink after shift and that will be that. Sol leans down, rubbing the rising knot on his shin, grimacing at Owen, who'd made something of an unmanly squeak when the lift dropped. *You'll get used to it, boy.*

Back down on 1300, the cage comes to a halt. Motioning Owen out in front of him, Sol gives Torsten a friendly slap on the shoulder as he exits the lift. "First round's on me later, hey, old man," he says. Torsten nods and smiles and that's that.

Further up the shaft, the spark, kicked up from the shovel Sol banged into a moment ago, is burning into a thick smear of the grease that coats the lift cables.

It drops down onto a dry patch of timber.

The old sorcerer kneels in the dark, fanning the spark until it becomes a flame. As it did before, as it ever will.

  Soon now.

  We are sharpened, like a blade, each time.

  Soon.

  We are sharpened, or we are broken.

2.

"We need to find him!" Sol, soot-faced, wild-eyed and filthy, strains at Nancy's arms wrapped around his chest. "We need to find him, now, *now!*" The blood streaming down from the deep cut on his head runs into his eyes; he blinks, tries to shake it free but it's pouring too fast and he can't see. "Goddamn it, let me loose!"

"Sol!" The boys are hollering, trying to get him under control by main force. Their own faces are streaked with ash and sweat and grime and maybe the runnels of tears, they're panting and coughing and shivery at what they've been through, what they're just now beginning to process. It'd taken them long, terrifying, lung-stretched minutes in the smoke and the dark and the wet heat, staggering along in a ragged group, Nancy carrying the unconscious, bleeding Sol after they'd dug themselves out of the last drift, the one that had caved in on them just a few feet from where they'd needed to get to. Mercifully close enough that they could pull themselves out, yelling and choking through the dust, bruised and cut and skinned up. Billy leading them out from the Penn to the Tramway, those long minutes a quarter mile deep underground before finally, finally, up and out, pissing their pants from fear until they could all get out of the burning mine, pulled up in a ragged, sweaty, huddled group. All of them but one.

Owen, left half-buried in the cave-in, the heavy, collapsed timber that had killed him at least pulled from atop his skull. No time for anything else. No time for sentiment.

And now that Sol is awake again, he's going crazy.

He pulls forward, winging his elbows back, trying to connect with Nancy's jaw, skull, teeth, whatever it takes to get the big dumb fucker to let him loose. He just needs one quick second for the bastard's arms to relax from around behind him, and he'll be loose and he needs to go now, *now*, while there's still a chance. Sol has already seen it before, he *remembers*, he knows what will happen, what is happening. Another set of arms wrap around his chest from the front, pinioning his own and stabbing him tight, back to belly, against Nancy. He snaps his forehead forward, feeling the satisfying impact as Michael's nose crumples to the side; he drives ahead again, trying to cut loose.

"Goddamn it, let me go, you fuckers! There's still time!"

Michael reels a step back, hands held to his face, cursing a mumble through his fingers and trying to stop the sudden gush of blood down his chin, but Nancy heels backward, lifting Sol from the ground so his legs lose their push forward, like that old Greek boy that Hercules wrestled, a story he was told once. Hercules lifted that boy off the ground and he was fucked, whatever his name was, like Sol is now, he realizes, and *goddamn you big faggot let me loose I have to go!* He flails around, kicking backward with his heels, twisting side to side like a half-landed trout, until he feels more arms, long and lanky

and tough as old leather – that would be Flynn – pinning
him tighter against Big Nancy, the voice growling in his
ear that he needs to stop, that it's too late, too late, it's
done.

"*It's not fucking too late you fucking fucks!*" Sol screams
it, knowing they won't understand, pushing his head
around Flynn until he can catch Billy's eye. Billy is
standing there like a statue while the other miners at the
collar of the Tramway push past and by, shouting their
own nonsense, running through the smoke that's settled
on the hill. A hive of activity all around, men hollering
for the Draegers, water, shovels; some are cursing the
Company, some yelling for friends they know were
down the Penn, trying to find them. All of them rushing
towards the black plume of smoke boiling out from
under the Pennsylvania's headframe. Even with the fire,
the air feels too cold, too sharp; there's a dry smell of
new snow even around the stink of burning mine timber
and the sulfurous fog from the arsenic-rich smelter pits,
that heavy, healthful air that smothers down around
town and is killing them, day by day, like the dust in
their lungs.

For a second everything seems to slow, go quiet and
hard, and Sol can see each individual small, pebbly white
flake of snow drift down amidst the lazy black flecks of
ash from the burning mine. He's failed, once again, and
the Penn is aflame. Somewhere, lost down there, his boy
is burning.

Sol doesn't open his mouth this time, merely stares
at Billy, knowing that he, of all the men in this town,
barring one, understands. Billy's mouth is slightly open
and he's panting, a slick of drool shining on his lower
lip, which he wipes with the back of his sleeve, smearing
more soot across his face. His eyes are bright white holes

above the dark of his filthy cheeks. Sol holds him with his own eyes, willing him to listen.

Billy, he says, silently, *we need to find him.*

It's not too late.

3.

Marked Face scrubs a thumb across the corner of his mouth, wiping away a yellow streak of undercooked egg. They're in the same diner they were at a day ago, a year from now, whenever, hungover and bleary, but that time they were eating their eggs while the old Indian watched. The situation is reversed now; Marked Face ignores them, stolidly working his way through his eggs and hash, pauses from time to time to loudly slurp from his mug of tea.

"Bad business, hey," is all he said when they sat down. "Dangerous, those mines of yours." He doesn't even flinch when Sol tries to jump across the table at him, hands racked into claws as if he's going to tear the old man's eyes out. It's all Billy can do to hold Sol back, to calm him down and quiet his shouting before they get kicked out of the place. Already the other customers seem less than pleased that a dirty old Indian from up the rez is sullying the establishment with his presence, but the stack of gold coins ostentatiously piled in front of his plate makes the owner and waitress more amenable to his patronage. Now, two sooty miners are trying to start a fracas. Everyone in the place has heard of the Penn fire by now, though; it's all that anyone is talking about and, just now, they're inclined to be a bit more forgiving to brother workers. But still, it's unseemly and the diner's owner is weighing propriety against that stack of gold.

"C'mon now, you two," he says, finally. "Take that shit outside."

Marked Face doesn't bother to look up, just quietly belches out of the side of his mouth, following up with another sip of tea. Billy makes placating gestures toward the proprietor with his free hand, the other clenched around Sol's biceps, holding him. He can feel the muscle shake and contract with the heave of Sol's chest, the air raked in in angry gasps. Sol's entire body is tight and jittery, his nostrils wide and white-ringed, pupils huge and black in his eyes.

"Send me back, you fucker," Sol finally whispers.

Marked Face pushes a last bite of egg onto his fork with the side of his finger. He raises it to his lips and then chews it slowly, methodically, before reaching into his mouth and removing a small fragment of shell, which he places back on the plate with a deliberate motion.

"I won the bet, chief."

Marked Face belches again, wiping his lips with the back of his sleeve. His eyes roam the room, aimlessly.

"I won the bet, fucker!"

At Sol's shout, the proprietor of the diner looks up again, frowning, but Marked Face shows no response, merely scratches idly at the back of his wrist, still looking around the café. Billy tightens his grip on Sol's arm and makes shushing noises.

"Uncle," he says.

At this, Marked Face's eyes swing around to rest on Billy's own. Billy feels the press of the old man's gaze like a physical thing; he feels the familiar pinch in his

guts, like he did when he was a boy and knew that the
fists would come out. Now, though, the fear is sharper,
because he knows that Marked Face is not merely just
a scary old man, a bastard with hard hands who never
shied from using them: he's something more. It doesn't
sit right with Billy's own government-scrubbed mind.
There's no such thing as magic, or medicine, or whatever
you wanted to call it, unless it's money or guns or disease.
That's the real medicine. And yet he knows what he's
seen, what he's been through. His belly is tangled up
inside him and he wants to shit himself at the expression
in his uncle's eyes.

"Why, little Sagiistoo," Marked Face says in the true
tongue, blank-faced. His eyes, stony and shining black.

Sol starts to speak but Billy cuts him off. "Sol's right,
Uncle. You said you'd give him what he desired. I
remember it, Uncle. *I remember*. I don't know just what
the hell you even are but–"

"What I am? *What I am*, Nephew?" Marked Face's
eyes go even harder, above a slow smile. "I am a man of
the People. *I am Marked Face*, who has killed a hundred
hundred men with his own hands. Marked Face, who
learned the secrets. I am a man who deserves respect,
Nephew." He pauses, the smile withering. "*Who are you?*"

Billy can't help himself: he hides his own eyes, stares
at the smear of yellow on his uncle's plate. Marked
Face has grown larger with his words, and Billy can
feel himself shrinking down. What kind of man is Bad
Bird, to stand up to him for so many years? The two of
them, always like stiff-legged dogs fighting over a rabbit
carcass. Who are these men that Billy thought were his
family? There's something almost palpable boiling out
of his uncle, crashing in waves against him. For the first
time in many, many years, Billy feels not the slightest

bit white, as if his uncle's presence has burned out what the government crammed down into him. Just now, he doesn't know what's left.

"I am no one, Uncle," he whispers, meaning it.

Marked Face laughs, seeing that the lesson is finally gnawing at little Sagiistoo's liver. "Yes, you are no one, Nephew. You see that now, hey?" He leans back in his chair, pulling his medicine back inside himself. No need for the whites to feel it, even if they don't understand the power that touches them. It just makes them uneasy, these hollow men who don't even exist as real things. But, for a moment, it feels good, letting himself become more like the way he was in times past, sitting straight and powerful again.

There is always a price that comes with using medicine though, and, for too long Marked Face has squatted up there on the reservation, biding his time, watching one day pass as another, empty and long. Waiting, left alone with his thoughts, his memories. Yet again he wishes that his brother would let himself out of that hospital. His brother, weak though he is, is the only one who truly understands him. It's only when they are together that life feels like it has much weight, great and terrible and full of sorrow that it is. At least it is something more than the numb, mocking days that step by now. He's lived too long, and yet he remains. But this is the way of things. There is no use dwelling on what merely is. The Above Ones have ordered this and who is he to quibble, he is only their tool. Their plaything, perhaps, like any other man. Marked Face knows that he must be strong, for himself, for his brother, for the boy. For all of them, he must be hard.

There is always a price with medicine.

"Old man," he says in the true tongue, knowing that his nephew will translate. He doesn't want the taste of the white words in his mouth, just then. "When last we diced, I told you that, if you won, I would give you the thing you desired in this world. This I have done."

"No, you fucking didn't!" Sol says, after Billy finishes. "All I wanted was my boy back. That's all I wanted."

Marked Face shakes his head. How to explain to the white that he, Marked Face, understands more of what the man wants than the man does himself? It is written there inside him, but this Solomon Parker cannot see it. The old white doesn't want this thing or that thing. What he wants is something far simpler: the chance to succeed. To change his world. *You are a failure, white man*, Marked Face wants to say, *or so you think yourself*. He's not sure which is more pathetic. These whites, empty as they are, are never satisfied, always hungry, and so fragile when they don't get what they want. *Solomon Parker, if you had seen and done and felt some of the things that I have*, he thinks, *you would crumble into dust. You are spoiled, like the rest of your race, like Sagiistoo has become*. Oh poor me, I have failed again. *If only you people understood that you cannot fight the whims of the Above Ones*.

Marked Face has played by the rules of the game, has delivered the thing he'd promised upon losing although, truly, it does not matter. The outcome will be the same. For whatever reason, Sagiistoo has been bound to this white man, their lives twisted together, their stories twined, so one must suffer for the other to grow. It is a strange thing. He sighs, shakes his head. He looks toward his stupid, empty nephew and can't help but feel a sadness. It is not quite time, not yet. Wait, Sagiistoo, it is coming. Wait.

"Very well, white man," he says, now. "We will play

again. Once more. If you win, I will grant you that favor, the thing it is that you desire."

Sol nods.

Billy doesn't say anything, this time, knowing that this is a terrible idea, one that will come to grief one way or another. He doesn't understand why his uncle is doing this, or how, but Sol doesn't seem to realize that there is always someone stronger than you are. Someone you can't fight. Someone who will always win. Sol just doesn't understand, and Billy knows that there is no way he will be turned aside, not now. All Billy wants is to get as far away from his uncle as possible, as far away from Sol. He gets up.

"Sagiistoo," Marked Face says, his eyes on the table in front of him. "There are some things you can't run from, Nephew. Not in this world or any other." He glances up and, for the first time Billy can remember, in all the years he's known him, his uncle looks sad. "Remember that. Some things will always find you."

Without a word, Billy walks out of the diner. He ignores Sol's shout after him, tries not to think about the look in his uncle's eyes when he stood, the one that reaches down inside him even now, wrapping around his guts. All he wants is to be away, to find a drink. He feels raw and brittle inside, empty, but that space is rapidly filling with fear.

On the sill of a high window, a glossy black bird sits, watching.

Sol watches Billy leave the diner, not bothering to call after him again. It doesn't matter; the only thing that matters is right here, right now. He stops a man passing their table and bums a smoke off of him. The man, seeing the soot and dirt on Sol's hands and face, gives him a sympathetic look and pats him on the shoulder.

"Just take the whole pack, pal," he says. "Things will be all right."

Goddamn right, things will be all right, Sol thinks, shaking out a cigarette and placing it on the table between him and Billy's uncle, who is watching him with no expression on his face. The old Indian shakes his head.

"What? Same bet as last time, yeah?" Sol rolls the cigarette closer to the old man with the tip of his finger. "Same bet. Let's get on with it, you piece of shit."

"No. A different bet, this time." Marked Face says. The bones are in his hand now and he rattles them over the table. "We raise the stakes. If I win, there is something you will do for me."

"What?"

"If I win, you will do *me* a favor."

Sol pushes down the unease he feels, and nods. Whatever it takes. This time it will be different.

A smile comes to Marked Face's lips, the black pits of his eyes shining.

"My throw, first."

Trouble and Bad Choices

— 1900 —

Stevensville, Montana

1.

Burn it all.

Elizabeth tugs another stiff-dried sheet down off the line and raises her arms, cracking the sheet down once, twice, trying to get the dust and pine pollen off of it. She holds it to her nose, breathing in against its scratchy, crinkled surface. It smells like vinegar and carbolic and the smoke from the fires in Idaho that are blowing east, which have been making the air hazy and hard to breathe for the better part of a month now. The laundry never smells clean any more: it either has the oniony, sour, organic reek of sweaty bodies and baby crap, before she washes it – a process that takes hours and hours of steamy, wet, scraped-knuckled and bent-backed labor – or there's this smoky, medicine smell when it's supposedly clean. This sheet in her hands *is* clean, but it stinks, stinks, and she's still going to have to heat up the iron and press it and all the rest of the linens, make the scratchy surfaces smoother, easier on the skin so it doesn't rub and chafe. Yet more hours spent hunched over, overheated and sweaty.

Just burn it.

The black bird, the fire-crazed one that seems to

follow her lately, squawks from where it's perched in a pine, watching her work. It squawks as if agreeing with her.

It's always so hot now. Elizabeth can't remember the last time she felt cool, rested, dry. Every day passes in sweating labor at one thing or another: laundry, cleaning the house, changing diapers, cooking. Every night she's up, again and again, to feed the baby, change his diapers – again – always just barely dropping back to sleep when the cries erupt once more. It's overwhelming. Sometimes, when Sol is off tending the tavern, she'll push a pillow into her mouth and scream, over and over, just scream, muffling it as best she can – but always the baby will pick up on her distress and join in so that she has to leave off and soothe him. No one ever soothes *her*, never. Sol does his best to help, in his bumbling, man's way, but it's a waste of time. A waste. Even when he pitches in, helps with the cleaning or cooking or any of the thousand little things that need to be done every day, it's more tiring than helpful. When he washes dishes, they're never quite clean and she needs to redo them; when he cooks, the potatoes get burnt and the meat dries out to the point that it's just better if she does it herself. Easier. He'll shrug and smile apologetically, but it still means that she has to do everything. She's raising two children, really: Owen and Sol. Sol's heart is in the right place but that doesn't make it any better. It should, but it doesn't.

Elizabeth rubs the back of her wrist across her forehead, smearing the sweat and dirt and the fine dust of ash that's always floating in the air lately. Her laundry basket is empty; looking down the line she sees sheet after sheet and a thousand miles of diapers, dresses, Sol's shirts and pants, all the million woven things that are part of their lives. Hours of folding, pressing, ahead of her again, the same chore that she does over and over and will keep having to do, day after day, in this merciless heat and smoky air. She can feel another scream building up inside her but clamps it back behind her teeth.

Burn it all, she thinks again, sniffing the air. Take all this damn laundry, all the sheets and diapers and shirts, pile it in a heap on the ground, and set it afire. Maybe take Owen and Sol and hike up into the Bitterroots, high up to some mountain spot, somewhere cool beside a lake, where it won't matter if there's smoke in the air because of the trees and the cold mountain water and the shade and all that they don't have here, down in the valley where the sun beats down mercilessly and the air settles thick and smoky with either no breeze at all or a sharp-edged wind that just kicks up more dust. If she looks west, she can see the mountains looming there, piney and sharp and cool, mocking her. She'll burn this laundry in a pile and then burn their little house along with it; they'll all turn their backs on this sweaty, dead-aired, smoky existence of chores and heat and wet rashes on the skin and go up into the mountains where it's cool and she can think straight, where she can relax for once. Where laundry doesn't make her want to scream and the wailing of little Owen doesn't send her into a desperate, hopeless crying jag. She and Owen and Sol will just burn it all and leave together, or maybe she'll just go by herself.

It's just the heat, she tells herself, again. Just the heat and the sweat and this air that's hard to breathe. At times like these, when the weight of her life seems to be pressing her down into the earth, cracking her apart, when everything about her feels broken and sick and crazy, she needs to remember, *remember*, that it's just the heat and the lack of sleep and the inconveniences that come with having a small child and a bumbling husband who doesn't make much money but who has a good heart and is trying to be a good provider, doing what he can to make their life better – she knows that – and these crazy, frantic thoughts she gets shouldn't be coming and they shouldn't mean anything when they do.

If only she had some help, though. There was that woman that Sol hired for a bit, but it hadn't worked out. She was an old harpy, that woman, always at Elizabeth for one thing or another, always judging her and tutting her thin lips. *Oh not like that, dear* or *surely you're not going to leave it that way*. All the time. Sol says he'll try to find someone else to pitch in, but she knows that word of how it had gone with the first one has gotten into town – *crazy Elizabeth Parker* – and they'll be lucky to find anyone else. She's stopped going to town, as much as possible; she knows the way they look at her. Sol brings home the groceries and the things they need from the store. *She's not feeling well*, he'll say, picking up the bag of sundries, *be right as rain in no time, though*. He's given up trying to convince her to come to town, even to go to service on Sunday. *Be right as rain in no time*.

It hasn't escaped her that he's spending more and more time at the tavern. Working, he says, trying to get us ahead, but he still comes home later and later, stinking of booze more often than not, a greasy look on his face and a rumpled, sweaty bag of groceries under his arm. It's fine, though, she prefers it that way; there's a time in the early evening, after Owen has been put down and the air is finally starting to cool off some, when she can sit on the couch and relax, feel almost normal for a while. She'll lay back, hands laced over her belly, listening to the silence of the house, the chitter of the finches and nuthatches outside. Just sit there, not thinking. More often than not, though, when Sol comes banging in the door, Owen will wake and begin screaming and the spell is broken, the peace and normalcy cracking around her like rotten ice.

From the house, she can hear Owen wailing now, thin desperate shrieks climbing out of the open window. He's a fussy, colicky baby, red-faced and angry more often than not. Even when he nurses, his face knuckles into an expression of indignant fury. It's irrational, she knows it, but she has the feeling that he hates her. Maybe because she's brought him into this hot, smoky, exhausting world from wherever comfortable place babies' souls live in Heaven. Sometimes he doesn't even look real, look human, as if that hatred that burns inside him molds his form into something unnatural. He'll be there in her arms, just a baby clawing at her breast, and then he'll become something dark and sharp, hard like a cicada, pinching and biting at her skin. More than once she's had to peel him off her, ignoring his furious screams, and leave the room, go outside, get away from him, heart pounding, sick in the belly.

She knows she's going crazy.

Elizabeth knows it, that she's not going to be right as rain, maybe not ever. She shouldn't have these thoughts, should just be able to be a normal wife and mother and woman and yet she can't, not always, no matter how she tries. After the incident with the woman Sol hired, he wanted her to go see his brother up at Warm Springs, maybe see about some help, but she refused. Now she wishes that maybe she'd gone. She hasn't told anyone about the things that she's seen that weren't there. Like dreaming while awake, remembering what never happened. She knows they weren't real, those things, she knows it, but there's a doubling that happens sometimes, when she can't tell where she is. When she is, maybe. What's real and what isn't. Just for a moment or two, but the spells, that's what they are, just spells, are coming more frequently. *I'll be fine when it cools off,* she thinks, *it's just this heat all the time and with the baby so small still and all of that. When it cools off I'll be able to think more clearly and Owen will sleep more and the colic will stop.*

She rubs her face into the scratchy sheet that's still in her hands, not caring that she's soiling it with the sweat and ash caked to her forehead. It doesn't matter: it's not clean anyway, nothing's ever clean any more. She's not clean, outside or in; there's something foul crouched inside her, leaking out the hotter and sicker she feels. She was so healthy once and now she isn't. Maybe that's why Owen hates her, because he can sense it in some baby way. Maybe she's poisoning him, he's sucking the foulness with her breast milk and it's infecting him too.

Owen continues to wail from the house. Elizabeth throws the sweaty sheet into her basket, tries to catch her breath. Her heart is thumping in her chest and for a moment she feels like she might faint; for a wild second she wants to just run, hike her skirts up around her hips and just run, run, *run*, not stopping until her heart bursts or she's so far away she can't find her way back. Instead, she packs it all down inside, once again, biting the scream back behind her teeth. She'll be right as rain in no time. Right as rain.

The bird squawks again and, when she turns, Sol is standing there, watching her.

2.

"What are you doing home?" Elizabeth asks him. Her face is flushed red and she's sweating, there's a smear of dirt on one of her cheeks and what looks to be an incipient pimple growing to the side of a nostril; wild tendrils of damp hair have escaped from the bun at the back of her neck and are sticking out to all sides. She looks beautiful.

What is he doing home? That's a longer story, for a certainty. One that Sol can't begin to explain, not yet anyway, if ever. He doesn't even have to look around to know where he is, when he is; Elizabeth still has that bit of pregnancy fat around her hips and chest and face, which rounds her natural boniness out in a way that makes his heart catch at the sight of her. He tries to freeze this moment in his mind, hold it tight so that he'll always remember it, no matter what happens next.

"Wanted to see you, is all," he says, finally.

Sol remembers everything that has brought him here, dropped down into this younger body that feels wrong, a body he can't quite recall ever having, even though he had, these years ago. He hears the rattle of dice that became a booming sound again, the singing, sees the hands holding his own and then the long fall into the black pits of eyes. He remembers it all, except whether he'd won or lost that last bet with old Marked Face.

Inside, later, Sol holds Owen, tries to still the boy's wailing. He was never particularly good at this; his hands always feel too big and rough and clumsy and he's terrified that he'll squeeze too hard or drop the boy. He sways a bit, humming something tuneless in his mouth, which only makes Owen cry harder, perhaps at the affront of it all. Elizabeth is banging around in the kitchen, putting some lunch together. She doesn't seem very happy to see him; his being here has maybe put her off whatever her normal routine is, the days that he was – *is* – down tending the little tavern in Stevi. Tending to his own belly, too, he remembers, pouring at least as many beers and shots down his neck as he did for the customers. No wonder he was never able to make a go of the place, even before what had happened happened.

"Did you get more cornmeal like I asked?"

"Ah, girl, I didn't." He tries jiggling the baby a bit, but Owen just bobbles his head along and continues to scream.

"Damn it, Sol, how am I supposed to cook tonight?"

"I'm sorry, Lizzie. I'll go out a little later, OK?" Sol shifts Owen to the other arm, trying on something of a side-to-side shimmy.

"Later, great." A pot bangs down over-hard onto the wood stove. "Fine. I didn't want to get the oven heated up anyway so we'll just have no bread. None. That all right with you?"

Sol remembers these fights. Lizzie was ever a stubborn and difficult woman, as much as he loved – *loves* – her but, after Owen came along, it was like they couldn't

be in a room together for five minutes without getting
at each other's throats like stalking cats. Another reason
he spent so much time down at the tavern. Lizzie was
always angry, always seemed to be sweaty and flushed,
bagged blue bruises under her eyes from the lack of
sleep. He tried to do what he could to help out but that
just made her madder; best thing he could do, then,
was to keep away and out of her hair. Best thing for the
both of them. He thought it would get better once Owen
got a little older, when he'd sleep longer through the
night; the wailing kept Sol up, too, after all. But people
had babies all the time, right, they got past it, like you
just did. Wasn't like it was a mystery that babies came
with a heap of inconveniences, after all, and it wasn't
as if Owen was an accident: they'd tried hard for years
and years, with some sorry disappointments along the
way, before this child had come to them. Sol wants to
think that they'll get past it all too, now. He lifts Owen
up to his shoulder, cupping the back of the baby's soft
head with one hand, patting at his little back with the
other, which serves no purpose aside from adding some
staccato to his wailing.

"Sol, he's just hungry." Lizzie strides in and peels Owen
from his shoulder with a brusque motion, dropping into
the rocker and pulling out her breast with businesslike
efficiency. The baby immediately quiets, going to work
on his meal, tiny hands rhythmically clenching and
releasing. The sight of Lizzie's breast, swollen and blue-
veined and stretched, the brown around the nipple
darkened, pebbled, wrinkled tight, sends a jolt through
Sol's belly. He can feel his prick stiffening.

"What?" Lizzie's glaring at him.

"Nothing, just looking is all. Forgot for a minute how
pretty you were."

She blows out a puff of air. "Maybe go look somewhere else, Sol. Like at the grocery store for what we need for dinner, OK?" She turns her body away from him, a gesture that hurts far more than it should.

"Sure, honey. Anything else you need?" She shakes her head, not looking his way. "All right," he says, ignored, picks up his shapeless hat from the table by the door. "I'll be going, then. Have to stop at the bar, check in on things, but I won't be too long, OK?"

"Take your time."

At the tavern, which he'd called Potter's after someone he once admired, Sol stares at his reflection in the yellowed mirror behind the bar, wondering at the man looking back at him. He's young – well, younger – but not the way he remembers himself being so. His hair is still brown, as is the stubble on his cheeks, mostly, a bit flecked with grey around the sides of his chin is all. Skin smooth, more or less unwrinkled, tending toward the leathery at the corners of his eyes from a boyhood spent outside, squinting into the sun behind the ass end of a plow horse. Those eyes, though, they're not like what he remembers, not at all. The eyes look his age, his true age, whatever that actually is by now. They look tired, wary. Busted-down some from everything they've seen. They're an old man's eyes in a younger man's face. Sol knows that he himself, now, is really something like an old man wearing a younger man's body, though, so fair enough.

He raises his glass to the kid he'd hired to help out, Chase or Jace or something along those lines. It's been years since he's even thought about him, after all. Pretty much the only thing he remembers now about this boy is that once he'd walked into the back room and caught him with his hands down his trousers, no doubt thinking about some girl or other as he committed an abbreviated version of the solitary sin. The boy's jaw had dropped but Sol had just said something like *hey maybe lock the door first*, having been a young man himself once. Full of vinegar and that terrifying feeling of being full up with everything that pretty girls brought with them, once you really started to notice them, everything they could put in your head with a simple glance of their eyes, a toss of the hair, sway of a soft and round buttock under a skirt. Even the homely ones could do it because, really, it didn't much matter at that age.

Had he already caught Chase or Jace, or whoever he was, grabbing a quick jerk in the back room during a slow time? Or was that still yet to happen? Sol wonders if that's what his life is going to be now, a stuttering repetition of all the things he's already done, over the next years until he catches himself back up. People he's met, things he's said, all of it. Lizzie once told him a story, another one of her Greek ones, about some old boy who thought to fool the gods when he'd wished for the gift of seeing his future. He'd been granted it, and the poor bastard went crazy, turned out; Sol hadn't quite understood it, at the time, until Lizzie had explained that the man in the story had lost the gift of hope, knowing everything that would pass, merely stepping along in the long line of footsteps in front of him, powerless to change his future.

Maybe that was to be his own fate now, yet another bad debt come home to squat on his chest. But that's bullshit, though, isn't it. There are always choices to make: you might not make the right one or get what you want, but you can at least try. Sometimes that's all you have.

He watches Chase or Jace fill his glass with another jot of whiskey, the golden-dark fluid shining in the dim light coming through the bar's dusty windows, which need a wiping. The fuck is he paying this kid for, anyway, except to jerk off in the back room when Sol isn't around, maybe pour him the odd drink in the middle of an afternoon. But he's the only one here now, aside from the kid; Potter's has never been what you'd call a thriving concern, and it's still early in the day, after all, when most people are doing whatever it is they do for work, not sitting in a dim bar, alone, drinking and bitching in their heads about the state of the windows. The bag of groceries lies neglected on the stool next to him, cornmeal and whatever else caught his eye: little peace offerings, in a small, cheap way, all he can afford, some huckleberries that have come into season, a little jar of apple butter put up last year for those too lazy to make their own.

Sol swallows half his whiskey in a hot, eye-watering gulp and thinks back – *forward* – to what's brought him here, to this failing little bar of his and a wife who's going crazy in installments and to his son, a boy he'd let die again a few years from now. And now this bag of cornmeal and impulse-bought sweets and cheap, bullshit whiskey that half makes you want to puke it up as soon as it goes down.

He knows about, remembers it all, now, the fight – the first fight, when Nancy knocked that goddamn idiot Faraday bang the fuck out (accidentally to be sure, it wasn't Nancy's fault) – and then the riot, later, at the Neversweat, Sean Harrity taking the shot at him, well deserved because of what Sol had done, probably, treachery and false dealing, after all, which had kicked the whole thing off. Good men dead in the gunfire and smoke and swinging truncheons, all because of Sol's bad bets and a fuck-up at the end of it. But Sol can also remember, now, though he didn't at the time, that first bet with Billy's uncle, throwing those scarred Indian bones; there was Nancy's fight – again, somehow – and then the riot that had never happened, that time around.

The second bet with the old Indian, going back to the Penn and still losing his boy, losing Owen, letting the fucking mine burn down around them all, just as it had before.

Now here he is, wondering what's going to come, if he has the chance to save Lizzie this time, before her mind finishes its cracking, before it tears loose of its casing and she burns their house down around her and Owen again. Burned it, just like the Penn, years from now. He'd gotten home to Lizzie before, on a fluke, just in time to pull her and the baby out of the flames, beat out her burning dress and blow fresh air into Owen's tiny lungs until he could breathe again. Lizzie watching him from the ground, cupping her forearms to her chest and laughing and crying and screaming nonsense at him. He'd saved Owen and then shipped Lizzie off to Ag up at Warm Springs, hoping they could put her back together there. That hadn't worked out, of course, and soon enough he'd sent Owen off to live with Ag and Sara and the rest of their brood, temporarily at first and then permanently. Telling himself it was for the best. Leaving them to raise his son while he, Sol, wandered around for a few months, trying on work as he could get it, drinking his share to be sure, getting in some fights and some other trouble, stumbling around in the daze of a man who's had his foundation shaken away from him. Eventually he'd made his way to Butte and found something akin to solidity again in the mine work, losing himself in the dark and wet and dusty tunnels, finding himself once more in the use of his muscles and the satisfaction of hard work done well, the companionship of tired men at the end of a long shift, washing the dust out of their throats with a beer and whiskey follow.

Those years after Lizzie hadn't been perfect, to be sure; there had been plenty of pain and heartache and trouble and bad choices, but that's what a life was and his had fit him snug, like a well-worn pair of pants. Even at the end, debt-deep into Harrity, fearing for his safety as those bad decisions came home to nest, Sol had felt solid and secure, in a way, with the messes that he'd made, the natural outgrowth of all that had come before.

Now, back here, he doesn't know what the hell to make of any of it.

Best not to fucking think about it. He doesn't want to know who or what Billy's old uncle, Marked Face, is all about. Indian magic or witchcraft or some kind of demon out the Bible or what, Sol doesn't want to know. Just doesn't. He's learning that, when faced with something so far out of the pale of anything else in a life, something so defiant of understanding, it's best to just shunt it aside, as much as you can, don't even look at it sidelong, if you can help it. He isn't much of a religious man but, now, understands a bit more about old Thomas the doubter from the Good Book. Some things are just too big to take in, some thoughts are stronger than the person thinking them, and, in that case, best to just to ignore them and get on with things, much as you can.

Here it is, Sol thinks now. Another chance, maybe. Even if he's just here to step through those same, sorry footsteps as before, there's fuck-all he can do about it, so better to just button up and get to it. He'll be damned, though, if he isn't at least going to make a stab at getting things right, this time; even if it means that whatever else happens turns to shit, he isn't going to just sit on his ass and watch it all happen again.

In the back of his mind, though, is another thought he's trying to ignore: he hadn't saved Owen, last time he'd had a chance, down the Penn.

The fire had burned him up, same as before.

3.

Billy is brought back with a slap, as only seems right. Instinctively, from long practice, he curls down into himself like a pill-bug even though, at some level, he's thinking *I'm not a fucking kid any more*, and then the next slap tells him that he is, the hard, open hand that cracks his head sideways. He can smell sweat and booze and something faintly smoky and any nascent defiance crumples then because he knows where he is, even with his sight slippery in his head and his body stumbling towards the corner of the shack where at least he'll maybe have something covering him on a couple of sides. A slap and a slap again, wordless and sharp, sending him backwards; when he gets himself turned away from the hands there's a swift foot to his asshole, lifting him up tippy-toe as he scampers towards somewhere at least half safe.

"Where have you been, boy?"

Marked Face's voice is low, rough, graveled angry with drink and whatever it is that makes the man himself. Billy feels his belly drawing up tight inside, even as he tries to make his body the smallest possible target. He hides his face in the crook of his forearms, does his best to shrink up his torso so his kidneys aren't laying out there for a punch or another kicking. The last time, he'd pissed blood for a week, his uncle never even breaking a sweat. It's not just inside himself, now, that Billy feels small and weak; he can tell where he is from the smell in the air and the skinny press of his wristbones on his forehead, curled fetal as he is.

He's back again, up the reservation at his father's cabin, the scrawny white boy home from the government school. His short hair itches the back of his neck and there's that familiar tightness at his crotch from the too-short school pants, the collar strangling his throat, clothes rough-woven and overly starched, stinking of lye. He remembers everything: the last thing he'd seen as he walked out the diner's door a moment ago, years from now, was Marked Face staring across the table at that blind, stupid old man, Sol Parker. Billy doesn't understand it, any of it, but here he is again, once more getting the shit kicked out of him by a bastard of a relative who's half a foot taller, fifty pounds heavier, and a thousand times meaner. Home sweet home.

"I said where you been, boy?"

Billy turns his head, peers over his shoulder at his uncle, who isn't his uncle at all, although that isn't really any good thing. Bad Bird snaps his open hand down again, rings a glancing blow off Billy's temple, forcing him to tuck tighter down into himself.

Where have I been?

Later, sitting across the little table from his father, eating white bread with cheap sausage gravy, it doesn't seem like Bad Bird is even drunk. It's tough to tell with his father: there's often a stink of whiskey about him but Billy rarely sees him actually drink. It's as if, somehow, the smell of liquor is just steeped into his body and leaks out his pores from time to time. Bad Bird is a violent, mercurial man, often giving the appearance of being entirely out of control with liquor but, over the years, Billy has come to wonder if his father's behavior is simply the natural outgrowth of whatever instability landed him at Warm Springs. Will land him at Warm Springs. Drunk or not, though, the old man had never missed an opportunity to slap the shit out of him, if not do something worse. Billy rubs the scar at his shoulder, remembering, and then realizes that the scar isn't there. Not yet, maybe.

"They treat you OK, up at that school?" Bad Bird speaks the old tongue slowly and deliberately, his low, plodding, breathy voice at odds with his quickfire temper, the one that can and will flare up in an instant, like kerosene on an open flame. It's not even so much that his father is meaner or harder than other men: he's unpredictable, is what he is. Bad Bird will go from maudlin sappiness to fisted anger to lazy indifference in a space of time where other men will yawn or let go a good fart; it's this kind of behavior, combined with that vaguely boozy stink, that makes most people think Bad Bird is just another Drunken Injun, instead of merely crazy.

Billy shrugs, mutters something about how it's OK, the school, knowing that Bad Bird will expect the courtesy of a verbal response. A shrug alone is disrespectful. Like all these old men, his father and Marked Face and the rest of those goddamn sad chiefs are fixated on respect, a commodity in short supply these days. Any more, they don't get it from their women and they've never gotten it from the whites so they goddamn well better get their due from their pissant children. *You show me some respect, boy, or I'll slap it into you.* In the old tongue it sounds a bit more poetical but the message is the same, particularly delivered a beat in front of an open hand.

"Why are you back, Sagiistoo?" His father reaches out then, taking hold of Billy's skinny forearm and squeezing it tightly, looking deep into his eyes with an expression of love. There's no other word for it. Billy knows his father loves him, just the same way he knows the old man is crazy. Despite himself, despite the slapping and the anger and the piss-pants fear, Billy can't help but feel an answering twist in his chest. Bad Bird is mean and depressed and crazy and full of hatred but he's still his father, one of the few ties Billy has to something, anything really. He's never had a mother, not a living one, hasn't had a home since being shipped off to the white school, and there they're taking away what's left of his race, bleaching the brown from his skin from the inside out. Bad Bird is one of the few things in this world that ties Billy to it, one shabby link to something that's bigger than himself. It's – was, will be – the same way with Sol; these men are family, blood or not, good and bad and everything in the middle but family of one sort or another.

"We're on a summer break, Father. Go home, hey, see the people, show them how we are, right?" Billy remembers this, just as he knows that this is the last time he'll be home, that he'll never go back to the school. Soon after this time he met – will meet – Sol, and life will go the way it did. But does it have to?

He looks down at his skinny wrists, dirty and scratched with faint scabs from one thing or another. They feel wrong, these arms, so much smaller and weaker than he's used to, than what he knows in his head to be his body. He feels uncomfortable in this one, a grown man dropped in a teenager's, a thing too light and fragile for the weight of his years. *A strange thing* doesn't begin to describe it, but if anything has changed in him over the course of this last while – those years from now – it's maybe that he's becoming a bit more Indian again, the brown beginning to seep back in, and he's able to see a little through the shallow pale of whatever it is that lives over the real world, the world that the People knew in the old times. The world of the stories which, before, he'd thought to be just that: stories. Bullshit songs to explain the inexplicable, make apologies for the shameful and talk up the noble. Now, though, seeing what he's seen, what he *is* seeing, maybe there's more to the stories than that. Maybe he's unlearning some of what the whites have taught him to know and is truly seeing the world for the first time, the real one, in the way that Bad Bird and his uncle and the rest of the old fuckers have seen it from the beginning. Seeing it the way that it is, baffling and mysterious and full of contradiction, but real.

Or maybe, just maybe, he's following the family path and going as crazy as his father. Anyone's guess, really.

"You seen Uncle around?" It slips out before he can catch it, reel it back in.

Bad Bird leans back, looking at him thoughtfully. He murmurs something under his breath, scratching at his neck. Eventually, still staring, he shakes his head with a grimace, then turns to the side and spits, taking care to rub the gob into the dirt floor before looking back at Billy, nodding.

"Thought maybe you looked different, boy."

Billy stares at his father.

"Let me tell you a small story," Bad Bird says. "And then I will tell you another, about your uncle, my brother Marked Face."

• • •

One day, Bad Bird said, *in the before times, after the sadness that came to him, Maatakssi sat on a flat stone, talking with Raven about the nature of the world. He was full of grief, and had many questions about why the things that had befallen him had come to pass.*

"Look there, two-leg walker," *Raven said, pointing with his foot at a line of ants that were winding around and around a dry branch.* "Where are those ants going?"

"They're going nowhere, Raven," *Maatakssi said.* "They are merely making circles."

"Yes, they are making circles. But watch." *Raven hopped down next to the branch and, with his sharp beak, made a deep crack in the wood. Tap-tap-tap, went his beak, and the crack opened. When the ants reached the fissure, some of them continued making their circles but some turned a different way, going around the crack and circling the branch in another place.* "Do you see?" Raven said.

"I see ants, Raven, nothing more than that. Stupid insects that only walk in a circle again."

Raven gave the branch more hard taps with his beak until it split in two, one piece falling to the ground.

"Maatakssi," *he said.* "This branch,. Is it new, or is it still part of the one it broke from? And these ants on it, where do they walk? The same branch or another? They are walking circles again, yes, but the circles are different now to the ones they made before, are they not?"

Maatakssi saw that Raven was right, that the ants were making a different path.

"Maatakssi, Maatakssi," *Raven said, giving a bird's version of a smile.* "Listen: do you think those ants know where they walk?"

Billy looks at his father, who says, "Now I will tell you about Marked Face."

4.

Sol feels the presence of Elizabeth next to him in their bed. From her breathing, steady as it is, he can tell she isn't sleeping, no more than he is. The old featherbed is oversoft and saggy and the weight of her body pulls his own towards her; he has to tense the muscles of his stomach to keep himself from being drawn down into the bed's gully with her, against her. As much as he wants to. He can smell her scent, milky and damp and faintly sweat-smoky, calling to him, after all these years that haven't yet passed. His prick is hard again, but mostly just as an afterthought, a purely bodily expression divorced from the way he feels. Sure, he'd like to get atop her, unlimber himself and slide inside her like they once used to do, so often, once, hot and frantic, bashing lips and teeth into one another but, more than anything, what he wants is to be just close to her, once more, now that he has the chance again. Earlier in the night he'd tried, sidling up against her turned back, pressing his chest against her and hooking an arm over her hip, hand on her belly, his other arm folded uncomfortably back behind his shoulder. The feel of her stiffening, though, drawing away with a slight but noticeable motion, sent him back to his own side of the bed, where he lays on his back now, staring up at the ceiling, willing his own breath to come still and regular.

It's hot in the bedroom; he'd forgotten just how dense and stagnant the air had hung that last summer they were together. Stifling, even when the windows were open. From the crib next to the bed he can hear Owen whimper and snuffle, smell the dank fragrant heat of him, small as he is. Strange to see and hold this little lump of flesh and bone and know that, years from now, the boy will be stretched long and lanky, a spot-faced youth, taller than Sol himself, already, trying on a man's life for the first time, to see the fit of it. A life that will be cut short in the burning dark unless Sol can steer things better this time.

This feeling of love for the baby seems familiar again; he remembers before, that first time around, the sense of pride and completion when he'd hold the boy, something that, at the time, seemed faintly unmanly, so powerful was the feeling, but was his nonetheless. A fierce, protective urge that is nothing but stronger now, knowing what will pass in the years to come. He knows that *legacy* is a pregnant, stupid, selfish word for what he feels: what this baby is is nothing more or less than the possibility of something good, that Sol helped to make and will try his damnedest to shape into the best kind of man that the boy can be. Owen isn't so much Sol's legacy as the chance for him to add a mark into the positive side of his own ledger, something, someone, to be weighed against all of his own failures and fuck-ups.

Strange to think these kinds of things now, again, when he'd felt this way the first time around and still had shipped Owen off to his brother as soon as things had gone south, with barely a second thought. Washed his hands of the boy, of his noble thoughts and his responsibilities, just as quick as he could, once life got a bit hard.

This is what he ponders as he finally drops off to sleep, wakening sometime later to the feel of Lizzie atop him, a knife at his neck.

"Why are you here?" she says, the warm, sweaty weight of her pressing down into him. "Why?" she says again, before he can speak, the point of his tarnished old pocketknife dimpling the skin under his Adam's apple. Though it's shameful to admit, Sol has a hard-on pressing painfully against his thigh, trapped under her leg, whether from racy dreams or Lizzie's insistent pressure or just because he has to piss. He's always been a heavy sleeper, so who knows how long she's been on him, squatting over his prick like that. He hopes she's asleep, having a nightmare maybe, but he also remembers how it went with the woman he'd brought in to help after Owen had been born.

He tries to answer his wife, with what he doesn't know. Anything, something, but her hand reaches out, damp and clammy, pressing down over his lips, pushing them closed. The knife pokes more sharply at his neck.

"Why, Sol? *Why?* Is it real, this time? *Is it real?*"

He wants to explain that they've been given another chance, but then she starts to cry, shuddering, tears dropping hot onto his face, shameless uncontrolled sobbing that crumples her down into herself until her forehead is resting on his chest. Gently, slowly, he frees an arm, sliding it around her back and pulling her close, wedging his other hand between them to free the knife from her now nerveless fingers, the blade forgotten in her sorrow. She's saying something, caught beneath the sobs, over and over into his chest. He can't hear it so much as feel it, murmuring through his ribs. It takes a long time for him to peel the meaning out from the sound.

There's something wrong with me, she's whispering, again and again. *There's something wrong with me.*

It feels natural, later, when her tears dissolve into exhaustion and the press of her head against his chest slides into the feel of her lips at his neck, and then they're kissing, gently at first and then insistently, not thinking, just drawing into each other. With a practiced motion she slides him into her, straddling across his legs. One of his hands is at her hip, guiding her movement, the other clenched in her thick hair, fist against the base of her skull. After all these years, Sol thinks, it's like it always was, clenching his teeth at the end and pulling her hard against him.

When he wakes up in the morning, he's sweating in the sheets, his bladder near to bursting, and she's gone, as if she'd never been there at all.

Lizzie ignores him after he gets up, busying herself with cooking his breakfast and sitting down with Owen for the baby's own. Sol watches her as he eats his eggs, which are overcooked and rubbery as usual. She's sitting there in the rocker with the baby at her breast like the Madonna. Finishing his meal, he scrapes the plate into the trash and, when the boy is done eating, Sol tries to take him from her but Lizzie turns away, slinging Owen onto a hip and carrying him into the bedroom and his crib.

"He needs a nap," she says, brusquely; whatever tenderness there was from the night before has evaporated in the sunlight that's already uncomfortably warming up the house, though it's early yet. Sol thinks it strange that the baby would need to sleep again so soon after waking but he's no mother, after all, and has learned by now not to contradict Lizzie on matters of maternal process.

He cleans himself up, splashing tepid water over his face and through his hair, brushing his teeth and marveling again at this new face, so different from the one that's glared back at him out of mirrors for the last umpteen years, angry and broke-down and accusatory. Lizzie is outside at the pump when he comes back out buttoning up his shirt, pulling his belt tighter around a surprisingly lean belly. Her generous ass is rounding the thin, over-washed calico of her dress and yet again Sol feels the tug of blood in his new, younger man's cock, even given that he'd wet it just a few hours before. This insistent sex drive takes him aback some, although he of course remembers those days, years ago, this hum of randiness that's coursing through him at the mere sight of a shapely rear end. But Lizzie shrugs him off as he tries to ease up behind her, pressing up against her suggestively, so he's forced to content himself with just working the well's pump handle a time or two, up and down, splashing water out, which seems onanistically ironic, really. When he tries to carry the wash tub for her, though, Lizzie snaps at him, peevishly, pulling it from him so that a goodly portion of the water spills, and then she stomps back towards the house. Sol watches, forlornly, that ass of hers swaying with every step.

"Guess I'll be headed to the tavern, then, honey," he calls out.

She ignores him.

It's maybe not his fault, then – well, not entirely – that he's drunk before noon, not just tipsy but flat-out drunk.

There are no customers this time of day and perhaps his inventory check got a little too exacting and personal, wanting, as he did, to ascertain the exact depths of various whiskey barrels. But he's finding that *ill-equipped* doesn't begin to describe how he's set up to deal with the situation he's found himself in and this is perhaps the easiest and most straightforward way to handle it all, drinking it out to a distance where it will get a bit smaller, letting him sidle up to it, inch by inch, until he's ready to take it in at that more manageable size.

It's maybe not his fault, either, that the way he gets through that day doubles and triples and doubles again, as the calendar flips. Each day passes in an increasingly drunken haze, each night sweaty and tense and largely sleepless, but without the release of that first night he'd come back, with Lizzie's thighs wrapped around him, her tears smeared on his cheekbones as they'd made love. As they'd just fucked, really, he thinks more often; it doesn't seem like there's much love left in her to make, as he sees it. Had it been this way before? From the distance of years he'd remembered things, bad as they'd gotten, with a rosy glow, at least up to a point. The two of them together, one flesh, deep in love, until Lizzie had gotten sick and everything went bad. But, before then, it had been perfect, hadn't it? Sol's realizing now, with the experience of time – since lost – that maybe what he'd really pined for had simply been that feeling of first love, the one that burns hot and sharp and breathy, painful and ill-made though it usually was.

The more he ponders it, staring into it from the depths of glass after glass of the mediocre whiskey that he serves in his tavern to the occasional patron – but usually just himself – Sol begins to remember things as they truly were back then: the way they are now. Lizzie, angry and tired and disgusted with a life that she chafed against, with Sol and Owen and the lot of it, as if she'd been somehow caught instead of walking into it with open eyes. He himself, hardly home, at the tavern most hours of the day, and drunk for most of those hours. Two people like poles of a magnet, circling around the baby and the life they'd somehow fallen into together, forever pushing each other apart.

Weeks of this sodden, maudlin existence, the understanding dawning ever brighter, day by day, that this golden time in his life which, to Sol as an old man, had been the years he'd yearned for the most, with that warm ache of nostalgia were, close up, just another set of years. Maybe their juxtaposition against the way it had all fallen apart so quickly, and that Sol had spent so long afterward merely drifting, angry and grieving for what he'd lost, had helped to build them up as something more lovely than they were, before the end.

Or maybe it was all just the drink-sodden, sappy memories of a sad old fucker, by then, with a soft prick and only the occasional working girl to attend to it, that served to shine these years so brightly. Years that now, seen for what they were, were as dirty and cheap as the rest of his life. You always remember your first, they say; Sol remembered his, a neighbor girl back behind a stack of bales, the proverbial roll in the hay. Lizzie was the first woman he'd ever loved, though, a perfect specimen of the human female, he'd thought, at the time. Really, she was a fading, crazy bitch and he'd been nothing but a drunk. An incompetent provider, lousy husband, lousy father. An overall failure. Shakespearean tragedy it wasn't, but a tragedy nonetheless, now that he's near enough to see it again. He knows he's being maudlin, that the whiskey isn't helping but, once started, it's hard to stop some of these sorts of thoughts.

Sol has the uncomfortable realization that maybe all the things in his life that he once thought were good are merely shitty memories that will fall apart when next he sees them. Sitting in Potter's, by himself, watching the dust motes dance in the hazy light leaking in through the dirty windows, he takes another drink, refilling his glass with an automatic motion, his vision bleary but his pouring hand ever steady. It's good to have a skill in life, to not be a complete incompetent at everything, he thinks. The whiskey pours into the smudged, greasy glass, just to the top, not a drop spilled. At least, at something, he's a true artisan.

More and more, he's beginning to understand that things are broken, that this isn't going to work. *Lizzie* is broken, so maybe that's why he's here: to cut with this life, take Owen and leave. Go somewhere the boy will be safe. Get Ag to take Lizzie to his hospital. Maybe last time, after the fire, it was just too late, the press of her guilt weighing the crazy down too deep into her. Sol doesn't want to just up and quit on her like that, even feeling as he does, but maybe that's how it needs to go.

The whiskey burns hot down his neck, splashing into the pool building in his belly, firing his insides until there's nothing to do but pour down another shot to drown it. Who cares that it's barely three in the afternoon and he's sitting by himself? He doesn't have anywhere he needs to be.

He's maybe not even entirely surprised when the bell over the door dings and the boy sits down beside him.

5.

Billy leans over the bar and takes a glass, slides it to Sol who, obviously drunk as he is, neatly and gracefully fills it with whiskey, right to the top.

"Cheers, Sol." He knocks it back, gagging around the sweet heat of it.

"Thought I'd see you sooner, Bill."

The both of them calm, blasé, as if meeting again in this new past, younger, different, is something that just happens every day. Even given what they've been through before, they're acting overly serene. Relaxed, bored even. Trying not to face the entirety of the strangeness of it all.

He shrugs. "Had some things to take care of, up at the reservation. Still got to get back up there for a few days, finish a couple things up for my father. Figured I'd come see you first, though. Check in."

"How's your dad?"

Another shrug. "How's Elizabeth?" Sol doesn't answer. A pause, a swallow. "Owen?" The strangeness a bit closer now. He polishes off his whiskey, refills it.

"Hey, is that kid supposed to be drinking in here, Sol?" A tubby, spot-faced young man with greasy hair

is coming out of the back room, looking a little sweaty,
maybe from the crate he's lugging.

"It's fine, boy. Why don't you go ahead and take the
rest of the day off, hey? I got things covered here."

"You sure, Sol?"

"Yeah, get out of here."

The boy gives Billy another doubtful look and then
goes in the back, coming back a moment later with his
apron off. He leaves it wadded, dirty and stained, on the
bar as he walks by, nodding to them both. Ding of the
doorbell and then Sol and Billy are alone again.

"Hard to find good help, Billy."

Just like that, they're back to it. Not five minutes
together and there's the opening, same as the last time,
all those years ago that hadn't yet passed.

Hard to find good help, son. Billy, hungry and broke, that
time before, down in Stevensville for no other reason
than trying to get somewhere away from the fists and
that his feet had somehow brought him here, a town like
any number of other little towns. Hungry and broke and
here, already, and maybe a job, brown as he was, even.
Man he doesn't even know offering him work, just like
that. Just looked at him, eyebrow raised, standing there
dirty and skinny in the road.

*I'm a good worker, sir. I can help out, if you need someone. I
can do pretty much whatever.*

Sol had just pointed to the stack of crates he'd been
carrying in and then it was years and years together,
after that. Good years and bad and all the rest, all that
had happened, and now they're right back to it, circled
around once more.

"I'm a good worker, Sol," he says, now. He's looking
the other way to hide the wet in his eyes. Billy isn't
even sure why he feels this swell of emotion. Maybe

there's just been so much out of kilter lately that seeing the familiar again, feeling it, makes it that much bigger. Maybe it's the idea that these years without Sol in them would have felt hollow; maybe there was a fear there that things would be different, this time, worse. It's why he'd stayed away from Stevensville for so long, almost didn't come at all. A worry that something would have gone bad, that Marked Face had poisoned it. But now here they were again.

"Might could find a spot for you then, son," Sol says, reaching over to squeeze Billy's skinny shoulder. "Might could find a spot for you."

Evening now, and they still haven't talked about things, about what's passed before. It's there in the room like that elephant you hear about. Billy has a hint of the feeling of *maybe I'm just crazy*, a fear that, if he brings it up, Sol will shake his head, furrow a worried brow. *Say what now?* Or maybe Sol feels that way too. But Billy knows, *knows*, deep down, that he's not crazy, that what's happened has happened but, still, there's a shyness about bringing it out in the open. He wants Sol to go first, to break the seal on all that memory but, so far, even several whiskeys to the good, neither of them has taken the step.

Instead, Sol has spent most of his time talking about Elizabeth and Owen and the tangled mess their lives have become. That maybe there's nothing he can do about it, either. Nothing he can do to make it better, now that he sees it for what it is.

"I think I got to just go, Bill," he says, finally. "I just got to go. You can keep hold of the bar for me for a while, can't you?" Seeming to forget, with the whiskey, that this Billy is fourteen. "Just for a while, is all. It don't seem right, but I think Owen and I need to go, at least for a spell. Lizzie isn't getting better, Billy, she's not. She's worse, maybe. I try to do what I can but Lizzie has problems and she needs to get them sorted out. Maybe having us around isn't helping. I'm worried." About as close as he's gotten to bringing up what came before, about what she did.

Billy hadn't known Elizabeth, that other time, aside from seeing her at the hospital sometimes, later, when he'd go to visit his father. He'd arrived in Stevensville after the fire, the last time, and he has only Sol's memories of her to build her image in his head.

"You sure about that, Sol?" he says now.

"Hell no, I'm not, Billy. How can you be sure about something like that? But I got this feeling. Feeling like nothing I do is going to go right with her. So maybe best I just leave. Take Owen and go."

"What are you going to do with him, Sol? Baby needs a mother."

"I know that, Bill, don't act like I don't. I know it. But maybe best if I just take him to Ag and Sara for a spell, until things get sorted out with Lizzie. They'll take him in."

Billy doesn't want to say it, doesn't like to even think it. Not about Sol, who he knows is a good man. But it sounds just like what happened before: Sol just upping stakes and leaving when things got hard, for which Billy knows Sol has beaten himself up over the years. Guilt at letting things happen as they did, compounded with the guilt at abandoning Owen with the Rideouts. One reason he never went to see Lizzie at the hospital, after the first while.

Sol might not see it, but maybe he's just doing what he wants to do, not what's right. Maybe he's convinced himself, but that still doesn't make it a thing that should be done.

"I think you need to think on this more, Sol."

"Goddamn it, Bill, I've been doing nothing *but* think on it."

"Well, maybe just wait a little longer, OK? Give me a chance to get up to the reservation, finish up what I need to do there, then I'll be back. I'll help you however I can, Sol." That's why I'm here, now, he thinks, and maybe together we can sort it out, this go-round. If not, we'll just make the best of a bad thing. That's what you do. You help your friends. You help your family and together you just work things out. Might not turn out perfect, but you had to stick. You don't leave family, Sol. Didn't anyone ever tell you that? Billy tries not to think that he himself is doing just that, getting away from Bad Bird. But he'll be back, he's not *leaving* leaving, he's just opening up some space for a time.

"Help how? What the hell are you going to do, Billy?"

Billy turns, looks at Sol. Both of them want to say it, bring it into the open, what passed before. Perhaps all that matters is that they both know and that, knowing, they can head off the bad that would come, a month or so from now. Lizzie and the fire and everything else. Even leaving it unsaid, they know and they'll make it better. He tries not to think about the Penn fire. They'll make it better, this time. His father has told him some things, about his uncle, he understands it all a little more. They'll fix it. There's a way to make it right.

"I'll do whatever it takes, Sol. Just give it a month, OK? We'll figure it out."

Sol won't look at Billy, but stares into his whiskey. Part of him wants to just stop caring, because he feels like maybe he's just walking through those footsteps ahead of him, that, no matter what he tries, it will go bad on him, one way or another. That that's to be the course of his life, maybe. Repeating the same mistakes or building worse ones out of bad decisions and stupidity.

He knocks his drink back, gritting his teeth. That's bullshit, though. Coward talk. Whining. Fucking weak. Billy's right. He's not going to just run away – because that's what it feels like, whatever the reason – at least not yet. He'll stick it out but he damn sure isn't going to just let things happen the way they did before. Fucking stand up and take what comes. Yes, Billy is right, and they have some time. Not much, but there's time to straighten this out. The fire didn't happen until September.

He'll get Lizzie to the hospital this time, drag her there tied up if he has to. Come visit her. Get her healthy and then she'll come home and they'll start again. It's what he should have done before, if he hadn't been so blind and stupid. He'll be ready, this time.

"All right, Bill. A month."

6.

But it wasn't a month.

Smoke in the air, still. Something is always burning, that summer. The fires in Idaho and Washington have been going for weeks. Ash blown east dusts the trees, the ground. Billy walks down to the little mission church. He looks up at a sun the color of a trout's belly, glowing through the haze like an ember. Something is always burning, lately.

It wasn't a month. Sol's house burned only a couple of days after Billy left Stevensville. He'd barely made it past Missoula when he heard the news and turned around. Sick in the gut, heart charred to coal inside him. It was a mistake thinking that everything was going to be just as before. On the same schedule, a repeat of that other time. Things change. They should have fucking known it. Didn't matter where that month went, or why. Things change. They'd made a mistake, and now Owen was gone, again.

He opens the church door, sees Sol sitting down at the front, elbows on his knees, head down. His hands are working the brim of a battered, brownish hat, pulling it in slow circles, around and around. The church is otherwise empty; Lizzie is nowhere to be seen. The air hangs hot and heavy, dust swirls in the light that lays across the small coffin that's not much bigger than one of the box planters outside, home to wilted, fading orange flowers. It's hard for Billy to understand – though he *knows* it, it's hard to *understand*, internalize in a visceral way – that it's Owen in that little wooden box. Owen, a baby, shriveled and burnt, as if presaging his fate as the young man that he would have one day become, the young man that Billy remembers: lanky, all elbows and knees, dumb with the lack of years but filling up with a life that was just starting to blossom. Years from now, when Billy knew him.

Owen, with his spraddled, sprawling stride, pushing the heavy ore-cart up and down the track all day. Owen, counting out the fifty rocks per cart – *no more, no less, goddamn it* – while the rest of them damn near piss themselves, laughing into their sleeves. Owen passing out in the Stope after half a beer and most of one whiskey, night after night, waking as often as not to something wet stuck in his ear: a finger, a beer-soaked peanut shell, a lump of well-chewed tobacco. Owen, Sol's boy come back, who will die in a fire down the Penn in 1916. Who's died in a fire in his own house, now, all these years before.

Sol doesn't even look up when Billy sits down in the pew next to him, just continues to twist his hat around in circles. Billy looks down at his own hands. He's afraid to say something, to meet Sol's gaze even. He picks at a rime of dirt under one of his nails, to give himself something to do. So he doesn't have to think. Just dig the dirt out, move on to the next finger. He's so focused on trying not to think that he doesn't even notice Sol's fist before it cracks into the side of his head.

● ● ●

"It's your fucking fault. *Yours*." Sol's following left hits Billy's raised shoulder and, fortunately, Sol is very much a right-handed man, his off-side punching weak and loose. That first shot has rung Billy's chimes something fierce and it's all he can do to scramble up and drop over the end of the pew, painfully, onto his hands and knees, do what he can to put something, anything, between himself and Sol, who is doing his best to clamber over the end of the bench and down onto Billy's skinny frame. With an agility born of desperation, Billy hoists himself upright and behind the second pew, separating himself from Sol with one low length of pine.

"Sol! *Sol!* Stop!"

"*Your fucking fault, Billy.*" Sol's brow is crumpled over bloodshot eyes; his teeth are bared, clenched as he spits the words through them. "You killed him."

"Sol!" He backs up again, sideways, bumping into a low table at the end and knocking over a candle that's burning in a mason jar; it falls to the floor and the glass cracks into several pieces. Even scared as he is, Billy has the presence of mind – given all that's happened – to stomp on the candle as he backs away, to kill the guttering flame.

"Sol, stop!"

Sol can feel with a remote, distant sliver of himself that what he's doing now is wrong. That Billy Morgan is his one last friend, the one man caught up in this shitty mess who understands it as much as Sol does, even if that means not at all. They're in it together though, for better or worse, have seen it together, the whole sorry snarl of it. Billy, who's been at Sol's side through the good and the bad and the much, much worse. Billy, who Sol damn near loves like another son.

But now, while his real son lays crisped and shrunken in a coffin the size of a breadbox, all Sol can see when he looks at Billy Morgan is Owen. Who would be alive now if it weren't for the boy in front of him. The boy who convinced him to stay, when he was ready to take his son and leave. To keep him safe. Instead, Lizzie had caught him off-guard, did what she did, a month too soon. Owen wouldn't be dead if Sol had just left when he wanted, before Billy made him stay. Billy, whose fucking uncle had brought him here in the first place. Fucking Indians and their fucking witchcraft. Fucking Indian bastards.

Sol knows at some small and faraway level of thought that the logic is wrong. That it's the mad product of grief and anger and everything shabby that lives between those two things but, now, all he wants to do is grab hold of the bastard. Who's right here in front of him, as if the fact he showed up somehow makes it all OK. He wants to wrap his hands around that bony throat, choke the life out of him, like it had been choked out of Owen by the fire and the smoke. Maybe whatever has gotten inside Lizzie, whatever drove her to do what she did, has cut free and crawled into him, too. Sol doesn't care, he can't think through this sudden stabbing knife of fury in his head that's come upon him, from where, he doesn't know.

He knows this is wrong. He can't think, can't reason, but there's something about a favor, a *favor*, and then the thought is gone though he tries to hold on to it, the thought passing into his rage. It's wrong, it's wrong, but it doesn't matter.

He hears laughter, or maybe it's only his own gasping breath.

With a quick motion, he stretches across the low pine

bench, grabbing Billy by the front of his ill-fitting shirt, pulling him closer. He raises an arm. Sol can feel the tendons pop in his good right hand as he makes the fist.

"Sol!"

Billy shouts it before the fist comes down, hopes that he'll be heard. Sol doesn't pause, though; there's no time to dodge so Billy does the only thing he can do, which is to hurl himself backwards, hoping to absorb some of the punch that way. From the burst of pain strobing his vision as his nose breaks, he presumes he wasn't all that successful, but his head is at least still on his neck, most likely. Stumbling back, eyes streaming tears, blood pouring down his lips, he pulls Sol forward with the fistful of shirt he has. Their legs tangle together and they go down in a heap, Sol's weight pinning Billy to the floor underneath.

Billy arches, bucking upward, trying to get an arm between them. He gasps for air around the forearm Sol is pressing to his throat now with slow, sickening downward insistence, pushing the wind out of him. He can feel himself starting to black out so he uses a trick he learned as a boy, trying to fend off Bad Bird or Marked Face when they got in one of their rages: he spits, the surprise of a mucky bloody spray, right into Sol's face. Sol flinches backward for an instant, just long enough for Billy to snake one skinny arm up and jab his thumb into an eye.

There's a howl and the pressure on his neck eases slightly, which allows Billy to draw a breath and try to twist his way out from under Sol, but then the forearm comes back down on his Adam's apple with a force that makes him gag, head arching forward, guts churning. He flails, trying to get hold of the other arm, down by his side, before it can come up and bring another fist crashing into his face. Sol's leaning far enough back that Billy can't even reprise a spit, though he hasn't the air to do so anyway. The only hope is that Sol will come back to himself before he finishes killing him.

Sol's arm pulls free of Billy's weakening fingers. When the hand is raised above him, Billy can see not a fist, but the glint of broken glass, a shard of the cracked mason jar held in Sol's cut, bleeding fingers, like a knife.

He needs to tell Sol the things his father had told him about Marked Face. If he could just get the air in his lungs, he'd explain it to Sol and maybe they could set things back to right. Maybe not to perfect, but back somewhere closer to right nonetheless.

All Billy wants, right now, is a second's reprieve, one short, shallow breath. That's all he needs, to get the little sentence out: *I know how to fix it.*

Instead, the world being like it is, the glass comes down, down towards that hollow spot below his jaw, where a swollen vein throbs above Sol's heavy wrist. Even as Billy tries to twist away, he's knows it's too late and that, now, he'll never be able to tell Sol those six quick words.

I know how to stop it.

Billy barely feels the glass as it goes in.

Appearances

1910

Butte, Montana

1.

"Goddamn it, get your fucking hands up, you nancy."

The kid just cowers so Sol gives him another slap upside the head, not sparing the weight of it. Sends the fucker stumbling sideways. Before the boy can get too far, Sol lets go with a left, staggering the little shit back to somewhere closer to facing him.

"Sir, stop, OK..." The boy is trying to hunker down into himself, shoulders up, neck bowed. "Listen, I didn't know–"

Sol slaps him again. "I said get your fucking hands up. Try to be a fucking man, all right? You just going to stand there and let me hit you?" He looks over at Faraday. "You believe this little bastard?"

"Kids today, hey Sol?"

"Fucking kids today is right." Sol slaps the boy once more, harder this time. "Hands up, shitbird. Jesus." Finally, scrawny little Michael Conroy, who once fancied – will fancy, although by now Sol barely thinks of any of that – himself a pugilist, raises his arms in a weak imitation of a fighter's stance: chin down, fists up and in front of his nose, left foot forward. As an intimidating spectacle, it's not much, given that Michael is what,

fifteen now? All of a buck-ten, short, spindle-limbed and
bony, a wild, dirty shock of hair that sticks up on most
sides of his head.

"There, that wasn't so hard, was it, son? Need to
rotate those fists in some, though, like that. No, don't
drop them, just turn them. There you go." Sol looks
back to his colleague. "What do you think of that stance,
Nick? You're the professional and all."

Nick Faraday gives an appraising eye. "Looking good,
lad," he says. "You make sure to keep those hands up
and in front of you, and step into your punches, using
your hips, like, but not too far, eh? You got to keep
yourself balanced." He demonstrates, slowly showing
the progression of punch from the plant leg all the way
through the hips and torso and shoulder to make it land
with weight. "You got to punch with your whole body,
kid, see? Don't just punch with your fuckin arms."

In the middle of one of Faraday's illustrative remarks
about the merits of a high-handed stance, the proper line
of force from fist to foot, Sol takes a quick step forward
and drives his own fist, as hard as he can, into the boy's
unprotected gut.

Once Michael is done gagging and puking into the dirt
at their feet, Sol and Faraday each reach down, grab a
skinny arm by the pit, and hoist the boy upright. Michael
sags against their hands, wobbling, sobbing for air and,
soon enough, just sobbing.

"I'm sorry I didn't know I didn't know I'm sorry–"

Sol slaps him, not too hard this time, just enough to
focus the boy's attention. "Shut up now, son. Just shut
the fuck up, hey? OK?" They step him over to the alley
wall, stand him up in a heap of garbage. "Now, can we
let you go, or are you just going to fall over and puke

some more? Huh?" Sol slaps him again.

"*I'm sorry I'm sorry—*"

Another slap because, Jesus, even as a kid Michael's mouth runs too busy, teeth chattering on with no connection to brain. Fucking little raconteur, still, isn't he. "Goddamn it, I said shut up. Shut it! Boy's not much of a listener, hey Nick? Maybe he's simple. You simple, son?"

"No s—" Michael stops himself and smacks his swollen lips shut, shaking his head with excess vigor. "Mm."

"Well, there now, you see, Nick? Not simple at all, turns out, our lad here."

"Wonders never, Sol."

Sol hardens his expression, pressing one extended finger into Michael's chickeny chest, pushing him tight against the wall. He's careful not to step in the sodden, stinking pile of garbage and ruin his good shoes. "Maybe not simple, but *fucking stupid*, though, huh? *Stupid*. And do you know *why* you're stupid, you little Irish fuckhead, Michael Conroy of County Dipshit?"

Michael's headshake turns into a quivery nod. He's crying hard now, and Sol wants to slap him a few times more, just on general principle, for being a whiny, snot-nosed little crybaby, but the work is done and he's on a fucking schedule, no time to indulge his pleasure. Instead, he just gives the boy another hard poke in the sternum, one that will leave a sharp round bruise and hopefully serve as a reminder, at least until hunger or laziness gets the better of the kid and sends him back to his larcenous ways. He's been warned once before this, Michael; the next warning won't be as gentle, not at all. There's a way things are done: there are rules and there are appearances to maintain. Exceptions are not made, not for anyone, not even a skinny teenager who looks like he hasn't had a straight meal in a week. No exceptions for anyone.

Sol stabs the finger once more. "You are *fucking stupid,* Michael Dipshit Conroy, *because you know you don't steal from Sean Harrity.*" Punctuating each word with another poke to the chest. Sol can't resist, and gives the boy one last hard slap upside the head. "Now get the fuck out of here. And hey: if I even *see* you again, I'ma kill you."

So it's not the greatest work in the world, slapping around teenaged petty thieves and all variety of whores and debtors and Chinks and junkies and whoever else happens to need it on the day, keeping Sean's growing collection of fuck-cribs and hop houses and gambling joints on an even keel, but it's work and Sol is good at it, very good at it, turns out. It fits him, this work, fits the man he is now, and it's even enjoyable at times. He always has money in his pocket, girls when he wants them. He's a respected – if not respectable – member of the community. He gets up late every morning after the long nights, has his coffee and breakfast in a clean, well-appointed room. When he goes out, he's well dressed and sharp looking. There's never dirt under his fingernails and he smells of expensive, spicy aftershave, good tobacco.

Not for him, twelve hours down a fucking hole in the ground, wet and filthy, ripe with stink, skin rough and blistered, spine and joints and knees aching from the work. Paid shit and likely to die from one day to the next, if not by accident or negligence than certainly once the miner's con settles in his lungs. Fuck that. He'd never even thought to come back to Butte this time around but things had worked out as they had and here he is, but sitting pretty for once.

He's taking a break now after checking in on some of the girls he looks after, relaxing in an overstuffed, comfortable easy chair, a glass of good, smooth whiskey in one hand – the kind he never saw before at the Stope, or any of the other shitholes he used to frequent – a cigarette in the other. Later, if he feels like it, he'll get his prick sucked by Maggie or one of the others, maybe that new one, the young tart whose name he can never remember, with that big, round, soft-looking ass.

Sean is a piece of shit and, sometimes, Sol finds what he has to do distasteful but, quickly enough, that distaste goes back to wherever it's come from because, really, it doesn't fucking matter. He doesn't care any more, about much of anything, really, so why even bother trying. If there's anything Sol has learned in his life, lives, it's that: nothing really fucking matters, not when you lean down and look it hard in the eye. Everything is transient, the good and the shit and all that squats in between. Life might keep you up at night, give you bad dreams, sometimes, but that doesn't matter either, because anything, everything, might be taken away from you from one minute to the next, no matter what you do. No matter how hard you try to stop it. Life is stronger than you are and will roll out how it will and fuck you if you get in its way. So best, then, to just get what you want while the getting is there and anyone who tries to come between you and your desires can go fuck themselves.

It's hard and it's cold and it's selfish but that's the fucking world, isn't it? This one, or any of the others, so fuck it.

He hadn't come to this understanding quickly, or easily, but come to him it had, eventually. Seems obvious now, really, but it hadn't always been that way and look at the fucking mess he'd made of everything, over and over, until he realized the way of things. OK, sure, he wasn't maybe never going to be voted Man of the Year by the Order of Hibernians, but here he was, beholden to no one – aside from his employer, whom he could leave whenever he fucking well liked – with this glass of good whiskey and a smoke and the prospect of a cock-sucking later from a young girl with lips that were as full and soft as her ass. Seemed pretty all right, those things, when you gave them your notice. There was some saying about the unexamined life, the gist of it Sol doesn't remember; far as he can tell, upon examination, his life looks pretty sorted, now and, if there were aspects of it that chafed around the gizzard, well, best just put those to the side because they were doing fuck-all good for him, were he to fret about them. Just button up and get on with it, like his mama used to say. Get over it.

Funny how things had worked out, though, him here in Butte, which was just about the last place he'd expected to fetch up, and working for Sean Harrity, of all people. But here he was.

After the thing with Billy, those years ago, he hadn't spent much time in jail. There were circumstances, after all, extenuating, really, plus it was just some Indian kid, as the law saw it. Not much sympathy there, really, world being the way it was. When Sol had gotten out, he'd gone on a bender that gave a whole new level of meaning to the word. By the time he'd gotten back to himself some, Ag had already taken Lizzie up to his hospital so there wasn't much of anything keeping him in Stevensville, what with his tavern shut up and his house burned down. So he left.

The next couple three years passed in a bit of a haze, what with drinking too much and maybe the little shine of lunatic he'd taken on. Best not to think on that, either, when it came up in front of him as it did from time to time. Just have another drink, do something to occupy himself. He found work when he really needed it, those years, but for the most part, he was a bum. Just a bum but, really, that didn't seem to bother him much.

Sol the bum, who drank himself blind for damn sure, often as he could, got in plenty of fights, wound up in jail more times than he could count, for one thing or another. Shuffled from one town to the next, leaving a trail of blood and booze and mayhem. At some level, he kept expecting to see that old snake-haired Indian turn up, smiling that smile of his and shaking those little marked-on bones. But he never had and, really, Sol knew that he himself was done with gambling. Knew that like he knew little else in this life, could feel it in his belly.

Funny, too, that the one vice that had landed him in the shitheap that had been his life before, what with his debts to Sean Harrity and all the sorrow that that had started, the games with the old Indian, tobacco for heartache, that one vice was gone, now – *pouf!* – subsumed in all the myriad others he was trying on for fit. And they did feel snug and well cut to his frame, damn near all of them.

And even funnier that it was Sean Harrity, Sean fucking Harrity, professional asshole, once the bane of Sol's life, who had been the one to pull him out of that last downhill collapse and get him set back to rights. Turned out that a man Sol had beaten damn near to death up in Helena, over a disagreement about a young lady – although perhaps *lady* was a bit of a strong word for the girl in question – had been a man for whom Sean himself carried very strong feelings, of the negative sort. That accidental favor had been parlayed into bail money and, once out of jail – again – the prospect of employment in the bustling, up and coming metropolis that was Butte, Montana, the Richest Hill on Earth. Where one Sean Seamus Harrity was a rising star in the scum-drenched, drink-soaked and shit-smeared underbelly of that particular society.

Sol can't help but laugh, now, because it's a hell of a thing: here he is, couple few years later, rich as Croesus – relatively – in his well-made soft clothes, clean-shaven and perfumed like a Paris whore. Old, expensive whiskey and good, ready-made cigarette to hand, feeling the hum of blood in his prick at the thought of that little girl's lips that will be working it soon enough. David Solomon Parker, professional villain, strong right hand to none other than Sean Harrity, top shitheel of Butte. Sol Parker, with his nice room and fat wallet and bruised-up, scarred knuckles, knife in his boot and fuck anyone who looks at him sideways because he's *Sol Parker*, Sean Harrity's man, meanest bastard that walks the streets of this fucking town.

Hell of a thing.

2.

The women say that no man should live longer than his days in this world; that, if a man does somehow manage that feat, the shock of it will sunder him.

Such was the case for Siinatssi, to be sure, for, when he returned from the Other Lands, the kind and loving and respectful young man his brother had known had become something else entirely.

Maatakssi wept to discover this, and understood that the Above Ones, in their anger, had tricked him as payment for his own arrogance. For they had given him, as promised, one boon and one punishment, and yet they were indeed the same thing, as the old women said: a return to life for his brother Siinatssi.

But the brother that left was not the one who came back.

Life went on, as it does, and Siinatssi and Maatakssi became great chiefs, the fathers of a nation. They had many wives and sons and daughters, and sons' sons and daughters' daughters. In this place they had come to, fleeing the anger of Old Man, they made the People.

For many upon many years, the People thrived, led by the two brothers. Maatakssi was a war chief, wily and strong in the ways of battle, fearless, leading the People to victory against all of their enemies of that time, the Cut-Noses and the Flat-

Heads and the Hanging-Ears, many others. His war club had notches uncountable and his foes shivered to hear that the great Maatakssi was taking the field against them. Siinatssi, his brother, became a mighty shaman, heavy with medicine; he had come back from the Other Lands with powers that no other man possessed. Twice-Born Siinatssi, he was called, who could speak with the dead and the beasts and the spirits of the air. Siinatssi, who could bend the world to his will and do wondrous and terrible things.

The two brothers were the leaders of a great People, whose numbers spread like the stars in the sky. From war band and medicine lodge they ruled the People and built a nation. But, alas, this was not enough for Siinatssi, who chafed that he must share glory with his perfidious brother, who had killed him those years ago. Siinatssi felt a burning in his heart that had been kindled during his stay in the Other Lands, which is a place of want and greed and ravenous, unending hunger for those who do not belong there. From time to time a spirit would escape from that cold place and find its way into a mortal; such a thing had happened to Siinatssi and what crouched there inside him now led him to betray his brother, Maatakssi, who had made him the man he now was.

So, in the dead of one winter night, Siinatssi and his sorcerer kin bound poor Maatakssi, cutting the tendons of his legs and plucking out his eyes. They removed his tongue and carved the sigils into his flesh that would prevent his soul from finding rest, and then they raised their knives to pierce his heart and free his spirit to an eternity of hollow wandering, empty and starving. But Siinatssi, at the last, broken and mad though he was, could not condone the killing of his brother, the rape of his spirit, just as it may have been. He stopped his sons and nephews from their task, saying, "This is enough," *and then he leaned down to kiss his blinded, crippled, weeping brother.* "May you have peace, Maatakssi," *he said,* "but you will not have it with the People. They are mine now, and we will make a great thing without you, who killed me and made me who I am."

He reached down and took the pouch from around his brother's neck where the bones, given to Maatakssi by their father, Old Man, were kept. "This, I take from you, brother," *he said.* "I have taken your legs and your eyes and now I take your medicine. I take your name. All that you once were is my own, now. It is as if you have never existed. Now go, nameless worm, crawl to the west until you reach the great water. Do not turn back. I, Siinatssi, who have eaten the spirit of my once-brother, Maatakssi, say this to you."

And with that, he and his kin turned and left.

Weeping bloody tears, Maatakssi crawled on hands and knees, blindly, towards the great water, for days that became weeks that became months. Ever westward, his flesh cut by rocks, his throat swollen and raw with the blood from his severed tongue, the hollows where he'd once had eyes burned by the sun. In the mornings, he sucked dew off the grass and dined on insects and the nodding heads of grasses; he drank from creeks and seeps if he found them, digging tubers and cresses from their banks. More often, he went hungry and thirsty, and wasted away to a skeletal shell of the man he once was, begging for a death that he could not find. Finally, Maatakssi could go no farther, and lay down to die. He closed his lids over empty sockets and waited for the Above Ones to claim him at last. Maatakssi had been well punished for his arrogance and the sin of killing his brother, the son of Old Man; he was now ready to greet the Above Ones with humility. These were his thoughts when he fell into sleep on that last day.

Instead of the Above Ones coming to gather in his spirit, he was awoken by Raven, his old friend and betrayer.

"Well, this is a thing, Maatakssi," *the bird said, squatting on his shoulder.* "Truly you look like shit."

Maatakssi had no tongue and could not speak, he could only manage a thin croaking sound to express his anger at Raven, inviting him to have relations with himself, should the bird be able to manage it with such a tiny prick as he carried under those ratty black feathers.

But, of course, Raven, being what he was, could well understand the croaking of Maatakssi, who sounded not unlike some of Raven's wives. Raven laughed to see that there yet remained a spark of life in his young friend, the foolish two-leg walker who'd sought in his arrogance to trick the gods themselves. His laughter died, though, to see the bloody tears weeping down his face, once Maatakssi's defiance had waned and he again merely awaited his release from the Above Ones.

Sighing, knowing that he would one day regret it, Raven made a decision, then and there, and flew off to find Nihaat, his friend Spider, who watched over the tribe of the Big-Bellies. Nihaat was a cunning and powerful creature, who might be able to help young Maatakssi, fool though the boy was, but the cost would be high.

For, even in the weeks and months since Maatakssi had been banished from his tribe, Raven had seen that the People, under the power of Siinatssi and Siinatssi alone, were already becoming a terrible thing.

The cost would be high, but there was yet a chance that they could be saved, that Siinatssi himself could be drawn from his evil path, with the help of his brother. Raven looked upon poor eyeless Maatakssi, seeing the life he had built in this world, seeing the grief that would come to him, before the end.

3.

Bad Bird is droning on about Raven and the stupid old one, Maatakssi, always the old stories, but all Billy can think about is how much he hates these goddamn fucking cows.

He hates the warm stink of them, their empty looks of bovine stupidity and, more than anything, hates the endless piles of steaming, mucky shit they produce. These piles of shit that, right now, as he does most days, he's lumping into a heap to be taken away for fertilizer. Hour after hour, day after day, Billy Morgan, chief shit-mucker at the Montana State Hospital for the Insane at Warm Springs, bends and lifts and stretches and drops one hot, fragrant pile of cow dung after the other. An artisan, is what he is, he tells himself. A cowshit artiste.

He's made a sizable dent in the current pile so that now he can take a minute to light up a cigarette, to stretch his back and unclench his locked-up fingers from their grip around the splintery handled pitchfork. Roll his shoulder in its socket to loosen it up some, work the stiffness from the scar tissue that's piled up inside the joint, where the glass had gone in. Ten years ago now, and still it hurt like a bastard, most days. Just luck, or Sol's poor aim, maybe, that it had found his shoulder rather than his throat that day. Damn near killed him anyway, from the bleeding. It had cut deep, and gives him no end of grief now, still, scarred up as it is.

Sol would have finished the job back then had big old John Tierney and his huge, horsey wife not come in and managed – just – between the two of them, to pull Sol off him, pin him to the ground long enough for Billy to get up and out of the mission church, streaming blood and hollering for help. The sheriff had thrown Sol in jail for a couple few days, just long enough for Billy to get far out of town – *and best you not come back, son* – told in no uncertain words to hightail it on out of Stevensville. Didn't matter the circumstances or who was wrong or right, *just go on, boy*. And so he did, eventually fetching up back at the reservation with Bad Bird, wild-eyed with grief and the shock of it all, arm pinned to his side under the thick wrap of bandage around his shoulder and chest.

Bad Bird had been sunk into one of his black depressions, had barely looked up when Billy came into the little cabin, just rolled over on his side and faced the wall, ignoring his son's hysterics. After a time Billy went out and found himself a drink, and then another one, and another, until his shoulder and heart didn't hurt quite so much any more.

"Can I have some tobacco?" Bad Bird says now, half-sitting on a big milk can, hand extended for a cigarette.

"I don't know, don't want to interrupt your talking, Father. Plus you're probably too tired out from all the help you're giving me here with this goddamn manure." Bad Bird has spent the morning telling stories, watching his son do all the chores, not lifting a finger. It's not that Billy minds the stories or even the laziness, it's that he has to listen to the same old shit every day, over and over, at least when Bad Bird is calm and lucid and out of his bed. These months of close acquaintance with his father, even given what went before, have done nothing but chafe.

Wordlessly he rolls another cigarette and passes it to his father, who leans forward for a light and then closes his eyes, smiling, as he pulls the smoke into his lungs. Billy leans on the handle of the pitchfork and, for a time, they're quiet, smoking in silence that's only punctuated by the flabby sound of the occasional cow fart.

Strange that he's wound up here at Warm Springs, this time around. Of his own volition, before his father even. After Stevensville he'd bounced around the reservation some, drinking a bit but mostly just moving from one thing to another without much in the way of thought or ambition, just following himself along from day to day. Picking up work mending fence and stacking hay and the like, as he needed, aimlessly shuffling from one job to the next, which at some point brought him near Butte: a place he'd never wanted to see again, but here he was, just down the road from it. It was as if there was a pull there, the place a low spot, high as it is, that he'd been slowly rolling toward.

Billy hadn't been particularly surprised then, when, one day on the road outside Anaconda, he'd stopped to help a man whose cart had busted an axle and, when the man crawled out from underneath the contraption and dusted his long frame off, had proved to be Sol's brother, Dr Rideout. One thing had led to the next, Dr Rideout seeming to take a shine to Billy and, sure enough, here he was now, working as an orderly and general dogsbody at Warm Springs. Wrangler of crazies, ice-bath dunker, carpenter, cowshit artiste.

"Have you boys seen Owen?"

Mrs Parker is standing in the barn's door, a worried expression on her face. "He's run off again."

Billy checks a sigh. It's better to just indulge her with these things; easier anyway. Funny that, that other time, Mrs Parker had been so convinced that she'd killed Owen, burned him up in the fire, even though the baby had lived. Now, this time around, when she actually had done the thing, she believes with all her heart that her boy is around somewhere, always running off, the scamp, as boys do. Seeing her every day makes Billy sad, but also just tired and exasperated. With her and the lot of them, the nuts and loons and defectives that make this place their home. It's an uncharitable thought, he knows, but wrestling clean diapers onto grown men – and several needed them – getting covered in their shit, bit at and kicked, day after day, uses up your charity pretty quick. The wailing and screams, the women who would spit at you and then try to suck you off, the ranting about conspiracy and things that weren't there. Billy doesn't know how Dr Rideout does it; he's a damn saint to choose these people as a life's work. It's only Billy's respect for the man that's kept him at the hospital this long. There are easier ways to make a living and, now that Bad Bird is sorted, off the reservation, where people can look after him, there's not much else holding Billy to the job.

"Haven't seen him, Mrs Parker," he says. "Expect he's around, though. You know how boys are."

Elizabeth is shaking her head *no*, picking worriedly at the hem of her sleeve. "Yes, you're probably right, yes," she says, still shaking her head. Her brow furrows and she puts a well-chewed fingernail to her teeth, nibbling at it. Her hands red and chafed, the nails ragged, quicks inflamed by her ceaseless fidgeting. She gets agitated easily and, once she starts, it can be hard to settle her down again.

Billy extends his half-smoked cigarette towards her, raising his eyebrows in question. Sometimes it's best to just distract Mrs Parker, derail her one-way train of thought as much as you can. Sure enough, her eyes light up and she reaches a hand out, greedily. The patients aren't supposed to smoke, and Elizabeth Parker is damn sure to be kept away from fire. Hell with it, though, Billy thinks, he's right here and can keep an eye on her. Poor lady is carrying around a pile of shit for a life and, if a damn cigarette can make her happy for a bit, let her have one.

"Shouldn't give that one tobacco, Sagiistoo," his father says in the old tongue. "That one is crazy."

Billy cocks a glance at Bad Bird. "Pot and kettle."

"Rile her up. She'll burn down this whole place and us with it."

"What is he saying, Billy?"

Billy turns back to Elizabeth. "He was just saying how pretty you look today, Mrs Parker, standing there in the light like that. Like a angel, he said. Careful with this old man, though: he's a charmer."

She blushes, looks girlish for a moment. She's still a beautiful woman, Elizabeth, when the pain and fear drop away from her face and leave her eyes, rare that it is. She looks like a woman half her age and it's easy to see what drew Sol to her, when that happens. It makes it even more sad to see the expression die, as quickly as it arrives, shut up as the worry comes back.

"Are you sure you haven't seen Owen? It's almost lunchtime." The gnawed fingernail goes back to her teeth, the stub of the cigarette forgotten in her other hand. "I need to go find him."

Before she can turn and leave, Billy steps over and takes her wrist in a gentle grip, stopping her. "I'm sure he'll turn up, Mrs Parker, but I'll just take that cigarette, OK?"

He smokes the remnant as he watches her hurry off towards the main building. He can hear her calling for her dead boy.

"Crazy, that one," Bad Bird says, a strange look in his eye. "But they say us crazies see the world as it really is, don't they?"

"They say a lot of stupid shit, Father, whoever *they* even are." Billy knows the things he himself has seen, and doesn't like the thought.

"Told you she'll burn this place down one day, that one," Bad Bird says, nodding towards the retreating Mrs Parker.

"You're probably right, Father." Billy twists the last bit of cigarette out under his boot. He stretches his back, rolling his bad shoulder one last time, looking grimly towards the long line of stalls he's yet to muck. "I got to get back to work. Don't suppose you're going to help." But Bad Bird has already resumed his low, breathy chanting, eyes closed, sitting there on his milk can, motionless as a tobacco-store Indian.

Well, to hell with him. As Billy steps into the first stall and stabs the fork into the pile of hay and warm shit, he tells himself again that it's not a bad life he's found, this time. Better in some ways than the one that came before, the one he tries not to think about. More and more it's just a kind of strange memory, losing its reality with the passage of years that are rolling toward it. He's young and healthy – mostly – now, he has a job and a friend or two and there's even a girl up at town who seems to maybe have a bit of shine in her eye for him, a state of affairs he needs to investigate further when he can find the time. Even if he's mucking shit, day after day, diapering crazies and the rest, at least he's not down in a dark, wet, fearsome hole in the ground, that will one day be the death of him. Here, a lunatic might stab him or a cow kick him in the head but, if that happens, at least it will happen on the ground, not buried under it.

It's not a bad life, not at all. Maybe not the one he would have picked for himself, not exactly, but pretty all right, most of the time. It's not a bad life but, looking over at his father, still chanting the old songs, Billy wonders if he'd change it if he could.

4.

Sol's been dreaming about the fire again. There's a faint, lingering whiff of smoke in his nostrils and his throat hurts, dry and scratchy. Whether from dream-smoke or from shouting himself awake, he isn't sure. More than one of the girls has complained about Sol's tortured, thrashing sleep, the mutters and shouts and grinding teeth, that keeps them awake. Sometimes when he wakes up his fingers are clenched so tight into fists he has to pull them free in aching stages, until he can straighten them all the way, leaving dead white half-moons in his palms from the press of the nails. When the girls complain Sol merely growls *then don't stay over*, as if it was their choice, when, in fact, Sol is the one who's brought them there, bought their time. Sometimes, the touch of a warm woman, even a stranger or a working girl, in the middle of the night, is what he needs. Just to be able to press his nose into the back of a woman's neck, smell the perfume and sweat and clean or dirty hair and all the rest of the things that makes up the scent of a female.

That spell is always broken the next day; he'll wake up, hungover more often than not, and look at the blousy, puffy eyed tart in the bed next to him, stinking of under-clean linen and a dirty crotch and other men's semen. *Don't stay over,* he'd say. If they bitched about his thrashing around he'd tell them to just drink more or use more dope – *that'll make you sleep* – or just shut the fuck up, now get dressed and out of his room.

Sol's alone today, bleary and dry, his head aching in time with the pounding on his door. Maybe it's the hangover or the nightmare or a combination of the two, but he feels uneasy, for no reason he can put his finger to. He doesn't want to open that door, face whatever might be coming. He just gets these sorts of feelings sometimes. Woman's intuition.

Looking out the window, he can tell it's late afternoon, the sun hanging large and low in the sky; the room, nice as it is, is still hot and close and Sol can feel the sweat running down his ribs. He lifts an arm, sniffs experimentally, pulling away from the stink of himself, dirty pits and stale booze. Again, he tells himself that he's going to stop drinking so much but, any more, he needs it just to sleep, most nights, lousy as that sleep is when he gets it. It's medicine, really, vital for his health and all that. Man needs to sleep to live and maybe he needs to drink to sleep so there it was. Sol just wished he didn't usually feel like day-old shit in the morning.

The hammering at his door continues as he levers himself upright, wiping a handful of sheet across his chest to dry the sweat some. *Bang bang bang* on the door or maybe it's just inside his head. He takes a long drink from the mason jar full of water, now tepid and flat, that he'd put next to his bed whenever he'd finally gone to sleep. The sun had been up, that much he remembered.

Bang bang bang.

"Hold the fuck on, all right?" he mutters.

Bang bang. Hollering from the other side of the door.

"Sol? Sol, you up? Wake up now."

It's that fat fucker Mickey Doyle. There's no love lost between the two of them, what with Mickey believing that Sol has usurped his rightful place as Sean's number two, but fuck him: it's not Sol's fault that Mickey is stupid – although a shade smarter than that halfwit Faraday, to be sure – and that he lacks initiative and forethought. He's big, Mickey, and that there is the sum total of his accomplishments in life, the entirety of what he adds to the Sean Harrity enterprise. Big and dumb and *bang bang bang bang.* "OK FOR FUCK'S SAKE, MICKEY, I'M UP!"

Entirely pissed off now, forgetting the unease, Sol stumbles over to the door, sheet over his shoulder like a Roman, dragging in a train behind him. His dick is hanging out but who cares, let Mickey see it. It's a fine piece of work, after all, unlike whatever sorry little bean the fat fucker is hiding under that gut of his. *Haven't seen your own pitiful little cock for twenty years, most likely, so take a look at this one, you flabby Irish bastard.* He yanks the door open.

"WHAT?"

Mickey stands there for a moment, blinking stupidly at the sight of sweaty, disheveled, half-nude Sol Parker, prick hanging out for all the world to see. "Sol," he says, finally. "You're up."

"Of course I'm fucking up, you dipshit. You been banging on my goddamn fucking door for twenty minutes. What? What do you want?"

Fuck you. Sol can see the line of Mickey's thoughts in the play of his fat, stupid face. Like reading a book. *Fuck you. If you got the fuck out of bed I wouldn't need to keep pounding at your door.* It's humiliating for him, Sol knows, being sent like an errand boy, and he knows that, one day, Mickey will try to test Sol, try to take his place. He's so transparent that he may as well be shouting it.

"Sean wants to see you," Mickey says instead.

"And he sent you to fetch me, huh? Ain't that cute, Mickey. Finally, a use for your limitless talents." *Here I am, fucker. Whenever you like.* Sol can't help needling the big dummy, although it's probably not the smartest thing to do just now, stood here with his dick out, by himself, hungover and, more to the point, unarmed and about a hundred pounds smaller than the man. He can see the muscles in Mickey's jaw bulge outward as his teeth clench, but Sol knows that, if there's one thing that Mickey is afraid of, it's Sean Harrity. So maybe Mickey's not so stupid after all, really, because it's nothing but smart to be afraid of that evil fucker.

"Hang on, just hang on a minute. Whiskey on the table if you want it," he says, placatingly, pointing his chin to the bottle, which has barely an inch or two left in it.

"I'm fine." The jaw muscles relaxing a bit.

"Well, I'm not, Mickey, so pour me one, hey? Got a thirst, first thing in the morning. Afternoon, whatever. Got a thirst."

"Boy's a faggot."

"Well now, Sean, who are we to judge? Ain't like we don't have our own vices." Sol is ensconced in one of the huge easy chairs in Sean's office, the city office, not the little hole behind the Piper where threats were made and the more gutter sorts of activities planned. This is the office of a respectable businessman, where a civil, and vastly more lucrative, sort of illegality is attended to. It's a place of buttery soft leather chairs, thick Persian carpets, shining brass spittoons. The smell of pricey cigars, a sideboard full of the finest liquors. The walls are paneled in some sort of dark wood – mahogany? teak? – and the gleaming desk, of a matching color, is the size of a rhinoceros.

This room's a place where Sean can meet with his betters, the Company men and their assorted clingers-on, the lawyers, politicians, the like, in an environment better suited to hide what he, Sean Harrity, is: an Irish piece of shit, a thug from the alleys of Dublin who has no reservations about much of anything, if it benefits him in any way. A prick with delusions of grandeur, come to bustling Butte to seize that gleaming brass ring. The American fucking dream and all. Here in this office Sean can pretend that he's merely a businessman, one who had particular resources offered by few others; he was a well-connected gentleman of society, Sean Harrity, and never mind his grammar or the broken knuckles. A self-made man like our own Marcus Daly, pulled up by his bootstraps using the sweat of his brow and that natural cleverness that comes with being a son of Erin.

"Still, Sol, a shameless queer. Unnatural, is what it is."

Strange, then, to be in this room of gentlemanly business aimed at the cream of Butte society, staring at huge, gangling young Eamonn Mallon, standing there, all shoulders and elbows, head down in shame. It's perhaps inevitable, being here in Butte again, that Sol would cross paths with some of his boys, but it still feels odd. First Sean and Butte itself, then Michael, and now here's Nancy: it's as if Sol's life is always going to settle out around certain features. Like a shaken gold-pan, swirled and jostled, leaving the flecks at the bottom of the dish when the water pours free. Maybe, if Sol's life is shaken out, Sean and Nancy and the rest of it are left there gleaming in the wet, that it doesn't matter whatever sand and gravel or what else makes up the remainder: the color is always there hiding somewhere, ready to show.

Or maybe the universe just isn't very creative, with only so many ideas to hand. Best not to think about that shit anyway; any of the before never happened. He's never known Eamonn Mallon, who everyone called Nancy, no matter what he remembers.

"Bit harsh, Sean. Just a kid, really."

"Heaney caught him sucking off one of the fellas in the back room of his place, Sol. It's disgusting, is what that is. Aberrative." Sol can tell Sean's pleased with that five-dollar word, as he repeats it. "Aberrative. Good Book has something to say about that kind of behavior, you bet your asshole it does."

The boy's head hangs lower. He's breathing so hard Sol can hear it, a thin wheeze of fear or humiliation or both. It didn't matter what had happened before – *didn't fucking matter* – but Sol can't help but feel a hitch in his chest, seeing him like this. That big kid was – *would be, whatever* – one of the best of Sol's crew, back before, and this isn't right. Who gives a shit what he put in his mouth, who he fucked? World is hard enough, already, and Nancy is who he is and besides, who are you to fucking judge anyone, Sean. He can't stop his mouth from opening.

"Yeah, but come on, cut the kid a break," Sol says. "You Irish are a nation of sheep fuckers, hey? Lonesome shepherds, all that? What's that word you used? *Aberrative*? Seems like the Good Book probably has something to say about that kind of behavior too, Sean."

As soon as the words leave his lips he knows he's made a mistake. Sean will tolerate some joshing around in private – just a bit, mind – but making him look a fool in front of the boys, in front of an outsider, worse, isn't to be countenanced. Sean Harrity isn't a big man, or a particularly hard-looking one. He's average height, average build, average everything, really. Maybe that's part of his success: he seems less than he is, so people underestimate him. Sol knows from experience that whatever is inside of Sean, though, is as cold and mean as a riled snake, when it comes out. There is nothing that Sean Harrity will shrink from, nothing, no matter how distasteful, if he feels it is in his own interests. Sean doesn't move now, doesn't even blink, but Sol still feels a wash of fear in his guts, his pucker knotting up.

He forces out a half-witted laugh. "Kidding, is all, Sean. Lies spread by the English, right? That sheep thing. Dumb joke. Shouldn't have said it. So there's my apology, then."

Sean just stares at him, for a long, long moment, holding him with his eyes until Sol's ass begins to sweat in sympathy with the sick in his belly.

"Shouldn't have said it," Sol repeats.

"This boy here, this poof, he's Irish, too." Sean finally says.

"That right?"

"Shame that a son of Saint Pat would stoop to such behavior. You hear me, lad," he says, raising his voice, pointing at Nancy. "Fuckin shameful."

"Ah, Sean." Sol trails off, not having anything more to say. His guts are just beginning to unwind and he needs to quit while he's ahead. Why the hell is he even here? Just to hear Sean up on his pulpit, castigating the poor kid? Sol knows for a fact, from one of the working girls, that Sean himself is partial to having a dick-toy stuck up his ass, so it seems more than a little hypocritical to berate Nancy for maybe enjoying the real thing.

"Yeah, but look at him, though, Sol, hey? What do you see?"

Ah. Now he gets it. Again, the irony of it all is a bit much. "I see a big kid, Sean. Real big."

"Yeah, Sol. Big fuckin nancy-boy, though, ain't he. But maybe we can come to an accommodation, Mr Big Nancy. I don't know, though, sullying my establishment with your shameful fuckin behavior. Word from me, you'll never find work in this town and I don't care how big you are. I know people, hey Sol?"

Sol grits his teeth. "That's right."

"So, a big faggot – literally – like you, what's to be done?" There's a long pause, as if he's mulling it over, but obviously Sean has seen the opportunity from a long ways off. Funny, again, how it all keeps coming back to these same old things. Eventually, Sean nods, winking over at Sol and then looking back Nancy's way.

"Tell me, lad," he says, "big fella like you: you ever done any fighting?"

5.

"Come on now, we're not fighting, right? Come on, Mrs Parker, it's me. It's your friend, Billy. I'm just trying to help you. So let's put that down, OK?"

Jesus, how does she keep *finding* the things? This is supposed to be a hospital for dangerous, crazy people, some of whom are sure to hurt themselves or someone else and yet, again and again, Elizabeth Parker somehow winds up with something sharp in her hands. Granted, it's just a little paring blade this time, but it doesn't matter: knives cut, and Billy's damn sure not interested in having that blade stuck in him, anywhere. Little lady like Mrs Parker got to looking a lot bigger with something sharp in her hands. The goddamn lazy kitchen staff, leaving shit like this around, maybe one of the other orderlies but, whoever it was, it's not right, at all, that this poor girl is standing there on the other side of her bed, keeping it between them, crying and shouting Lord knows what as she holds the little knife to her neck.

"*Get away!* I deserve this. *I deserve it so get away!*" Elizabeth is weeping, her words caught and bouncing between sobs until they're mostly incomprehensible.

Yet again, she's found the way to her salvation, a release from it all in these three inches of sharp, pointed metal but, again, she won't go through with it. *"Get away!"*

One quick jump, Billy thinks, a jump right across the bedframe and a pop on the jaw would give him time enough to get the knife away before she cuts herself. Or him. One fast punch, didn't even have to be that hard, just enough to stagger her for a second, and then we're fine. But *shit*, he doesn't want to hurt her. The thought of punching a woman, one old enough to be his mother – not to mention everything else about her, Sol and the rest – the thought of just up and smacking her doesn't sit right, even if it's for her own good.

"Get away! You stop!"

She's not yelling at him, now, but at James, another of the day orderlies, a big simpleton who's come barging into the room, running over, hollering like the idiot he is. Billy and James don't see eye to eye, never have. He's cruel to the patients, James, and Billy suspects that, from time to time, he takes liberties with the women. The inmates at Warm Springs are tiresome, exasperating, dangerous sometimes, but they're sick and it's not their fault they're that way. The temptation to slap around the more recalcitrant has come to Billy, from time to time – for sure it has – but the patients are people, human beings, and should be treated with as much respect and kindness as the staff can muster. James musters very little.

"Put it down, Mrs P, or I'm gonna hafta come get it, and none of us are gonna like that, are we?"

"Goddamn it, James, I got this. Just get out of here, OK? I got it."

"How come the lady's got a knife, Bill? That your fault, Chief? You fuck up again? That right?"

What Billy wants, right then, is to pick up this little table he's standing beside, pick it up and bust it right over the head of this stupid cracker, settle things. Drop the table down on that bald, spotty head and then, once James is down, stomp him to a paste for all slights, perceived and imagined. For the cruelty and the rest of it. World would be a better place without this fucker in it. Billy has been getting these rages sometimes, that seem to appear out of nowhere, touched off by some little spark of incident. A burning anger inside him that wants to come out, needs to. He's gotten in some fights, up at town which, fortunately, haven't yet led to anything too terrible. Maybe more just out of luck than anything. These aren't the mostly good-natured scuffles that used to happen after shift, back when he was a miner. Holding his own with his crew against some other, drinks at the end of it once the cursing and bleeding stopped. These fights are something worse, something black; fury – at something, anything – boiling out until it's all he can do to still his fists, pull his boots in.

It reminds him, more and more, of his father and Marked Face. It scares him.

James is big, but he's stupid, callow. Age and treachery beats big and dumb any day. Billy's older than his time: he may only be twenty-four on this calendar but he has many, many years of fighting dirty behind him, learned from his father and Marked Face and the government school and the rest of it. Queensberry-rules fisticuffs isn't for him. There's no glory in losing with dignity, not when your flesh and bones are on the line.

"Huh? I *said*, that right, Chief?"

The table is just a step away and that gurning grin on James's face is calling for it but, right now, the important thing is getting the knife away from Elizabeth before she hurts herself or someone else. *Later, James, you stupid bald bastard.*

"Come on, now, Mrs Parker, let's just have that little poker, OK? I think Owen's probably looking for you, right? Owen? Let's go find him, me and you, OK?" Billy speaks in the low, sing-songy voice you'd use to calm a skittish horse, extending a hand – slowly – out across the bed that's between them.

"Oh fuck this."

James lunges forward towards Mrs Parker and, before Billy has a chance to think about it, the table is in his hand, swinging. It's just cheap pine but the weight of it across the bridge of James's nose feels glorious, landing hard enough for the leg to splinter off in his hand. James lets loose a squeal – high-pitched for a man of his size and crumples to his knees, head in his hands. Figuring that the cards have been played at this point, Billy doesn't hesitate to come forward and, with a judicious application of fists and boots and the remnant of the little table, finishes the work. James, whimpering, tries to crawl away, under Mrs Parker's bed, but Billy grabs him by his belt and drags him out, then uses a combination of a foot up the ass and some pointed cursing to get him out of the dormitory. As the adrenaline begins to wear off, Billy regrets what he's done, necessary or not, and he knows that it's not the last that he's seen of that situation. There will be consequences, almost certainly. James is too dumb to learn from his mistakes. Well, fair enough, nothing that can be done about it now.

When he comes back, Mrs Parker is sitting on her bed, head in her hands, crying. The little knife is next to her, forgotten now. Billy sits down beside her, the bedsprings shrieking under the thin, stained mattress, the sag pulling them together. Elizabeth leans into his shoulder, crying so hard it sounds like she's gasping for air; Billy puts an arm around her back, patting her awkwardly. She shouldn't have seen any of that, him and James, regardless of whether it needed to happen or not. Too much excitement, good or bad, is hard on a lot of these patients, many of whom are just trying their best to keep things together in the face of whatever storms rage in their mind. Dr Rideout had explained it to him, but it's obvious if you looked at it. Hot, raw emotion just spins these poor people up, to no good outcome, usually. Keep them calm, encourage them to pick weeds in the garden, help with the cows, shuck peas, whatever: gentle, pastoral therapy designed to quiet whatever it is in them that's broken and can't be fixed. And here he is, breaking a goddamn table over a man's head in front of a patient with a knife in her hand. Jesus.

"I just want to go home," she whispers, turning her face into his chest. "I want to go home."

"It's OK, Mrs Parker, it's OK." Because what's he going to say? *You're home here, with all the other crazies. The suicidal, the murderers, the defective, the deranged. With me. All of us who see the real world. Welcome home, Mrs P.*

"I just want to go home, Sol," she says.

Later, Billy's having a cigarette out on the back porch, sitting on a step, watching the sun go down. Dinner's over and he's off shift, though he usually sticks around for a while, just in case the next crew needs any help. A pint of whiskey is tucked discreetly against his ankle and, from time to time, he lips it, just enough to take the edge off. He doesn't even look up when Dr Rideout sits down next to him, just wordlessly passes him the bottle. It's cheap, lousy stuff, and the doctor hisses after a small sip, to tamp down the burn. For a long time, they're quiet, watching the sun sink, listening to the click of the early bats out for mosquitoes. Even this late in the day, it's hot still; the air smells of dust and pine and, with the wind on, the faint smoky stink of the mines those miles away at Butte. He's rolling himself another cigarette when Dr Rideout speaks.

"Give me one of those, will you?"

Billy doesn't say anything, just lifts an eyebrow, as the doctor is a non-smoker. A non-most-things, really: he rarely drinks, no more than a sip or two, of an evening with Billy – as far as he, Billy knows, anyway – doesn't smoke, doesn't swear, doesn't whore or engage in any other vice that is obvious. His family, his church and, most importantly, this hospital are the extent of Dr Rideout's interests. The guiding force in the doctor's life is the work of helping others, as best he can, which, to all appearances, makes Agamemnon Rideout happy. Dr Rideout is a serious man, but there's usually the glint of a smile in his eyes. Endlessly patient, calm, gentle, he's almost a caricature of what a doctor should be, really, Billy thinks. Strange that he and Sol – loud-mouthed, drunken, impatient Sol, and that's the way he was, *then*; Billy's heard rumors from up at Butte as to what, who, Sol is now, and none of it sounds good – strange that the two brothers, brought up together, are so different. They have different fathers, so maybe there's some kind of truth in blood that mattered more than how you were raised or what your name was or wasn't. Although, it is true that Sol, like Dr Rideout, has, or at least had, that thing about him that made him take others under his wing. The boys in the crew, Billy himself, certainly, gathered in by the man that Sol was, looked after as best he could. So maybe Sol and his brother weren't too different after all, at least once.

He hands Dr Rideout the cigarette, gives him a light. There's a long inhale, a pause, and then a hacking, racking cough.

"Good God, that's awful," Dr Rideout says, when he can breathe again. He passes the cigarette back to Billy. "Every once in a while I feel the need to try to smoke again, see if there's something I'm missing about the process. You'd think I'd be smarter about it, by now, because every time it's just as terrible as the last. Good God." He shakes his head, spitting discreetly to the side.

"Live and learn, Doctor."

"Live and learn." There's a long pause and then Dr Rideout says, "Bad thing today, Bill."

Billy sighs. Here it is, then. "Yeah, a bad thing. I'm sorry, sir."

"Sam James can go fuck himself, Billy. He won't ever be back here, that's for certain."

Billy wouldn't have been more shocked if one of the cows had come up and started declaiming Shakespeare. Dr Rideout almost never cursed, and certainly nothing saltier than the occasional *damn*. He glances over, can see that the doctor is seething, rims of his nostrils round and white in his reddened face.

"Miss Summers was in the hallway, Bill, saw the whole thing. I don't like to say it, but I'll just admit, now: I wish you'd done more, even, because Miss Summers went on to imply that James has been, well, *bothering* some of the women. You know what I mean. Why didn't the silly woman say something before now? Do I have to have you break tables over all of the employees' heads? Just in case? Good God, Billy." Dr Rideout stands up, takes a few purposeful steps one way, another, before returning to his seat, somewhat anticlimactically.

Billy feels a stab of guilt for suspecting the same thing about James and not mentioning it to Dr Rideout. He should have said something from the get-go, same as Becky Summers should have. If he'd been wrong, so be it, but the Doctor should have known. Either way, it didn't make what Billy had done in front of poor Elizabeth any better, though.

"How's Mrs Parker, Bill?"

"Ah, she'll be all right, I guess. Just a bit riled up, confused. You know."

"That poor woman. She gets so much worse when the weather gets hot, you notice that? Every summer. Sometimes I wonder ..." He trails off, and they're quiet again.

"I ever tell you just how hard my brother had to work to land that girl?" Dr Rideout says, eventually. "It was really a bit pathetic. She wouldn't give him the time of day at first, which did nothing but make him more determined. If you knew my brother, you'd see the humor in that, let me tell you. Drove him absolutely crazy that she didn't fancy him. I guess in the end he just wore her down." He sighs. "And look how that turned out."

Oh, I know your brother, Billy's thinking, *knew him, anyway, and it doesn't surprise me a bit, hearing that*. The Sol he knew was never one to let something come between him and a thing he wanted.

"You ever wonder, Bill, how things might have turned out in your life if you'd just made a different choice, done something else, maybe, once upon a time? What you'd do if you could take another shot at it, knowing what you do now? You ever want to just start over?" He sounds sad.

Billy doesn't know if Dr Rideout is still talking about

Sol, or maybe about himself, some lost, lingering regret, maybe, an opportunity missed, a girl left waiting, something that aches in the quiet hours. It wouldn't do to lecture the doctor, but Billy wants to tell him that the life we have is the one we get and, no matter how you might want to try it, changing it up is most likely just going to come to grief. One way or another, if his own experience is anything to go by.

Life is just a series of things that you have to get through. Make the best of it that you can. Billy understands that more and more, as each year passes.

He never wants to see his uncle again.

They watch the sun finish setting. Listen to the clicking of bats and the soft hoot of a barn owl, hunting.

6.

"Goddamn it, get your hands up, Nancy."

Sol reaches forward, grabbing the boy's wrists, lifting them closer together and raising them a few inches. Turns them inward some, lining up the fists where they need to be. "Here, like this," he says, tapping the top knuckle of one of Nancy's thumbs. "See how this knuckle points right at that opposite shoulder? That's where you want to be throwing from. Keep your hands lined up like that." He leans down, slapping at the kid's front leg until he pulls it in a little. "And goddamn it, quit sprawling your leg out like that. You can't punch if you're standing there like you're trying to step over a big puddle."

"Sorry, Mr Parker." Nancy turns his head, then murmurs something else into his shoulder.

"That you said?"

The boy won't meet his eyes, just mumbles, "Don't like being called that, Mr Parker. Nancy. I ain't no fairy."

"What? Of course you are, son. And no one's business but your own, that. Now come on, hands up and let's see what you can do to this bag." Sol steps behind the big gunnysack filled with sand, which hangs from a beam in the warehouse he's using to skim a quick veneer of pugilism onto Nancy. Who, if anything, is even more hopeless as a boxer than he remembers. That training hadn't quite taken, first time around, but maybe he'll be better now, catching him young like this. At least the boy is still huge, and hopefully just as tough as before. Sol leans his shoulder into the back of the bag and waits for a punch, but Nancy just stands there, hands dropping to his side.

"I ain't no fairy, Mr Parker. Drunk is all I was. Just fuckin drunk." Nancy's head sags.

Oh Christ. Sol steps out from the bag, reaching a hand up to Nancy's shoulder and giving it a squeeze. "Son," he says, "don't much matter if you're queer or not. Thing is, people are going to think that about you now. If it was a mistake, well, it's been made, and you got caught at it, more's the pity. You ain't the first boy to get liquor in him and take a pleasure that ain't quite the usual. Hell, I knew a man once got caught with a horse. And you know what they say about them Basques down Boise way, the shepherds. Lonesome, right? Just like you Irish." He gets half a quick grin, maybe. "But son, if you've got inclinations that aren't necessarily towards women, that's your own business, just like I said. You don't let no one tell you how to live your life, OK? Maybe it was a mistake or maybe it's a phase or maybe that's just the way you are. Life is fucking hard enough, so why quibble over shit like that? You keep your chin up, hey?"

Nancy nods, back to looking miserable. The boy already knows, Sol can see, knows that he's different. World isn't kind to those who are different, after all. Sol wonders at what point Nancy came to terms with it all, before, because this conversation had sure never happened, first time around. Maybe there'd been someone standing in, playing Sol's part, or maybe Nancy had just figured it out on his own. But Sol doesn't want to think about that first time, before, any of it. Not this, not the rest of it. Didn't happen, didn't matter. Just focus on the here and the now and get this boy to the point where at least the punters will take a chance on him. Make some money.

Sol gives him a slap on the arm. Much as he doesn't like it, doesn't want the reminder, it's comfortable, though, being around Nancy again, callow as this one is. "OK, kid, now listen: I want those punches to land hard, hard, *hard.* Big as you are, you're never going to be quick, so you need to make your punches count. Man told me once that every punch had to land with the weight of a baby dropped off a building. So you think about that when you're dropping those big hambones of yours: baby falling off a goddamn building. *Bam.* OK?"

"That's a awful thought, Mr Parker."

"Goddamn it, son, you know what I mean." Sol steps back behind the bag, snugging his shoulder and ribs against it to keep it still. "Now fucking hit me like you mean it, Nancy."

"Kid looked good tonight, Sol," Sean says, pouring them both generous shots of whiskey from the bottle he keeps in the drawer in his desk. "*Sláinte.*"

"Cheers, Sean." They knock the glasses back and Sean refills. "But were you watching the same fight I was, tonight? That boy is terrible, can't box a goddamn bit. All he did was stand there and soak up that old rummy's fists until he got lucky and dropped a haymaker. Come on, Sean, bullshit."

Sean shrugs. The big poof was no boxer, for sure, but at least he'd won tonight's fight. He'd been knocked right out of his first fight not a minute into it, dropped his guard and caught a cross to the chin, out like a light, and from a man more than twice his age. But still, the kid was huge and had shown he knew how to take some punches. If he could be taught to keep himself covered he'd do all right. Men always liked to bet on the big boys. They'd get the kid into some more fights and maybe he'd make them some money; if not, well, there were ways to encourage that. The fight business was just a hobby anyway, these days. It reminded Sean of his youth, the brutal affairs they'd put on in Dublin, where men would half-kill one another – if not finish the job by accident from time to time – in the squalid little holes where he'd come up.

Looking around his office, Sean knows full well where the *real* money is: sucked straight from the Company's tit rather than peeled away dollar by dollar from the lowliest of their employees. Still, though, he loves the spectacle of the fight, the sounds and smells of it. Maybe at heart he's still just a Dublin gutter rat in a nice suit.

Thinking of money reminds him. He reaches into his jacket and removes an envelope, tossing it on the desk in front of Sol, just far enough away that he has to reach for it.

Sol takes the envelope, hefting it in his hand appraisingly, frowning. He opens it, riffles the stack of bills inside with a thumb, the frown deepening. "Bit light, hey?"

Sean shrugs again, knocks back his whiskey and refills the glasses once again. "Business has been a bit light, hasn't it?"

"Jesus Christ, Sean, no, it *ain't* light. You know the take from my places just as well as I do, and my places are solid."

"Hey now! I won't have it with the blasphemy. You fuckin well know that."

Oh Jesus fucking Christ's hairy ass, Sol thinks. *By the sweating balls of the Virgin fucking Mary, go fuck yourself, Sean.* His employer likes to pull this bullshit from time to time, play the devout, aggrieved Catholic, Mass every morning, saints' days, all that. Sean is about as devout as Sol is – not at all – and probably hasn't seen the inside of a church since he'd last robbed one. It's just another in the series of constant, aggravating tests Sean puts his underlings to, more fucking bullshit to illustrate just who the boss is and who is the goddamn servant. The higher up Sol's gone in the enterprise, the more he's been tested until, now, damn near every little thing had to have some jab in it. Same as Sol does with Mickey, he supposes, but it fucking rankles, this way of doing things. That's the way of the world, though, isn't it? The strong and the weak. There's always someone stronger than you out there.

But this light fucking envelope. Sean damn well knows every penny that comes in and goes out of his places, knows that those Sol minds are as profitable as ever, more so. But what is Sol going to say? Call Sean a liar, a thief? That's exactly what he is, but Sol can't say a goddamn thing, but just scoop up his meager earnings and thank the master for his generosity.

Sol looks around the office, willing his teeth to unclench and his heart to slow. Sean isn't any smarter than he is; a bit more of a bastard maybe, but Sol can likely hold his own there, any more, after plenty of practice. Wasn't no reason why Sean was the only one who should be sitting there like that, grinning like a cat with a broke-winged bird under his paw. Wasn't no reason that Sol shouldn't be on *that* side of the desk, with a string of businesses and properties and a bank account the size of a fucking barn. He meets Sean's eyes, holds that smiling gaze as long as he can. Uncomfortably, he's reminded of Billy's old Indian uncle, just then, that flat black look that hits you with weight. Eyes like dead babies. There's always someone stronger, isn't there.

"Problem, Sol?"

You bet there's a fucking problem, Sean. "Nah," he says. "And yeah, guess maybe business has been a bit light, lately. I'll get it turned around, hey?" He swallows something hot and bitter, keeping his face as placid as he can.

Sean winks, pours them another shot.

7.

Things at the hospital have finally settled into something of a relaxed rhythm, lately. The weather has cooled off some, though it's bound to turn again; the break in the heat has made Billy's work easier, the patients seem a shade calmer, hell, even the cows seem to be shitting a little less. It's almost pleasant being at the place, some days. Sometimes it seems more like a slightly gone-to-seed hotel, with the garden in bloom and the flowerpots full, men and women idling away the hours in rockers on the big veranda. If you don't look too close, see the crazy eyes and wild hair, the piss-stained pajamas. If you don't listen to the muttering and occasional weeping, Warm Springs could pass as something other than a lunatic hospital, on these cooler summer days, the sky huge, blue as a robin's egg, clouds like fat sheep grazing lazily overhead.

And then Bad Bird runs off. One day to the next, vanished. Poof, gone. That old goddamn bastard is nowhere to be seen, and Billy is the one who has to go find him.

"Be quick about it, Bill," Dr Rideout says, a severe, fatherly hand on Billy's shoulder. "It doesn't look good for us, having patients just strolling away like that. I know it's not your fault but, still, it doesn't look good at all. We're supposed to be looking after these people, keeping them safe." *Keeping the community safe*, is the unspoken addendum to that. Some of their patients were dangerous. Bad Bird, well, enough said. "It's not your fault, Bill," Dr Rideout says again, frowning, "it's our shared responsibility, all of us."

Yeah, it's not my fault, Billy thinks, *not my goddamn fault at all. I don't even want to* be *here any more. I'm trying to work up the sand to quit this place, and then this happens. Damn sure won't be able to quit for a while, after this, now, not in good conscience. Goddamn it.*

His father is just one old man, though, right? He can't have gotten far and there's one place he's going to be headed: back to the reservation, back to his little shithole cabin. Like a badger to his den. He won't have gotten too far.

It takes Billy most of two days to make it back to the reservation on the old horse he's borrowed, two days where he's expected to come across Bad Bird every minute and instead comes up with nothing. He doesn't fool himself: he's no tracker, not some old chief wily with woodcraft, who can glance at the ground and immediately know who passed, when, and what they'd had for breakfast. But, shit, there are fucking roads right up to the rez and he can't imagine that his old father – who *is* one of those old chiefs, but he's also lazy – would have elected to skip cross-country when there's a nice, easy path to where he's going, where he can maybe even beg a ride from some passerby. It's been an irksome couple of days ambling along on this swaybacked, stumble-stepping horse not far away from the glueyard, playing Injun. *Him go-um that way.* That goddamn old bastard of a father of his.

It's late on the second day when he reaches the cabin, his ass and lower back screaming from the unaccustomed effort of riding, particularly on a broken-gaited horse like this old nag. From a distance he can see a light in the one window, which hangs oblong and out of true in the wall. The whole place looks like a good fart would tear it down, the walls rough-boarded and splintery, grey with age, the entire structure listing to several angles at once. Billy is hot, tired, greasy faced and irritable; he just wants to round up the old fucker and, after a night of sleep, start making the long way back.

What the hell was Bad Bird thinking, anyway? He wasn't in the hospital voluntarily: Billy had filed the papers, got the signatures, put his father away for the man's own good, after that last fracas when he'd nearly stabbed the census taker come to count him. He's lucky he wasn't in jail. But who knew just how much Bad Bird understands these things, even lucid; he's the product of another time and the white man's ways – The White Man's Ways, Billy hears, those implied, ponderous capitals whenever his father says something like that: The White Man's Police, The White Man's Money, that kind of thing – he's the product of another time and probably just assumes that if his own two feet will let him go somewhere, he can follow them. Even after years of reservation living, Bad Bird still thinks himself a free man. Billy doesn't know if that's admirable or not.

Right now it's fucking irritating, though, deeply, truly irritating and, as he loosely ties the horse to the post in front of the house, promising to come back in a minute to get the saddle off and rub him down, Billy is composing his aggravation into something akin to a coherent speech, translating it laboriously into the old tongue to lend it some weight to his father's ears. With a bowlegged, sore-assed limp, he walks up the couple of porch stairs that are angled like bad teeth, and pushes himself through the door. "Father…"

"Sagiistoo." Marked Face smiles back at him from where he lounges on the frayed, stained cot that serves as Bad Bird's bed. He raises an old, worn bag made out of a bison's scrotum. "Tobacco, Nephew?"

There's a long and slow moment as Billy tries to pull back in the breath that's gone out of his chest. Marked Face here like this, just like that, after all these years, after all that his uncle has done, twisting and folding Billy's world up into something that's almost unrecognizable now. He hears his father's words.

Now I will tell you about Marked Face.

He hasn't seen his uncle since the diner in Butte, years ago, years from now. A very different life from now. Bad Bird had just shaken his head, when asked. *He'll turn up, in his own time,* the old man said, *he always does.* Looking at his uncle now, the things his father has told him about the man don't seem real, even though he knows them to be true. Marked Face just looks like any other old Indian, Billy's own fear of him notwithstanding: white-haired, weatherbeaten, shabby. But that look in his eyes, the feeling of presence, that can't be ignored either. Particularly given what Billy knows now, about the terrible things his uncle did, to get his medicine. The things that crouch behind those dead, smiling eyes.

When we were boys, Sagiistoo, Bad Bird had said, falling into the sing-song chant he used when telling stories, *the People were still strong and the whites few on the ground. This was before their big war, and there were not many of them, in those days: there were the trappers and the traders, some occasional passers-by. But then that gold was found by the water to the west, and more and more of them came. They crossed our lands with impunity, they hunted our game. Sometimes they shot at us with their rifles, raped our women from time to time. And it wasn't always rape, because the traders brought whiskey with them and, in many of our kin, a powerful thirst was kindled, such that they would trade their women for a time – or the women would trade themselves – for that medicine water.*

And it got worse, and worse, and worse.

Seeing the force arrayed against us, most of our chiefs counseled patience, diplomacy, but some of us, like my brother – and, for a time, myself – wanted to drive all of the whites out of our lands, kill every one we encountered, in terrible ways, to dissuade others from coming. The old men – who were more like old women, we thought – these old men were merely afraid. They were dried out and used up by their years, but we, the young and the strong, we would drive these intruders back whence they came, with the force of our own arms. And so we tried: we attacked any group of whites we could find, provided they were in small enough numbers. We killed some of the traders and trappers who had become our friends, betrayed their trust and cut them down, knowing that, because they were of the whites – that empty, hollow, hungry race from the stories – they would eventually betray us too, so best we do so first.

It was a terrible time.

We killed men. Women. Babes at the breast. We roasted them on fires, we sliced off the men's stones, we gave them the slow, cutting death, making it last as long as we could. It sickened me, but I joined in this because I thought it was the right thing to do.

But we were fighting a losing fight, and we knew it. Even then, we knew, in our dark, nighttime thoughts. The whites were simply too strong, with their long guns, with their sickness, and the numbers that only increased, no matter how many of them we killed. Even more of the chiefs began to counsel appeasement, compromise, giving up our rights to the land where we had lived for a thousand thousand years, letting our deer and our bison fall to the bullets of the whites. Our women went hungry, our babies died, so that the whites could find their gold, take our hunting and then our land.

But you know all this. You know it. These are the sad stories we tell now, when the older stories have been forgotten. These have become the true stories of the People.

Listen, though, and I will tell you how my brother got his medicine.

Marked Face was a handsome man in his youth. Forget the scar, forget the white hair and age and you can see it, even now. He was handsome, he was strong, fierce in the fight; my brother was the kind of young man the rest of us aspired to be like, in those days of hopeless war. And, because he was the man he was, he took for his first wife the most beautiful girl in our band, maybe the most beautiful of all the People. Dove was tall, like a pine, slender like a cat-tail, curved as, well, I am no poet. Just know that she was lovely. Men's heads would turn when she walked by, their voices go quiet. That was the power of her. She was graceful, humble, all that a man of the People could want. Her father was of lowly station but a good man, proud and protective of his daughter; still, he was honored when Marked Face bartered for her hand, and accepted the overly-gracious gifts my brother made for her. She, for her part, saw my brother's handsomeness, his fierceness, the honors that were accruing to him, and she welcomed him, whispering to her father to make the compact.

So it was: my brother, possibly the best of the young men, took the most desirable of our young women to wife. Soon enough, she was fat with a son. As it should be.

But my brother, ah, my brother was seething inside, all this time. Even then, newly wed to a beautiful girl of sixteen *summers, what should have been at least a brief spell of happiness, he was possessed by thoughts of the whites. We all were, all of us, by the callousness of that greedy people, by the insult to our lands and our way of life. But, in my brother, it had become a madness, bringing him to a dark place in his soul and then back again, to us. He left our band, without a word, merely going absent one morning; for many weeks, he was gone, seeking something he'd seen in those black dreams, leaving a young wife growing large with child. We said that he'd had a medicine dream, that he was bringing back something that would help us against the whites.*

Oh, but we were wrong.

The brother that came back from that vision quest was not the brother who had left. Like Siinatssi from the stories, who had died and come back from the Other Lands a mad, broken man, so had my brother Marked Face, though we didn't see it then. "Brother, I have found a strong medicine," *he said to me, taking me aside soon after his return.* "I have found that which I sought. I have been tested and deemed worthy and, now, the Above Ones have shown me what I must do."

Would that then, I had left our band, gone to the great water – anywhere, really – so that I would not have seen what I saw next, after my brother had left camp once more.

We found him, Marked Face, days later. Several of us were hunting, seeking what meager game the whites had left us, and we found him, his face smeared with her blood.

We only knew that it was Dove because she had been gone for a few days. "She's with her husband," *we'd said,* "making up for lost time." *Nudging each other, winking, thinking of her slender, curving form, wishing that we had caught her instead of lucky Marked Face. Now, what was left of that beautiful girl was little: her body had been butchered like a deer. From a nearby tree hung a haunch of her leg, along with*

*some unidentifiable portions. In one of the iron pots gotten from
a white trader, a stew of long bones bubbled over a low fire. But,
ah, the bones that Marked Face held to his lips then, they were
too small to be those of his wife. Not even her fingers, her toes,
the delicate lines of her ribs. Those bones were so small.*

*My brother tied one, well chewed, into his hair as we
approached, our mouths open and the sickness rising from our
bellies.*

*"Brothers," Marked Face said then, smiling as he swallowed
another mouthful of his son,* "I have found my medicine."

"Something to eat, Nephew?" Marked Face is saying,
jutting his chin to the rusty woodstove, the small bones
in his braids chittering against each other. On the stove,
a sauce-pot bubbles, giving off the wet coppery fragrance
of meat and blood and fat. He pats his belly. "I'm full,
myself, but there is plenty more there. Help yourself. Dig
in, boy, you look like you need it."

"Where is my father?" Billy says.

8.

"Get your fucking hands up, Nancy!"

Sol is rubbing the boy's shoulders, trying to loosen those huge flat slabs of muscle some. Nancy punches so wrong that he works everything too hard. The power should flow easily upwards and outwards from his plant foot, like he and Faraday had tried to teach him. Instead it just winds up as loosely flapped arm-punches, Nancy relying on the weight of his big hands and his considerable muscle to give it the requisite oomph. Artistic, it isn't. Sol has tried again and again, as has Faraday, to give Nancy at least the rudiments of form, make it a little easier on him, save him some lumps and soreness, add a bit of art to that muscle, but the boy is hopeless.

Not that it matters, though, tonight: this is a bullshit fight, pure and simple. It's fucking Nick Faraday himself, across the little ring, sitting on a stool of his own while fat Mickey Doyle rubs his shoulders. Faraday is thick-witted and his punches are soft but he knows something of the art of boxing, even Sol has to admit it. Nick's a pure technician: he doesn't have much in the way of strength or smarts but he knows these skills, somehow. One of those idiot savants, maybe, although with most things the savant part is sorely lacking.

"Listen, you got to get them up," he says, "your hands, otherwise you're going to get hurt."

"OK, Mr Parker, I'll try," Nancy says, wheezing air in. "I'll try."

"Fighters, one minute!" Pat O'Toole – that useless tosser – hollers out, with something approaching authority. Drunken deadbeat is what he is. Judge of a bullshit fight the limit of his abilities.

"Fuck are you doing, lad?" Sean Harrity is leaning in now, hissing in Nancy's ear so loud that Sol can hear it, even if Sean's eyes weren't pinioning his own just then. "Make this fuckin shit look right, hey? Don't just fuckin *stand there*, faggot." Sean stands up, fixes Sol with a look that makes the prior version seem like courting eyes, damp and loving and full of promise. "And Jesus fuck, Sol, *get your fuckin man sorted*. Or I'll fuckin sort him for you, right? There's money riding on this fuckin fight."

Yeah, there's money, Sean. A whole passel of stupid shits, too dumb to see what's there in front of their faces, will be putting that Friday paycheck in your pocket. That fucking Friday paycheck that I see fuck-all of, even though I'm the one that's doing most the work while you're up in your fancy office, smoking good cigars, drinking old whiskey and sucking Company cock. Don't tell me how to do my fucking job, you sheep-shagging Irish piece of shit.

"Yeah, Sean," he says, blandly. "We're on it. Eamonn here's just getting warmed up. Hey, Nance?" He gives the boy a slap on the shoulders, following it up with another deep squeeze of those thick, triangular muscles, and leans in towards Nancy's ear. "One more round and then down. Down in the third. Like we talked about, yeah? But Sean's right, Nance," he says, louder, looking up again, "maybe show a bit more life out there, kid. Don't let ol' Faraday just pat you around the whole round. Need to make this look square."

"Fuckin third, lad," Sean says with another flat look, before turning back to Sol. "Fuckin third, Sol. Jesus fuck, *do your job*. Fuckin third."

"Yeah, yeah, third, Sean. Third, I get it. Ain't like I never done this before." Sol gives Nancy another squeeze of the shoulders as that witless Irish bastard O'Toole yells out *Fighters!*

"Come on, Pat! That's a goddamn foul, son!" It's mostly lost in the collective, sympathetic male groan after Faraday's fist finds Nancy's crotch, doubling the boy over like a boiled shrimp. There's a long, loose second where it looks like Nancy is just going to drop, hands clenched over his balls, eyes rolled back in his head, but then he straightens up a bit, just in time to catch Nick Faraday's forehead with the bridge of his nose. Cue another groan from the crowd, melding with shouts of outrage this time.

The fuck, Nick?

Here it is again, Sol thinks. Another of those gold-panned moments, the color of prior experiences settling out from the gravel of whatever this life is. Fires, fights, fuck-ups. The lot of it. Nothing is ever easy, is it? No matter how many times he runs through things, it happens more or less the same way. The players may shift position, play different parts and have different names, but they're all reading the same fucking script, aren't they? It might look a little different from one time to the next but, really, just pick up the book and read your lines, whatever they are, this time around. Doesn't much matter what your part of the story is, because it all shakes out in the end.

OK, so maybe Nancy cut loose a bit more vigorously

than the situation warranted, at the beginning of the round, chiming Faraday's head with a surprising combination of heavy crosses but, if anything, Sean himself can be blamed for that. *Make this fucking shit look right. Don't just stand there.* Nancy is just a kid and has nothing in the way of subtlety, not now, anyway, if he ever really did last time, so maybe he got a bit excited at the start of the round and dinged up Faraday more than was actually needed. But Nick Faraday is a tough man, this Sol knows, no worse for wear after a couple three of those errant punches, so just settle the fuck down, Nicky.

But Faraday also has a flaming temper and no real way of easily stopping it once it gets burning so, now, he's bashing poor Nancy's balls in and trying to stave in the boy's face with a forehead. Just because Nancy had landed a punch or two. Jesus, Nick, it's a fucking *fight*, regardless of its inherently bullshit, dishonest nature; it's fucking *fixed*, so calm the hell down, you dumb shit, before you hurt the kid.

"Goddamn it, Pat! Are you just going to fucking stand there? *That's a foul!*"

"Shut your hole, Sol Parker, and let the boys fight." Pat gives him a look like he's a piece of dogshit scraped from a shoe. *That's going to get paid for, Pat,* Sol thinks, clenching a fist until his knuckles hurt. *Talk to me like that? That look? May be a while, but that'll get paid for.*

Sol is so furious with Pat O'Toole that his attention is diverted and he almost doesn't even see the long, looping, heavy hay-maker that cracks into Faraday's skull. Like a baby dropped from a building, that one – finally, but *now?* – then Faraday is down.

Sol closes his eyes. Pinches the bridge of his nose between a finger and thumb.

• • •

Back in Sean's office, later.

Not the opulent one, the gentlemen's sanctuary. Not the snuggery, the growlery, one of those European words for a fancy room where rich men take their leisure, far from the stink of the unwashed masses. No, now they're in the little shithole of a room behind the Piper, the one that's used for the closer, sharper, more emotional work of Sean's various enterprises. The one with the big shabby desk, the low, penitents' chairs, the suspiciously dark stains in the wood floor. Fat, smug-faced Mickey Doyle looming at their backs like a goddamn low moon squatting on the horizon. Sol can almost feel the press of Mickey's soft belly tickling the hairs on the back of his neck.

Or maybe that's just fear. Sean is pissed off, royally so, but come on, it's not like this is a firing offense. Firing, a euphemism, but still. Sean's gotten where he is by mastering his own baser urges, when the situation requires it, and Sol is a vital part of this enterprise. One of the most vital, if Sol is giving himself his due. Second man, all that. Responsibility. His ass is in for some chewing, that's for a certain, and his pocket will be lighter by the end, so best just get on with it. He's fucked up, plain and simple. Well, Nancy fucked up, but accidents happen, all right? Accidents happen and they'd make it right. First, though: first the theater.

Sean brings out a bottle of good whiskey from the drawer of his desk, makes a show of pouring himself a shot. He knocks it back, refills, and then puts the bottle away, shutting the drawer with finality. *Oh you cheap, petty fuck,* Sol thinks, eyes on the glass. *You wretched Irish bastard.*

"What'd I tell you, Sol," Sean says, lazily almost, his eyes not leaving Nancy, who's sitting, slump-shouldered, head down, miserably staring at his hands in his lap, the knuckles bruised and swollen, fingers twisted into a nervous tangle. It's even more pitiful a posture in such a big man, young as he is, too. Sol reaches over, gives Nancy a brief squeeze of the knee. *Don't worry about it, son*, that squeeze says, best as Sol can manage it. *You'll be OK. It wasn't your fault. I've got this.*

Sol looks at his employer. *I don't know, Sean,* he thinks. *You've told me lots of stupid shit over the years, haven't you now.* "Told me I needed to do my job, Sean. Told me third round, Nancy goes down," is what he says, though, mustering a tone of voice that has as much of the semblance of contrition as he can scrape up, just then. *But fuck you.* "Accident, though, all it was."

"Accident, hey?" The eyes lift from Nancy, swing his way, sharp on the inside. Sean's nostrils are flared, sure sign that he's working himself up into one of his posturing rages, the chest-beating horseshit that serves to reiterate *I'm the boss.* Been a lot of that lately, more than Sol really cares for, but what can he do. Sean *is* the boss, much as it chafes, times like this. Wasn't necessary for the man to do all this drama, put Sol back in his place, but there wasn't much to be done about it. *Let's just get on with it*, he thinks again.

"Accident, Sean. Boy's still learning, after all."

"Learning, is it?"

What are you, a fucking parrot? "Yeah, he's learning, Sean. I told you, it won't happen again."

"I lost money on this fight, because of your learner here."

"And I'll make it good."

"Oh, you'll make it good."

"Jesus, Sean, I said I'll make it good. You should know that by now."

"The fuck is that supposed to mean?"

Oh sweet Christ is this necessary? "It *means*, Sean, that I'll make it right. Pretty straightforward, really."

"Taking a tone with me now?"

Sol stills the anger in his chest, keeps his teeth from clenching. He's been through worse than this, he's learned control. None of this matters, anyway, not a lick of it. The things he's seen and done and seen and done again. Sean Harrity doesn't fucking matter, now or ever. It's a solid, smooth and slippery life Sol's learned to lead, by now – over-learned, maybe, with these unnatural years added and re-added to his total, a thing he doesn't like to think of – a life where nothing is able to grab hold of him and hang on, pull him down. This moment, now, is just one more thing trying to claim him but it won't, same as the rest, the good or the bad. Who knows if this moment will come back again, after all, in one way or another. Sol might dream poorly of a night, but this mode of being is a surprisingly liberating way to go through his days, really, skipping across the surface of things like a stone chucked flat at a pond. Solid, smooth, slippery.

He's calm again now, his jaw loose. Sean's just another actor, playing his role. Best just to get on with it. "Course not, Sean. I just want to make this right. I made a mistake, and I'll get it sorted, me and Big Nancy here. It's my responsibility, and I'll make it right. Like I always have."

"Like you always have." *Parrot, again.* "Seems like I hear a lot of those words, these days, from you. I appreciate that, though, Sol, I do. You're a good man." Sean opens the drawer again, pulls out the bottle of whiskey, setting two more glasses down on the desktop. He fills them, refills his own. "Here now," he says. "Let's all have a drink. We've had a disagreement, and maybe I got a little hot, but that's that. You're going to make things right, and that's that. Drink up, boys."

Nancy hasn't even had the chance to look up and reach for his glass before Mickey loops the belt around his neck.

Just pay it no mind, it doesn't matter. Sol stares straight ahead at the whiskey in front of him, trying to draw it into the full scope of his consciousness, blocking everything else out. Nancy's kicking and thrashing next to him, the panicked gasps, Mickey's strained, groaning grunts as he heaves his bulk backward, trying to use the leverage, the thick, narrow leather of the belt cutting into Nancy's throat. The boy's fingers are frantically grabbling at it, trying to get some purchase and dig it out of his flesh. Mickey's good with that belt, though. Sol's seen it before.

"Sol, I worry that you're not giving the job the entire amount of your attention, lately," Sean is saying, ignoring what's transpiring in front of him. "You're getting a wee bit sloppy, maybe, some would think. Your poof there had made his own side bets on tonight, did you know that? Fucked us, tried to anyway. Stood to collect a nice little payday from that little 'accident' of yours. Tried to right fuck us."

Bullshit, Sol thinks. *Nancy doesn't have that in him. Doesn't have the gumption, even if he had the savvy to do so. Where did you hear this? Mickey, maybe? That's a possibility and, if he finds out that's the case, there's going to be a reckoning for that fat fucker. A fucking reckoning, let that be said. Or maybe Sean has just made it up himself because, after all, this is just another lesson, now, isn't it? Sean Harrity, showing his underlings how it is, at the expense of one big, dumb kid. Don't make mistakes, boys and, whatever you do, don't think you can put anything past me. Sean Harrity, the all-seeing, all-knowing. Big men are a dime a dozen, after all, town like this, so who cares as to the truth of the matter at hand. Wrong place, wrong time, all that. Sorry, lad. There are always more men at the bottom.*

"This is an unpleasantness," Sean waves a vague hand, "but I'm thinking, Sol, that you needed a reminder, maybe. To pay more attention, like. Because, if this has slipped past you, what else has? And if it *didn't* just slip past you then, well, we have another problem, don't we. But I don't believe that, not for a second, Sol. I trust you. We've done a lot of good work together, and I trust you."

Yeah, you fucking trust me, Sean. Same as you trust everyone, trust them just enough to put the knife in when their back is turned. Don't worry, this won't get forgotten, Sean. The lesson is learned and will be paid for. Won't be today, won't be next week, but this will get paid. Same like Pat, like Mickey, a reckoning. There will be restitution for this.

Sol's ledger of wrongs grows longer by the day. Just because things didn't matter doesn't mean they could be forgotten. Seemed like, any more, it's the wrongs, the slights, that are the only thing Sol lets cling to him. Wasn't always this way, but that's the way it is now.

"Let's have that drink, Sol, hey? This will be done, soon enough. Let's just put this behind us. Focus on the future. The past is dead, Sol." Sean reaches forward, raises his glass.

Sol tries to ignore Nancy's weakening kicks as the life drains out of him. It's a real shame, and he's sorry, but none of this matters anyway, he repeats to himself. Weights it with repetition. Makes it convincing. None of it matters. The past is dead, just like Sean said, and it's all a fucking illusion, this whole sorry world. Sol doesn't want it to be this way, but there it is, so best not dwell on it. Maybe the next time will be better. If there is a next time, but who knows. Maybe he's living his life just waiting for it to start over. A life free of consequence.

He picks up his glass, keeping his head cocked away from Nancy, who is whimpering a thin wheeze now. Sol stares at the whiskey, admires the oily amber slick of it, the way it clings to the side of the glass when he tilts it. At least the pleasure of a good drink is a constant. One of those shining flecks of gold. He nods at Sean and brings the glass to his lips, savoring the hot astringent burn of the fine malt. Holds it in his mouth for a moment before letting it slide its fiery way down his throat. Sol closes his eyes with satisfaction, and can't help but think about the shape of the boy's lips as they tried to gasp out his name, can't help but remember it. He knows that it's one more thing that's going to stick with him, much as he'll try to shrug it off, like all the rest of it. One of many things to wake him up at night, maybe, whether they matter or not.

But, after all, though, his is a life free of consequence, isn't it? Near as he can figure things, anyway. And that's Nancy strangling next to him, *Nancy*. He owes the boy, from before. Owes him. Sol lets the anger come back – it's never far away, lately – and it burns like fine whiskey.

Maybe today is a good day for restitution after all.

And, really, what's the worst that can happen? When there are no real consequences, what's the worst?

The back of his chair hits the wall as he jumps upward, awkward in the room's tight space. The thick, heavy glass cracks into two big pieces as Sol slams it into Mickey's face, badly cutting his own palm in the process, liquor burning into the wound. One of the pieces is driven into Mickey's eye and he releases the belt around Nancy's neck with a cry, putting his hands to his head, falling backward.

Even in the moment, Sol is unpleasantly reminded of cutting Billy. Maybe Billy is living an image of this life, himself. What part is he reading, this time around? Still the victim? Or maybe Billy's breaking a man down like this, this time. Maybe he'll come for Sol at some point. Come to make things right, his own form of restitution.

Before Mickey has even hit the ground, Sol is moving, trying to get around the slow bulk of Nancy and over the desk to Sean. If there's anything Sol has learned over the years, it's that it's best to *act* when you act, quickly and to the point. Once you start a thing like this, it needs to be finished, fast as you can: doesn't matter how it's done, just finish it.

Sean's eyes are wide with surprise – comically so, really – and his jaw sags open although, when Sean's hand comes up with a pistol in it, a bit of the humor leaves the situation. Sol is almost past Nancy, bloody hand reaching forward, when the gun goes off. Later, he'll swear that the boy pushed him back, right there at the end.

9.

"*Where is my father?*" Billy says.

"Oh, I expect he's around somewhere, Nephew. I haven't seen him. You are sure you're not hungry?" Marked Face sits up on the cot, the little bones tied into his hair rattling softly. He leans his back against the wall of the cabin, smiling, pointing at the other cot against the opposite wall. "Sit, Sagiistoo, sit. You look tired."

Billy edges near the cot, uneasily. The room is over-hot, stifling, and the smell of the stew is making him sick. He can feel sweat at the small of his back. The cot gives a weary, low squeak as he settles into it.

"Where have you been, Uncle? It's been years."

Marked Face raises a hand, waves it vaguely. "Oh, around. The world is a big place, Nephew. How is my brother?"

"You really haven't seen him?"

The smile bleeds off his uncle's face. "When I say a thing, it is said, boy."

"He's the same, Uncle. Same as before. Back at the hospital, with me. Or he was before he ran off, couple days ago. I was hoping to find him here."

"My brother has always been a crazy one. I expect

he'll turn up. He always has, before."

"Before." It's a word that's become completely inadequate to the task of conveying its meaning.

"Yes, before. When we were young he was prone to go after visions. Our mother was the same, would talk to spirits that only she could see, would do very strange things. One of our uncles was this way too. At first, we thought that maybe Bad Bird was destined to become a great shaman but, really, his thoughts would just go out of his head, from time to time. And then all that we went through with the whites probably cracked him for good. It's a shame because, once, my brother was a good man. Maybe the best of us."

"The best of you."

"There's an echo in this room, maybe. Yes, he was the best of us. He had a beautiful wife. Not your mother, one before. Such a beautiful girl, but she died young. Maybe that hurt my brother's thoughts some, too. She died in a bad way, that girl. I can't even remember her name, now. A bird name."

"Dove." It's out before Billy even thinks it.

"Yes, Dove, that's it. She was a lovely one, Dove. Ah, those were bad times." He shakes his head sadly.

"Father told me that Dove was *your* wife, Uncle. That you killed her, that that's how you got your medicine. That you killed her and ate her. Ate the baby inside her. He told me." Billy is breathing hard. "That's how you got your power. And my father told me how to take it from you, Uncle. He told me how to use it."

For the first time he can remember, Billy sees a look of real surprise on his uncle's face. Gone is the smug sneer, the anger, that flat and watchful distaste that usually roosts there. Marked Face's eyes widen, the brow furrowed, jaw slightly open.

And then he laughs: long, loud, braying laughter, head bumping back against the wall of the cabin. It's disconcerting, to say the least. "*My power?*" Marked Face says once he has control of himself again. He rubs with a knuckle at the tears pooling in the corners of his eyes. "My power, you say?"

The fear is gone now and Billy wants to put a fist in the old man's face. Drop it over and over until his hand breaks, pound that goddamn smile down that old, lying throat. "Yes, your fucking power, Uncle."

Marked Face sits up straight, holding his hands out, palms up. Putting himself on display. "Behold me, then, Nephew. Behold mighty Marked Face, who has to get up a dozen times at night to make water. Behold Marked Face, who has no money, has one change of clothes, who lives in a falling-down shack on a tiny slice of poor government land. Marked Face, scourge of the whites, champion of the People! Marked Face, the powerful, whose prick will not rise any more and whose knees ache always. Behold my *power*!" He starts off laughing again.

It's too much. Billy is up and across the room, fist raised. Before he can bring it down, though, his uncle brings up an arm, quailing, seeing what's coming. With his free hand, Billy grabs Marked Face by his dirty, ratty shirt, pulling him off the cot. He seems to weigh nothing, like a husk. Billy pulls his fist back again, tries to push it forward. But he can't.

Marked Face is just an old man. A tired, rheumy eyed, shabby old man. Something has changed, either in his uncle or inside himself. Something is different.

He lets his uncle go, backing up until the cot hits the backs of his knees. Feeling weak inside, he sags back down to the cot, putting his head in his hands. He doesn't understand anything any more. For a long time, they're both quiet, not looking at each other. Something akin to shame hangs in the air between them, like a stink.

"Let me tell you a thing, Nephew," Marked Face says, finally, softly. He closes his eyes, head resting back against the cabin wall. "Bad Bird was always a storyteller, even as a boy. He knew all our songs, knew some that perhaps he just made up on his own. Maybe this one, about his poor Dove and this supposed power of mine, is one of those. I think maybe those stories got into his head, with his thoughts loose as they were. He was always obsessed with those stories of Maatakssi and his brother Siinatssi, the fathers of the People, too. Maybe he saw something of himself in those stupid Old Ones, saw a power in the world that is no longer there. Wanted to see it, needed it, maybe. He's always said he sees the world as it truly is. But he is broken, my brother, and he is mad. They are just stories."

"We have had our differences, my brother and I, have them still, though I love him and have tried to protect him, as best I could. I always have, even when we fought. I have lived a long time, Sagiistoo. I have maybe not lived a good life and have been cruel at times but, even after my brother gave me this scar, I have tried to protect him." Marked Face taps his cheek and is quiet again. "Ah, poor Dove," he says, finally, breathing out a sigh. "Let me tell you a thing, Sagiistoo, which will maybe help you to understand your father and the rest of it."

He sings:

10.

A short time after he had flown off, Raven returned to broken, eyeless, dying Maatakssi, lying in the dust, tortured and banished from the tribes of the People by his mad brother, Siinatssi. Riding on Raven's back, gripping tight with his many legs, was the one called Nihaat. In the true tongue, his name means Spider. Spider was ancient, old with power, wily and strong. Some say he was one of the Above Ones, cast out to the middle lands for some sin; some merely suspect he was a clever being who learned his medicine on his own. Regardless of who or what he was, Spider was a cunning creature, but one who did things for his own reasons. Truly, Raven must have had a heavy heart that things had reached the point that they had, if he looked to rely on the power of that trickster Nihaat. Rarely did anything come without a steep price, when Spider was involved.

"Here is the one of which I spoke, Nihaat," *Raven said.* "You can see that he's in bad shape. Can your medicine heal him?"

"It is already done," *Spider said, sounding offended that this mangy bird would doubt his ability. He hopped down from Raven's back, perching himself on a stone. Two of his front legs rubbed together in a way that, in a man, would look unseemly.*

But Nihaat was who he was.

Maatakssi was standing on strong legs, seeing the world again through the new eyes that had appeared in his head. "Thank you, noble Nihaat," *he said with his new tongue.* "Thank you for healing me in this way."

"It is nothing," *Spider said, waving one of his long, spindly legs dismissively.* "It is the least I can do for my friend Raven."

"Raven, I thank you as well. Forgive me for ever doubting our friendship." *Maatakssi knelt on the ground, pressing his forehead into the dirt in his shame.* "I will reverence you always; myself only, for I no longer have a People. I no longer have a name, even. I am no one, or anyone, nameless and with no place in this world, but I will reverence you always, noble Raven."

"Oh, get up," *Raven croaked, irritated at the two-leg walker's humility and theatrics.* "The name of a thing is not important and besides, you have a People, but they are sunk into evil ways without you to check the madness of your brother. I have seen it. Listen, now. You may weep to hear it, but you must understand this thing so that, through you, it can be made right. Listen:

"The People have become a terrible thing. A low smoke hangs over their camps, a smoke made from the burning meat and fat of the bodies of the men and women, the old and the children. It has become a place of horrors. Siinatssi has become convinced that he has found great medicine in eating of the flesh of men, that, by doing this, he takes of their strength and the strength of the spirits that cling to their fear, their pain, as they are butchered. Siinatssi thinks this medicine will allow his band to cover the whole Earth, to rule it as he sees fit. So he and his kin kill their own people, without mercy, to get at this flesh. True, there is a power in this, repugnant though it is, but it is as the snake eating its own tail. The circle is closed and, soon enough, Siinatssi and his followers will eat themselves hollow, from the inside, will become nothing but empty, ravenous spirits.

"This, you must stop. Siinatssi and the People are the creations of the Above Ones, children and grandchildren of their friend Old Man. To let them be destroyed in such a way would be a great sin. Many of those folk are my friends, too, and I mourn to see them used in such a way." *Raven looked away at this.*

Maatakssi wept to hear this fate of his People, which had come about in such a short time through the evil of his brother. "But what can I do, Raven? I am one man, with no medicine of my own. How can I stop my brother, Siinatssi?"

Feeling a fear deep in his chest, Raven looked over at Nihaat, who was again rubbing his front legs together in that way of his.

"Maatakssi," *Spider said,* "perhaps I can help you in this thing. As a favor to my friend Raven, who I do not like to see grieve in this way."

"What would be the cost of your help, Spider?" *Maatakssi asked. Even he had heard rumors of Nihaat's bargains.*

"Cost? Pah, there is no cost. I told you, I do this as a favor to Raven, and to stop an evil thing. My own people, the Big-Bellies, would be threatened by this power of your brother, and I must look out for them. We will help each other, you and I. Is that acceptable?" *Maatakssi nodded, but Spider said,* "You must ask for my help, Maatakssi." *This was a condition of Nihaat's medicine, that it must be freely asked for in so many words.*

"You must choose this path or turn from it, Maatakssi," *Raven said.* "To save the People and, in saving them, save your brother Siinatssi, who has used you so poorly, from his own evil, even though the cost may be greater than you can imagine." *He paused and looked away.* "You must decide for yourself."

Maatakssi was silent for a time, weighing his decision. It was tempting to simply go from this place, to make a quiet life elsewhere and leave the People to whatever fate the Above Ones had decreed for them in this world. To let his brother Siinatssi suffer as he had. But, he knew, the People were where they were because of his own sins, so he said, "Nihaat, great one, will you help me to save the People from the evil of my brother?" *Raven, from his perch in a nearby tree, closed his far-seeing eyes, knowing a bit of the future, as he did. It was a terrible bargain he'd made, but it was the only way to help the two-leg walkers that were his friends.*

"Maatakssi, I will help you," *Nihaat said, smiling, and the contract was sealed. What he did, he did for his own reasons.* "Lie down in the dirt now, Maatakssi, and let me stand on your chest." *Maatakssi did so, and Spider hopped down from his rock, onto his chest, where he did a dance that only Nihaat knew, moving his many legs in a particular pattern and singing a medicine song. He danced for long hours, singing as the sun went down and the moon rose, heavy and full. Finally, exhausted, he hopped back up to his rock.* "You may rise, Maatakssi," *he said in a weary voice.*

Raven flew away, croaking something that sounded like weeping.

Maatakssi stood up, but had no sooner made it to his feet than a powerful cramp gripped his guts, forcing him back to his knees with a cry. There was a hot, shooting pain in his belly that folded him over. Gasping and shaking, he vomited and vomited again. Three, four times, more, he gagged up his belly, spitting the mess out in front of him. He was hot, feverish and, before he fell into darkness, he was sure he could see shapes moving in the puddle of sick. White shapes that looked like tiny men and women.

When Maatakssi came to, the sun was high in the sky and a band of slick, naked, white creatures were squatting in the dirt in front of Nihaat, listening attentively to his quiet speech. Maatakssi blinked his eyes to see this. The people looked like men and women, but their skin was pale, their eyes light. They looked like humans who had been washed in some bitter fluid that had stripped the color from them. As one, they stood, bowing their heads for the blessing of Spider, and then they ran off in small groups.

"What have I done?" *Maatakssi asked.* "What are those things?"

Spider was smiling, but he also seemed sad, in his way. He was a changeable creature, powerful though he was. "Maatakssi, I have kept my side of the bargain," *he said.* "Soon enough, your new children will grow strong, and they will stop the evil of your brother, Siinatssi. These new children will spread over the land and learn great medicine, and they will destroy the People. It is the only way to save them from becoming an evil thing. One day, maybe, your People – and mine – will rise again. That I cannot see. But if your brother is left unchecked, they will descend into darkness for all time.

"Maatakssi," *he said then,* "our bargain has concluded. Do not hate me for doing what needed to be done. Do not hate yourself, for this is the way things needed to pass. Raven knew this. Sometimes the Above Ones are cruel, to allow such things to happen, but that is the way of things. They constantly test us, to make us stronger, some say, although others say they do so simply out of boredom. I do not know. But the guilt you feel now will be a reminder of that first sin of yours, the murder of your brother that first time, which set this all in motion. A lesson, for you. Maybe this was always the plan of the

Above Ones. Who knows the minds of gods?"

And, with that, Spider left, and Maatakssi never saw him again.

As Nihaat promised, the whites grew strong and eventually destroyed the People, taking their hunting, driving them from their lands, covering them with sickness until they were barely anything, only a few poor remnants left, by the end. Maatakssi saw this, condemned by the Above Ones to walk the Earth with the People, feeling every child's death, the rape of every woman, every man's drunken tears. This was his fate, until he could end it.

To this day, in the tongue of the Big-Bellies, the word for white men is Nihaat.

11.

Billy feels like he could sleep for days. This room is so hot, airless; his head is throbbing and he feels sick, breathing in the stink of boiling meat. He just wants to rest. Be by himself. Think. He knows what he's seen, what he remembers, Sol and the bets and the fires and the rest of it. The past circling around and again to bring him to this place, now. Like Maatakssi, cursed to live beyond his years. He'd come to terms with it, in a way, even though he didn't understand any of it, had tried to forget it. But, now, seeing Marked Face like this, hearing what he's said, he doesn't know any more. He can't trust his uncle. If ever there was a trickster, it's Marked Face. There's something itching at the back of his mind, though, and he doesn't want to let it lean any closer to his ear.

"What am I supposed to understand, Uncle?" he asks, wearily. "It's just another story."

"Yes, you have it exactly, Nephew: *it is just a story*. Here is the thing: those stories long ago got into your father's head, as I have said. Maybe he doesn't even remember what really happened to Dove, that she was taken and raped by the whites, pregnant as she was, used so harshly that she took her own life in her shame. My brother's thoughts were already loose when this happened, like our mother's, our crazy uncle who heard the spirits. What happened to poor Dove maybe drove him past the edge. He was never strong, my brother. Who knows how these things work. If not that, then the years of war with the whites, the sickness, losing our land, all of it. My brother belongs in that hospital of yours, Sagiistoo. You do the right thing, looking after him. I am old, and can't do that nearly as well any more. Our days are drawing to an end, my brother and I; you must keep him safe until that time."

"Uncle, I remember, though. *I remember*. With my friend Sol and the fires and the rest of it. You were there, Uncle. *You were there*. Sol remembered too."

"Nephew, did my brother tell you the story about Raven and the branch? The ants? My brother was obsessed with that story particularly. He was convinced that he saw the true way of the world, this one and all the others that came before."

Marked Face sighs, getting up and crossing the room, sitting down on the cot next to Billy. He takes one of Billy's hands in his own, the fingers bony and scarred and twisted. He won't meet Billy's eyes. "Nephew, remember this: remember your father, my mother, that uncle of ours. I'm sorry, I don't know anything of what you say. I haven't been anywhere but around this reservation, for years upon years. It's good that you have that job, there at that hospital. My brother, he was about your age when it started to go bad for him. The stories were so strong that they made a world for him, different than this one. You say your white friend remembers me? Maybe you believe so strongly that your stories have confused the world for him, too. I don't know how these things work, Nephew. Sometimes, though, I think lives and stories get twisted together. Me and my brother, my brother and his tales of the Old Ones, you and this white man. I don't know."

Billy's breath is hot in his chest; he can feel the pulsing of his blood inside him. His head pounds even harder. He turns to look at his uncle, searching for that cold, mocking smile but, when Marked Face raises his gaze from the floor, all Billy sees is deep sadness there.

"My brother was about your age, Sagiistoo. Remember that. There is only one world, Nephew. As cruel and bitter as it is at times, there is only this one. We are those ants walking around the branch, maybe but, even broken, the branch is the same. Take care that my brother's stories don't crawl inside your head, Nephew. Sometimes I wonder if we are cursed, the People, because of the things we have had to endure. We can't all be strong. There is no shame in this. You need to find your father and go back to that place, hey? You need to go back to that place so you can be kept safe."

First and Last Warning

1917

Butte, Montana

1.

Sol looks around his office from behind the huge, darkly polished desk. The whiskey glass in his hand glints in the glittered light of the cut-crystal chandelier, the one he'd had installed a few months ago at ridiculous cost. It's maybe a bit overlarge for the room, but it's impressive, nonetheless, an icy monstrosity of a thing looming down from overhead. It had taken a while to get used to, to subdue a vague urge to duck when he walks under it but, now, he wouldn't have the fixture removed for any reason.

It might not fit the room, not exactly, but neither does he: they are both cold and massive things that dominate this space.

He carefully lights up one of his cigars, trying not to wince on that first inhale. He's been smoking them for a few years now, but has yet to really get a taste for them. They're still a bit reminiscent of burning trash to him but, like the chandelier, that smell is a part of the room and it belongs. Sol only smokes the cigars – again, the most expensive ones he can find – in this opulent, absurd office of his. He enjoys the whiskey – oh, that he enjoys – and the soft leather of his chair, the massive bulk of the huge desk in front of him. He loves that low, jaggedy light dropping from the chandelier and the way that sound in the room muffles and dies in the thick rugs on the floor, gets trapped by the shelves of unread, leatherbound books that line the walls. As for the cigars, well, even Sol has sacrifices he must make, these days. Appearances must be maintained.

Alone with his whiskey and this horrible cigar burning the taste of garbage into his mouth, Sol can't help but chuckle at what a fucking caricature he's become, when he thinks about it, infrequently though that is. David Solomon Parker, the boss, these seven years now. Lucky seven, he would have called it, back when he was a gambling man. Not any more, though; he's done with all that. Now he's only the boss.

He owns taverns and hop-houses, brothels and cribs, diners and cafés and hardware stores and apartment blocks. He has a gold-ringed finger in a hundred pies, legitimate and not; here in this very room he does business with Company high-ups and their associated minions. He lunches with the mayor, from time to time, is a member in good standing of the Ancient Order of Hibernians – although he is about as Irish as a rabbi – the Elks, Odd Fellows. The Sons of St George, for good measure. Laughing at the irony of it, given his line of work, Sol contributes from his deep pockets to the WCTU, the Society for the Suppression of Vice, the Florence Crittenden Rescue Circle.

His suits are bespoke, his house a mansion, and the size of his bank holdings – those that exist on paper – would gag Midas himself. He dines with the most lovely or well-connected women of Butte and fucks only the very finest of whores. Old as he is, Sol is the one of the most eligible bachelors in town these days, truly a catch.

Even as fat has he'd gotten lately. He slaps his belly, appreciatively. The flab just adds more substance to him, more weight.

A fucking caricature.

The dreams still get him, sometimes, at night, but that's nighttime and the days make it worthwhile, usually.

The end of Sean Harrity had been an ugly thing. By the time it was over, what was left of Sean's face was almost unrecognizable as a man's, the back of his skull pounded to a splintery mush against the floor. Sol's screaming drowning out Sean's own, by the end. Until quiet came back, just the gasp of breath, Mickey mewling from the floor. The bones in Sol's right hand had never healed straight. Nancy, though, poor Nancy died from the gunshot wound after a couple of bad days. The bullet he'd taken that, by rights, should have been Sol's. It was a shame, but there it was. Best not to think on it overmuch, now. That was years ago; it was done. Might come back at night from time to time, the memory shivery and sweaty, but it was done.

As for consequences: here they were. This office, the money, the women, the lot of it. Another joke in the long series of jokes that comprised his life. Some funny, some not, but none of them mattered once you got the trick of seeing them for what they were, seeing life for what it is: a fucking joke.

It turned out, logically enough, that the people with whom Sean did business, legitimate or not, were more interested in continuity than anything else, so when word got out that Mr Sean Harrity had left Butte for parts unknown – Hell, in this particular case – Sol merely stepped in as the heir apparent, came into his own. He'd always had a skill for making men trust in and rely on him; running Sean's business was not unlike running a mucker crew, writ larger and more complicated, for sure, but Sol had a knack for it. It was mostly man-management, at the root of things. Build relationships, find capable men as employees or partners, and treat them in the right way. The boss as a stern parent, magnanimous as required but taking no shit.

Of course, he'd made some mistakes; that was natural as he was finding his feet. Some of his new business associates saw a vacuum, tried to cheat or chisel away at the edges, if not outright take the bread from his plate. Sol had had to take some action, then, here and there, make an example or two. He found that, now, he had something new to add to his reputation: he was feared, even more so than before. Sol Parker was the man who had removed that evil bastard Sean Harrity, and that wasn't a man to take lightly. Sol, then, well, best step careful around him. Show the appropriate respect.

There's a light, hesitant tapping at the door. "Yeah," Sol calls out in a puff of garbage-smelling smoke. He rinses his mouth with a wash of good whiskey, tries to peel out the taste of cigar. "What?"

The door opens a crack and one-eyed Mickey Doyle sticks his head in. He mumbles something Sol's way, that watery, remaining eyeball of his staring at the floor.

"Goddamn it, Mickey, how many times do I have to tell you to just come in? Quit sticking your head in like a fucking muttering jack-in-the box and come over here." Even now, after all this time, there's still satisfaction in goading the fat fuck. Although, any more, Mickey isn't even fat, is he? He's unhealthy looking, is what he is, loose-limbed and shambling, the skin hanging off him like a suit that doesn't quite fit any more, which Sol imagines is more or less the case. His color has yellowed. Sallow, poorly shaven face like chicken skin. A pucker of scar reaches from his left cheekbone to his brow, crumpling that side of his face into an uneven, unseemly mass over the empty socket.

Mickey is paying, still, for the lies he'd told about Nancy, the ones that had gotten the boy killed. Easy enough for Sol to just kill Mickey and be done with it, but these long years of fear and servitude are so much better, so much more just. Sol is honestly surprised that Mickey has held on this long, really, what with the state of his health, the ulcers and the nerves and the constant, whispering fear that Sol is finally going to make good on what he promised and do something to him that will make what happened to Sean seem like a kiss from a beautiful girl. *You got to earn your life back, Mickey. Convince me that you deserve it, after what you did. Otherwise, what's going to happen to you is going to give nightmares to the hardest fucking men in town, hey?* At first, he'd wondered if Mickey had anything left inside him, if he would try to come at him in one way or another. If he'd ever had anything, though, it had departed along with that popped eyeball. Sometimes a fight is over before it really begins.

And, to be honest, it's entertaining, trying to push Mickey to the edge of things. It's a perquisite of power, really, to play with a man like this. Godlike, in some small way. That's the extent of Sol's religion any more, a belief that, if there is a deity, it's only there to fuck with those creatures weaker than it. Tomorrow he'll yell at Mickey for coming into the office instead of sticking his head in, as ordered. Always keeping him off-balance.

Mickey is standing there now, in front of the big desk, eye on the ground, worrying an envelope in his hand, smoothing a finger and thumb down the edge of it, over and over. "Well, you just going to stand there, Doyle?" Mickey looks up, startled, and starts to sit in one of the heavy leather chairs facing the desk. "The fuck are you doing? Get out of my chair!" This last said at a bellow, Sol half-standing from his own seat.

Mickey pops up like that jack-in-the-box again, taking a step forward, to the side. Rubbing at that envelope still, though, in his distress, he seems to have forgotten that it's in his hand. It's hard for Sol to keep the smile from his face. *Why does he even stick around?* he thinks, from time to time. *World's a big place, just go.* But Sol's forbidden it, and Mickey just doesn't have the sand in him to disobey. It's fascinating, really, just how thoroughly broken a man can get, given the proper pressures.

"Well? That for me? And I'll thank you not to grub it all up like that, shitheel."

Mickey remembers the envelope then, quickly passes it over to Sol after smoothing it one last time, and stands there uncertainly. He waits for whatever derision is coming next.

Sol opens the envelope and stares at the contents. "Go on, then," he says, distractedly. "Get out of here." He reads the telegram again, those eight short words calling up a wash of forgotten feeling from down low in his chest. He finishes his whiskey and pours another, the cigar burning abandoned in its tray, smoke curling upward, hanging around his head in a pall.

Sol knocks back his drink, pours another.

2.

ELIZABETH PASSED. SERVICE TUESDAY. COME WARM
SPRINGS. – BILLY

It was bound to happen, sooner or later. Just a matter of time, really. Maybe for the best, when it came right down to it, because it wasn't like she'd had much of a life. These were the kinds of things one told oneself, and it might have been true, even. Regardless, when Billy tries to make himself believe it, the words feel hollow.

He'd handed the form to the Western Union man, paying the fee without comment. Left, then, walking down the road to the crappy little tavern he frequents more and more these days. He never used to be much of a drinker, was afraid of what it would do to him and, yet, here he is, damn near whenever he can. It doesn't appear to have done him much harm over the years, though, aside from this gut he carries around, the dugs that sag on his chest. He's fat. Never thought to see that day, but here it is. Fat Billy Morgan.

The bartender gives him a nod, pulling up a mug of beer for him, scraping off the foam with a paddle. Billy nods back, acknowledging a couple of the other regulars, tired, shabby old fuckers like himself, and takes his beer back to his normal corner table. He's a regular, too, but not a talker. The bar is just a place, fairly quiet, usually, where Billy can be alone with his thoughts. It's mostly empty inside, the air thick and lazy with cigarette smoke and the low mutter of conversation, punctuated by the occasional cackle.

Billy takes a long, slow sip of his beer. He's still in his orderly's whites and, when he brings his arm up to light his cigarette, he sees the splash of blood brown-dark against his sleeve. The stain doesn't want to come out. He shakes his head and sighs, pulling the smoke into his chest.

He'd been the one to find her, tucked away in one of the cow stalls. Sitting there leaned back against the wooden wall, a surprised, puzzled look on her face. The hay wet underneath her. Maybe the end is always a surprise, even when you bring it on yourself. Was there a moment, right there at the last, when she thought *no wait* even though, by then, it was too late? *I take it back.* More likely the look on her face is just pure physiology, the sag of muscles after the animating force has left. But, still, it almost looked like she was just sitting there, biding her time, waiting to get up, wondering why she couldn't. Regardless of the reason, Billy just wishes that she'd looked more peaceful. *Passed*, he'd written. Such a quiet euphemism. As if she'd just gone somewhere. Which Billy supposes she has, not that he really believes that she's anywhere now. It's a pleasant fiction, though. *She's gone to her reward. She's with the angels now. Called home.*

It had taken him a while to write the text of the telegram, before settling on *passed*. Not that he would have used one of those more flowery phrases, particularly given who he was sending it to, but *Elizabeth is dead* seemed too harsh, too final, even to him. And he damn sure couldn't have put down *Your wife has finally cut her throat.*

He takes another swallow of beer, smokes quietly for a while. How did she keep finding ways to hurt herself, he wonders. It was a mystery to him and all the other orderlies. After so many years at the hospital with her, Billy thought he knew all her little idiosyncrasies, could plan around them. But, sure enough, once or twice a year, he or one of the others would find her with a piece of broken glass, a kitchen knife, once an awl from the shop. The only thing that even made it remotely close to acceptable – which it wasn't – was the fact that she would always cause some kind of drama, once she had the thing in her hand. Cry, scream, rage at them. As if, deep down, she wanted someone to stop her, to help her.

But not this time. For one reason or another she'd just taken a shard of glass, from wherever it was that she found it, gone into the barn and quietly laid her neck open. Died surprised and alone, surrounded by cowshit and hay that needed mucking.

Wait, I take it back.

Billy drains his beer and fetches another from the bar. *It's not your fault,* Dr Rideout had said, squeezing him on the shoulder. *You did everything you could.* Wasn't enough, though, was it? *She was a tragic woman, really.* He respected Dr Rideout mightily but, right then, he'd felt a flare of anger. Elizabeth Parker wasn't a tragedy. Tragedy implied something had just happened to her. There was no responsibility in it, it said nothing had been *done* to her, when, really it had. More and more, Billy thinks that the terrible things that happen in his life are just because he, himself, is in it. That he's poisoned it. Twisted everyone's stories into his own, maybe, like his uncle had said, that time. Could be, if Billy had never known Sol, never met Elizabeth, she would have been just fine. The two of them would have raised up a baby into a man and did whatever it is that married people did after that. Dug a garden, maybe. Sang in the church choir on Sundays.

But even Billy knows that's all bullshit. Sometimes his thoughts get away from him, though, which happens more and more these last years. Particularly when he's feeling low. Some days it's hard to even get out of bed, to crawl out from the weight of the blackness hanging over him. Other days it's as if his mind reels out from itself, bringing him along to places he shouldn't be going. Showing him thoughts he shouldn't be having. He worries that he's becoming like his father.

Billy isn't crazy. He tells himself that, regardless of the things his uncle had said. The things his father had said, about seeing the world a little too truly. Even with the depression and the rages and that other side of things, when nothing looks quite right, not exactly, when things are just a shade out of kilter, he knows he isn't crazy. He's not like his father, not at all. But maybe he's getting closer. Just maybe, some days. It would be a lie if he said he didn't fret about it, which is why he's stayed at the hospital all these years. The job is still as lousy as it always was, even more so, in some ways, now that there are so many more patients and the staffing hasn't kept pace. Dr Rideout does everything he can, but funding and the board and all the rest of it. Being an orderly – head orderly, these days – is a shit job but Billy feels safer at the hospital. Just in case, just in case.

He never thinks about that other life he thought he once had. Tries not to, anyway. There have been times when he's wanted to confide in Dr Rideout, tell him the story, his fears, but he's never been able to bring himself to do so. So, instead, Billy just does his best to shrug his thoughts away from all that but, sometimes, it sneaks up on him, an echo of the person he once was. Thought he once was. A particular image, the sound of a voice, a smell. Another life. Or maybe Marked Face is right, after all.

These days, the person Billy wants to talk to the most is his uncle, but the old man has been gone for years. Gone back to wherever it is he goes, just up and vanished again. From time to time Billy heads back up to that little cabin but it's always empty. No one around the rez claims to have seen him, the same way no one has seen Bad Bird in all the years since he disappeared. Billy still expects the telegram, though, the one that will begin *REGRET TO INFORM YOU*. Someone will have found the old man; one of those old men anyway. *Gone to his reward. Called home. Passed.* With each new year it's more and more unlikely that either Marked Face or his father are still alive. After all, they're old, they've been old Billy's whole life and he's north of thirty now himself.

A world without those old Indians seems somehow wrong, though. Lacking. They've always been there, those two, even when Billy barely saw them. Even when he hated them, feared them. Their very existence tethers him to his own. Their stories are twisted together with his. Without them he doesn't have much. Dr Rideout, maybe, who is a colleague and a friend, but the doctor has his own family, his own anchors. The job? No. Maybe this shitty little bar and the cheap beer and his own fat belly hanging there over his belt. Is all that enough to hold him down to his life? Once, he'd had Sol as family but that was in that other life he didn't like to think about, the one that never happened.

Billy wonders how Sol will take the news about Elizabeth. Grief? Relief? Indifference? Never once has Sol come to Warm Springs to see his wife, not in all this time. Twenty-five miles, all it is, but not once. Now that Sol is such a big man, or so Billy understands, there have been a number of large cash gifts to the hospital endowment, money to pay for this or that. Money for Sol Parker to buy off his conscience, Billy thinks, stunted though it may be. You can't buy your way out of family, though, whatever Sol might believe.

He hasn't seen Sol since their fight, years ago. Some days he thinks to go to Butte, to find him, but he never does.

Afternoon becomes evening and one beer becomes many until he finally stumbles out of the bar and begins making his way back. As he weaves blearily down the road, he looks for signs of his father, looks for Marked Face, but Billy is alone.

3.

"A Bolshevik, is what he is."

Sol nods at Marcus Connor, looking up over his forkful of *canard en sauce crémeuse*, the duck fatty-sweet in his mouth. The Company security director is a big, bovine man, who makes Sol look svelte in comparison. A former Pinkerton, though, Connor is not one to be trifled with, as the scars across his knuckles attest, the flattened nose. Just another thug, done up in an expensive suit, Sol thinks, a hard man wrapped soft. Like me, feeling the tightness of his waistband against his expanded belly.

"That a problem, is it?" Sol doesn't really need to ask, but he has to play his part. He chews and swallows another buttery forkful. Philippe's duck is over-rich, like most of the dishes at *La Maison*, that pretentious Gallic mainstay of Butte's upper crust. Sol knows that, later, he'll be shitting himself hollow from all of the cream and butter and fat, but, like the cigars, dining at the *Maison* is a part of his new station in life. Deals are started over *steak au poivre* and *blanquette de veau*, closed over *raspberry charlotte* and oversweet wine, with a tiny coffee in a cup the size of a thimble. Never mind that Philippe himself is a Québécois junkie with a taste for rough trade in men,

321

has never once been to the Paris he claims as his home.

"Everything is good, Mr Connor, Mr Parker?" He's there now, hovering over their table like a moth at a light. Better be good, with the money he's into Sol for.

"Yeah, it's great, Phil, like always," Sol says. Too rich, too fatty, it's great. With a fey clinch of his hands over his heart, Philippe flutters away to another table of worthies, his chef's whites gleaming.

"Can't have those Wobbly types riling up the men, Sol. You know that." Connor methodically scoops another mouthful in. He's the type of eater that starts in one quadrant of the plate and devours outward, at a steady pace, one forkful after another, not bothering to savor or enjoy or maybe even taste. Food as fuel. Sol wonders if anyone enjoys Philippe's food, actually, or if the place is just an elaborate joke pulled on them all.

"Mm," Sol nods, mouth full. Swallows. "Can't have that." Maybe a bit too wry, in tone, from the glance up from Mark Connor. Sol shakes his head, tries to be more serious. "Productivity, all that."

"Productivity, Sol. War's on. This needs to be an example."

"War's on." Who gives a shit about the war. "So..." He leaves it hanging.

"Man's a problem."

"That, I gathered." Sol sets down his fork with a quiet clink. "So?" He repeats it. It's not necessary, he knows what Connor is after, but he likes to make the man say it. Or at least hedge close. "Just what is it that you want, Mark?"

Connor doesn't say anything, which is something of a disappointment, just raises a hand and makes a gesture like something blowing away. A piece of fluff on the wind, poof, gone. Sol sighs. "You say the man's name was again?" Already knowing.

"Frank Little."

Sol hadn't gone to the funeral. Why would he, really, he hadn't seen his nominal wife in years upon years. No need to stir up any of those feelings. The telegram had done enough of that, forced him to remember in daylight hours those things best pushed to night. Elizabeth Parker, née McDaniel, gone to her grave, at last. Overdue, really. She'd been in that hospital for years, after all, and what kind of life was that. From time to time Sol would send a donation to Warm Springs, call it good, and that, even, was more than he needed to do. Above and beyond. He was a taxpayer – mostly – and it was a state hospital so there you go.

More than thoughts of his once-wife, pushed so far to the back of his mind they rarely peeked out, it was seeing the name *Billy* that gave him pause. Billy, from that other life he never considered, or did so as little as he could. Billy, his friend, almost-son once, who he'd done his damnedest to kill this time around. Fucking stabbed with a piece of glass. More than once, over the years, he'd meant to go find the boy, make things right. Billy was the only other person in this world who could understand him.

Somehow it had never happened, though, and Sol was honestly surprised to hear that Billy was even still alive, as if because he, Sol, had ceased thinking of him, the man had ceased to be. But there he was, now, right at the end of that telegram and not twenty-five miles away. Living a life, whatever it was. How does *he* do it, Sol wonders. Does Billy consider the man he once was, and try to live up to that ideal? Or, like Sol, had he just taken this next chance around, grabbed it by the fucking throat for once and squeezed? Sol is seized with a sudden desire to call for Mickey, get him to bring around the new Knox that Sol's had shipped all the way out from Massachusetts, fire the contraption up and drive them to Warm Springs. Mickey may be mostly a plaything, any more, but his one actual use is as a chauffeur; the man has something of a way with mechanical things. It's maybe the only skill left to him, or maybe just the thing he clings to. Machines are predictable, after all, Sol supposes.

But no, he won't do it. Won't call for Mickey and go. Wouldn't be right. Maybe *right* wasn't the word, but what would Sol say, seeing Billy, after all this time? *Hey Bill, sorry about the shoulder and how's things?* Part of Sol worries about judgment and part of him worries that he's been forgotten. Not forgotten-forgotten, but flushed away by whatever Billy has now. If Sol doesn't ever think of Billy Morgan, the idea that he's still there, but maybe has washed his hands of Sol, is strangely upsetting. Sol doesn't want anything of that before life, not a goddamn thing but, knowing that there's a link to it, still, tenuous though it might be, is an odd comfort. Why hadn't Billy ever come to see him? Never once, not in all these years.

ELIZABETH PASSED. SERVICE TUESDAY. COME WARM SPRINGS. – BILLY

Well, he hadn't, and that's it, isn't it.

Usually, he doesn't involve himself in these things, not any more but, somehow, he feels he owes it to Frank. Whatever that even means now. Sol doesn't know why, exactly, he feels this way, unless it's that he's been thinking overmuch about the time before, since Billy's telegram. Stupid, really.

His hat is shucked down low and itches against

his brow; the bandanna pulled to his nose stifles his breathing, sucked in and blown out with every breath. Again, he wonders, as he has for the last several minutes, just why he's here. He doesn't need to be. He doesn't owe anyone anything. Not a goddamn soul.

Frank's eyes are wide and he's gasping for breath from the punch to his belly. Must be a lousy way to wake up, that. Faraday punches him again and Kelly, the Pinkerton on loan from Connor, stuffs a rag in Frank's mouth, holding it down while he and Faraday go to work on Mr Little. *An example*, Mark Connor had said. Shame, really, but needs must and all that. Faraday leans back, opening a space over Frank and raising an eyebrow inquisitively. Sol shakes his head. It's not that he's against beating a helpless man, as a general rule, but still.

This whole fucking thing isn't sitting right with him. He knows Frank Little, after all, had known him – before, anyway – admired him. And it's not as if the man hadn't been given fair warning, too, ample reason to back off, just go, and yet here they were. Bravery or foolishness or some hybrid of the two, but, whatever the reason, Frank had made this bed. Just a shame that Sol has to be the one to tuck him into it, and it makes him mad, raises feelings he tries to keep stunted and mute.

Outside of the boarding house, now, Frank humpled over, gagging around the cloth in his mouth, dragged between Faraday and Connor's man, Kelly. Into the back of the automobile, another punch or two to keep him docile. Mickey behind the wheel and, in a few quick minutes, they're at the rail trestle outside of the Penn.

The Pennsylvania had burned, again, a year or so ago. No one dead, oddly enough, this time around. All the miners up and out safely. The quick investigation, after, and then the mine back open, the report's ink still wet.

Just an accident, was the Company's verdict. Regrettable, but there had been no loss of life, after all. Promises were made for future improvements, but the miners had seen that for what it was and, again, they'd struck and rioted, bitching about safety and hours and the rest of it. Regardless of the validity of their complaints, a riot is a riot, though, and Sol's men had had to crack some skulls that day. Another shame, really, but best not think about that. Well paid for their troubles, at least.

But, goddamn it, Frank had shown up shortly after that, the idiot, to organize, then ignored all the warnings and, now, here they were.

Out of the car, Frank held up by Kelly while Faraday commences to pound on him southpaw again. Left, left, left, right, left, left. Frank's strong chin broken and bleeding now, thin hair hanging down into his eyes, lips split, eyes swollen shut.

"OK, that's enough, Nick. Nick! Enough." Sol grabs Faraday's arms. Man gets like this, so het up he can't stop himself. Not that it really matters now.

"Shouldn't say my name," Faraday gasps, heaving some wind back in, massaging the knuckles of his left hand with the palm of his right. "Don't say my name."

What does he think is going to happen here?

"Fine, whatever," Sol says, not wanting to engage with a fool, stepping past him and pulling down his mask. No need for it now. "Set him down." Kelly drops Frank to the floor of the trestle, props him back against one of the struts. Sol doesn't want it to be like this. He wants it quick, if it has to be, but orders are orders and this is what he's been paid to do. Again, though, he thinks *why am I here?* He wants to just turn around and walk away, leave Frank to the others to finish things but, because Sol *is* here, there are appearances to maintain.

Checking a sigh, he levers himself into a squat and faces the bashed-up remnant of Frank Little.

Frank is mumbling something, over and over. Sol leans closer, concentrates until he can make it out. "Give me a minute, boys," he says. Doubtful looks. "You think I can't fucking handle this?" Sol snaps. "I said give me a fucking minute, so go to the fucking car." He turns around, knowing that he'll be obeyed, and leans closer to Frank.

"That you said, Frank?"

"Thought it would be different, this time." Frank says it slower, trying to make the words cleaner around his broken teeth. "Thought it would be different, this time."

"Made the wrong choice, is all, Frank. And I am sorry for that. Really I am."

A laugh, a dying, broken thing coughed out from that cracked jaw. "Never was a choice. Sometimes you just gotta do the right thing."

Ah, Frank. "There's always a choice, son," Sol says. "Might just be between lousy options, but it's always there. Thing is, though, thing is that it just don't matter which one you pick, most times, so you can't let it get to you. That's the only way to get through this fucked-up world, Frank. Only way."

"You really believe that, don't you?" Frank's head lolls back against the trestle strut. "You really believe that."

"What do you mean?" There's no reply so Sol gives him a little slap, harder until he's regained some attention again. "What do you mean?"

"Thought it could be different." Frank trails off again, head slumping to the side. He mumbles something else, one short, squared-off word, then he passes out. Sol leans back on his heels, wondering if he'd heard right. What it meant. Best not think on it, maybe. Words he says often, so often he should put it on his fucking crest: *best not think on it.* He stands up, feeling the sharp cracking in his knees – *I'm too goddamn fat* – and walks back to the car, telling the boys to finish things up. He gets in the back and shuts the door. Sol turns his head away, towards town, picking at a rough patch of skin on his palm. Trying to ignore the commotion.

The next day, Frank Little's body is found hanging from the trestle, a note pinned to his thigh. *First and Last Warning,* it reads.

First and last warning. It was what Connor had required, so they'd done it. The whole sorry shit of it, they'd done it. First and last warning.

In his office, door shut, Sol thinks back to that last thing that Frank had said to him. That look of understanding in the one, bloodied eye, the one that could still open. Understanding and pity and something that couldn't quite be read. *Damned*, was the word, although Sol doesn't know which of them Frank had meant.

Damned.

First and last warning.

4.

The room is too warm. There's a sparkly berg of a chandelier overhead, too big for the place, hanging down low and clinking from above, so much that Billy wanted to duck when he walked under it. Like it's going to drop down on him, bury him alive in crystal shards. The rugs are thick and walking on them was like plodding through sand, each step an effort to push past. The leather chair he's been sat in is oversoft like the carpet, drawing him in unpleasantly. But it's quality, right, this is the kind of discomfort that the rich buy for themselves, because they can.

It stinks in here, smells like burning trash, or cigars, both of which smell more or less the same to him. He lights up a cigarette mostly to give himself something to do and, if the smell of it masks that leafy reek of cigar, so much the better. He looks around, at the huge desk, the color-coordinated – unread, for sure – books that line the shelves, the brassy mass of a spittoon. He shakes his head at the excess of it all. It's a room that says *look at me*, that lacks any notion of subtlety. A room that says *I'm rich, I'm important, I'm somebody*. He's surprised that Sol hasn't had the whole goddamn place gilded, a shining monument to his own magnificence.

Billy wasn't surprised, not really, that Sol hadn't made Elizabeth's service. It had been a rosy conceit that he would come, that, finally, the two of them could maybe, somehow, use the opportunity to reconcile their differences, reconnect maybe. But they weren't even differences, any more. More just a kind of neglect. Not indifference, but a studied distance of sorts. They were perhaps the only two real people in this world, after all, the only two could see it for what it really was. Or were they? Billy doesn't know, doesn't like to think those kinds of thoughts, the ones that tend to spin him away into places he'd rather not go. He no longer knows just what he believes about much of anything.

One cigarette smoked, he lights another. Petty, really, goddamn petty for Sol to keep him – *him* – waiting like this. Sat here in this low, spongy chair – Billy swears that the legs have been sawed down to leave the occupant staring up at that railcar-sized desk – sat here to smoke and fret and wait on the pleasure of his betters. Making folks wait is the prerogative of the powerful and insecure, really. Fine, Billy can wait. He has plenty of cigarettes.

"Billy!" Sol says as he comes into the room. Bluff, glib, hand extended like a politician. Is Billy expected to kiss a ring? Fortunately just a handshake. "Good to see you, Bill."

Yeah, I'll bet. Spent damn near a week trying to get an audience with Your Majesty.

The first thing Billy thinks: Sol's fat. No other word for it. Sol is a fat bastard, stretching out what looks to be – at least to Billy's uneducated eye – a very expensive suit. Tortoiseshell buttons and the like. Sol's crammed into it like a sausage in its casing though, pushing at the seams. The heavy, ornate gold watch-chain across his belly looks like it's pulled tight to bursting. Sol. He was never a small man: short but broad, is how Billy remembers him, but the broad of muscle, strength. This man, with his blousy, jowly face and rolling, tubby gait seems less than he once was, even though, technically, he's more. Whole lot more, really.

The hand that shakes his is damp, soft.

Boy's fat as shit, Sol thinks, shaking Billy's hand. The hell happened to him? The Billy he knew, the one he remembers, was lean. Hard, strong. Even as a kid, this time around, all elbows and ribs, there'd been a kind of wiry power to him. But this Billy, he just looks unhealthy. Flabby gut, tits like a woman's pushing out against that shabby shirt. Bags under his eyes, sag at the jaw. Hair looks a little thin, even, creeping up from his temples. How long had it been since Billy had even washed that hair, gotten it cut? If Sol had passed him on the street, he would have thrown him some change.

OK, sure, maybe he himself has a bit more around the middle than he used to, but at least he doesn't look like a fucking derelict. Some busted-up Injun down off the rez. Don't matter where he came from, though: Billy just looks like shit.

And why is here here, *now*? The doings with Frank Little last night have riled Sol, damned if they haven't, so why today, of all days, has Billy fucking Morgan turned up on his doorstep?

Billy tries to restrain the urge to wipe his hand on his pant-leg, and watches Sol lumber into the big chair on the other side of the desk. Again, he's struck by the disparity in height, as if Sol is sitting on a booster seat, looming down over his own, low chair. It's a cheap trick but, he has to admit, it's effective. Sol, the boss, perched up on his throne like Jehovah. He sits himself up straighter, tries to even things out some.

Why is he even here? What did he think he was going to get out of this? Some kind of satisfaction? He was fuming, at the service for Elizabeth, so angry he could spit, even though he'd suspected, already known, maybe, that Sol wouldn't show. But to see that poor woman laid to ground with no one other than Dr Rideout and himself in attendance, listening to the minister's distracted, rushed, uncaring speech – he'd called her *Eleanor* – it had set Billy's blood to boil. Dropped into one of his black rages, that came more and more often of late. Twenty-five fucking miles away, and the mighty Sol Parker couldn't be bothered to spare a couple three hours for his wife. *His wife.* Mother of his child.

Don't worry about it, Bill, Dr Rideout had said. He'd given up on making allowances for his brother, long ago. Made his peace, forgotten him, at least enough so that he didn't seem to get too bothered by it all. Billy couldn't forget, though. As much as, now, he's estranged from Sol, they're tied together, somehow. Best to not think on just how, but their lives were joined in some way, by shared experience, maybe. Don't think on it but still, *still*, Sol not bothering to attend Elizabeth's funeral put Billy in a fury. So here he was. Finally badgered himself a meeting with glorious Solomon Parker, king of goddamn Butte. He can feel the anger coming again.

"Missed you at the service," he says.

Missed you at the service, hey? What kind of bullshit is that, you pompous fuck? Sol can tell Billy is pissed off. Sees it in his face, he's not even trying to hide it. Just who does he think he's talking to? Sol's surprised at how angry it makes him, just seeing Billy sat there like that, wearing that pissy expression and after all this time. It shouldn't be like this. He'd expected some joy, maybe some regret, something at least with some sweet to the sour but all he feels, now, is anger. Who the fuck is this man, calling him out? *Missed you at the service*. As if Billy fucking Morgan has any goddamn right. Putting on airs, the rest of it. Who the fuck is Billy Morgan, anyway? Some goddamn Indian from the reservation, that's all. Given a white man's job. Another fat drunk, another suck on the state. Oh, boo hoo, the poor tribes, fucked by the whites. Doesn't fucking matter, though, does it? It happened and maybe that's just the way of things. The strong fucking the weak. Things might change in a life but *that* never will, chief. Way of the fucking world, isn't it?

Also doesn't matter, the rest of it, what maybe once passed before, between them. What was it Sean said? *The past is dead*. Just a vague memory now. If that, even. He's Sol Parker. Sol *Fucking* Parker. Half of fucking Butte is his, and this shitheel sat down in front of him is putting on airs. *Missed you at the service*. As if the fat fucker has any call on Sol's time. It's an effort, born of long practice – his business, after all, relies on corralling one's own baser urges, at times – but Sol peels a smile across his face, the regretful, rueful one he uses when the occasion demands it.

"Yeah, bit busy, I was. Sad thing, though. Tragedy."

The anger is on him now, clinging to his back, whispering. *Tragedy*. Billy wants to jump up, over the desk, and pound that false fucking smile into the old man's skull. The smile that says *oh I'm so sorry* while tacking on *but I don't give a shit*. Does Sol think it looks real? Does anyone? How on God's green Earth has Sol gotten to where he is now, if this is the kind of false, transparent bullshit he sells? But maybe that's the point, Billy realizes. Maybe, once you get to a certain station, you don't have to try any more. Maybe it's better to let other people just see how little of a shit you actually have to give them. *Fuck you*, says that smile, and what are you going to do about it?

"Sad," Billy says, "but maybe for the best." Hating every word of it, trying to calm himself. "She's in a better place now." *Really? What the hell is he even saying?* But, seeing Sol, after all this time, it's put him off. Seeing Sol is *real*, no matter how angry it's making him, no matter all the roil of feelings in his belly.

"Maybe it's for the best," Sol agrees, looking down at Billy. Damn right it's for the best, and should have happened years ago. No reason she had to linger on as long as she did, crack-minded and broken as she was. The girl he'd loved had died, long time ago; what was left wasn't Elizabeth. Didn't take a doctor to figure that out.

Billy's scratching at the side of his nose now. His skin hangs loose on him, like Mickey's really, only darker. Boy looks terrible. Again, Sol thinks, *why is he here?* Does he want money? A job? Fine, to either of those things, they're in his power to give. Or is he just here to ride that high horse, to berate Sol for some perceived slight. *Missed you at the service.* You know what though, Bill? I missed *you*, all these long fucking years. I missed you. There it fucking is. Apparently, though, there you were, not twenty-five, thirty miles away, and did you come see me, even once? No. *No.* OK, fine, we had a bad spell there, but I would have apologized, had you come see me. Apologized, and meant it. I was in the wrong, but not in my right head, at the time. Circumstances. But *no*, after all we went through, not even a fucking telegram, but here you are now, not to say hello, not to reconnect, but to walk that goddamn high road on me. *Missed you at the service*. Not even a *how you been*, not a *been awhile*. You piece of shit.

This is a mistake. Billy knows, now, that he never should have come here. There was no plan, no reason, just that he felt that he had to see Sol, finally, to tell him about Elizabeth, there at the end. *She seemed OK, mostly, and then she was gone*. Trite story of a life, that, in nine simple words. *She seemed OK, mostly, and then she was gone*. Why had he assumed that Sol would even care? A man who for almost twenty years hadn't even bothered with a visit? Stupid, is what it was, putting feelings on Sol that weren't there. Maybe the Sol he'd known, once, but not this one.

Billy stands up to go.

"Saw your uncle, other day," Sol says. "Whatshisname, Scarface?"

Billy sits again.

"Marked Face. You saw him?"

"Yeah, Bill, what I said. Saw him down on Utah. I don't know, begging change or something. Just standing there."

"Just standing there?"

"Jesus, Billy, did I stutter? Yeah, just standing there. Looking pretty much like he did before, last time we saw him. Older, maybe. Looked like shit, really. A bum."

"Last time?"

"Good lord, Bill, there an echo in here? You going simple on me, maybe? Yeah, last time." Sol reaches into his desk drawer, pulls out a bottle and a couple of glasses, fills them with whiskey, and pushes one across. "Here, where are my fucking manners, though, hey? Let's have a drink. Sláinte."

Billy takes the glass, necks it without thinking. "Cheers, Sol." Just like that. Old drinking buddies again. Suddenly, all of it in the open again, staring back.

"Funny, seeing him like that. Been a long time. You ever talk to him?"

"No." His uncle's been gone for years, vanished, and now here's Sol, just seen him the other day.

"Hard to believe, really."

"What?"

"You know, all of it." Sol waves a hand around, taking in the office. "All of it. This. What happened. The rest of it. Sometimes it don't seem real, even. Keep expecting to wake up back in our place down in the Patch. You remember that spot?"

"Shithole." Billy's not sure he does remember, not really, so how can Sol? Stories, twisted together.

"Yeah, that's for a certain. Times change though, hey?"

Billy looks around again at this stupid lair Sol's made for himself. His opulent little hideaway. He doesn't want to ask the question that's in his mouth, give it any credence. Any weight. To think these thoughts that maybe he shouldn't, knowing what he does, but he can't stop himself.

"You change it, though," he says, "if you had the chance? If you could wake up, like you said, back before? Start again?"

Change it?

Ah, Billy, you can't ever go back, Sol thinks. Not like it was. Don't you know that? It's there, and then it's gone, and what you find if you get lucky enough to see it again isn't what you left. It will never be the same.

You might step through the same sorry shit, but you're not the same person any more, are you? You think that the man you are now can be the man you were then? It's gone and you can't go back, Bill, so don't talk to me about changes.

There's a long pause.

"Why are you here, Billy?" Sol says. "You want something from me, that it? Well, that's fine. Maybe things didn't really turn out for you, this time, to look at you, anyway. So what is it you want, then? Just ask, and then you best be getting on, OK?"

"Fuck you, Sol."

It's out before he can reel it back in. The words squatting there in the back of his throat, maybe, just waiting to jump out. The anger still whispering at his back. *Fuck you for all of it, Sol, for this hopeless life, on the edge of crazy, for your fucking part in making it. For dragging me along into your bad choices and mistakes and the rest of this sorry fucking mess. For ruining the good we had, once. I'm so tired of it all. I don't want this. So fuck you. There it is. Fuck you.* Regardless of how he feels, the past between them, Billy knows it's a bad idea to have said it aloud. Because it's not just Sol, any more, sat across from him, behind that battleship of a desk, is it? That's Sol Parker, *Sol Parker*. A man to be feared, who is starting to rise now, face purpling with anger.

"That you said, Bill?"

No backing off from it now, though.

"Fuck. You. Sol. Follow? Fuck you. There's your echo. Hear that? *Fuck you.*"

Sol almost looks amused, now, even with those hard eyes and a face turning the color of brick. "Sure about that, are you, Billy?" Quietly. Knuckles white, tendons on the backs of his hands raised like ropes.

"Fuck you, Sol."

"All right then, Bill."

Quieter yet, even.

On a window ledge, outside the building, a dusty raven sits watching.

5.

Boeuf Bourguignon tonight. Over-salted, over-rich – again – the meat on the tough side. Philippe nowhere to be seen, maybe sleeping his dope off, maybe at something else that Sol would rather not think about, certainly not over dinner. Mark Connor across from him once more, plowing methodically through his food like a horse at the trough.

"Just a small one, though, right?" Connor murmurs through a full mouth. "These things have a way of spinning out of control."

You don't fucking say, Mark. Sol doesn't like the sound of any of this. He's in a mood, too, has been for a couple of weeks now. First that unpleasantness with Frank Little and then the thing with Billy. It wasn't right, and the taste of it lingers in his mouth like this lousy food. He pushes his plate away, disgusted, the meal half-eaten; what appetite he'd stoically gathered earlier is long gone now. *Always back to fire, aren't we. Round and round we go, la la la la la.* "Spinning out of control?" he says. "Jesus, Mark, that's a goddamn understatement. You ever been down there?"

"Course I've been down there, Sol. Well, been a

while, but yeah, I've been down there. I understand the difficulties."

"Difficulties."

"Yeah, *difficulties*, Sol. There a problem?"

"There are a lot of problems, here, Mark. *Loads,* hey? You should be able to see that."

"Maybe I got the wrong man, then."

Ah, fuck. It won't do to alienate Connor; a lot of money flows from the Company through him, straight into Sol's pockets. And besides, he wants to know that, if this thing is done, it's done right. Spinning out of control is a fucking understatement. "Nah, I've got a good man for this. Steady. Powder boy, owes me some."

"Who?"

"You really want to know that?" Eyebrow cocked.

"No, no, I guess I don't." Connor scrapes away the rest of his food, washing it down with a swallow of wine. He leans back. "Listen, Sol, we've got things in place for this. That's kind of the point here. One of them."

"You'll excuse me if I'm not brimming with confidence about that. A lot can go wrong."

"You're an engineer now, are you?"

"No, I'm not a fucking engineer, Mark. What I am is not an idiot. You get a fire going way down there, who knows what's going to happen? Even best case, it's fucking risky."

"It's a *safety system*, Sol. State of the fucking art, all that. Jesus, you think the Company is going to risk their own mine if the engineers aren't sure with this? Been tested, the lot of it. New technology."

The restaurant is entirely empty. Connor's booked the whole place out. Still, they're at the farthest table, talking in hissed whispers.

"Whose idea *was* this? Yours?" Connor leans back

with a wry expression that asks if Sol thinks he'd ever actually answer that. "Fine, OK, fine. At least not on 25. How about 3? 5 even. 25-level is too goddamn deep."

"That the whole point, Sol. Show everyone the system works, calm down the Union. Get them back to work. Besides, there's that other part of things."

"Move them, then. Easy enough to do. No one will think twice."

Connor shakes his head. "25-level. Those crews stay where they are."

That's the second act of this farce, pinning the fire on supposed Bolsheviks, a couple of the union organizers that have been doing the most harm lately, with their slowdowns and speech-making and the rest of it. Ten thousand men had turned up for Frank Little's funeral and the mood since has gone from bad to worse. They're on war production and the Company says they can't be having these slowdowns or, God forbid, the strike that they can all feel coming. So some ACM genius, Connor or someone higher, has decided that a fire a half-mile underground, started by anarchist saboteurs, is the order of the day. Show off that shiny new fire safety system while they're at it, show the Union that the Company is concerned about their wellbeing. And get those men back to work, full speed, sharpish. Make those numbers.

Sol shakes his head again. "Jesus, Mark."

"I'll ask you again, Sol: we have a problem here?"

All it will take is one word and he's out of this. Out. It will hit him in the pocketbook for a while and Sol has his eyes on some expansion that will require capital, investors, those Company men who have come to respect and rely on him, little that they know of the actual details of just what he does, most of them. Maybe Sol is finally in a position to peel back away from some of these dark things he's doing, like that shameful thing with Frank. Because that's what that was: *shameful*. He admits it now, is willing to. Regardless of whether it matters or not. Regardless of the things Frank said.

Divest some of his seedier holdings and responsibilities, then. Move further into property and the like, that's what Sol wants. He has money, plenty of it, but just not enough to do what he wants on his own. Not to mention the more important part of it: those men, his fancy friends, who will cut through the red tape, get his permitting sorted, contracts, labor, distribution, the lot of it. Won't never happen without those boys. If he cuts Connor loose, like he wants to, now, might be he'll never get back into this position, leastways not for quite some time, and he's not getting any younger.

Fuck.

"Course there's no problem, Mark. None at all."

In the deep hours of night, later, Sol's sat up in his bed, the four-poster with the canopy, whole damn thing the size of a tennis court, almost, drinking a whiskey to calm the roiling in his gut. Whether from Philippe's shitty rich beef or nerves, it's tough to say. He really needs to get rid of this bed, though, find something more cozy, he tells himself for the hundredth time. Something smaller. After so many years sleeping on a narrow cot, this lumpy mattressed monstrosity of a thing has just never been comfortable. Plus it's so big that one uneasy part of his mind is always expecting to wake up and find someone squatting there in the dark with him. He shudders at the thought, pushing it back down wherever it came from. He gives another glance down to the far end of the bed, miles away.

Near as he can tell, though, tonight it's just him and

Kitt, his latest paramour. That's how she refers to herself: *a paramour.* Which, near as Sol can tell, is simply a five-dollar French word for *working girl*, because that's what she is, even if she costs a damn sight more than five dollars. Never mind that nothing as crass as cash ever changes hands; Kitt is recompensed with jewels and furs and all the other trappings of a kept woman. A *paramour.* Jesus. At least she's beautiful and, thankfully, easy company. She keeps her mercenary nature well hidden. Sol doesn't begrudge her that nature, of course. Most everyone has to have a trade in this world. Hers just happens to be charm and beauty and lips that are big and soft as pillows, not to mention her unbridled enthusiasm, feigned or not, for some of the more nuanced acts of carnal sin.

Her back is turned to him now; he rests the base of his whiskey glass on the swell of her warm, generous hip, scratching idly at his cheek with his other hand. Sol doesn't know if it was his gut or another nightmare that woke him, this time. He has that sweaty, jittery feeling that comes with the dreams but they don't always wake him. He's used to them. If one can ever really get used to such things. It's automatic, any more, waking, reaching over in the dark for the whiskey decanter, pouring without spilling a drop. A learned skill. Sitting up, waiting to calm again, hoping sleep will return. Sometimes it does, but not often enough for his liking.

He thought it had been squashed down, but memories of the past have been popping up, more and more, since seeing Billy, since what happened after. Since Elizabeth, too, maybe, before then. He thinks about her more than he'd like. Thinks about Owen, too, that other life he's tried to forget. Look at him now, though, he tells himself, yet again: this big old house, all his money, the fine whiskey and the finer girls. A beauty like Kitt curled up against him? Warm and sweet-smelling and soft, his come in her belly and the knowledge that all it would take is a nudge and those lips will be around him once more. The Sol from before, that busted-down old fart, would never have had a girl like that, not in a million years. And never mind the particulars of the transaction because, when he's with her, she's good enough at what she does for him to have no trouble suspending disbelief, at least until he finishes maybe. After that, no matter, she's good company and he enjoys being around her. She looks good on his arm.

And, really, how long had he been happy with Elizabeth? A few good years, that was about it. Never mind that those years are the ones his mind constantly tracks back to, if he lets it. Rosy glow of memory, all that was; every time he calls it up it just gets another polish until now it's almost too bright to look at. No way it was like that before, he knows it. They were just two people together with fights and accidental gas and everything else that goes with being a couple. Nothing is ever perfect.

Would he go back, though? Wake up again in that shitty old shack, like Billy had asked?

That time he spent before, running his mucker crew, drinking with those boys, fighting and whoring and gambling, those memories have some of that same false polish on them, he knows it. Easy to remember the bad times, too, though, all that went before with the job and being broke and all that shit with Sean. Maybe that's his problem: those other lives are so sharp around the edges, the good and the bad both standing out in high relief. This one, it's just flat, really. There's good and there's bad but even the standouts feel squashed and hunched.

This right here, lying in a warm bed with a beautiful woman, that should be a high; that shameful fucking thing with Frank, a low. And they are, they are, but somehow it's just not the same. It's attenuated, weak, like it's happened to someone else and he just happens to have acquaintance with it.

So now, even knowing what he does, that he couldn't ever be the same man as he was before, would he go back, given the chance? Try again, one more time?

It's childish, but he closes his eyes and makes a wish. He tries to pull it to him by force of will. *Just one more chance*. That's all I'm asking. At least let me decide, with the choice right in front of me. Make the bet or not. Easy to speculate on the answer, but let me decide. He listens for the rattle of Indian bones.

But, of course, when he opens his eyes again, there's not a goddamn thing.

Eventually, Sol dozes back off, startling himself to wakefulness by the whiskey spilled onto his belly. He jerks up and catches sight of the old Indian, Marked Face, crouching there in the dark at the end of the huge bed, like a cat come to steal his breath. Leering, the bones in his hair rattling softly. Sol yells, an unmanly squeal, and tries to scrabble away. The old man opens his mouth, too wide. Croaks like a raven, crawling forward towards him.

The spill of whiskey, or maybe his hollering, wakes him, for real this time. There's no one at the end of the bed, there never was; it's just another fucking nightmare. His belly is wet with malt and sweat and he's shaking.

Kitt reaches out a hand, comforting him, still sound asleep. It's one of the girl's most attractive features, her ability to sleep through just about anything but also so easy to rouse when Sol gets to needing her during the long, shuddery nights awake. He closes his eyes, concentrating on the warmth of her hand, the soft press of her ass against his hip. He rolls over, sidles up behind her, buries his nose in the nape of her neck. He matches his breathing to hers until he finally drops back off, a long time later.

Marked Face watches from the darkness at the foot of the bed while the old man sleeps.

It is almost done, now.

The boy is ready. Finally, after all these long years, he is ready. All that Marked Face has done, the pain and sorrow he has caused, has been to bring this time to pass, to prepare his nephew for the trials that come. Poor Sagiistoo is the point of the spear and now we shall see if he breaks.

Marked Face can feel the excitement of the Above Ones.

His brother, his own part played, waits in the place where it will end, once again.

Past the end of things is a beginning.

"I have one last favor to ask of you, white man," Marked Face whispers, with words that lack sound. "You, who the Above Ones have bound to my nephew. There is a thing you will do for me."

Slithering like Lenaahi, Snake, he comes forward and pours the dream into the white man's ear.

Listen, Solomon Parker –

6.

– Listen, and I will tell you of the end of Maatakssi and Siinatssi

You whites, those children of Maatakssi, called forth by Nihaat, the one called Spider, spread across the Earth. Your kinfolk grew great and strong and their numbers were without end, their power without compare. They returned to the lands of the People and drove the tribes to destruction, with their shooters and their sickness and their medicine water. Horrible dreams at night came with them, and the People never had rest. They wept for Siinatssi to save them with his own great medicine, but it was as Raven had foretold; evil had hollowed out the insides of Siinatssi and his children, and left them with nothing but a gnawing hunger, one that could never be sated. The medicine had abandoned them, leaving only this hunger.

Finally, now that he was on the edge of becoming nothing but a spirit, Siinatssi's broken mind cleared, for a time; he was given a vision and understood what he must do. Perhaps the Above Ones, looking down, whispered in his ear. He gathered his pouch and his tobacco and his traveling things and left the People in the night, alone. He knew that he must find his brother, Maatakssi.

Maatakssi had disappeared, though, long ago. It had been years since any of the People had seen him, though he had become a terrible legend. Maatakssi, who had betrayed the People and created these empty, hungry white men who were killing them; Maatakssi, who had been driven mad by what he'd done, madder even than the sorcerer, Siinatssi. Some of the old women would say that they had seen Maatakssi here or there, in this cave or by that grove of willows, but these were merely stories to scare the young children into obedience. Maatakssi was gone, and Siinatssi knew that only Raven would be able to find him.

So Siinatssi sought the bird out.

Raven, though, even that creature was hard to find, and it took Siinatssi many years to do so, a story that is for another time. For Raven, seeing the world truly as he did, knowing how things would come to pass, had long ago witnessed this destruction of the People and known that Nihaat's terrible trick was the only way to save even a remnant of the tribes from Siinatssi's madness. Sorrow had overtaken the bird, and Raven spent long years alone, away from his wives even, growing thin and silent, his feathers gone dusty and brittle. But, at the sight of poor Siinatssi, even Raven's cracked heart was moved and he agreed to lead him to his brother Maatakssi.

When Raven brought him to the spot, atop the mountain that was shaped like an ear, Siinatssi could not help but weep, seeing what he had wrought. Nihaat, ever helpful, had placed a veil over the place, a spell that prevented any from finding what remained of the wretch that Maatakssi had become. But Raven's eyes were sharp, and no veil, not even one made by Spider, could block his vision.

By this time, Maatakssi was more beast than man, filthy, hair matted, wordless. He sat surrounded by empty barrels of his children's medicine water, covered in his own sick, a constant stream of tears running down his face. The old women say that the river at the base of that mountain was created by the flow of Maatakssi's tears but that, again, is another story. I was speaking of the end of the two brothers.

The mountain was a sacred place. Being shaped like an ear, it heard the dreams that crossed from the west each night once Sun had gone to his sleep. These dreams would rumble through the bones of the Earth and crawl into the skulls of the People who slept on the Earth's skin. But now, the burning drink of the whites, or perhaps Maatakssi's tears, seeped into the mountain, causing those nightmares and terrible thoughts that came in place of the dreams from the west. My brother, oh my brother, *Siinatssi thought, weeping harder,* what have we made, the two of us. Truly, we, the sons of Old Man, have been cursed by the Above Ones. We have been damned for our sins.

Siinatssi stilled his tears as best he could and took the cup of medicine water from his brother's hand He cleared away a spot, and sat down. "Brother," *he said,* "it is I, Siinatssi. I have done you a terrible wrong, for which I have no hope of forgiveness. But Brother, we must do something to save the People." *Maatakssi made no answer and showed no awareness, merely wept silently at what had come to pass.*

Siinatssi tried again, more words that went unheard. He stood up then, and danced his most powerful dance, sang his strongest song, but he was empty, you will remember, hollow and always hungry. Filled with madness and a great anger that clouded his vision at times. His medicine was gone. Still, for many hours, he danced and sang and exhorted his brother to listen, to no effect, until, finally, Siinatssi sank to the earth and wept again.

Raven watched all this and, with a deep sigh, shimmered, then, and changed his form. He regained the shape of Old Man, which he'd abandoned long ago, after his sons had left him.

He reached down, touching each of his sons on their head,

clearing their minds and bringing them back to themselves. Holding their hands together, he called upon the Above Ones.

"Surely my sons have been punished enough, Above Ones," *Old Man said.* "Please take pity on them. It is I, your friend, who asks this." *Old Man lowered himself to the dirt, his own tears making mud of it.* "Please take pity on my sons."

The Above Ones are cruel. They are spiteful, even, at times. They toy with their creations, but they are not entirely heartless. Looking down then at pitiful Siinatssi and Maatakssi, seeing the grief of Old Man, the Above Ones saw anew this world, saw the many mistakes they had made in building it yet again, while forming it out of the chaos of the before times. They saw the terrible state of things now: the sickness of the land, the dying animals, the grief of the People who walked the Earth. Perhaps they felt guilty even, although who can tell the feelings of people of that kind. But maybe this had something to do with what they did, or maybe their motives were other.

"Siinatssi, you are almost a spirit," *they said.* "You have let evil magic eat you hollow. Why should we take pity on you?" *Siinatssi hung his head in shame.* "And you, Maatakssi, you brought those whites into the world, the ones who are destroying the People and this land we made for them. Why should we take pity on you?" *Maatakssi put his hands to his face and wept again.*

"But perhaps there is a way," *the Above Ones said,* "for you to show us that you have learned from your mistakes, that you are no longer the cruel and selfish men you once were. Your fate will be bound with that of your People, and with their choosing you will be judged."

The Above Ones showed them, then, what it was they

required, giving Maatakssi and Siinatssi a vision of what must be done, the fate that they would have to endure to right the wrongs they had made. Perhaps those gods smiled, then, too. They were great gamblers, and the place in which they lived could be dull at times, after all.

The brothers looked at one another, understanding. They wept and held one another, sorry for all that had come to pass. They embraced their father, pressing their heads to the dirt, after, begging his forgiveness for their many sins.

"I forgave you so long ago, though, my sons," *he said to them, the tears hot in his eyes.* "So long ago."

Maatakssi and Siinatssi turned to face the sun just coming up now, shining down on the top of that mountain, glowing like a watchful eye. They opened their arms and accepted the will of the gods. They knew what they must do.

7.

Billy listens to the screams. The wail of the sirens and the sharp clanking clatter of the fire-bells. Smoke pours out of the Speculator's headframe, a black billowing cloud of soot and ash and rising sparks. He's sweating, shaking with the memory of the Penn, real or not; that long-ago flight in the dark and the wet, the asshole-pinching terror as he and Sol and the crew fled the flame and the smoke, in those times that never happened. He'd thought – convinced himself – that he'd forgotten all of that, but the banging of the bells and the banshee sirens bring it back, pound it behind his eyes, tighten his chest. It's hard to take a breath, not just because of the sore, busted-up ribs Sol's boys had left him with, a couple of weeks ago: the smell of the smoke, acrid and sharp in his nose, is pulling his throat closed with remembering.

He limps back down the hill, fighting the crowds that are pushing towards the Speculator, moths drawn to the flames, to try to help or merely to gawk at the spectacle of tragedy. Billy elbows men out of the way, ignoring their curses, his broken, half-set arm shouting at him and the breath hot and gasping in his chest, until he's well away from the press of men. He can still smell the bite of smoke, hear the yelling and the sirens and the bells, so he keeps stumbling along, always downhill, away from the fire. It doesn't matter where he goes, he just needs to get away.

Eventually, much later, he finds himself in a dim, ragged little tavern down in the Patch, empty save for the bartender. Billy shakes his head when asked the latest, says he doesn't know – *don't fucking know, all right?* – just wants a beer and another and another.

He shouldn't even be in Butte, he should be back at Warm Springs, but he's been kept here. First the week or so of convalescence he'd needed after Sol's men had beat the shit out of him for his insults; after that, he'd decided to stay in town, to look for his uncle. Nowhere to be found on Utah Street or anywhere else, though, Marked Face, and Billy wonders if Sol had been lying about seeing him in the first place, for reasons of his own.

He thinks about those men down in the Speculator who maybe won't be coming out, their last panicked moments in the dark; he thinks about Sol and Flynn and Michael and the Dans, about running for their lives wrapped in that same terror. Them, the lucky ones. He thinks about Owen and beer follows beer until he can't think straight, any more, which is just fine by him. That's the goal, tonight.

Hours pass, and the tavern fills with angry men.

The headline reads:

33 KNOWN DEAD; 162 MISSING
GRANITE MOUNTAIN DISASTER WORST IN

METAL MINING HISTORY
BUTTE STAGGERS UNDER PARALYZING EFFECT
OF TERRIBLE LOSS OF LIFE
EVERY MINING OFFICIAL IN BUTTE AIDING IN
THE GHASTLY RESCUE WORK

Sol's shaking hands lower the *Butte Daily Post*. For a long minute he thinks that he's going to be physically sick, to puke down into his own lap. His breath comes short and fast and doesn't bring much air with it. He's sweating, the muscles of his back and belly gripped tight to his bones. The stink of smoke in the air, which cuts even through the cigar reek that impregnates the walls of his office, brings back too many memories of that time before. The whiskey he drank earlier is burning his guts. He feels old, old. His true age for once, not whatever the lines of his face say. Although, today, the two are probably in sync with one another.

He knew this would happen and yet he went ahead anyway. Out of greed. That was it, pure and simple. He's condemned who knows how many men to death, so that he could buy office blocks and businesses. Condemned them to burn and smother and suffocate in the dark, just like his boy.

Sol has damned himself, just like Frank had warned, before he'd killed him, too.

Damned.

Instead of puking, the sick bubbles out of him in laughter that, once released, he can't stop. Laughter that twists close to tears and back again. It doesn't matter, he tells himself. It doesn't matter even though he knows it to be a lie. Frank was right. He's damned, and this is his punishment. It would be horrible if it wasn't so fucking funny. Fire, flame, smoke, over and over and over again. He's still laughing, head between his knees, holding his ribs and trying to stop himself, when Marcus Connor pushes into the office.

"I couldn't stop him, Sol." Mickey is standing behind Connor, holding his hand to his bleeding nose. "I couldn't stop him." Whatever he's going to say next is cut off by the door that Connor slams in his face. He's white as a sheet, hair standing on end, soot smeared across his cheek, eyes wild.

"What did you do, Sol? *What the fuck did you do?*" he whispers. He strides over to the big window on the far wall, pulls the curtain shut. "No one can know about this. Sol!"

It takes long, long moments for Sol's laughter to stop. He leans back, wiping his eyes, giving Connor what he knows is a ghastly grin. The grin of a dead man. Damned. "Did what you told me to do, Mark, that's all. 2500. Like you said. New technology. Bolsheviks, though, fucking Bolsheviks, hey?" He clamps his teeth down over the laugh he can feel trying to claw out from his throat, again, scraping up out of his belly. "I did like you said."

"I never said any of that, Sol. *I never fucking said that.*" The damage control is beginning already, before responsibility can come to squat like a vulture on a carcass. "We *never talked about this.* You understand? Sol! *You understand?*"

Sol closes his eyes, so he doesn't have to see Mark Connor, and leans further back in his chair. Oh, he understands. Wasn't no way that any Company man would wind up with a smear on him, because of this.

Tragedy and all, but the ACM had done everything they could to prevent this kind of thing. New fire safety system, after all! Sure, it needed some work, maybe. But those anarchists! Terrorists! They're the real enemy here. The Company would make some sad statements, pay off some families – cheaply as possible, of course – talk about further safety concerns but it's best for all of Butte – all! – if we get back on production footing, soon as we can. The whole town benefits from Company productivity; we all benefit. We all suffer when work slows.

Surely you can see that?

Connor would come out of this wary but untouched. Never mind his masters; they were never at any risk to begin with. Hell, even Sol was clear of danger. Probably come out of this to the better, even, if only to ensure his silence. Although, really, what could he ever say?

"Oh, yeah, Mark," Sol says now, eyes still closed. "You bet I understand you." He opens the desk drawer, starts to pull out a bottle. "Drink?"

"*Drink? Now?* Come on, Sol, you're not serious. Listen, I shouldn't even be here. Best we don't see one another for a while, right? Let the dust settle–"

"Smoke."

"What?"

"Let the *smoke* settle. Maybe a bit more apt, phrase-wise."

"Jesus, Sol, really? Whatever you want to call it, we need to stay away from one another for a bit, couple few months maybe. We'll make this good for you, don't worry. The Company looks out for its own, and you've been a good man for us to know. Done good work. This is a shame, what happened, but we'll get past it, all right?

We'll get past it."

Sol smiles a lazy, crazy smile at that. *The Company looks out for its own.*

"Sol, are we good here? Look at me. We good?"

He nods. Oh, we're good. Never better, Mark, never better.

"Course we are."

Sol reaches into the drawer again. Connor has his hand on the office door when Sol pulls out Sean's pistol and shoots him in the back. He gets up, walking over, and shoots him in the head. Keeps shooting and, by the time Mickey comes bursting in again, the pistol is empty, smoking in his hand.

– *Listen, Solomon Parker.*

He remembers the dream, then. It comes to him, echoing like gunfire, rattling like dice on the floor.

He understands, now, sees what the old Indian had showed him in the night. Sol knows what he has to do, where he needs to go, to finally make this right.

He's damned, but there's always a choice.

There's always a choice. Right, Frank?

Take the bet or not. The price, he'll pay it whatever it is. One last wager, then, for the sad remnant of his soul. It might be a case of too little, too late but, for the first time in many years, he feels his luck coming back.

"Mickey," he says. "Get Faraday. I need him to find someone for me."

8.

The wind is sharp in Billy's face when the hood is finally pulled off. It's dusk, by the looks of things; there's a low bonfire kindled and Sol drops the burlap sack down into it. It flares up after a moment, washing his face with light. Sol squats down, slowly, taking a seat on a low, flat rock. He uncorks a bottle, drinks a long swallow and then silently extends it, eyes still on the fire.

Billy's wrists are sore and chafed from the scratchy jute rope that had bound them. He has bruises and scrapes on knees and elbows from where he'd fallen as he'd been dragged on the long, steep, wordless walk to wherever he is now. The end, he guesses, one way or another. Sol's man hadn't been any more gentle when he'd scooped him up this time and, drunk as he was, still, Billy hadn't put up much of a fight. A couple of jabs to his broken ribs had folded him over like a jackknife; he'd been tossed into the back of an auto, his wrists efficiently tied, head bagged. Sol's employees were good at what they did.

He looks around. They're up high somewhere and, near as he can tell, he and Sol are alone, Mickey and Faraday nowhere to be seen. He steps forward, taking the bottle from Sol, and drinks. It's good whiskey, smooth and hot. Billy sits down on the other side of the fire and, for a long time, neither of them speak, just stare into the flames. The summer night sags to an end and the darkness wraps tight around their little circle of light. There's just a sliver of moon but the stars are strangely absent, although, as far as Billy can see, the sky is clear and cloudless.

They pass the bottle back and forth and Billy finds himself getting sleepy, even though he knows that this is likely his last night on this Earth and, as such, he should try to savor it. Take a memory of it with him if, wherever he's going, such things can follow. He's oddly calm, content. The thought of escape, of cracking this bottle over Sol's head and running down the hill and away somewhere, anywhere, doesn't even really register as an option. Billy feels more peaceful than he has for years. Maybe it's because his choices, such as they ever were, have been taken away.

Whatever happens will happen It's liberating, really.

"Been thinking a lot about what you said, Bill." Sol speaks, abruptly. "About taking it all back. Trying again."

"Yeah?" Billy drinks, passes the bottle back. It's almost empty.

"You think we just never made the right choices?"

A long pause, and then Billy sighs. He picks up a little stick, scratching it in the dirt between his feet. "I don't think it matters, Sol."

"Of course it matters."

"No, I don't mean it like that. I mean that it was always going to wind up like this, one way or another. Stories get twisted together, my uncle told me once, and I think he's right. You maybe just got caught up and pulled into mine somehow. I don't know."

"Your uncle, hey? That sorcerer, or whatever he is, is the reason we're here."

"Shit, Sol. He's no sorcerer. He's just an old man, nothing more than that. Just an old man. I don't understand any of it, but none of that other stuff ever happened. I know you think it did, but all of that bullshit, it never happened. I told you, you just got caught up." Billy pauses, drops the little stick. "There's something wrong with me, Sol. I think I'm sick, like my dad. I need help." He looks around. "Although, I suppose this is good enough. Whatever you're going to do, let's just make an end to it, all right? I'm tired."

Sol looks up, fixes Billy with a sharp eye. "You really think that? After everything."

"Sol, I don't have the answers."

A short bark of a laugh. "Shared crazy, hey? And stories getting twisted, is that how you put it? Now, that would be a thing. That would be a thing indeed. You reckon we should both be down at that hospital, then, with my brother?"

"I don't have the answers."

"Yeah, well."

They're quiet again as the night pulls onward.

Billy's dreaming of a bird, huge and black, almost the size of the sky itself. Or maybe he himself has become small, like an ant. He feels no fear, though, only a soft contentment that's washed with sadness. It's peaceful, lying here, watching this beautiful black thing on the air. The bird soars above him, fixing him with one dark eye that begins to glow red, becoming almost unbearably luminous, so much that Billy has to look away.

The raven speaks, then.

The perspective shifts and he sees himself, lying by a dying fire, atop a mountain shaped like an ear. Low voices bring him awake.

The dawn sun is bright, glowing orange, looking up at the mountain. Billy isn't surprised to see his father and his uncle squatting in the dirt, next to Sol. They're staring at one another, intently, and then Sol nods. He picks up the marked bones that lay where he tossed them, hands them back. "All right," he says. "I will, then."

The three old men turn to look at Billy as he pulls himself upright and, for one odd moment, it's difficult to tell them apart.

Sol stands up, slow and wobbly on tired knees. He walks over, looking at Billy. His eyes are wet and, without saying anything, he takes Billy in his arms, pulling him tight to his chest. "I'm sorry, Bill," he whispers. "I'm sorry for all of it. I didn't understand, but you were right." He holds him for a long time and then takes a deep, shaky breath. Releasing his arms, he puts a hand to the side of Billy's face. "Always loved you like a son, boy," he says, softly. "Always did. Even as I was fucking things all up for you, I loved you like a son."

Sol turns and walks off before Billy can respond, heading down from the little clearing, away from the sun. Billy tries to speak but his throat is tight shut, aching. Even now, beat to hell, ribs aching, and with everything that's come to pass, he still loves Sol, too. He wants to say it, but he can't.

Before Sol drops below the crest of the hill, he turns. "There's always a choice, Bill," he shouts, "and you're a good man. A better man than I ever was." He smiles, and then with another step he's gone.

It takes Billy a long moment to collect himself. He dries his eyes, then, and crosses the little clearing to stand before his family.

"Behold Siinatssi," he says, in the old tongue, the language of truth and substance, remembering the words of the raven. Somehow, it's not even surprising to Billy, finally seeing his family as they are. Maybe the great bird in his dream has brought him understanding or maybe, finally, he truly is seeing the world as it really exists. The thought doesn't worry him now. Crazy or not, this is his world.

"Behold Siinatssi, Sagiistoo," his uncle says, "but you will learn that a name isn't important." He looks weary, sad. "I am sorry for the tricks, for causing you pain and doubt, but things must pass as they do. From chaos our true nature is shown. That is ever the way of the Above Ones."

"They are a hard people," Maatakssi, his father, says. "Sometimes a thing must first be nearly broken, before it can find its strength. For my part, I am sorry I was not stronger for you. I was never strong enough."

Siinatssi and Maatakssi close their eyes, remembering long-ago things, and tears run down their cheeks. For a moment, the water shines in the sun, although their faces are dark, shadowed.

"Sagiistoo, my son," Maatakssi whispers, "it has been so many years. So many terrible things we have done, so many wrong choices. But, perhaps now, with your help, we can make them right again, at least for a time."

"Take our hands, Sagiistoo," Siinatssi says, his eyes open. "You must see a thing, and then you must decide. It is time for this to end, in one way or another. The People are waiting."

"So the Above Ones have decreed," Maatakssi says. "They await your choosing. No doubt they have long ago made their wagers. Would that this thing had not passed to you. I am so sorry, for everything."

Billy steps forward and takes each man's hand with one of his own, feeling the dry, heavy solidity, the sharp bones and stony knuckles. He looks into the black pits of their eyes, and then he sees it. Holding tightly, he falls forward into the vision of what could be, if he chooses to make it so. It's only their grip that keeps him upright as he sags against the weight of it.

He watches himself shovel cowshit in the hospital barn. Sitting with Dr Rideout, of an evening, smoking a cigarette and sipping mediocre whiskey, watching the sun sink and listening to the soft cries of hunting owls. He sees himself, older, taking a girl in his arms. The cry of an infant. The smell of cooking dinner. A little boy plays in the yard. The sun rising and setting, rising again. Fights with the woman, making up. The boy, older now, helping him fix a sagging barn door. Grey in the woman's hair, smile lines around her eyes. A small house on the hospital grounds, paint peeling, window out of true, but warm inside. Bread baking, the glow of soft lights. A bed that sags in the middle, pulling him towards her. Arm around her hip, nose at the nape of her neck, breathing in. The sun rises, sets, rises again, over and over. Scraping for money, tired of working over-hard for too little pay. On the porch with a boy become a man, a baby on his knee. A funeral, the house empty again. A sore back, and knees that crack, needing to get up and piss three times in the night. Whiskey and a cigarette during the evenings, mostly alone, visited by his family at times.

It's not a bad life, not at all. Maybe not the one that he would have picked for himself, not exactly, had he been able to choose from all the particulars, but one that would fit him. A life that he knows he'd never want to change.

A good life.

Things shift, and he sees himself, a boy again, hiding from the fists of his father and his uncle, those madmen or sorcerers or whoever, whatever, they are. Cruel, hard, full of anger at this world the gods have made, that they themselves have brought to pass. Broken from what they've seen, what they've done, the weight of their endless lives. Memories cracking them apart. Cursed, damned by the Above Ones, against whom they'd sinned, long ago.

Billy sees the sorrows of the People, the whites covering the land. He watches the last remnants of the tribes pass into nothingness.

But the stories roll backwards, then. He sees his father, sitting on this mountain, surrounded by whiskey barrels. His uncle dancing, making a feeble medicine song. He watches the history of Maatakssi, of Siinatssi. All those that came and went. The history of the People, his people, his family. That thing that tethers him to this life across a thousand thousand years, roots him, although this is a bitter fate to share.

He hears the laughter of the Above Ones, the rattle of dice.

In his mind, Billy can still see the bird in his dream, soaring over him, brushed with a sadness as big as this mountain, eye red like the sun.

His self drops away, then, into someone else, caught up and twisted into the story he watches.

A spear, in his own hand now. He feels the roughness of the shaft, the weight of it. He's running, this person he's become. Another man, faceless, runs with him; they're sprinting towards the wives in the long-ago, before the People. The breath rasping in his chest, the pounding of his heart. The other man begins to pull ahead, and Billy feels the anger, from which he suffers at times, growing.

He sits on the porch, smoking, listening to hunting owls.

He runs, raising the spear.

Choices, forking.

The tapping of a beak on a branch, the wood fissuring.

Tapping, banging, booming.

Booming.

The Night Announcer

—◆— 1900 —◆—

Stevensville, Montana/
Warm Springs, Montana

Flame and smoke.

Once again.

The room is hot and close, smoke from the wildfires to the west floats lazily in air that feels like treacle in his lungs. With the back of his sleeve he rubs the sweat from his forehead, blinking in the dim light that seeps under and between the curtains. He always hated that she kept the room so dark, the drapes shut, but that won't matter for much longer.

The lantern's weight stretches at the ends of his fingers, as if seeking release.

Elizabeth won't be home for hours yet. She and the baby are where he left them, with his brother and Sara, visiting in town, doing the shopping. It will be hard for her, but it's the right thing to do and Ag will take care of them. His brother is a good man. Maybe the way Sol was, once, before he fucked it all up. He'd like to think so.

But you can always change who you are.

Lizzie will get help, and Owen will be safe. Let them start over. He won't be there with them, but they'll be all right. That was the wager, this time; that was the price. Nothing is ever free and no life is without consequence, not even one like Sol's. Regardless of what he may have thought before, he knows the truth of that, now. Perhaps the last game was something of an apology, a reward, maybe, for his part in Billy's story, that life twisted with his own. Whatever the reason, Sol knows that, this time, when he'd handed the marked bones back to the old Indian, he'd finally, truly won.

His luck has finally come home, at last.

He swings the lantern and lets it go. There's the crack of glass and the bite of kerosene. A thin puddle slops across the dry wooden floor toward his feet, pooling around the leg of the empty crib. Hazy waves shimmer in the air, climbing up his legs. He takes the matches from his pocket, scratches them alight.

Sol Parker takes a deep breath, tasting the smell of warm bedsheets and the powdery sweetness of a baby's crib, the sharp tang of wildfire smoke. The smell of a life.

He drops the burning matches at his feet.

The flames rise around him and he smiles to hear the raven at the window, calling his name.

Listen.

I remember the East Wind was howling, pushing Maatakssi and his brother Siinatssi across the great water on a skin boat.

I remember the wind and the raging water. I remember crying and praying to the Above Ones for succor; we cried and prayed to Old Man for forgiveness. "Let us come home," we cried, "Take us from these waters."

Old Man turned his ears from his sons and instead we came to the place of the People, battered and wet, tired and sore. We pulled our boat to shore and kissed the land; we gave thanks to the Above Ones for saving us.

Some say Old Man did not turn his ears from his sons Maatakssi and Siinatssi at all, but that he himself came to the lands of the People, searching for his lost children. Some say that he watched over his sons in a new form, watched over the People who became his grandchildren.

We came to these lands and, for a time, it was good. Game was plentiful and the weather still. We talked to Black Bear, and to Beaver in his lodge. Particularly we reverenced Raven, though, who was always our friend.

For a time, it was good, but we became lonely, for we were the only two in the lands of the People, and we longed for wives. We asked Siyakohah where we could find wives to give us sons and daughters, but Black Bear did not know, nor did Beaver at his labors. Raven, though, had seen many places in his travels.

"I have seen a people," *he said,* "east along the great river. They are traders from the north lands. Maybe they will have wives for you."

"Are their women strong? Are they beautiful?" *we asked.*

Raven shrugged. "Truly, it is difficult for me to tell you two-leg walkers apart. Now I must get back to my own wives, who will be missing me." *And with that he flew off.*

We headed east along the gorge of the great river. We decided to race, that the first to reach the northern traders would have first choosing of their women. We ran, racing towards our new wives.

Dr Agamemnon Rideout reaches up to help Elizabeth out of the cart. Owen is in Sara's arms, sleeping peacefully. Setting Elizabeth down, Dr Rideout straightens the black band he wears on his sleeve, his expression weary. He slides one arm around his wife's ample waist, kisses her on the top of her head. He takes Elizabeth's hand, then, gently leading her towards his large house behind the hospital. Soon enough there would be time to get her settled into a ward but, now, she needs the comfort of family.

Later, at dusk, he sits on the porch at the back of the main hospital building, watching the sun set. He rolls a cigarette and passes it to the old Indian sitting beside him, even though technically it's against the rules. The old man nods, smiles, reaching forward for a light. He has long, white hair, the ends of his braids tied with raven feathers. His seamed face crinkles into a satisfied smile as he pulls the smoke into his chest. Lately they've taken to sitting like this, of an evening, doctor and patient enjoying the end of the day, smoking and listening to the soft hooting of hunting owls.

I will tell you one last story.

I will tell you how man came into the world.

In the early days, when this world was young and only partly built, the Above Ones made a man out of river mud. The man was ill-formed and the mud difficult to work with, so the Above Ones became angry and moved to destroy it.

Old Man, who was in the form of Raven that day, watched this from his perch on a tall pine. Before the Above Ones could destroy their half-made creation, Raven said, "Above Ones, why are you angry with this thing?"

"It does not move, Raven," *they said,* "it only lies there."

"It has no legs," *the bird said.* "Give me one moment."

He flew off and came back with two sticks in his beak. He put them into the half-made man's body and the man stood up. The Above Ones were pleased, and enjoyed watching the man walk around, although soon they became angry, and again moved to destroy their creation.

"Above Ones," *Raven said, before they could crush the man,* "why are you angry with this thing?"

"It does not dance," *they said,* "it only stumbles around."

"It has no eyes and cannot see, Above Ones. Give me one moment." *He flew off once more, returning with two stones in his beak, which he placed in the man's head for eyes. The man blinked and began to move in a purposeful manner, mimicking the steps Raven showed him. Once again, the Above Ones were pleased, and enjoyed watching the man dance.*

The Above Ones made more and more of these mud men and had great pleasure from their new creations, putting them to this and that and dicing upon the outcome, until they lost interest for a time.

Raven knew the fickle nature of the Above Ones, though; he knew that they could be cruel with the things they had made. Always a responsible bird, he vowed that he would watch over these new people and be as a father to them, given the part he had played in their creation. This is why we reverence Raven above all others, and give him the prime parts of our kills.

Like the world itself, we men are imperfect things, but we can be made better.

Listen.

I am Sagiistoo, the Night Announcer.

I am Maatakssi.

I am Siinatssi.

I have been all these people, and I have been others.
I have played many roles in these many worlds.
I have told you: the name of a thing is not important.
I remember.
I am memory.

Once, Sagiistoo, the Night Announcer, was tested and made the choice at the end of things, on a mountain shaped like an ear. Sagiistoo of the People. Sagiistoo, the point of the spear. Who did not choose the easy life of one man but went back, to the beginning, and made a new path. Who brought the People into being once more, and reworked the shape of the world.

This I did, although I am not the man I was then.

The point of the spear did not break, that time, but cut the branch like the beak of a great bird and, after many years, we are brought back to this place once more. Things passed a different way, but we are here again. It is the story of the world I sing to you, and it has been sung a thousand thousand times, in a thousand thousand ways. I remember the stories, and those other roles I have played. Memory is the legacy of my family, or perhaps it is our curse for long-ago sins.

The Above Ones are cruel, as I have said all along, and they try to break us, but the People remain. That is the test, again and again. Novelty is a rare thing for those gods. But they are not heartless, and there are these moments of peace, of happiness, which fall to me even now, as I draw near the end once more. I can feel my time approaching and, soon enough, I will seek out the unlucky boy, as once I was sought out. My part is different, this time, as is his. A name has no meaning, as I have said again and again: there is only the role itself.

There will come another moment, and a man of the People will be tested. A choice will be made, a wager won or lost, and *we will begin once more.*

Some fear this fate but I choose to see hope, because the Above Ones made many mistakes with their creations and the People have many flaws yet. But we are sharpened each time like a blade; we become more perfect with every pass. The old women say that, when the People have been completed and made whole, this will be the end of Time because the Earth will have lost its purpose.

I say, perhaps then this world will be a paradise and the Above Ones will leave us in peace. Perhaps there is the novelty they seek. I am a hopeful man and this is what I believe, but then again I have had my fill of gods.

Listen, I will tell you a secret:

Some days, I think that maybe I am just another lunatic in this place.

Perhaps I am just a man who let the stories crawl into his head. Just an old man with feathers in his hair, who shovels cowshit in a barn and sits smoking tobacco in the evenings with his white doctor. But then I feel the warm bones in the pouch I keep next to my skin and I remember.

I remember Raven, the smiling bird, flying above me, eyes bright like the sun.

I remember the joys, the laughter of my children and my children's children. I remember the sadnesses, the mistakes, even then. I remember the beauty, and also the terrible things that came to pass for the People, my children, my kinfolk, before they were saved. The coming of the whites again, for other reasons, but coming nonetheless. For such are the gods' designs and those people must play their part, even now.

I remember all of these things.

I am tired and it has been a long life, bringing me to this place. Near the end, once more. Close to another beginning.

    It is I who sings you this tale.

AUTHOR'S NOTES

This not a Native story. I want to be especially clear with that, because it's important. This is a "Native" story, by which I mean it does not reflect any particular tribe or culture; when writing *The Trials of Solomon Parker* I very deliberately set out to anonymize those elements because, frankly, I'm not a Native and those aren't my stories to tell. That said, I've lived in the Western US for almost the entirety of my life, and Native stories are part of this place. I'm of the belief that anyone should be allowed to tell a type of story, if perhaps not a certain particular, so long as it's treated with respect, and that was the goal here.

The "Native" elements of this book, then, have been picked and chosen from a variety of indigenous traditions from here in the West, and assembled into something that reflects them in the general rather than the specific. The "myths" themselves I simply made up, but are modeled on the kinds of stories that appear across all sorts of cultures, not only Native American ones. Some things that I left intact are the (translated into English) names of Marked Face, Bad Bird, and Night Announcer, which are the Blackfoot words for badger, bat, and owl, respectively, although the "Native" words I used are fabrications. I couldn't resist keeping the Gros Ventre trickster Nihaat in, as-is, because I liked the fact that his name became the word for "whites" in that language; the rest of his role in this story, aside from his association with the Big-Bellies, is my own fiction. Raven, of course, appears as a character in a variety of tribal mythologies. The story of Rabbit Woman and Moon's carrot is based on the Blackfoot myth of Feather Woman and the Great Turnip, which is itself of course similar to the stories of Pandora, or Adam and Eve and the tree of knowledge.

The flavor of these "Native" parts of the story owes a great debt to a number of genuine Native writers, particularly James Welch; his book *Fools Crow* I've probably read half a dozen times, if not more, and is absolutely magnificent. The idea for my story about the original creation of the whites was inspired by Leslie Marmon Silko's in *Ceremony*, although hers (a contest between evil sorcerers) is terrifying and, in fairness, much better.

Finally, even given the setting and cosmological framework, as the epigraph at the beginning of this book suggests, *The Trials of Solomon Parker* is, in some ways, a loose retelling of the Biblical story of Job. Which, again, is itself a common sort of myth across cultures, this idea of powerful beings making wagers on the actions of their own tormented people. It's a grim sort of idea that has always fascinated me.

Moving on to some history, then.

Butte, Montana, was an amazing place during the period written about in this book. It was a classic boomtown and, at 100,000-plus people at its peak, the largest city between Denver and the Pacific coast. These days its population is a third of that, and Butte has something of a faded grandeur to it. Some fun facts: Butte was the second city *in the world* to have electric lighting (the first: Paris, France) and the oldest continuously operating Chinese restaurant in America is in, you guessed it, Butte.

The hill on which Butte sits has been a mining site from the 1860s onward. First, gold and silver; then, as technology (and investment) improved and mines were able to go deeper and grow more elaborate, copper, the metal that made Butte's fortune, and its name: the Richest Hill on Earth. Fueled in part by the new demand for electrical wiring, copper drove the boom that turned Butte from a small mining camp to a cosmopolitan industrial city. People came from all over the world to get in on the rush, and money was being made hand over fist, particularly by those at the top of the heap. Several of these titans of industry collided over power and influence, the so-called Copper Wars which included, among others, William Rockefeller, Marcus Daly, F Augustus Heinze, and the fabulously corrupt William Clark. Clark was a Gilded Age robber baron of an easily recognized type; no friend to the working man, flaunting his wealth, he used his money, influence, and lax morality to eventually purchase a position as a US Senator.

With the copper boom came some of the things that one associates with a boomtown: disposable income, vice, and crime. For a time, Butte had all three in spades. What Butte also came to be known for, however, was its important position in the nascent Labor movement during the early parts of the twentieth century. The Gibraltar of Unionism, it was called, the scene of many pitched battles of Labor against the ACM for workers' rights and improvements to workplace safety. Life as a miner was tough and dangerous; Butte and the surrounding environs were the sites of a number of major industrial disasters, not to mention the day-to-day injuries and occasional deaths that came with mine work. Over all of that was the specter of very real health dangers posed by working conditions, including the dreaded silicosis, AKA miners' consumption.

I've conflated or modified some of this history to fit the story in this book. There were in fact deadly fires at both the Pennsylvania and Speculator/Granite Mountain mines (among others), although of course the cause of the latter was not as I described it. These fires resulted in catastrophic loss of life and highlighted the dangers that miners endured every day. The broad strokes of the "Bloody Tuesday" riot here come from the "Bloody Wednesday" riot of 1920, when ACM guards opened fire on striking miners, killing two. IWW organizer Frank Little was an American labor leader who came to Butte after the 1917 Speculator/Granite Mountain fire (not the Pennsylvania in 1916) and was later abducted from his boardinghouse and killed, left hanging from a railroad trestle with a sign warning other activists to stay away. No one was ever convicted of his murder. While Little was an actual figure, I've fictionalized details of his time in Butte for purposes of this story.

Finally, while I tried to stay close to the actual conditions in the various mines, and the processes used to get the ore out, I've fudged a few details here and there or likely simply gotten some things wrong. The various mines honeycombing the hill under Butte were in fact connected to one another (later standardized), making it a maze of hot, wet, dusty tunnels that were eventually allowed to fill with groundwater when played out. This water soon oxidized into acidity and dissolved out various remaining metals like arsenic, copper, cadmium, and so forth; that toxic soup then leached into the environment. Butte has been left a very polluted and poisoned place, the home of the largest Superfund site in America. With mining petering out and largely moving overseas in the decades after World War II, Butte's economy has largely collapsed, leaving it a shell of its former glory.

If you're interested in more of Butte's history, I recommend Michael Punke's *Fire and Brimstone*, Janet L Finn's *Mining Childhood*, and the WPA's *Copper Camp*, among others. It's still an amazing place to visit... a trip to the Mining Museum (and associated tour down a mine) and the Butte Labor History Center is a great way to pass a few hours. Maybe afterward go have some Chinese food at the Pekin Noodle parlor, and a beer and a shot at one of the bars, breweries, or distilleries... raise your glass to the Richest Hill on Earth.

ACKNOWLEDGMENTS

These sections are the one part of any book that is actually consistently enjoyable to write. That said, it is my duty and pleasure to thank (and in no particular order):

Once again, my wonderful agent, Jennie Goloboy, who somehow managed to sell this book, even if she confessed to me afterward that she had no idea how she was going to do so.

All of the fantastic Angry Robot crew. Alphabetically: Marc Gascoigne, Mike Underwood, Nick Tyler, and Penny "Marmite Yourself Before You Spite Yourself" Reeve (publicist to the stars and also me), who are all, hands down, absolutely lovely people to work with. Also, uh, still alphabetically: my editor, Phil Jourdan, who through some vague, mystical editorial Zen alchemy helped turn a convoluted manuscript into this book.

Copy editor Paul Simpson, who, among other things, smoothed out and clarified many tricky tenses ("it's someone in the future back to the past remembering forward … is that a *was* or *is* or *had been* or …?") while leaving intact the voice I was going for.

Amazing cover artist Steven Meyer-Rassow, because

just look at the covers of my books (and an extra shout-out here to both Steven and Marc – wearing his art-director hat – for tolerating my many, fussy suggestions).

All of my writer friends, who are such a great, supportive cast of misfits. To the previous suspects in the back of *Dr Potter's Medicine Show* I'd like to add: Wendy Wagner, for book-tour Powell's conversations and just generally being awesome; Peter McLean, for sending me a magazine with my first print review, all the way from England; and Dr Adam Rakunas, also for book-tour interviewing and for opening his home up to my plague-ridden presence on more than one occasion, plus flaming rum drinks. There are plenty more writer friends to thank, but hopefully there will be more books in which to thank them.

Beta readers for this book include: Tex Thompson (also a writer friend; fine you're in here twice, Thompson), and the always fabulous Megan Fiero and Randi Mysse Ristau (who also did some amazing pro bono photographic work for *Dr Potter's Medicine Show*, the acknowledgment for same being too late to make it into that book so thank you in retrospect for that).

Brent Richford and Juan Manuel Valdez, who moaned that they weren't in the last book's acknowledgments but, fair enough, are my greatest of friends and have done all sorts of supportive things over the years, so they've earned it. Fine, are you happy now?

Everyone who came out to see me yammer and wave my arms around on my last book tour.

My family, just because.

Delia, my canine support unit, to whom I say *hah*.

And, finally, again, Tara "Tata" Fields, for all of the

long ridiculous list of things she's done to help with this book nonsense since it got started, from beta-reading to non-eye-rolling to crafting promotional things to just being supportive in general of this weird second job of mine that eats up my time, that I love doing, and which I never stop griping about.

Thanks, y'all.